It's got to be Perfect

Claire Allan

POOLBEG

This novel is entirely a work of fiction. The names, characters and incidents portrayed in it are the work of the author's imagination. Any resemblance to actual persons, living or dead, events or localities is entirely coincidental.

Published 2010
by Poolbeg Press Ltd
123 Grange Hill, Baldoyle
Dublin 13, Ireland
E-mail: poolbeg@poolbeg.com
www.poolbeg.com

A catalogue record for this book is available from the British Library.

ISBN 978-1-84223-433-4

Typeset by Patricia Hope in Sabon 11/15.5
Printed and bound in the UK by CPI Mackays, Chatham ME5 8TD

www.poolbeg.com

Note on the Author

Claire Allan describes herself as a journalist, author, mammy, wine-drinker and occasional nutcase – not necessarily in that order. She lives in Derry with her husband Neil and their two children Joseph and Cara. She continues to work as reporter and columnist for the *Derry Journal*. When she is not working, she fights a continuing battle to lose weight, break her handbag addiction and win the affection of her two-year-old nephew Ethan, who looks at her strangely a lot of the time. She cannot sing – not even a note – but does enjoy trying.

You can find her at **www.claireallan.com**, or on Facebook or Twitter.

Also by Claire Allan

Jumping in Puddles

Feels Like Maybe

Rainy Days & Tuesdays

PUBLISHED BY POOLBEG

Acknowledgements

First of all, this book was written with you in mind. Especially if you are thirty or over and still feel uncomfortable in your own skin, or haven't met The One or have never looked good in a pair of skinny jeans. If you were ever five and dreamed about your wedding day/being a mammy/running your own company and perhaps life hasn't panned out that way, then this is for you. And this is especially for you if you think your friends/family have it all sorted and just haven't let you in on the secret for perfectly painted nails and nice interiors yet . . .

Writing this book was easy. It was easy because it was fun. Seriously, I loved it. Almost every minute. For the minutes when I just kind of liked it, I had my in-built fan club urging me on. For this book, in particular, three people kept me going. My very best friend Vicki, my writing hero Fionnuala Kearney and my inspirationally gorgeous Auntie Raine. Thank you.

For those moments when I needed reminding that I have an actual life and don't just make lives up for other people – thank you to my family. My husband (of the long-suffering variety) Neil and my two children, Joseph and Cara. Words cannot express how much I love you all.

Mammy, Daddy, Peter and Emma, thank you for being the best family ever.

Lisa, thank you for everything – from riding shotgun for me when I drove to Dublin and back in a day for TV3, and riding shotgun when I got us lost on the longest drive in the world ever to

Trim, to riding shotgun while we drove very many places where you would listen to the same old talk time and time again and always look interested. This one is for you.

My extended family, as always, must get a mention and it would be remiss of me not to mention my niece here. When I was writing this book and creating the character of Darcy, my sister found out she was pregnant. Fast forward and Darcy Bo (inspired by me, I like to think) was born and she is my squishy girl. Along with her brother, Ethan, and her sister Abby, I am a very lucky auntie indeed.

Of course the staff of the *Derry Journal* and Johnston Press NI must get a mention – especially the girls in the office – and most especially Erin. We may have had one or two of those Annie and Fionn scrapes in real life before we settled down and became mammies within a week of each other.

Writing a PR storyline was amazing fun – not least because I could let my imagination run wild (and I did – the nipple-tassels, I must stress, are entirely my own invention) but one very glam and lovely PR lady by the name of Gráinne McGarvey may have shared a story or two. *Merci beaucoup* for the Singles Night inspiration.

I don't use acknowledgements usually to get all mushy and personal but while I was writing this book I was going through the pregnancy from hell with my amazing daughter. There are people who kept me sane and this is one way I can think to say thank you to Dr Claire Sweeney of Cityview Medical Practice.

While we are on a mushy vibe, this book has helped raise money for a very special charity: "Camille's Appeal". Camille, who makes a special appearance in this book, is the daughter of a friend of mine and is perhaps the bravest little girl I know. I auctioned a mention in this book for her charity and an amazing woman called Tor Pickles donated £250 and nominated Camille and her mother Hayley for a mention. I am proud to know all these people and to fight beside them whatever way I can. Please, if you can, have a look at www.camillesappeal.co.uk.

On a cheerier note, ah, my Northern Girls – Emma Heatherington and Fiona Cassidy – what great craic we have shared and I am happy to be on the Poolbeg bus with you. Indeed, darn it (mushy again) I just love my fellow Poolbeg authors – big up to Sharon Owens, Anne Dunlop, Anna McPartlin (who genuinely does make me shoot wine out of my nose on a regular basis) and Emma Hannigan who is just amazing.

Which brings me to the Poolbeg team – who have fought our corner relentlessly in the toughest market this country has known. You are amazing, all of you. But especially Paula Campbell (and not just because I am duty-bound to kiss her ass). When you can sit, drunkenly, across the table from your publisher and have a great craic, you know that you have landed on your feet. Also big thanks to my editor Gaye Shortland who never misses a beat.

I also have to thank my agent, Ger Nichol, who continues to buoy me up and keep me going. Thank you doesn't seem enough.

To the booksellers and journalists – all at Culture NI and Books Biz NI or anywhere – proving that us Northerners have a valid voice, thank you. To Lynsey Dolan, for being inspirational, funny and introducing me to Lady Antebellum, thank you.

And finally to you – who have parted with your hard-earned cash when hard-earned cash isn't exactly free and easy at the moment – for buying this book, thank you. To all who email, Facebook, tweet and stop me in the school playground, God bless you all.

For

Lisa,

A friend, a sister and an inspiration

1

I wouldn't say I was jealous of Fionn. Just because she was getting her happy ending while I was plodding along waiting for my life to start. She deserved her happy ending – I believed that entirely. But still, as I watched her walk out of the changing room in her stunning shot-silk gown, her eyes misty with emotion, I couldn't help feeling a little green around the gills with envy (and the remnants of last night's vodka).

"She's gorgeous, isn't she?" the over-enthusiastic shop assistant almost squealed, and I nodded.

"Do you really like it?" Fionn asked, her face begging me to say yes.

"I do," I said, and I wasn't lying. It was a stunning dress which accentuated my friend's natural beauty but when I choked back a tear it was because I couldn't ever see myself in her position – no matter how carefully I had planned every aspect of my life. You see, I had this wonderfully crappy habit of messing things up. If there was a degree in being a fuck-up, I would have passed with first-class honours.

"I'm so glad you like it," Fionn said, waving her hands in front of her face to try and stem her tears, "because I really think this is the one. This is my wedding dress, Annie. *My wedding dress.*" She emphasised the words while twirling around like some sort of demented overgrown fairy princess and the shop assistant actually did squeal with delight at this stage.

I just sobbed into my hanky. In a most undignified manner.

"Like a princess," I said, sipping my wine. The buzz of the bar had lifted my spirits and Fionn and I were three-quarters way down a very fine bottle of Sauvignon Blanc.

"I was, wasn't I? Like a Disney Princess."

"Hmmm," I answered. "Cinderella."

"Or Ariel. I like her wedding dress best of all. The way it sparkles in the sun when she kisses Eric in the last scene." Fionn sighed dreamily, before sipping from her glass again.

I raised my eyebrow – or at least I think I raised my eyebrow. The wine was combining with the previous night's vodka and it was possible that any facial gesture I tried to make at that moment looked more like I had developed some weird facial tick.

"Okay, okay," Fionn blushed. "I know I sound like an eejit, but Emma is going through a particularly fierce and ferocious Disney Princess phase at the moment and it's about all I can think about. Every moment of every fecking day some cheerful tune is dancing through my head."

I smiled. Fionn was not taking to motherhood all that well. That's not to say she was doing too badly at it, but since she had moved in with Alex in the run-up to the Big Day she was finding it challenging to come to terms with the demands – and viewing habits – of his five-year-old daughter, Emma.

"But I can't just tell her I don't want to watch them, can I? Because if I do, I'll be the Wicked Stepmother and, believe me," she said with emphasis, "I've seen enough of those movies to know that doesn't bode well."

"Emma loves you," I soothed. "And it's just a novelty having a woman about the house to indulge her princess fantasies with."

Fionn nodded. "I know, but promise me this. The next time I come into work with fairy-dust on my cheeks, can you point it out to me before the ops meeting? I don't think it does well to have me looking like an overgrown schoolgirl."

"I don't know about that," I laughed. "I think Bob liked it. You brought a little colour to the office that day."

Ah, Bob. (Or "Bawb" as Fionn and I usually called him, in a faux-American accent.) He was our boss and obsessed with client portfolios and, it seemed, little else. I didn't think he actually had a life outside of the office, which was why he liked to exert as much control over his minions (as he had been known to call us) as possible.

Fionn shuddered. "I don't want to talk, or even think, about Bawb just now. It takes away from the whole wedding-dress, fairy-tale experience. And I don't want anything to take away from that."

Which was precisely the reason I didn't explain to her how the last twenty-four or so hours of my life had been the most spectacularly painful of my existence. If she didn't want Bob to ruin her dream wedding-dress day then she sure as feck didn't want to hear about Chewbacca.

Have you ever made a mistake? You know, a big, huge mistake which makes your heart sink to the pit of your stomach and the contents of your stomach try and escape through your mouth every time you think about it?

It was one of those things which seemed like a good idea at the time. I was wanted. I was fancied. I was irresistible. But that was then.

Lying there, in the stale air of my bedroom, with the exceptionally hairy arm of my mistake draped over my stomach – clammy with sweat – I felt my mind whir and my head thump. Too much vodka on an empty stomach – it was never going to end well.

I glanced at the clock on the chest of drawers and my heart thumped harder. It was 10.29 a.m. On a workday. So not only was I trapped under the weight of a man who was a walking *before* advertisement for a good back, sack and crack wax, I was also approximately eighty-nine minutes late for work.

I glanced at Chewbacca lying beside me. He was out for the count. I moved my head closer to his, wondering if he was actually dead, but the stench of booze-breath wafting out with every exhalation was enough to reassure me that he was very much alive – if comatose.

I lifted his arm, weighed down by the sheer volume of hair on it, and inched my way out of the bed – doing my best to leave him sleeping. I wanted him awake, and out of my apartment – but preferably not while I was still naked. The last thing I wanted was him to wake and get a notion that there was a chance in hell of a repeat of the previous night's performance. Even though my hazy memory told me it had been quite pleasurable.

It was 10.33. I wanted (needed) a shower, but that would only make me even later for work and even further into the bad books of Bob who by now was probably halfway to a stroke. I lifted my phone to call him, but then it dawned on me: I could just get ready and get to work as soon as possible. When he asked where I had been I could say I'd been out meeting a client. It wasn't unheard of, and it might just work. If only I could get Chewbacca out of my flat any time soon.

After a speed-wash with a sponge, I slipped into my suit and dabbed on some foundation – although I doubted even the finest Clarins had to offer was going to make me look anywhere near human. Pulling a comb through my hair and tying it up into a topknot, I slipped my feet into a pair of court shoes and glanced back at the clock: 10.43. And he was still sleeping.

I tried slamming a door. I even set off the alarm clock and had a very loud conversation with myself. Not so much as a flinch. I pulled the duvet off the bed – hoping the cool would shock him awake – but then I wasn't reckoning on his carpet of self-insulation.

It was therefore supremely ironic when it was my phone ringing with a call from my boyfriend that actually woke him.

"Hello," Pearse said, his voice showing his confusion. "Where are you? I tried phoning you at work. They said you weren't in yet. I tried calling last night too – you didn't answer."

Pearse Campbell liked to know where I was and who I was with at every hour of the day and night. Having gone off radar for the last twelve hours would not have gone down well with him. Not at all.

"I'm with a client," I lied, my face blazing. I was sure he would know I was fibbing. He could read me like a book – even over the phone.

And it was at precisely that moment Chewbacca chose to shout, loudly, "Babe, do you know where my boxers are?"

It was 11.23. The underwear had been located and returned to its rightful owner shortly after Pearse had given orders that we would talk later, muttered something about how could *I* do this to *him* and hung up. I had got rid of my mystery man-beast and was now fighting against the traffic to make it into the office at all before lunchtime. Bob would not be happy, client or not. This day was not going well and that sinking feeling in my stomach was back – which did not sit easily with the hung-over feeling which seemed to have taken over my entire body.

I drove on demented, pushing all thoughts of Pearse and the battle that would ensue later to the back of my head. I just didn't have time to think about it now. Okay, this day was a balls-up – but if I didn't get my ass into work pretty damn soon, it would be the most spectacular balls-up day of all time.

I was somewhere between weeping with relief and crying with fear when I pulled into the communal car park and secured the last parking space. Jumping out of the car, snagging my tights as I went, I dived through the rain to the office, stopping only momentarily to plaster a look of nonchalance on my face before entering.

"Oh Annie, how nice of you to join us!" Bob crowed from across the open-plan room. My colleagues, well aware of the seriousness of my offence, didn't even look up. Apart from Fionn, that is, whose Bambi eyes gazed at me, begging me silently to keep my cool and not ruin her dream day which would, of course, end in the Great Wedding-dress Trying-on Extravaganza.

"Nice of you to notice," I bluffed back, with more confidence than I felt. Perhaps if I pretended that everything was just tickety-boo, Bob would be lulled into a weird sense of security and forget just why he had cause to be angry.

I walked to my desk and sat down, lifting the phone from the cradle and rattling in an imaginary number while my computer booted up. Bob just stood, for a few seconds, open-mouthed, before storming into his office.

An audible sigh of relief rose from everyone outside.

"Where were you?" An email from Fionn pinged into my inbox.

"Long story. Nothing exciting," I lied. I had already made the conscious decision not to tell her about Chewbacca or Pearse – not when we were going on a wedding-dress hunt. What a downer that would be.

"Where were you?" An email from Bob pinged into my inbox.

"With a client," I lied. I had already made a conscious decision that I would not crack under pressure, ever.

"Which client?" he asked.

Fuck. I couldn't cope with this kind of pressure. One false move and it was P45-land for me.

"A new one. I'll tell you when it's a little firmer. Don't want to risk it. It's a big one." I pressed *Send* and crossed my fingers, hoping that would buy me time.

"It better be," he replied and that was that.

Now that my job remained secure, I just had to clean up the other pieces of my life.

It was, I admit, hard to get into the spirit of work – despite the whiteboard behind my desk detailing all our up-and-coming campaigns – several of which I was in charge of. Being an account executive for NorthStar PR was rarely plain sailing, but there were times when I found it nigh on impossible to get excited about the latest branding of the local supermarket or some fancy perfume.

I tried to ignore the fact that one of our major campaigns for the month was to be Manna – Pearse's restaurant – and that my involvement in "keeping the client happy" might have just gone disastrously wrong.

Instead I turned my attention to our campaign for the new "adult" shop, Love, Sex and Magic, which was set to open in town amid a furore from right-wingers everywhere.

It wasn't a sleazy shop, per se – I mean it was all really in good form – no seriously hardcore stuff – but we still knew we would have a killer of a time putting a positive slant on it when the local do-gooders were already planning a protest on opening day – complete with placards and everything.

Bob wanted this to work. He really, really wanted it work. He was even trying to convince myself and Fionn to dress in French Maid costumes while handing out leaflets outside – but I figured that was more to satisfy his own seedy desires than anything else. We had, however, been talked into dressing as magician's assistants and it was my job to source suitable costumes. Did I just say life in PR could be dull?

"FSB?" Fionn emailed.

Ah, Fake Smoke Break. Even though neither of us smoked we still allowed ourselves the periodic traipse out to the smokers' corner of shame for a gossip, away from the glare of our computer screens (and Bob's eagle eye).

"I think he would kill me if I dared move from my desk," I jotted back and she smiled sympathetically.

Truth was, I wanted to avoid her as best I could, in a bid to keep my disastrous morning under wraps. And I genuinely did think Bob might kill me.

Reaching for two paracetamol from my desk drawer, I swallowed them down with some water and started phoning.

I was starting to feel almost jolly, until, that is, the phone rang and Pearse barked a hello at me. From the noise in the background I could tell he was calling me from the restaurant kitchens and this show was one all of his staff were enjoying.

"Hi, Pearse," I whispered, careful not to prick Fionn's curiosity. The girl had bat ears – anything in a twenty-foot radius was fair game.

"So, are you going to tell me what happened?"

Oh God. He couldn't really want to have a meaning-of-life-the-universe-and-everything chat just now, could he?

"I'm at work," I replied.

"And what? Your job is more important than me and our relationship? Is that what you're saying?"

In any other circumstance I probably would have gone to him. I would have made my excuses to Bob – on the pretext of the forthcoming campaign for Manna – and cleared off to talk things through. I would have apologised and told him I didn't know what had come over me (except I did, and it was a hairy big fecker from Donegal) and begged his forgiveness.

But sitting there in the office it dawned on me that I wasn't quite sure if I wanted him to forgive me. Surely I wouldn't have done what I'd done – or who I'd done – if things had been perfect? Pulling at a loose thread in my laddered tights and watching the material unravel, I sighed.

"I can't, Pearse – things are mad here. But I am sorry."

"Well, what about after work?"

"I have to go a wedding-dress fitting with Fionn," I said. "I can't get out of it."

"I'm sure you could, if you wanted to."

His assumption that I would be able to stop doing whatever I was doing in order to be at his beck and call was really astounding. It shocked me that I'd once found it alluring and sexy. Once. Perhaps that was the keyword in all of this.

I could imagine him standing proud in his chef whites, his minions running round him, listening to him ordering the little woman around.

"I'm sorry, Pearse. If I could get away, I would," I lied.

He put the phone down, his anger obvious by the slam of it against the receiver. Oh, this was not going to be good.

2

"Taxi!" I shouted, stumbling from the bar.

Fionn was doubled over behind me – a mixture of finding my attempts to hail a taxi hilarious and an urgent need to pee.

Glancing back at her, her hair ruffled and blowing in the wind, her make-up long departed from her skin, she looked so much less the blushing bride than she had done just three short hours ago.

"Seriously, I've got to pee," she whined, her smile changing to a grimace and then to a look which could only be described as sheer desperation.

We could, I realised in the cold light of the following day, have simply gone back into the bar we had just left. But that would have made too much sense. It was only fitting that, given the way my day had gone, I came up with the inspired idea of visiting Manna for a quick after-hours pee.

It had gone eleven and the last of the diners would be sampling their after-dinner whiskies and G&Ts. Pearse would be propping up the bar with a pint glass of iced water in his hand (he never drank on duty) and the bouncers knew me well enough to let us in to use the very stylish ladies' toilets.

Landing in might even earn me some brownie points. So far I'd had six text messages and three missed calls from Pearse and, in my dazed and confused state, I felt that me showing willing to actually talk to him might be a good thing. We could also phone a taxi from the more dignified surroundings of the restaurant bar and, once Fionn was safely on her way back to Alex and Emma, I could start to sort things out with my perhaps-ex-boyfriend.

"Manna!"

"*Manna, do do, be doo doo!*" Fionn howled, bursting into the old Muppets' classic song. "Lead the way!"

We were still scatting our way through the same song – with some impressive free styling I have to add – when we arrived at the doors of Manna, Fionn now trying desperately not to grab her crotch like an incontinent three-year-old.

"Lemme in!" I shouted before realising that this was not the best way to help me wend my way back into Pearse's good books.

A surly bouncer with a monobrow eyed me up and down.

"S'me. Annie. Is Pearse there? We need in!"

He looked at us suspiciously and called to a passing waitress, who after squinting out into the dark night was able to confirm that I was indeed Annie and that Pearse was indeed in. Opening the door, Monobrow gave a half-smile as we darted across the bar to the ladies' with not so much as a thank-you.

"Oh God, oh God, oh God!" Fionn moaned as she bustled into a cubicle and sat down.

I hoped against hope there was no one in any of the other stalls. I dreaded to think what they might imagine was going on. And then it struck me – an awful memory of a stall, and a hairy-backed Donegal man and groping. There was definitely groping.

"Oh crap," I said, sitting on the loo and leaning my head against the cool stainless steel of the minimalist cubicle.

"Are you okay?" Fionn asked, her voice having come down a few octaves to its usual tone as the urgency of her toilet trip passed.

"Oh me? I'm fine. Just fine." My voice was probably a little too cheerful and my actions a little like a bad lead in a cheap pantomime as I pranced out to the sink with false confidence. "Right, let's get you a taxi!"

Fionn yawned. "Yes, home would be a good idea. Let's hope I don't wake Emma. Or Alex for that matter."

"Just take your shoes off and sleep on the sofa if you have to. I'm sure they won't even notice." Lifting my mobile, I tapped in a number and ordered a taxi. Then the pair of us emerged from the bathroom with faces as straight as they could be.

"Annie!" Pearse called as he walked across the room.

Fionn grinned at him. "I got a wedding dress. I'm going to be a princess and you two," she said, gesturing at both of us in a fingers-pointed-in-a-pretend-gun style, "just have to be next!"

Pearse looked at me and back at Fionn while I just grinned, trying not to let the stinky air of tension in the room get to me.

"Yes, well, we'll see!" I smiled and breathed a sigh of relief as a taxi horn beeped outside.

When she was gone and it was just Pearse and me standing in the middle of an empty dining hall, I felt very foolish. It was wrong, I knew that, to come and see him – even if we had been desperate for a pee.

It was hardly the best place to have the conversation we were about to have – even if I hadn't been three sheets to the wind.

"Shall we go home?" Pearse asked and I nodded, although I wasn't sure what home he was referring to. We had been together two years but still lived apart. Perhaps my reluctance to move into his admittedly stunning house on the hill had been my subconscious telling me that one day I would wake up next to a hairy-backed man after a night of wanton sex in my own grotty flat.

Speaking of which, feck, there was no way we could go there. I hadn't had time to strip the bed sheets. The whole place probably still smelled of stale booze, cigarettes and very rude sex. The whole sorry mess suddenly felt very sordid.

"Can we go to yours?" I asked pathetically.

He nodded. I guessed he knew why I was not so keen to go home.

We drove in silence. I wanted to start talking so many times but there isn't much you can say in that situation. Pearse sighed, very loudly, several times and swore at passing cars but it was the tinny din of the car radio that kept me awake as opposed to any big old heart to heart.

Pearse's house was a thing of dreams – and testament to the success of Manna. Sleek and stylish, with the same minimalist style as his restaurant, it wouldn't have looked out of place in the interior pages of a glossy magazine. The smell of polish, bleach and the after-scent of Yankee Candles (sandalwood) hit me as I walked through the door and into the lounge. Pearse got busy, switching on the gas fire and lighting some of the aforementioned candles before making me a cup of hot chocolate.

"Will we talk now?" I asked, as I curled up on his squishy chenille sofa.

"I need a shower," he responded. "It was sweaty in the kitchen tonight – can't risk crotch-rot setting in."

And when he put it like that, who was I to argue with the man? He sloped off to his designer bathroom with his perfectly polished chrome power shower and I pulled a chenille throw over my shoulders and fell into a deep sleep.

When I woke my hand brushed against the chenille and for the briefest of moments I wondered if I was back with Hairy Back. It took a while for me to realise where I was, and that it was morning and that Pearse and I hadn't had the chance for our big chat yet. I stretched and walked to the kitchen – parched – in need of a long cold glass of something. Finding a carton of cranberry juice, I poured myself some. God knows what Pearse thought of me now – but then, he had been the one to leave, to go and shower his sweaty privates, and given the utter cosiness of his living room it had been a given that I was going to fall asleep. If he had wanted to chat to me, he could have woken me. I wouldn't have minded.

I noticed a note on the worktop. "*I've gone to the market. I tried to wake you last night, but you were out of it. I've left you a change of clothes in the spare room. We'll talk tomorrow. P*"

So, I cringed, he had tried to wake me. I'd probably slobbered in his direction, or snorted or something equally unfeminine. I was certainly in the bad books if my emergency set of spare clothes were laid out in the spare room and not in the master boudoir. Swearing under my breath (and swearing again when I realised I had twenty minutes to get to work on time) I pelted up the stairs and threw on the cream A-line skirt and mint-green twin-set Pearse had left out for me to wear, along with a string of pearls, some cream court shoes and – his pièce de résistance – some American Tan tights and clean underwear. Ah, my very best respectable-girlfriend outfit which he liked very much indeed. In his mind, I guessed, it would have been perfectly lovely if I always dressed as if it was still 1956.

As I poked in my bag for my trial-size Flash Balm and loose powder, I called a taxi and prayed it wasn't one of the days when the grumpiest dispatcher in Derry was manning the phones.

Of course, God was not that kind to me. As Grumpy answered the phone he didn't give me time to state my request before he launched into a tirade of swear words at some poor driver who had taken a wrong turn on the school run.

"Excuse me," I muttered to his ranting voice.

"Excuse me," I repeated, but a little louder.

"Excuse me," I repeated, but a good deal louder.

"Wha'?" he eventually muttered.

"A taxi, please," I stated.

"And there was me thinking you were ordering a pizza," he said gruffly and I could hear him puffing on a cigarette. It seemed the smoking ban didn't extend to his little office.

Rolling my eyes, and feeling my headache kick in behind my eyes, I stated my destination and asked him to be quick.

"Five minutes," he said and hung up and I knew, just knew, it would be at least twenty and by that stage I was expected to be at the office, with the magician's assistant costumes in tow. I sent Fionn a quick text asking her to pick them up and then headed straight for Pearse's alphabetised bathroom cabinet. I scrolled my eyes over to P for paracetamol and downed two.

I would talk to Pearse tomorrow. *Mañana* would be D-day because Friday nights always belonged to Manna. I knew that.

Arriving in work twenty-five minutes late – but carrying a tray of pathetic apology-attempt doughnuts from the neighbouring bakery – I smiled at my colleagues (Bob included) and made my way to my desk where Fionn had kindly laid out two of the most garish pieces of satin and nylon I'd ever seen.

It wasn't long before Bob sidled silently over. Sometimes I wondered if he wore those Heely shoes with the wheels underneath. He never seemed to walk – more glide in a slightly creepy way.

"Late again," he said.

"Yes, I'm sorry. Couldn't get a taxi. I brought buns." I offered him a chocolate-sprinkled doughnut and watched his eyes light up – just for a moment.

"No more late mornings, Annie. The rest of your colleagues can manage to make it on time. Pull your socks up or look for something else."

"I'm sorry," I muttered again, resisting the urge to snatch the doughnut from his hands and grind it into the floor with the heel of my shoe.

"Yes, yes. You should be," he said, biting into the bun and sending a shower of crumbs everywhere – including onto the garish nylon – before turning and gliding off again.

"FSB?" a message pinged from Fionn some time later.

I nodded in her direction. I dug my prop packet of cigarettes out of my bag but couldn't find my prop lighter in there. Then I remembered lending it to Chewbacca. Surely he hadn't made off with it? Pink plastic? Hardly likely.

Fionn looked as bad as I felt and as we walked through the back door to the smoker's enclave – a Perspex bus-shelter-type structure NorthStar had erected on the edge of the car park – she pulled a pair of dark sunglasses over her eyes.

"I'm never drinking again," she said dramatically.

"Feeling that bad?"

"Are you not?" she asked, incredulously. "I think the third bottle of wine did it for me. We should have stopped at two. No, actually we should have stopped at one."

"I'm not feeling great, but I've had worse hangovers," I said honestly, thinking back to yesterday – which of course I still hadn't told Fionn about. But looking at her now she certainly didn't look as if she had the constitution to deal with my confessions about my night of something-or-other with Chewbacca. Feeling my stomach turn a little (a strange combination of guilt and downright horniness) I didn't think I had the constitution to relive it just now either.

Fionn took a cigarette from her prop packet of Marlborough and pretended to light up.

"So did you manage to get in the door without waking Alex or Emma?" I asked as I got one out too and started to fake-smoke. (We always put on a good performance just in case Bob was spying on us.)

Fionn smiled. "Actually, I had a lucky escape. Emma was having a sleepover at her mum's so I had Alex all to myself. And," she said with a wink, "it would seem he doesn't mind Drunk Me so much."

"Lucky you," I said with a smile.

"Well, indeed," she smiled back, "but I'll tell you something for nothing. My thighs are killing me today."

"Show off!" I teased.

"And you? Did you make it up with Pearse? Whatever it was that was bugging the pair of you?"

"I fell asleep, more's the pity. On the sofa – so I've a crick in my neck but not so much as a sore thigh, never mind a pair of them."

"Well, it's the weekend. There's always tonight."

"I doubt it. It's Friday. It's Manna's busiest night, remember? I'll not see him. It will be me and a bottle of polish tonight, sorting out my God-awful pit of a flat."

Fionn laughed. "I'm sure it's not that bad. Sure there's only you in it. I share with the messiest man in Ireland, a five-year-old and enough Barbies to open a branch of Smyth's. I sat on one of the feckers this morning. I'm sure I have a plastic-boob-shaped bruise on my arse just now."

I thought of my flat – the awful mess it really was in. When I left the day before it was stale with sweat and dust and general mess and I wasn't looking forward to going home to sort it out. Especially with a hangover – but needs must. In some ways, though, it was the least I could do. A penance of a Friday night on hardcore cleaning before I finally got to talk to Pearse.

"Penny for them?" Fionn asked.

"We don't have long enough," I said with a wry smile. "Bawb will be wondering where we are so we'd better get back in. He's already threatened my job once already this morning."

"He has not!" Fionn said incredulously.

I nodded and gave a half-smile. Maybe that was part of my penance too.

The biggest part of my penance, however, seemed to involve the aforementioned campaign outside Love, Sex and Magic. Looking down at my blue hot pants and nipple-tassels (sewn onto a lurid bra top complete with dazzling sequins), I wondered if I would have been better fixed wearing the French Maid's Outfit. My ass would definitely have been warmer.

It crossed my mind that if my parents were still around (not that they were dead – they had merely retired to the Costa Del Tax Haven), they would have despaired. Four years at university and this was how I spent my working day – dressed like a cheap trollop and trying to convince the local old-biddy brigade that the shop was not a modern-day version of Sodom and Gomorrah.

"The shop, as you may see from the name, is also about love. Love is good – and this shop can be used to purchase items which will promote loving relationships in committed couples. These items don't have to be known as sex toys." (There was an audible gasp at that) "If you prefer they can be marketed as marital aids."

A small woman with greying hair and yellowing teeth, dressed in a prim and proper twin-set and pearls, looked me straight in the nipple-tassels and said: "My dear, there is no room in any Christian marriage for a butt-plug."

There is some logic you can't argue with.

I took a deep breath, allowing me just enough time to gather my thoughts, and replied: "But this shop sells all sorts. Honestly. Maybe you should have a look and see?"

"I think not," she muttered, turning back to her group of cronies and encouraging them to waft their placards higher than ever.

Bob walked over, a smile on his face. I expected him to be apoplectic that I hadn't managed to quell the protest but instead he rubbed his hands together in glee.

"The newspapers are here – and UTV. We're guaranteed some cracker coverage over this!"

Oh great, I thought, cringing. Me and my shiny blue bottom would be centre-stage on the evening news. This would be even more humiliating than the time I was snapped dressed as a giant latte promoting the latest coffee shop in town.

If Darcy – my sister – were here, she would be positively glowing with joy at my humiliation. It wasn't that she was a bad person, and she wouldn't do it in a hateful way. She just had a wicked sense of humour and would enjoy adding the picture to her growing Facebook folder of "Annie pulls an 'Annie'" pictures – humiliating myself having been a big factor in my life so far.

But thankfully Darcy was in Dublin and she never watched the UTV news so I knew, on this occasion at least, I would escape her mockery. All I had to do was make it through the next hour with my nerve – and my costume – intact.

This was so not my scene. Of course PR work as a concept *was* my scene. I loved it – but this, touting marital aids, or sex toys, or butt-plugs was not. I was quite prudish really. I rarely, if ever, did anything out of the ordinary.

3

I couldn't really explain why what happened with Chewbacca happened. To be utterly honest, I couldn't really remember it. I knew it had been a hard day at work. Bob had been in best "Bawb" mode – where every sentence out of his gob was a cliché and every time he so much as looked at any one of us he was shouting about targets and thinking outside the box etc.

I didn't want to think outside the box. I wanted to climb in the box, with a bottle of vodka, and shout out from the corners that he could go feck himself.

Trying not to make myself seem too much like a bona-fide loony tune, I decided to forgo the box and opt simply for the vodka. I'd phoned Pearse just on the very off-chance he would leave the restaurant for the evening and come and keep me company. It was a Wednesday night and even Manna couldn't be that busy on a friggin' Wednesday night, I reckoned. But, busy or not, that place was his baby and I, well, wasn't, obviously.

"But I've had a rotten day at work," I whined.

"I'm busy," he huffed. "I'll come over later," he added, his voice full of promise.

I wasn't in the mood for promises. I just wanted a boyfriend who was there when I needed him – not just when he needed me. Fionn had it – every night she went home to a gorgeous man who, even though he had a young daughter, still made time for just them.

I could have handled coming second to someone's child – but not someone's fecking restaurant. The bloody garlic chips would surely be safe in the hands of one of the other chefs.

So it was in a fit of pique that I'd hit the bar on my own and it was in a fit of something – loneliness, lust, whatever – that I'd found myself trapped under a strange man the following morning.

Now I should point out that I wasn't a slut. I didn't normally shag around. I found it enough of an effort to maintain a relationship with a significant other – all that shaving legs and dressing in skimpy undies nonsense. Going out and taking a random stranger to bed was unheard of for me and yet the evidence was undeniable. You can't wake up in the buff amid your own discarded clothes and covered by another human being without reasonably believing you had done the down and dirty.

I remembered, vaguely, meeting Chewbacca. I'd been on my third double vodka and stuffing my face with my third bag of Bacon Fries when he'd asked if I had a light.

"I don't smoke," I'd replied and he shrugged. But then, of course, I remembered the lighter kept solely for my FSBs with Fionn.

I'm sure he must have thought I was mad, or an arsonist, or both, as I fished in my bag and handed him the luminous pink piece of plastic.

"Thanks," he smiled and bought me a drink.

Of course I let him buy me the drink in an act of wilful feck-you-Pearse frustration and the next thing I remember was, of course, waking up under him. I didn't even know his name. Names just didn't seem important when you were on your fifth orgasm. And the following morning I just hadn't had the time to ask as I tried to get him the hell out of my flat and out of my life. Guilt is a terrible thing. If it wasn't for guilt . . . well, who knows . . .

And yet as I walked back in the door that Friday evening, tired from my day pimping the local sex shop, there was a faint trace of him still there – and it wasn't all down to the moulting.

I dragged my hair back into a ponytail and changed into my old grey trackie bottoms and T-shirt. Strange as it was, I felt a lot more glam in my trackies than I had in my sparkles and spangles.

Stripping the bed off, I pushed the windows of the bedroom open. I desperately wanted and needed a shower, but there was no point in soothing away the stresses of the day before deep-cleaning the scene of my crime. Picking up my discarded outfit from Wednesday night, I cringed. I imagined him stripping it off me – or, worse still, me in some drunken state of madness performing a weird striptease. Please God, I thought, may that memory be simply a figment of my imagination and not an actual flashback. I bundled the suit, along with my bedclothes, into the washing machine and whizzed around the room, picking up two discarded wineglasses, a pizza box and my missing pink lighter from the floor. Lifting a foul-smelling saucer with three cigarette-butts stubbed out into it, I wondered for the umpteenth time just what the hell had I been thinking? I never let anyone smoke in my flat and yet this mystery man had crossed that line – and a million more.

Then I set about doing my best Mrs Mop job with the polish and Hoover. It took almost two hours before I could look at my flat and see it as my home again and not just the scene of some dirty sex-ridden crime. My candles were burning, my rooms were aired out and everything was fresh and clean. I was just about ready for my shower – which would be followed by a luxurious soak in the bath. There was no way I could soak in the bath without scrubbing off the grime of the day first – otherwise it was just like lying in dead-skin soup.

It was only then that I could sink back and start to relax. Yes, of course, I still had to deal with Pearse and the mess our relationship was in but, as that wasn't going to happen any time soon, I figured I'd just make the most of a night on my own.

When the flat was clean, I loved it. I could see past the rickety windows and the fading carpet when everything was in its place. I could pick out the character in the sloping ceilings and sash windows and think I could never, ever live in a fancy new build like Pearse's. (Even if his house was warm and stylish and all the things mine wasn't.)

Pouring an overly liberal dollop of bubble bath into the tub, I pulled on my fluffy dressing gown and tied my now-wet hair up on top of my head.

My bathroom was huge – too huge maybe. I couldn't reach the door while I sat on the toilet which always made me nervous. I had an irrational fear about it. I preferred to have the safety of knowing I could reach the door to check it was locked in the event of an intruder breaking into the house while I was mid-poo. Despite the fact I had two locks on it.

But my huge bathroom was one of the characteristics of my higgledy-piggledy home which made it so unique. The top floor of a sparklingly ancient house, the bathroom was the same size as the living room, while the galley kitchen only fitted one person comfortably. Pearse refused to cook in it – there wasn't room to toss a pancake never mind sauté or blanche anything (not that I actually knew what that meant – but it sounded fancy). Half of the living room was a dining room and my bedroom was large enough for three double beds with just one small radiator stuck below the draughty window. (It only had one double bed, mind you.)

And yet, when it was clean and tidy like this, I couldn't imagine living anywhere else.

Not that I had the option. Of course I joked about living with Pearse, or him living with me. I was always fielding questions about when we would move in together – and I knew it was mostly because many of my friends wanted a good nosey around his house – but, when I thought of it, he had never asked me. And I certainly wasn't going to ask him to move in here – he barely even stayed the night. We always went to his place – or he would visit mine for an after-hours booty call and then clear off home.

That's not to say he was a bad person. He didn't treat me that badly. He told me he loved me and bought me nice jewellery and took me away on the (very) occasional romantic weekend (generally to places where he could check out new restaurants). But when it came to commitment he seemed reluctant – and, as I sank under the bubbles and thought about the conversation we were going to have the next day, I realised that I was too.

It was hard to know what to cook for a chef. Pearse was a fussy sort, while my usual repertoire of meals for one consisted of pasta and sauce or potato waffles with a garnish of lettuce and tomato – and it was ordinary lettuce too – none of your fancy curly-leaf stuff.

So when Pearse visited for lunch I was always a little flummoxed and on this occasion, knowing that he was coming over to confront me about my terrible indiscretion, I felt even more flummoxed than usual.

"Leek and potato soup is easy," Fionn had suggested down the phone that morning. She was quite the cook herself and liked to offer her recipes at a second's notice.

"The only leek and potato soup I can be guaranteed not to feck up is the kind out of a can," I replied and while she tried to offer me her best bread-making tips for a side dish, I was already planning a trip down the crusty-roll aisle in M&S. This was not just any food – this was make or break food. My shoddy cooking could not be relied on to save the day. Not, mind you, that I had decided the day needed saving.

I had lain awake most of the night, mulling it over in my head. While my dalliance with the Hairy-backed One had not been intentional, could I really love Pearse if I had let that happen? And would I have been out, drinking on my own, chatting to strange men, if he had loved me enough to spend a decent amount of time with me?

Of course I couldn't have this conversation with Fionn just now – excited as she was at the thought of a garlic and herb ciabatta – because I couldn't bring myself to admit to her just how utterly ridiculous I had been. I had enough fish to fry in the shape of Pearse and I would deal with Fionn later.

"You're so lucky," she crowed. "A romantic lunch, maybe a glass or two of wine, and a little afternoon delight. I'm taking Emma to McDonald's while Alex and the ex meet to talk over what's going to happen while we're on honeymoon." She lowered her voice to a whisper. "I hate to sound awful but I hope she doesn't make it difficult. I love Emma and I'm ready to share my life with her but I wouldn't mind at least a week with just Alex at the start of our married life."

"I'm sure Rebecca will have a little compassion about something so important," I soothed, all the while knowing that Rebecca was not known for her compassion about anything Fionn-related.

"You and me both," Fionn said, her voice returning to normal. "Look, enjoy your lunch. I'll get you a spare Happy Meal toy from McD's so you don't feel you missed out. And enjoy the afternoon nookie if you get the chance."

In the background I heard a precocious voice ask what *nookie* was and Fionn said a hasty goodbye before leaving me settled on a tin of soup and some fresh-baked grocery bread. I decided against putting a bottle of wine in the fridge to chill – I wanted my faculties about me for what was to come.

By the time Pearse arrived I was regretting that decision. I could have done with a bottle of wine. Or two. He smiled at me – not warmly – when he arrived and walked in. There was no kiss on the cheek or tender embrace, but I could hardly expect it, could I? I felt in many ways that he was looking over my shoulder just in case I had any other part-time lovers secreted away.

"I made lunch," I offered as he walked through the living/dining room. I had set the table – functionally, just the basics. "It's only soup and crusty bread, but since it's cold out there I thought it would be nice."

Neither of us commented on the frosty atmosphere inside as well.

Pearse sat down on the sofa, the furthest point in the room from my non-fresh cooking, and looked up at me.

"We need to talk," he started and I nodded.

I sat down opposite him. "I'm sorry, Pearse. I don't know what happened. Well, I do know what happened but I'm not sure why."

He nodded – a weird expressionless nod. I'm not sure whether he cared about what I'd done – despite the flurry of text messages – or was beyond hurt. He was giving nothing away. Nothing at all.

"Who is he?" he asked, tone flat.

I blushed because, of course, I didn't really have a clue who he was. "No one important. It was a silly, stupid thing of me to do."

"Yes, well, you're right. It was." His tone was still flat and yet I felt as if he was shouting at me. "I mean, I can't actually believe you would think so little of us to risk what we have for the sake of a one-night stand."

I sat for a moment, taking in what he was saying. I had risked "what we have" but then I had to wonder what it was we did have. The way Pearse was talking, we had it all. Truth was, he was little more than an associate I met once or twice a week. Yes, there was a certain kudos in having him as my boyfriend but there was little actual boyfriend behaviour going on these days. And if I questioned him about it, he would get annoyed and tell me I should be grateful that he was working so hard "for us". But I didn't see how he was working for *us*. The quality of our relationship certainly had not improved. I had spent birthdays and holidays alone. I had been unable to talk to the one man who was supposed to comfort and care for me when I had a bad day or needed a hug. I had even spent our two-year anniversary sipping Martinis on my own in the corner of Manna while Pearse worked and congratulated himself on how far *we* had come.

And it wasn't like I had a share of the restaurant stashed away somewhere, or drew a wage from it, or even got to share in Pearse's house, drive his car or enjoy any of the trappings of his success. How he was doing this "for us" was beyond me entirely.

"I've been thinking about this – a lot," he said, cutting through my thoughts. "In fact it's all I've been able to think about these last few days and, much as it hurts me to say it, I don't know if I can forgive you."

His words seemed well rehearsed, robotic even. It was almost as if he was reading a speech straight off an auto-cue, or if he had prepared this talk as if it were one of his many after-dinner speeches. Oh God, he had probably even made flash cards.

I knew this was my moment. I had two choices. I could beg him, plead and cry for his forgiveness, and promise to be the perfect little trophy girlfriend from now on. Or, I could be honest.

"I'm not sure I want to be forgiven," I muttered, and he had the decency to look shocked. My reaction had obviously not been in his script. "I love you, Pearse," I said, resisting the urge to add "in my own way". "And I wish this had worked out. I honestly do, but how can it? I think we both know that we want different things out of life." And in that moment I meant more – much more – than wanting to sleep with different people. I had been holding on to Pearse, perhaps long after I should, because I hoped he would be my happy ending but it was dawning on me that he never was going to be. Not unless he changed. Not unless he really wanted to.

This was *his* moment. It was his chance to beg me, plead and cry for another chance and promise to be the perfect trophy boyfriend from now on. Or he could just be honest.

"You're right, Annie," he said sadly. "And I wish this had worked out too but I think we need to cut our losses."

I nodded.

"But about the dinner on Wednesday – can I ask you a favour? Please don't mention this. Please pretend everything is fine and don't make me look like a loser."

He looked so worried and so pathetic that I could not say no. I was also keenly aware that NorthStar had arranged the charity dinner and it would not benefit either Pearse, or me, to feck up the proceedings at Manna.

And then he left. His losses cut. His soup uneaten. A dirty big garlic and herb ciabatta staring me in the face. And I walked to the cupboard, took out the still warm bottle of wine and opened it anyway.

In the bottom drawer of my dresser in my cavernous bedroom was a scrapbook. It was not so much a collection of my favourite pictures and ideas as a Life Plan. I'd even laminated the cover one weekend when I was working overtime.

I had added to it over the years but basically the plan hadn't changed. Finish school. Go to college. Get a degree. Find a decent job (okay, so I failed on that score). Buy my own home. Meet someone. Fall in love. Date for approximately two years. Get engaged. Perhaps live together – although this was not vital. By the age of thirty-three get married. Have our first baby within a year or two – definitely no later than thirty-five. I didn't want to risk scrambling my eggs.

It all seemed perfectly doable, especially when I was lucky enough to keep on top of the first few goals. Okay, so the job wasn't my dream job and my flat wasn't my forever home but I'd got there all the same. When I met Pearse Campbell, at the age of twenty-nine, I figured I was set. I was perfectly – absolutely one hundred per cent – on track for getting engaged at thirty-one, married at thirty-three and popping out our first little one at thirty-four or thirty-five. It was all happening like a dream. It's just a shame that the "madly in love" bit hadn't fallen into place.

When we'd met I'd been convinced he was the one, but now looking back I wondered was that because I wanted to believe it so much. I liked my life being ordered (contrary to outside appearances) and he slotted in nicely to the plan.

And we did have fun. Our first few months together were everything a relationship should be. We sat up into the small hours talking. We stayed in bed all day. I hung around Manna like a fragrant smell, sipping wine and making him laugh as he cooked. I put on 7lb in the first year, dining on rich foods. I dread to think how much I would have put on had we not also spent a considerable amount of time bonking away the calories.

When we'd been seeing each other five months and three weeks, we told each other we were in love. We were out for dinner (a competitor's place, of course) and over the lemon sorbet he looked deep into my eyes and told me I was very special to him and he thought he was in love. I thought I was in love too and we glided out of that place on Cloud Nine.

It would only be a matter of time, I was convinced, before he proposed and we were sent hurtling down the road towards married bliss. Only it didn't happen and after a while I didn't mind that it didn't happen. We were content and in our routine. The only time I felt a pang of jealousy was when Fionn flashed her diamond in the office and announced her forthcoming nuptials. Even then, however, I think I was only jealous of the ring. It was starting to dawn on me that I, perhaps, was starting to fall *out* of love with Pearse and that we would never be ideal marriage material. It made me incredibly sad to feel that way because he was the kind of man many a woman would give her right Jimmy Choo for. He was handsome. He was successful. He had even been on the telly.

I knew that if he asked me to marry him I would probably say yes and we would rub along nicely – well, adequately if not nicely – but surely marriage should be about more than rubbing along adequately? Fionn and Alex were mad about each other – Pearse and I were just comfortable with each other. Sometimes it felt as if I was a box simply ticked on his to-do list. One less thing to worry about. Girlfriend? Yes, I have one of those. Available for corporate dinners, parties and family gatherings at a moment's notice. And she's not the worst-looking either. She won't show me up. Not much.

Maybe I wasn't the only one with a laminated Life Plan.

Yet still I felt sad watching him walk out of my flat for what would no doubt be the last time. I was there, thirty-one and back at square one, with not as much as a decent prospect on the horizon and a whole can of worms to open when I told family and friends that I had broken up with the man they all perceived to be Mr Wonderful. (I figured, technically, since I'd done the shagging around, I had also done the breaking up. Of course, when I retold the story I would leave out the details of my indiscretion.)

I flicked through the scrapbook, running my fingers over the pictures of pretty dresses – one of which looked a lot like Fionn's – and sipped my wine again. Of course I knew I was officially supposed to be off the drink but these were desperate times. It was a Saturday and I was alone. And I would be alone even after the restaurants and pubs closed. And – if I'm honest – I was afraid I would be alone forever. I admit I was starting to feel all melodramatic and Bridget-Jonesy and was about three seconds away from putting on an old Celine Dion CD and blasting out tunelessly about being "All By Myself".

Instead, however, I crawled into bed, my Life Plan beside me, and fell into a deep sleep.

5

On Sunday mornings Fionn and I had a little tradition. I was terribly impressed that, even though she was so very much in love with Alex, she hadn't broken our habit of going out for bacon sarnies and a nice steaming cup of tea at approximately 11 a.m. each and every Sunday.

If it was dry and relatively warm we brought food out to the park and sat on one of the old green wooden benches and put the world to rights. If the weather was horrendous we went to a local café and if we were completely broke we had bacon sandwiches in one of our houses.

Today was a park day. It was cold enough, but not freezing, and we promised we would go for a long walk afterwards. After all, Fionn had a wedding dress to look gorgeous in and I was to be the bridesmaid with the mostest. The last thing I wanted was to look like a one-woman mountain beside the naturally slim and gorgeous Fionn – no matter how much it was her day and she was supposed to be the main attraction.

I also figured the walk around the park would give me ample time to break the news to her about the big break-up.

As soon as Fionn saw me, she twigged something was up. In fairness, it was probably down to my gaunt expression, lack of make-up and general Mother of Sorrows look. In fact, I had shocked myself when I looked in the mirror earlier that day – and saw my mother looking back. My hair looked greyer. There were a few more lines around my eyes and my whole appearance had taken on that of a sad old spinster destined for a life of loneliness with perhaps the occasional cat for company.

"Are you okay?" Fionn asked, setting down the polystyrene cups of hot tea on the bench and stretching out her arms for a hug.

I hadn't cried before then – because, to be honest, I wasn't that sad about saying goodbye to Pearse. But there in the park, with the thought that the only person ever to hug me again might just be this woman sitting across from me, I let out a big old snottery yelp of tears.

"Jesus, Annie, what is it?" Fionn asked, her soothing tones replaced by blind panic.

"I'm all alone!" I wailed and put my head in my hands. Somewhere in the back of my mind I figured that, as I'd already crossed the line of crying in public, there was no point in being precious about making a total eejit of myself now.

"I'm here," she said.

"But you won't be, not after you're married and all familied up. Where will I be then? Just me."

"You'll have Pearse," she offered and I wailed louder.

(I fully accept that this was not my finest hour.)

When eventually I was composed I explained that, no, I wouldn't have Pearse.

"But surely this is fixable?" she offered, handing me the cup of strong tea.

"No, no," I said. "It's not fixable and I don't think either of us wants to fix it."

She looked puzzled for a second. "Then it's a good thing? If you don't want to fix it, it's a good thing that it's over."

"Except," I sniffed, "for the fact that I'm alone."

"There are worse things," she said.

But then again she would say that – as someone unlikely to ever be alone again.

"And who's to say you'll be alone forever?" she went on with the confidence of someone who reached thirty-five before she met her Mr Right. She had already confided in me that before she met Alex she had resigned herself to a life of spinsterhood. "Love tends to happen when you least expect it."

Meeting him had been a bolt out of the blue and now, just twelve months later, they were planning a wedding and a very lovely happy ever after.

"You're right," I sniffed, trying to pull myself together. "Of course you're right."

"But it's okay to be upset," Fionn soothed, rubbing my hand gently. "I have to say I'm a little shocked. I just expected you and Pearse to be forever."

"Did you really?" I asked, genuinely intrigued, because even though I was now in bits at my alone-ness I can't say that I myself was too shocked that Pearse and I had parted ways.

"I suppose I did. You've been together a long time. You never seemed unhappy – well, not much anyway."

I nodded, wondering to myself if not seeming unhappy was the same as being happy. Surely the one you love should make you delirious? They should make you want to lose the run of yourself and do mad things like bunk off work to spend the day in bed or perform a mad striptease. My mind flashed back to Chewbacca – his hairy arms, which were strong and muscular and had pulled me to him as if I weighed six stone – and I tried to remember the last time I'd lost the run of myself with Pearse. Generally we were both too tired for mad-passion sessions. And he had never, ever pulled me towards him and growled (yes, actually growled) with raw animal passion.

"Penny for them?" Fionn asked.

"To tell you this story, we need something stronger than tea and a setting a little more discreet than a park on a Sunday morning," I said. I also needed to build up the courage to tell her exactly what had pre-empted my relationship break-up and, even though she was my dearest friend, I wasn't sure she was up for hearing about my night of amazing nookie with a stranger.

"So how are you?" I asked, trying to change the subject. "How did things go with Rebecca?"

It was Fionn's turn to grimace. "She's not being awkward as much as being –"

"A bitch?" I interjected.

Fionn shook her head. "I'd like to think not but she said it would be hard for her to change shifts for a full week to give us that time without Emma. She has no one else who could mind her and, while she would like to help out, she just doesn't know that she can."

I sighed. Of course Rebecca could work something out. Surely she could take leave from her nursing job if necessary to mind her own daughter? I said as much to Fionn who just nodded quietly.

"But I don't want to make a fuss. It's hard enough being a part-time mammy as it is, without kicking up a stink and Emma thinking we don't want a bar of her near us on our honeymoon."

Ah, there it was – the Wicked Stepmother fear again.

"I was just hoping Rebecca would be more understanding," she continued. "I mean it's not as if she's jealous or anything. Her and Alex, well, it was a long time ago and didn't really mean anything. I doubt he'd even feature on her radar these days if they hadn't had a child together."

I nodded, thinking that there was no reason why Rebecca wouldn't still be jealous even if she didn't want Alex to herself. I didn't want Alex and yet I was jealous of what the pair of them had. Who's to say, with my reckless behaviour of late, that I wouldn't stoop so low as to use a defenceless child (if I had one) to throw a spanner in the works of their happy ever after?

I wanted to think that I wouldn't and I was pretty sure that on the Big Day, when I stood beside them at the top of the church, the smile on my face would be utterly genuine. But in a way, a small way, I could understand where Rebecca was coming from.

"I'd still say she's jealous," I offered and explained my theory (of course leaving out the bit where I would possibly do the same in her position).

"You might be on to something there," Fionn said, running her fingers through her hair and sighing. "But I mean, what me and Alex have – it is lovely, but there's nothing to say it isn't around the corner for her – or you for that matter." She gave me a warm smile.

Somehow, somewhere deep down, I doubted it *was* around the corner for me, but I simply smiled back. I'd had enough of emotional trauma for one day and I couldn't stand the thought of another mad crying session in the park.

"I'm sure Rebecca will come round, given time," I offered. "It will be an adjustment for her. You know, it must be hard seeing someone else playing mammy to her daughter."

"But I'm not," Fionn protested. "Wicked Stepmother, yes," she said with a wink, "but not mammy. Emma loves her mum and I'm not trying to replace her. I'm only trying to do the best I can to be her friend."

"Five-year-olds don't have much of a need for adult friends though, do they?" I asked.

"Nor do they have a need for two mammies," Fionn replied, "even if one of them is slightly gone in the head."

"Are you referring to yourself or Rebecca?"

Letting myself into the flat, I switched on the gas fire and the telly for the *EastEnders Omnibus*. As I flicked on the kettle I realised I was glad of the distraction of Fionn's complicated stepfamily arrangements. We had successfully managed to keep the conversation as far removed from Pearse and hairy Donegal men as possible – which is exactly what I wanted.

Except, I don't think I really knew what I wanted. Sitting down in front of the telly – cup of tea and chocolate biscuit in hand – I wondered would I ever know what I wanted.

Sliding down into my worn but extremely comfy sofa, I pulled a throw over me and decided to lose myself in the misery of Albert Square.

Two hours later I was just getting ready for that dramatic drum-roll and end credits when my phone rang and I hauled myself from my Sunday afternoon stupor to answer it. No one usually phoned on a Sunday afternoon – leaving me to my alone-time with Pearse or my soaps. Of course, now that there wasn't any chance of any alone-time with Pearse in the near (or indeed distant) future, and my soaps were coming to an end, I had nothing better to do than answer the phone.

A deep, strangely familiar voice spoke. "Is that Annie?"

I struggled to place him. I was pretty sure he wasn't a client from work – and why would a client from work be phoning me at home on a Sunday – or any other day, anyway? And I was fairly sure he wasn't a long-lost family member or old friend.

"Who wants to know?" I asked.

"Ach, you're upsetting me now. Surely you know who it is?" he asked, with a hint of a smile in his voice.

But all my brain could do was draw a dirty great blank.

"I'm sorry," I muttered, thinking that for all I knew he could be a random crank caller who had picked my name out of the phone book or be stalking me from afar. "Can I have a clue?" Just in case it was in fact somebody really very important who would be mortally wounded by my not recognising them from voice alone.

"I didn't think I was that forgettable," he said.

I heard him dragging on a cigarette and it clicked.

Bloody Chewbacca.

But of course that wasn't his real name. I didn't actually know what his real name was – but it would seem exceptionally rude of me to admit that now. I couldn't believe I had actually passed my phone number on to this stranger while not knowing his name. I could only think that I had completely lost my mind when I'd let him into my life, my house and my knickers. But none of that mattered now – what mattered was that I was on the phone to him, not having a clue what his name was, and not knowing how to get myself out of this fix.

Shit and double shit. I had the urge the hang the phone up and pretend I'd never answered it in the first place. In fact, I would just pretend I'd never *met* this nameless creature in the first place, let alone let him into my life and then obviously given him my number. But then again, there must have been something about him that had intrigued me enough to pass on my phone number – even if it was just great sex. A relationship could not be based on that – but I didn't want a relationship with him. At least, I didn't think I did.

But in the absence of any other offers from strange men on a Sunday afternoon, I figured he deserved a hearing – if only I could get over the hump of not knowing his name.

"I'm only teasing," I bluffed – trying not to sound like a coquettish schoolgirl in case he got any notion he could get back in my knickers anytime soon.

"Glad to hear it," he said. "Look, Annie, I really enjoyed myself the other night and it sounded to me like you did too." He laughed – a dirty laugh which I somehow knew should have made me cringe but actually sent a shiver of excitement running up my spine. I was glad, in that instant, that he wasn't in the room with me and had no chance of seeing my face redden. When you think about it, however, that was a little daft considering just how much of me he had clearly already seen.

I giggled back – a little. I think I sounded okay and not demented. Truth was, I just didn't know what to say and my mind was still frantically trying to find some idea inside it as to what his bloody name was.

"Anyway, I wondered," he went on, "if we could, you know, do it again some time?"

Now when he said "do it", I wondered if he meant do *it*. And if so, wasn't he being a little presumptuous? Of course we had ended up doing *it* on our first, erm, date – if you could call it that – but that didn't mean I was the kind of girl who routinely did *it* on a second date – or a first date for that matter. It had taken me over a month to do it with Pearse – and even that was quick compared to my previous record. Contrary to what you may think, I was generally quite reserved when it came to the opposite sex.

I coughed to hide my embarrassment – vaguely aware that my limited responses were in fact creating an impression of me as a total feckwit.

"I mean, I'd like to take you out for dinner," he offered and I breathed a sigh of relief. I probably should have said no, but then as I've already explained I was lacking in other options. All I had to look forward to was being the spinster bridesmaid of my best friend and a lifetime of loneliness. My beautiful laminated Life Plan would mean nothing now – if I didn't find another man, and fast, I'd have to bin the fecker altogether. And I knew that sounded pathetic. And I knew I was a modern, successful woman who didn't need a man to define me. And I knew that I was terribly stupid to think that a man – and only a man – could really make me happy. But I wasn't good on my own. And even though my behaviour with him vaguely disgusted me, I found myself agreeing to dinner with the Nameless Wonder.

"Great," he said and I could hear him smiling down the phone. "I'll take you somewhere special," he vowed. "I was thinking of Manna. I've heard great things about it . . ."

"So you don't know his name?" Fionn asked. "And he wants to take you to Manna?"

"Wanted," I corrected her, sipping from a glass of Merlot and dipping into the box of Maltesers at my side.

Yes, again I knew I was supposed to be going easy on the drink and at this stage my liver was screaming out for a reprieve but desperate times call for desperate measures.

"I said I'd been recently, which wasn't actually a lie, and he agreed to take me somewhere else."

"But you still don't know his name?"

I shook my head and Fionn looked at me with a mixture of disbelief and, dare I guess, admiration. I'd thought she would have been utterly, utterly disgusted with the tales of my wanton misbehaviour with Chewbacca but she had, in fact, laughed her head off. "Well, that explains the sudden change of heart about Pearse!" she'd roared and I didn't correct that by telling her the end of my relationship with Pearse had been anything but sudden. Thinking on it, we had been in the death throes for a really, really long time. Denial was our best friend.

"I probably do know his name," I said, refilling her glass. "I just don't actually remember it at the moment. I'm hoping it will be one of those things which come back to me in the middle of the night. You know how you can just be dropping off to sleep and *bam* – in it pops?"

"I've heard one-night stands described in many ways but that's a new one for me," Fionn said with a wiggle of an eyebrow.

I plastered a look of mock offence on my face. "You know what I mean," I said and sat back against the sofa, again reaching for the Maltesers.

Once Chewbacca had finished chatting to me on the phone, I had gone into a bit of a spin. I wasn't sure if I had done the right thing agreeing to meet him again. I was not sure I had done the right thing meeting him in the very first place, if the truth were told. So I needed to talk and even though Fionn had enough on her plate and it was a school night and Bob would be thoroughly unimpressed with the inevitable whiff of stale booze in the morning, it was inevitable that I would call her. She didn't hesitate – her antenna for scandal on full alert – and within an hour of *EastEnders* ending and my phone call with the mystery man, she was sitting on my floor, drinking wine and coming to terms with the fact her best friend had – for all intents and purposes – acted like a complete hussy during the week.

"Feck me," she said. "You don't do things by half."

"I hadn't actually planned it," I explained to her. "And I don't really understand it. All I know is that something in me shifted and I ended up in bed with someone else. And I don't even know if I like him – in fact, if you had asked me earlier today I would have said it was all a mistake and I didn't care if I never saw him again."

"But you do want to see him again?" she asked, eyebrow raised.

"It can't hurt."

"Apart from the carpet burns from his chest hair," she said with a smile.

I laughed – a genuine out-loud laugh which made me snort just the smallest amount of red wine through my nose and all over the floor.

Fionn stayed over. It was easier than trying to get a taxi and we figured we could land into work together. With Fionn to push me on in the morning, it was also much less likely that I would be late. That had to be a good thing. Sure Bob had warned me about my timekeeping before but there was something in how he warned me about it last week that made me think this time he was actually serious.

So when Fionn shouted, "Wakey wakey!" in a much-too-chipper-for-seven-thirty voice, I resisted the urge to tell her to get to feck and instead hauled myself out of bed and under the shower. As I washed away the smell of stale red wine, I wondered had I been utterly out of my head to agree to a date with a man whose name I didn't know – but who I knew intimately in almost every other way? I admit I did feel a tad sluttish about it – but what worried me (then again, perhaps worried is the wrong word) – is that I quite liked the slutty feeling.

There wasn't much time for feeling slutty with Pearse – not after those initial few weeks and months anyway. It was hard to get yourself into a sexual frenzy with a sweaty, knackered chef with a faint, if permanent, whiff of garlic about him. And he seemed to find it impossible to get himself into a sexual frenzy with me at all – in fact, now that I thought about it, it was hard to remember the last time Pearse and I had had a decent romp. Sure there were duty-fumbles – but passion? Forget about it.

But with Chewbacca – I remembered with a flush of excitement – yes, he knew what he was doing. Perhaps our meeting up again would actually go well? Perhaps it would be for the best? Perhaps it was high time I stepped away from the constraints of the Life Plan and just enjoyed myself for a bit?

With a smile on my face, and a spring in my step (despite the slightly hung-over feeling in my gut) I dressed in my nicest, most professional skirt suit (pencil skirt, boobage-hugging jacket) and high heels with proper stockings and sashayed out the door behind Fionn, unafraid of what the week ahead would hold.

Sure this time last week I hadn't planned on splitting up with Pearse and launching myself once more onto the world of Singledom – but now that I had, I had a feeling it wasn't going to be so bad after all.

6

Bob was in remarkably chipper form when we arrived – on time – and with smiles on our faces. "Ladies," he crooned, "good morning and welcome to another wonderful week!"

Normally I'd have given him a death stare and walked to my desk but I was feeling generous of spirit and smiled back.

"Oh, did someone get some action?" he quipped and I felt myself blush. For all his by-the-book mentality when it came to the office, he was still able to make some amazingly inappropriate statements from time to time.

"And what business is it of yours?" Fionn asked matter of factly, with more confidence in her voice than I could have mustered.

Bob had the good grace to look a little flustered and walk off in the direction of his office while Fionn dissolved into giggles. "He can give it, but he sure can't take it," she said as she sat down and switched on her computer screen.

At around eleven (give or take time for the managers to faff about and decide to run things to their own schedule) we would hold our monthly ops meeting and discuss what campaigns were coming up, what was still bubbling along and needed a little help, and any pitches we were putting in for new clients.

It was generally about that time that Bob would announce

another jump in targets, and we'd all groan, have a bitch and then Fionn and I would clear off with our prop cigarette packets and lighters for an FSB and plan how to hurt Bob in a 101 ways no one had even thought of yet.

The routine of it all was at the same time comforting and utterly depressing. Yes, things could get weirdly exciting when we were given something weird and wonderful to sell, and sometimes the thrill of an upped target was enough to give me an injection of adrenalin and a new-found love for my job. But at other times I just wished I had some easy little job where I sat all day, knew my targets, filled them easily and didn't feel as if I had to beg people to spend money just to keep myself a hair's breadth away from my P45.

And of course Bob had made it fairly obvious last week that I was moving ever closer to the dole queue so there was no way I could slip up now. I would have to be one hundred per cent on my game – so spending thirty minutes Googling for advice on how to find out the name of someone you slept with, and who you were due again to meet for dinner, without actually having to admit you didn't have the wits about you to find out in the first place, was not a good idea.

Google didn't really provide any answers and Fionn seemed to find it increasingly hilarious as the day went on.

"Do you really need to know his name?" she asked during FSB3.

"Well, it would make it easier – you know, for phoning him, or storing his number in my phone – that kind of thing? I'm not sure he would be too flattered to know he is currently stored under the name of a *Star Wars* character."

"Well, it probably wouldn't surprise him. I mean he must be aware of how hairy he is and it mustn't annoy him too much."

I smiled, a conciliatory smile which meant I knew Fionn was right but at the end of the day I couldn't assume that he would be happy for me to spend the rest of our relationship avoiding calling him by his actual name. I mean, it was okayish now when we were only planning our second date – but should things progress, I imagine it would get harder and harder to hide the fact I didn't have a baldy notion who he was. Introducing him to my parents would be a fecker for one thing – not to mention the whole "I, Annie, take thee whatever-the-feck-you're-called to be my lawful wedded husband . . ." thing.

"You could just make up a name for him," Fionn suggested during FSB5. "I mean a proper name – not a *Star-Wars*-inspired name. And tell him you think it suits him so much better. Or better still just call him 'Stud'. I bet he would love it if you just called him 'Stud'."

I had immediate visions of myself in overly tight leather trousers and a spiral perm, stubbing out my cigarette with the heel of my impossibly high stiletto and singing about him being the one that I wanted while he shimmied and shook his carpet of excessive hair in my direction. No, no, that wasn't going to work at all – even if he did seem to be the kind of guy who *would* secretly quite like to be referred to as 'Stud'.

Every now and again a thought of Pearse jumped into my head. It would be over something silly. During the monthly meeting we were talking about a new slimming club we were hoping to represent. Pearse hated slimming clubs and all their restrictions. He would complain bitterly about the hordes of women who would take up the very popular seats at Manna and order a small plain steak with a garnish of green salad – no dressing allowed. He thought it such a waste of a good night out and for that alone I loved him (past tense – I reminded myself) because I was never, ever going to be the kind of girl who could settle for a small plain steak with garnish. Even my healthiest eating attempts would not see me stoop so low. I was the kind of girl who would go to the salad bar at Sainsbury's, on the premise of being good, and stock up on all sorts of creamy pasta delights before adding a token leaf of lettuce and a cherry tomato just to take the bad look off myself. (And it was amazing how often I could convince myself it was okay not to eat the lettuce after all because I had eaten the rest of my "healthy" salad with gusto.)

Later that afternoon "Hot Stuff" was playing on the radio and I remembered how – in the first flushes of our relationship – I used to sing it (badly) to him when he called to mine after a night at the restaurant, sweaty and smelling of spices. As the song played in the office I felt a little pang of regret but managed to push it away. It had been a long time since we'd shared a hot-stuff moment – those spicy moments had long since lost their appeal. There is only so much caressing from onion-flavoured fingers a girl can take before she too starts to develop a faint whiff of kitchen stink about her.

I'm sure Fionn was only too aware of my pangs of . . . something . . . I can't describe it as regret, over Pearse. She sent occasional emails throughout the day – generally with pictures of very hairy men in them or a witty line or two about the best way to get over one man was to get under another one.

Well, I had already done the getting under another one bit and I don't think I wanted to get over Pearse as much as I wanted to come to terms with the fact that, with the exception of a man whose name I didn't even know, I had no romantic life to speak of. Which brought me back once again to my Life Plan and the fact that it was spiralling away from me at a rate of knots. I wondered if I should just bin it – but then it contained years of deepest thoughts and hopes. It was me – and everything I ever wanted. And just every now and again, while I clicked on the latest image of Tom Selleck sent to me by Fionn, or jumped as Bob glided silently up beside me, I felt a little bereft that the Me I had wanted to be for so long was never going to happen.

By home time I was resisting the urge for a glass of wine and a kingsize Galaxy. I had to manage without drink – even if just for one night. It dawned on me it had been a very liquid week and, with payday still looming somewhere off in the distance, it seemed daft to assault my plummeting bank account with yet another trip to the off licence.

So instead I went home and promised myself a soak in the bath, a read of a good book and an early night. I figured distracting myself with someone else's fantasies in the form of a trashy novel, before falling into a blissfully sleepy oblivion, would be the perfect way to quiet the voices in my head.

Climbing the many stairs to my flat, my legs ached. It was strange how, even after all this time and all the many trips I had made up and down those stairs, they still had the ability to make my calves scream for sweet mercy.

Opening the door, I went straight to the bathroom and set about lighting the candles which were dotted around it. The only ones I didn't light where the sandalwood Yankee Candles which reminded me too much of Pearse. In fact, I picked them up and hid them in the cupboard under the sink. I would have binned them but, feck it, they were expensive and they did smell nice. I was sure one day I would be able to burn them freely without feeling this sinking sense of disappointment in myself.

I started to run the bath – an old roll-top which stood just left of centre in my cavernous bathroom. I dollopped in half a bottle of Sanctuary bubble bath and watched the foam grow and rise at a frighteningly impressive rate. I dipped the lights and closed the door. I don't know why I closed the door – it wasn't as if anyone had half a chance of walking in on me but I had to do it anyway. Even if, like the toilet, there was no way I could reach the door to make sure it was locked if I took a mid-soak panic.

I stripped off my clothes, showered quickly first, and then climbed into the bubbles, sinking down under them as I let the gorgeous rich aromas fill my nose. I lay there for ten minutes before I lifted my novel and started to read. While it felt strange not to have a glass of wine in my hand, or the phone at arm's length so I could call Pearse and chat about the mundane activities of my day, I started to read and stayed there until the water started to go cold and my fingers and toes wrinkled enough to resemble those of a shrivelled corpse. It was not a good look, so I climbed out, wrapped my oversized and fluffy dressing gown around me and climbed into bed – again with only my book for company. I could see the Life Plan, jutting out from under the chest of drawers where I had pushed it in a fit of over-emotional hysteria the day before, and I rolled over so it was out of my line of vision.

If only I could get it out of my head altogether.

7

Wednesday arrived and I still did not know Chewbacca's name. I did know, however, that I had to accompany Pearse to dinner that evening. He had called me early in the day to tell me that he was sending a dress over for me and that I was to be ready for six thirty.

I wondered, momentarily, what kind of dress he would have chosen for me. I had told him I had plenty of my own clothes I could wear, but he had insisted: "No, please, let me." I felt moved that he could see beyond his anger at our relationship break-up to treat me to one final gift.

Then again, he probably wanted to make sure, one hundred per cent, that I looked the part. This was sure to be a dress that would set tongues wagging.

And it was.

If the Taliban made evening gowns they would look like this one. In fact, the only things Pearse had left out of his choice of attire for me were the actual sackcloth and ashes. Or perhaps a giant scarlet *A for Adulteress* emblazoned across the front. There was a minimal amount of flesh on show – my hands and neck area were just about free. The rest of me was swathed in yards of heavy black material which neither flattered me nor made me feel remotely comfortable.

In fact, as I hobbled down the stairs of my house to the awaiting car, I could already feel myself break into a sticky sweat.

I had done my best – my hair was teased to perfection, piled high on my head in a funky up-do. I had accessorized as best I could with a chunky silver necklace and some gorgeous silver heels – but none of my efforts took away from the fact I looked as if I should be in the backstage crew of the local pantomime.

Perhaps Pearse was hoping I would fade into the background – just be there to hand drinks around and smile when necessary. But if he had wanted me to be invisible, he could have just uninvited me. I was only going out of a sense of loyalty and, if I admit it, guilt. I could just as easily have stayed at home and contemplated my date with Chewy – or washed my hair – or something equally exciting.

However, I felt so completely conspicuous – so totally awkward and uncomfortable in this get-up – that there was no way I was going to be able to fade into the scenery. My blazing red cheeks from the growing heat of the synthetic fibres would be enough to make sure I stuck out like a sore thumb.

I wriggled my way into the taxi and tried to take the sheen off my face with some pressed powder. A lot of pressed powder.

I arrived at Manna looking and feeling like one of the restaurant's signature dishes – cooked to perfection and emitting a fine aroma. Pearse was waiting for me at the door – a fake smile plastered on his face for his assembled guests to see.

"Annie," he said cheerily, "you look good."

I grimaced at him before forcing a smile onto my face and kissing him on the cheek. His skin felt cold, just like his entire demeanour.

"Let's go in," he said, gripping my hand in his and leading me through the throngs of the great and the good, smiling as he went.

He listened intently as partners were introduced. Occasionally he nodded in my direction but he didn't introduce me. He didn't tell people I ever had been, or was ever likely to be, anything to him.

The thing is, it then dawned on me, that during these types of soirées in the past – and not just when we had broken up because I had slept with someone else – he never introduced me as anyone important. Occasionally I got: "This is Annie. She works for NorthStar." But I never got: "This is Annie, she is my girlfriend" or "Meet my other half, Annie." Or "Have you met my lovely partner, Annie?"

No, I was Annie. Just Annie. Who worked for NorthStar. There was never any hint that I meant anything more to him than someone with good contacts with the local media and the ability to write a good press release.

That night was to be no different – except I was to feel as physically uncomfortable as I did emotionally. And all of it – every last second of it – was down to Pearse.

So I trudged about in my designer sackcloth and ashes with my smile never fading while inside all I could think of was that I wanted to be home and as far away from this lie as possible.

I didn't talk to Fionn about the night with Pearse. I didn't tell her that it had all gone on too long until he finally said I could go home at around twelve thirty. He didn't call me a taxi. I made my own way home, stripping off the horrendous dress as soon as I was inside the door and bundling it into a bin bag. I would return it to Pearse as soon as possible. Perhaps he could get some use out of it with his next trophy missus.

In fact, I buried the whole sorry affair in the back of my mind and carried on as normal.

I went to work and had a laugh with Fionn. She continued to find pictures of increasingly hairy men – some of which frankly disturbed me – and email them at semi-regular intervals. We had our usual Fake Smoke Breaks – except now with the thought of the dress of her dreams firmly in her mind, Fionn was actually considering taking a real smoke break or ten to curb her appetite. She had given up smoking three years before, but she still missed it. Desperately. I saw that faraway look of longing while we huddled in the smoking shelter outside work and her nostrils caught the faint sniff of a smoking butt smouldering in the overstuffed ashtray.

"Yes, I know it's bad for me," she said, "but I'm thinking, you know, as a short-term thing, it could stop me munching on Maltesers of an afternoon and that dress could look really spectacular on me."

"The dress already looks spectacular on you," I reassured her, but I don't think that's what she wanted to hear. I think she wanted me to say it was perfectly okay to give into a three-year-old craving that was refusing to die but, seeing as I was on a self-imposed wine ban and narky with it, she was looking for support for nasty habits in the wrong place.

"But it could look *really* spectacular," she said, gazing forlornly at a colleague trying to light a Silk Cut despite the wind howling round his lighter.

"But you would stink of fags and that's never a good thing for a bride," I challenged. "I mean, you want to be sexy and floral and beautiful – not yellow-toothed and smelling like you just fell out of an ashtray."

My mind flashed back to the staleness of my flat after my night of passion with the Hairy-Backed One and I tried to remember whether or not his teeth were stained yellow and whether or not he predominantly smelled of smoke. Nope – musky. He had a musky, masculine scent. A shiver of excitement shot through me. It was a nice smell.

"I suppose you're right," she said, thankfully not noticing the flush of colour rising through my face and turning my cheeks pink with the memory of a very musky man making me scream out in pleasure (or perhaps that was a reaction to the carpet-like burns?).

"Of course I'm right. I'm always right, sometimes . . ." I said, turning her physically away from the waft of smoke making its way towards her. "Maybe we should cut back on these fake breaks if you want to resist temptation."

"Very funny. Very funny indeed," she laughed. "And spend all day, with no reprieve, looking at Bawb and trying to figure out if he is *actually* half-human, half-robot? No. No, I'll not smoke. Promise. But don't take away the fake breaks. I need the fake breaks."

She looked kind of desperate and I felt sorry for her. She was showing a little extra strain lately. You would think that with a big wedding to plan she would be on Cloud Nine but she seemed distracted. As we walked back to the office – already having set a time for our next FSB – I vowed I would have a chat with her about it later and make sure she was fine.

Ideally we would have had that chat over a glass of wine, but I was determined not to break my self-imposed ban until my date with Chewbacca. Instead I vowed to see if she wanted a coffee after work and we could take it from there. I also wanted to ask her whether she thought it was worth my while shaving my legs before my big date on Friday night. It wasn't so much that I wanted her approval should I choose to jump into the sack with the Hairy One again – more I wanted to gauge whether or not he would even notice, considering how hirsute he was himself. To be honest, it could be a very nice plus point to any possible relationship – the ability to forget about the necessity of always being baby-bottom smooth in the leg (or other) department.

I sent her a cheeky email – having found a remarkably gory picture of a man with the longest ear-hair on record – and made sure to tell her that, as far as I could remember, this was one area in which Chewie was at least groomed – and then mentioned the coffee.

I watched her face for a reaction and she did smile and then typed back.

"Sorry. Can't tonight. Going to see Rebecca to continue the Honeymoongate discussions and then Emma is coming back to ours for yet another riveting Disney DVD. I'm plumping for *Enchanted* as at least in that the wee girl's mammy has had the good grace to feck off for good."

It had been easy – too easy, I suppose – for me to be so caught up in my relationship issues and complete breakdown of my coveted Life Plan that I had forgotten all about Rebecca and her unhelpfulness regarding the wedding and honeymoon. I knew Fionn adored Emma but surely she was entitled to a week of bonking and romance without the fear of an inquisitive five-year-old popping her head around the corner at any stage to ask a host of awkward and embarrassing questions?

I typed back: "Well, I'm here to talk about it when you want to. And if you don't think talking will do any good, I'm more than willing to help you plot a devious and evil plan to sort out the whole situation."

I did think, briefly, before I hit the *Send* button. I wondered, should Rebecca mysteriously fall off the earth the week before the wedding, would my emails be checked and possibly used in evidence against me? But I decided to live dangerously anyway. Anyone who knew me knew I didn't have an evil bone in my body – apart from maybe Pearse who was probably around now convincing himself I was the Wicked Witch of the West.

Fionn replied with a simple thanks and I decided it was best to leave it for then. She would open up when she was ready to and not a moment before – and, besides, it wasn't really any of my business.

Apart from my secret envy of the Fionn-Alex relationship, I also found the looming marriage hard to accept for another reason. Alex was essentially marrying the closest thing I had to a soul mate. He was the most important person in her life now – when I suppose I liked to think that once upon a time I was. In a non-lesbian way of course. I didn't have secret Fionn fantasies – it was just hard to accept that she was closer to someone else (a smelly boy of all people!) than she was to me. That thought alone reconfirmed to me that my previous relationship must have been ultimately flawed – because I never felt closer to Pearse than to Fionn. If I'm honest there were days when I felt more intrinsically linked to Bob and all his god-awful gobshitedness than I did to Pearse.

No, I had to step back and, for the moment anyway, leave this dilemma to Fionn and Alex to work out for themselves. And besides – I had bigger fish to fry. I had to actually try and sell some ads this month and I had to decide what to wear for my big date – including whether or not to consider sexy undies. I cringed when I thought of the combo I was wearing the last time I had met with

Chewbacca. They were at least black and matching – but owed more to the power of lycra and soft cotton than lace and sex appeal. They were built for comfort not for speed. Then again I hadn't been planning on showing them to anyone. And much as I liked to look semi-decent on a day-to-day basis, I was not one of those ladies who trussed herself up in sexy undies for an ordinary day at work. It would have made me feel really sluttish and neither Fionn nor I were sure that Bob didn't have some Super Sense or X-ray vision (after all, he was the man who could silently glide through a room) which would enable him to tell and then make some sleazy remark. His ordinary remarks were sleazy enough without giving him food for thought.

As if to prove a point, he appeared beside me just as I clicked onto a sexy undies website and I had to click as fast as my mouse would allow me before he had the chance to say something entirely inappropriate.

"Interesting," he said with a raised eyebrow.

"Love, Sex and Magic are thinking of stocking some of this stuff," I bluffed and he looked me up and down before smiling again.

"Yes, yes, good idea," he said. "But avoid the red lace. It's a little *too* slutty."

He walked off smiling and I decided I needed another fake break to get the mental image of Bob ogling me in a red lace basque out of my head.

It was hard to get through Friday without thinking about the big date. Not least because I still hadn't figured out how to explain the fact that I didn't know Chewie's real name. It would be interesting, to say the least, to try and get through the evening without making a complete eejit of myself.

I had decided in the end to avoid any overtly sexy underwear, although I had nipped in to Marks and Spencer in my lunch break and bought something new and just a little lacy. I had also shaved my legs, just in case. In a fit of madness I had coated myself in fake tan on the Thursday evening and tried to sleep amid the fug of sickly sweet fumes rising from my body. Thankfully, the effort of almost gassing myself with a mixture of coconut and chemicals paid off, and by Friday morning I had a healthy glow about me.

It didn't stop Bob singing the song about the Oompa Loompas from *Charlie and the Chocolate Factory* as I walked into work that morning but I silenced him with a withering look and a chocolate doughnut. He was a very lucky man not to have said doughnut rammed down his throat at the speed of light – and I think he knew it. He backed off pretty soon after and stayed in his office – which was a blessed relief.

It left me free to distract myself from my forthcoming date with booking ads and talking to clients and only very occasionally emailing Fionn – who still seemed to be in a bit of a fug. We had agreed to go shoe-shopping the following day to find the perfect shoes to go with her perfect dress but she didn't seem particularly enthusiastic about it any more.

She hadn't told me exactly what had happened with Rebecca on Wednesday night when they met to discuss the honeymoon plans but I knew that it had not been good and that she was seriously contemplating my offer to put in place a vengeful plan of attack against her partner's ex.

The thing that galled her most, I think, was that Rebecca had seemed perfectly sane and lovely up to the point that Fionn and Alex announced their engagement. In fact, Fionn used to say how she just couldn't believe that they all got along so amiably – especially when a young child was involved.

We *would* talk about it the next day though – whether Fionn wanted to or not. I made myself that promise.

In the meantime I would focus on my first date in a very long time. I felt a mixture of what can only be described as sheer terror and utter excitement. It felt thrilling – the thought of meeting someone new, experiencing those first flushes of lust again. And who knows what might come of it.

Sure it hadn't been in my Life Plan – which was still languishing under the chest of drawers in my room – but that didn't mean it wouldn't be a good thing. In fact, even though I wasn't sure if this particular man was the good thing I was looking for, I was increasingly confident that I was doing the right thing.

And, it was Friday, my week-long walk in the desert abstaining from alcohol was officially over, and I fully intended to enjoy a glass of two of crisp white wine while I got ready at home. I wasn't sure which I was looking forward to more – the drink or the date. And yes, I know that makes me sound like an awful lush but sometimes a girl just needs a drink – and when she is contemplating a new relationship at thirty-two is one of those times.

I managed to leave work a little early – in enough time to allow myself a long soak in the bath with the aforementioned glass of wine.

I took time to dress in a gorgeous black wraparound dress (no hint of Taliban-style cover-up necessary), with killer heels that would no doubt make me want to beg for an early death should I have to walk further than from the taxi to the restaurant. I slipped on some stockings too – which made me feel very naughty indeed. I just could not countenance putting on a pair of normal tights – regardless of what would or wouldn't happen as the evening progressed – ordinary tights made me feel like a frumpy fifty-something-year-old with neither the desire for nor probability of any kind of action any time soon. I wore ordinary tights a lot in the latter stages of my relationship with Pearse.

For the Hairy One I even straightened my own hair – slapping on a dozen different hair-care products to promote shine, minimise frizz, hold some volume and keep my hair looking fresh as a daisy amid whatever might happen.

My make-up was applied with precision – there was no mere slathering on of foundation and quickly dabbing at blemishes with a stubby concealer. I used Touche Éclat, loose powder, mascara *and* an eyeliner. This was a full-on assault on my face and, even if I say so myself, I was quite impressed with the end result when I looked in the mirror. I looked half-decent. Even a wee bit sexy. And as I spritzed some Thierry Mugler *Alien* on my neck, and down my cleavage, I *felt* a wee bit sexy.

The taxi arrived magically on time and I managed to make it down the stairs to the ground floor without killing myself (having long ago learned the lesson that you don't put the killer heels on until you have descended from your top-floor flat).

It did feel kind of weird driving on past Manna and not dropping in for a complementary glass of fizz and some stuffed mushrooms. But it also felt deliciously wicked to think that on that evening at least I might be getting my stuffing elsewhere.

We had agreed to meet at Karma – a modern, sleek lounge bar and restaurant on the banks of the Foyle which served the nicest tapas in town.

The barman gave me a strange look when I walked in, alone. He was used to seeing me on the arm of Pearse – on some of our many expeditions to check out the competition. I swear I actually saw a look of relief pass over his face when he realised that no one was following me in the door. It wasn't that they had anything to fear from Manna but the presence of Pearse Campbell in any restaurant in town sent people into a bit of a flap. As well as being the head honcho at Manna, he also fancied himself as a celebrity chef and had even been on *Ready Steady Cook* a couple of times. He was ridiculously proud of what he could whip together from just a sweet potato, cheap cut of meat and tin of olives. He wouldn't serve anything like it in his restaurant, of course, but that didn't stop him being proud.

I smiled in the direction of the barman, secretly relieved myself that no one was following me in, and I walked over and ordered a glass of Pinot Grigio. Scanning the room, I saw no immediate sign of a walking carpet so took a seat at the bar and tried not to gawp every time the door opened. I composed myself into a semi-comfortable pose, adopting a casually nonchalant look as if sitting at a bar by myself was completely natural to me. Although given that when I'd had my first encounter with the Hairy One I had been doing just that, it was a given he would think it was natural anyway. In fact, he would probably think I was a total lush. And a slapper. And what made it worse was that a lushy slapper seemed to be just the kind of woman he wanted to spend his evenings with. I had a dose of the collywobbles but thankfully copped myself on before I started gulping the wine like a woman on the verge of an alcoholic-induced coma.

I was just reaching the bottom of my first glass, in record time, when I heard the bell above the door ring – despite the noise – and I looked around and saw him. He was remarkably good-looking. I think in part this was due to the fact that he was fully clothed and the full extent of his hirsutism was hidden. He was wearing a suit, which was deliciously crumpled and his eyes were heavy with either desire or exhaustion – I couldn't tell from that distance. There were traces of his hairiness. A tuft of hair threatened to rise above his shirt collar and swamp his Adam's apple. His hands looked a little as if he was wearing some of those freaky werewolf pretend-hands from Halloween. Bizarrely, he was completely clean-shaven – which looked odd. Although I appreciated that if we were going to get intimate in any way, shape or form later, it would be much nicer not to have to deal with his bristle.

He looked around and I waved – a regal queen-like wave – and he smiled. He had a nice smile, and perfect teeth. They weren't even remotely hairy. I smiled back as he walked towards me and I muttered a "Hey". I would have added his name but I was still lamentably ignorant.

"Annie," he said. "Lovely to see you."

He looked me up and down, mentally undressing me in a way that sent a frisson of excitement shooting down my spine and straight to my special lady place. I blushed at the thought. And blushed harder that as a grown woman I was unable to think of my intimate areas as anything other than "special lady places". I would be a crap dirty talker.

"Lovely to see you too," I said and smiled. I was smiling a lot. I knew I looked like a fecking eejit.

He glanced towards my wineglass, the dregs of which looked miserable and said: "Pinot Grigio?"

"How did you guess?"

"We pinned a bottle back at yours that last night, don't you remember?"

I laughed nervously. There was no way I was admitting I didn't remember what wine we drank, or even that we drank wine at all. It would lead to all sorts of confusion and stress and me admitting I didn't know his name.

"Of course," I added.

He gestured to the barman who now looked even more confused, at the fact that not only was I not with Pearse, I appeared to be with someone else entirely.

"A bottle of Pinot Grigio, please?" he smiled. "Just put it on our tab."

"Of course," the barman replied.

I was relieved when a new glass was put in front of me. Something about this man, and his complete and utter masculinity, made me very, very nervous and very, very in need of a drink.

"Shall we get a table?" he asked, sipping from his glass.

I nodded. "That would be nice."

"I'm starving," he said, and something about how he said it made me very aware that he was not just talking about food.

As we sat and ordered a selection of tapas, I was surprised at how easily we made conversation. I mean I knew relatively nothing about this man except that he smoked and was, from what I could remember, an exceptionally good shag. I bluffed it enough through general chatter to find out that he worked in banking and was relatively well off. He didn't have a big house on the hill like Pearse – but he had a nice house by the sea with nicely proportioned rooms and, I imagined, a bathroom door within easy reach of the toilet in case of people-breaking-in emergencies.

I chatted about my job – the deadlines, the Fake Smoke Breaks and Bob. Some of it he apparently knew already from our first encounter but he didn't seem to mind listening again.

My salvation came over the king prawns when an equally handsome man in an equally crumpled suit walked over and said hello.

"Anton!" he said cheerily, reaching out for a manly handshake.

I had to sit on *my* hands to stop myself from jumping up and declaring: "Anton! Thank feck for that!"

Anton smiled back and the men chatted briefly about something or other. I wasn't listening. I was too busy internal-happy-dancing at finally knowing his name. As the mystery man walked away, I felt at last in my comfort zone.

"So, Anton," I said breezily, "shall we order dessert after this?"

"I thought we'd been through this," he said with a sly smile.

"Through what?" I said, alarm bells ringing. What had we been through? He hated desserts? He was on a low-carb diet? He had diabetes? Desserts were against his religion? He thought I was grossly overweight? He thought women shouldn't take the initiative in restaurants? The possibilities were endless . . .

"You agreed to call me Ant – you know, as in Ant & Dec."

"But I like Anton!" I said, missing hardly a beat and managing, I hoped, to conceal both my relief about the dessert issue and the fact that my memory of said conversation was just a black hole in space.

"I thought we agreed 'Anton' sounds a bit 1970s' male hairdresser?" he said.

"Oh, I don't know. My friend Fionn has a mad fancy for that Anton Du Beke character from *Strictly Come Dancing* and he's not gay," I countered.

"No, well, I know that. But he's a dancer. Not exactly a man's man. I prefer to present a more manly persona to the public."

With body-hair like that he didn't have to worry on that score.

He laughed. "My parents thought they were being trés chic when they named me Anton – cooler than Anthony but still getting the hint of a saint's name in."

"Well, both are fine with me," I said, secretly commenting that anything was preferable to Chewbacca or "yer man" or, as Fionn had suggested earlier that day, "Plunkett". (She had taken a call from a similarly oddly named customer and laughed herself silly that it could be my hairy-backed lover.)

"And where did Annie come from?" he asked. "It's not that common a name these days."

"My parents are John Denver fans," I replied. "I'm named after the song."

"Oh, what song's that?" he asked, surprising me by not bursting into a verse of the country classic – *"You fill up my senses . . ."* – the usual response to my revealing my name.

I toyed with the idea of answering "Grandma's Feather Bed" but I guessed if he didn't know a classic like "Annie's Song" he was unlikely to be completely au fait with Mr Denver's quirkier back catalogue.

Instead I answered straight and gave him a blast of the first line myself. He nodded – somewhere between faint recognition and fear that he was sitting in a very public place with a lady liable to burst into song at any moment. I started to wonder at that moment if this was all going to go wrong. At least Pearse had known "Annie's Song". He had even serenaded me with it once in a closed Manna after hours, back in the very early days of our relationship of course. It was at the time when I still thought he had a spark and excitement about him relating to anything other than food produce and cooking methods.

Still, I tried to push my doubts about Chewie – sorry – Ant to the back of my head and we continued with our meal. There was something undeniably sexy about him and I tried to focus on that – and the fact I did not want the effort of shaving my legs to go to waste.

As it happened, with a glass more of wine, we were chattering like old friends. Old friends, admittedly, who had feck all in common. By after-dinner coffee (which was of course ignored in favour of after-dinner wine) I was feeling hazy and starting to wonder if tonight would go the same way as the last time we had been together. I, at least, despite four glasses of finest Pinot Grigio, felt fully in control of my faculties which made the whole "Will I or won't I invite him back to my place?" dilemma a little more difficult. I didn't want to come across as a tart – although in fairness I knew there was a strong possibility I had achieved that goal last time – but I also didn't want Anton Dunne (as it turned out his full name was) to walk away. I wondered if that sounded desperate – it did a little in my head. But, even though he didn't have a baldy notion who John Denver was, I had to cling to the hope that he was a nice sexy guy and that perhaps there was a reason fate had thrown us together just over a week ago. And fate was a fecker – making me think my Life Plan was all on track and then throwing a hairy spanner in the works. The spanner had to have his purpose, though, and I hoped that would mean that with little awkwardness he would come back to my flat that evening. And that when I woke in the morning there would no hint of vague disgust at what, or who, I had done.

I looked at him, his dark, round eyes staring at me. I looked at his werewolf hands – and something about the carpet of hair creeping out from under his shirt cuffs made me feel a little funny inside.

"So," I said and he smiled, a deeply sexy smile.

"So," he replied and I smiled, not overly sure mine was sexy and not just a little demented but he didn't run screaming so I have to assume it was the former.

He reached out and took my hand, caressing it slowly, stroking my palm and then turning my hand over to gently caress my fingers. I looked at him again and he wasn't smiling – he was in fact looking as if he could pounce over the table at any moment and ravish me right then and there in the restaurant.

"Let's go back to mine," I said, in a voice a little higher than a whisper and he nodded.

"I'll just pay the bill," he muttered, leaving me sitting there in a state of high anticipation at what was about to happen. I went to the ladies' for a quick reapplication of lippy and a nice spritz of perfume and I checked my mobile phone.

"Have fun. Be good. And be careful," Fionn had texted and I smiled. I had no plans to be good at all – just very, very bad.

9

I got two hours sleep that night. And yet when I woke up I didn't feel overly exhausted – sore, yes – with a touch of that thigh-ache that Fionn had spoken about after her drunken night with Alex.

Anton Dunne was lying beside me, snoring gently. The room was thick with a haze of sweat and cigarette smoke. (Yes, I had let him smoke there again, despite my promises that I wouldn't – but, you know, I felt he deserved it after his sterling performance . . .)

I had a stupid smile on my face. I felt, for the first time in a long time, satisfied. Part of me fought the urge to phone Pearse up, just to let him know that I hadn't felt the need to fake anything with my new partner and to tell him if he treated his women with half the care and attention he used when stuffing a mushroom he might not have found himself single again.

Yes, I felt smug. I felt the smugness of a woman who had just had damn fine sex. And this time I could remember it. I could remember almost every touch, every kiss, every caress and every bite. (Oh yes, there was some nibbling going on . . . it was very pleasant.) I didn't feel even vaguely disgusted. I just ignored the hairy-back issue and instead luxuriated in running my hands through his chest hair. With my slut-red fingernails I felt very 1970s' porn star. It was so unlike me to be so free with my sexual favours that I felt positively wanton. Maybe this is what Madonna had been harping on about every time she told us women to express ourselves. Because, believe me, I felt empowered.

I climbed out of bed, leaving him sleeping, and stood under the shower letting the hot jets wash over me. I felt happy as a pig in shite, I realised. I'd had three amazingly wonderful orgasms the night before. I didn't feel even remotely hung-over and, to top it all, I had plans to go shoe-shopping with Fionn. What more could a girl ask for?

If there were any nagging doubts in my head – any teeny tiny voices telling me that this was not my usual behaviour and that I shouldn't play with fire for fear of getting burned, I hushed them with a rousing chorus of "Annie's Song". Oh yes, my senses were well and truly filled.

When I was dressed I walked into the bedroom and opened the windows to the bright spring morning. Ant didn't stir. Seemed nothing much stirred him. Glancing at my watch, I realised I had to be out in half an hour and I needed to make sure he was gone. Even though he had shared my bed twice, I didn't really know him and I certainly could not leave him unattended in my flat. I might not have had much in the line of luxury goods, but what little I did have I wanted to keep, and I certainly didn't want him hoking through my knicker-drawer.

"Morning, sunshine," I said breezily, watching the soft air from outside ruffle his back hair.

He grunted. It wasn't vaguely sexy.

"Ant, good morning," I said a little louder. "Rise and shine!"

He lay for a second, then turned with a smile on his face – and with one quick glance downward I could see that he was indeed rising and shining.

I was twenty minutes late for meeting Fionn and my hair was a little more ruffled than I had intended. I had dropped Ant off in the centre of town with the promise that we would meet again, and that he would call. I had parked my car and hotfooted it to Debenhams'

Café where Fionn was sitting, thankfully with a look of amusement on her face.

"So I've no need to ask how your night went then," she said with a smile.

"No," I answered, straightening my hair, "I don't suppose you do."

"And were you good and/or careful?" she asked with her best step-mammy-in-training voice.

"I was, he tells me, very good," I said with a wink. "But yes, Mammy, I was also very careful."

Fionn laughed but then she looked at me, that mammy-look square back on her face. "I just want you to be okay. I know you're going through big changes but I want you to be sensible with it. I don't want you to get hurt."

"I'll be sensible," I promised because I really didn't want to get hurt either.

I ordered a coffee and we sat back, sipping in silence for a few minutes, and then I realised that I didn't want this day to be about me and my liaisons. I wanted it to be about Fionn and her wedding and finding the most gorgeous shoes in the entire world to go with her stunning dress.

"Right, lady, should we get shopping then?"

"Just as soon as I've finished this coffee," she said. "I've seen some lovely shoes downstairs and fitted them on and they're perfect – but they are a bit, you know, different and I'd value your opinion."

"Hey, I'm all about the opinion," I said with a smile, which reminded me of something. "So, you know, when you're ready to tell me the latest instalment in the Rebecca dilemma, I'm all ears and ready to jump in with suitably bitchy and nasty comments where appropriate."

Fionn smiled, but it was a small smile and I could tell that the Rebecca issue was becoming less and less of a laughing matter. "I'll tell you later," she said. "And I might just take you up on that offer of plotting some dastardly plan to sort her out."

"Oh dear. Not going well then?" I offered.

"That, my dear, would be an understatement. But I refuse to get bogged down in this just now when there are very, very ridiculously pretty shoes in this very building with my name quite possibly all over them. Drink up your coffee and let's get moving!"

It was only the closest of friends who could have detected that she was gripping her own coffee cup a little too tightly and that her eyes were a little tired – and I was pretty sure it wasn't from an all-night bonking session.

"Right then," I said, setting my cup back on the table. "Lead the way to Shoe Paradise!"

Linking arms we headed to the shoe concessions and I darted in the direction of the gorgeous ivory satin-covered peep-toe shoes, embellished with crystals and with heels that would cripple even the hardiest of stiletto-wearing fashionistas.

"Oh no," Fionn said with a cheeky grin. "I have something altogether more fabulous in mind."

Intrigued, I followed her across the shop floor to a stand where – perched on top of the display – were a pair of bright pink satin-covered heels – so deliciously high and feminine I almost fainted. With delicate ankle straps, a small diamante buckle and the pointiest toes in Christendom, they actually made me gasp with delight.

"What do you think?"

"They are very, very beautiful but very, very pink," I said, resisting the urge to reach out and stroke them.

"No one will see them under my dress," she said "But I would know they were there and I would feel fantastic in them."

"Well then, my dear, you simply have to get them. You must feel fabulous."

"You are right, and I will," she said with a grin before lifting them and practically dancing to the sales counter to ask for a pair, boxed, in her size and ready to take home.

"I just feel like doing something a little different," she said as she handed over her credit card. "I'm always predictable and doing what people expect – but people won't expect me to wear bright pink shoes – not even Alex."

Again I noted the forced smile and I gave her hand a wee rub.

"We will talk about this," I said.

"Maybe later. Surely you have shopping to do? I mean, I know we were supposed to choose the shoes together but I got here early and had a look around – so now I feel I've robbed you of your shopping experience. So, my dear, I thought we could have a quick look at some bridesmaid dresses!"

I almost yelped in delight before remembering my face was a little sallow from the after-effects of my four glasses of wine the night before and my serious lack of sleep. Not to mention my hair still had that bird's-nest quality about it which was deeply unattractive. I could have said no, but Fionn looked so excited and, damn it, dress-shopping was exciting even if I did look like crap.

"Oh, you say the nicest things," I grinned and we headed in the direction of a local bridal shop where we hoped to bagsy a viewing of the very, very pretty dresses without an appointment. We had already discussed what we wanted and thankfully Fionn was not of the opinion I should look like a total feckwit and had imagined me sailing up the aisle behind her in a *Sex and the City* type creation – gloriously stylish and a wee bit sexy.

But I was open to trying anything on, well, at least anything that was not meringue-looking in design or quality. Thankfully the shop assistants were agreeable to our request – probably due to Fionn spending a small mortgage on her own frock there –and we were taken to a gorgeously opulent changing room where a rack of dresses was placed in front of me.

The same exceptionally enthusiastic sales assistant who had sold Fionn her dress tended to us and smiled sweetly as she looked me up and down.

"A Size 14," she declared.

"Size 12," I corrected. I was very proud of my Size 12 self. I worked hard at it. You couldn't date a chef for several years and not have to work hard at burning off all the nice food – not to mention the increasing quantity of wine you drank to get through the increasingly boring dates you shared with him.

"Ah, but bridesmaid dresses are cut smaller," she said. "You always go a size up."

"Well, in that case let's just call it Size 12 and ignore what the labels say," I said, not sure if the assistant was just trying to make me feel like a heifer. I wanted to tell her I was a very sexy woman actually and that my curves were amazing – and that a very hunky (if hairy) man had told me that just last night. But I decided to keep my smugness to myself and just show her instead how fabulous I could look in a satin gown.

"Well," I said to Fionn, "anything take your fancy?"

She fingered her way along to rack, a look of complete concentration on her face. "I like this colour," she eventually said, lifting out a champagne creation in finest duchesse satin and silk. I almost fainted at the very beauty of it.

"Oooooh!" was all I could manage in place of an intelligent response as she held it up against me and stood back to admire it.

"Try it on," she said, and I didn't need asking twice.

The sales assistant directed me to a small cubicle and handed me the dress before turning her back and starting to chat to Fionn about the plethora of accessories she could sell her which would add, no doubt, to the mammoth commission she had already earned from my friend.

I slipped my clothes off and slipped the dress on. It was strapless and boned – holding me firmly in all the right places and showing off my definitely Size 12 curves as perfectly as possible. The skirt spread out in a stylish A-line below the waist – which was decorated with a thin satin belt and gorgeously ornate corsage. Stopping just at the knee, it looked as if it had been made just for me and when I saw myself in the mirror I could not help but smile. I looked good – really good – even though the canvas on which I had thrown this work of art was a complete wreck at that moment.

I pulled back the curtain with a joyous "*Ta-daa!*" and watched as the sales assistant went into over-excited overdrive and Fionn burst into a flood of tears. And I knew they weren't happy tears. They were the tears of someone having a crisis. Believe me, I knew from experience that she was not a happy camper.

The sales assistant looked vaguely horrified, reached for a box of tissues and handed them over silently. She was clearly not used to negative emotion in her shop so she nervously excused herself, telling us to take our time and suggesting we try on another few dresses before making any decision. The cynic in me was sure that was her delicate way of telling me to change out of the dress before letting Fionn snotter all over it – but Fionn was clearly in need and there was no way I wasn't going to run straight to her aid – fancy dress or no.

"What's wrong?" I asked, sitting her down on the plush velvet sofa across the room.

She shook her head and sobbed loudly.

"You know you can tell me," I said. "Is it Alex? Is it fecking Rebecca? Or is it just that I look so much more amazing than you could ever have imagined in this dress and you now know that I'll be the best-looking girl there on the day?"

I should have known that it was not the best time to try and inject some humour into the situation. She sobbed all the louder, like she was actually in physical pain, and I started to get really worried.

"There might not be a day," she stuttered.

"What?"

"There might not be a da-ay," she sobbed again, her voice breaking further. "All this – dresses and pink shoes and everything – could all be for feck all. There might not be a wedding. I'm not even sure there'll still be an Alex and me any more . . ."

I caught a glance of myself in the full-length mirror across the room. There was me in the most beautiful dress in the world ever, with my jaw almost touching the floor. Seriously, the shocked expression on my face was almost of cartoon proportions. I looked ridiculous. And beside me I could see a woman in contortions of agony at whatever crap thing had just happened in her relationship.

Alex and Fionn were in trouble – this was not good. This was not good at all.

As suspected, Rebecca was involved. I managed to drag that from Fionn after ten minutes of sobbing had subsided. I had rubbed her hand for five minutes, then changed from the dress (a wee bit reluctantly) and escorted her to a nearby coffee shop which was thankfully still quiet.

"She doesn't want us to get married," she said. "She told Alex last night that there was no way she was going to change her shift patterns so we could go on honeymoon without Emma. She told him that if I wanted to be the 'perfect little mammy' I'd have to get used to Emma being around. But, Annie, it's not like I'm not used to it, is it?" She looked at me for reassurance that she was indeed a good mammy-in-training.

"Of course you're used to it," I replied.

"And the thing is, whatever way she talked to him, he agreed with her. He asked me would it be so bad if Emma did come with us and then I felt like a complete cow because, yes, it would be so bad. We have little enough time together anyway. And then he said I knew all along he came with baggage –"

"Aye, a big baggage called Rebecca," I interjected, increasingly angry with the woman who was scuppering what should have been the happiest ending in history.

"I told him I loved Emma," Fionn went on, "but that I loved him more – and that was, apparently, the very worst thing I could have said because I should love her as much. And I do love her – just not the same way."

"You'd be arrested if you did," I said with a small smile and this at least made Fionn laugh – well, more burst into a funny mixture of laughing and crying all at once. The noise made the old woman drinking tea across the shop look around, very alarmed, and almost choke on her fruit scone.

"So he said that if I didn't love Emma and couldn't accept her as part of his life, then maybe we shouldn't be getting married and he stormed out. When he came back he slept in the spare room. He *never* sleeps in the spare room. And I'm wondering how on earth we can fix it, and how on earth we reached a stage where he ever questioned my commitment to his daughter. For the love of God, I have almost maxed out my credit card on Hannah Montana goodies for her. I know all the words to the 'High School Musical' songs and, let's not forget, my choice of wedding dress has been largely influenced by the Little fecking Mermaid!"

I nodded and listened as best I could. There was only one answer to her question. There was only one reason that Alex was questioning how his fiancée felt about him and his daughter. And that reason was a loud-mouthed freaky nurse bitch called Rebecca.

"Oh Fionn, I don't really know what to say. Is there anything you want me to do?"

"I'm not sure there is anything you *can* do. I'm not sure there is anything anyone can do. If I thought it was as simple as saying, yes, Emma can come on honeymoon with us, I would – even if I wouldn't have him to myself. But then I have a feeling Rebecca would just think of something else. And what annoys me most about it is that he believes her. He sees what I'm like with his daughter but he believes her anyway." Fionn sighed shakily and took a sip of tea.

I have to admit I was pretty pissed off at Alex myself – but not half as much as I was pissed off at Rebecca. I'd only met her once – at Emma's birthday party. She was nothing much to write home about. She had a good enough figure. Her hair was kind of shiny but she had a face that looked as if she was permanently really, really annoyed about something. Even when she was smiling she had a vague look of 'I could kill you any minute' about her. She had been perfectly pleasant that day – and I could tell she was a good mum but I wasn't buying it, not for one second, that Alex meant nothing to her. Fionn had told me that Emma was conceived after a few fumbles between her mummy and daddy and that they probably wouldn't still be in touch if they weren't tied together by the existence of a precocious five-year-old. But I saw that day how Rebecca looked at Alex. I saw how she referred to all their joint experiences over and over again, as if to assert her ownership of him. If Fionn mentioned their engagement, Rebecca was able to segue that into a conversation about how Alex had mopped her brow as her perineum split in the throes of labour. You had to admire that – the ability to equate a romantic proposal in Venice to the tearing of human flesh and pooping on the delivery table. It was genius really.

But Alex wouldn't hear a bad word about her. Not that Fionn generally badmouthed Rebecca and certainly not to her intended. Generally such chat was reserved for our FSB's. She thought it wouldn't do her any good to get offside with the ex-girlfriend – but it seemed she had managed that anyway without even trying.

I was fecked off on her behalf – and slightly gutted that, if things really were going tits-up, I might not get to wear the most beautiful dress in the world ever. Of course I reminded myself I was being a shallow cow and instead switched back into one hundred per cent sympathetic-friend mode.

"Alex loves you. This will all be okay," I soothed.

Fionn nodded, before once again switching back into her calm and collected persona and saying we really should take a look in the local department store for a few ideas on wedding jewellery.

She only ever let her guard down so far – she was the complete opposite of me.

10

When Ant phoned that night I found myself agreeing to his coming over. I had intended a night to myself. There was a kingsize bag of Maltesers cooling in the fridge for just that purpose and I had already poured an ice-laden glass of Diet Coke to give my poor liver a chance to recover from the night before. I had changed my bed sheets and cleaned my room and was looking forward to slipping between the fresh sheets in fresh jammies with a good romance read and getting an early night.

And yet when Ant phoned. I was powerless to resist. He asked, and I agreed. To be honest, he didn't really ask so much as tell me he was on his way over with a bottle of Pinot Grigio and I found myself speed-shaving my legs and spraying some Alien between my breasts in a fit of excitement.

I had just about finished tousling my hair into that just-out-of-bed look when the intercom buzzed. I heard a husky, definitely hairy voice say hello and I felt myself blush from head to foot. This was ridiculous, I chided myself – but also deeply satisfying. I couldn't remember the last time I'd felt so excited about anything – apart of course from the most gorgeous dress in the world ever. I had certainly not felt this excited with Pearse any time in last few years – not even when he had whispered sweet nothings in my ear and caressed me with fingers that knew my body better than I knew it myself.

I knew what was going to happen before it did. Ant would run up the stairs, probably taking them two at a time with his long, strong legs. He would arrive at my door breathless from exertion and passion and hand me the wine. Before I would have the chance to open the bottle in my impossibly small kitchen he would have me pressed against the fridge and my just-out-of-bed hair would be a minute away from right-in-the-middle-of-the-bed hair.

It happened kind of like that. Except we didn't even make it to the impossibly small kitchen. I'm amazed the wine bottle didn't smash as it was almost dropped to the floor as he walked into the flat and took me in his arms. I guess my primeval instincts to save a good bottle of plonk were in top form as I somehow managed to rest it comfortably by the door before I was carried (yes, carried, and he didn't even look as if he was developing a hernia or anything) into the bedroom.

And then, dear reader, he ravished me. I don't use that word lightly. Or often. But *ravished* is the only way to describe just exactly what he did. I'm sure that excess of hair signalled an excess of testosterone or the like because he was as manly as he could be and when he was finished all thoughts of Maltesers and Diet Coke and a night alone with a good book were long gone.

In fact, all thoughts of almost anything, bar the stars swimming before my eyes, were gone. I was blissed out. So blissed out, in fact, that I ignored the fact that after he was finished – and he had shared his bottle of wine in record speed – he left and promised to be in touch soon.

It was only the next day, when Fionn's eyebrow raised to a whole new level during our Sunday morning bacon-bap fest that it struck me as anything other than perfectly normal.

"So, essentially, you're telling me he made a booty call?"

"A what?" I asked incredulously.

"You know, a booty call. He called, said he would come round, he did. You had a little jiggery pokery and he cleared off again. And you didn't even voice an objection." Fionn looked concerned, but mildly amused at the same time.

I felt myself blush but this time it wasn't with passion. Could Fionn have a point, I wondered? Was Ant likely to be only using me for sex? And did I mind?

I mean, I still had my Life Plan. I still wanted the same things I always wanted. And yes, that included finding the right man and getting married and having children. But did that mean I was never to have fantastic sex with a semi-stranger? Could I write Ant off because he had booty-called me – especially since I had very much enjoyed the booty call?

"It wasn't quite like that," I sniffed, my defences shooting up.

She smiled, sipping from her tea.

"Well, it was, but it's okay," I said. "Honest."

She smiled again and then reached her hand out and squeezed mine. "Annie, I'm glad you're having fun. Lord knows you deserve it. But, you know, I worry about you and I don't want you getting hurt. I mean, you *are* on the rebound. You've only just split with Pearse."

"Pearse and I were over a long time ago. I just didn't realise it."

"I'm only saying," she added, "be careful. You know very little about this man."

I could feel my hackles rising. I was a grown woman. I could make my own decisions and my own mistakes if necessary. And there was nothing to say Ant was a mistake. Nothing at all. There was only one way out of this and that was to change the subject, in perhaps a not so subtle way.

"So, anyway, how are things with you and Alex?"

Fionn's face fell. And I knew I was off the hook and, even though it probably made me a very, very bad person, I was glad of it.

"He slept in the spare room again last night," she said with a look of devastation on her face. "And Emma was staying around so she asked this morning why Daddy slept in the spare room. No doubt that nugget will make it back to Rebecca and by tonight she will be dancing her happy dance of success."

I tried to hide the grimace on my face – to show Fionn that I believed this was not as bad as she thought it was. But it was. Rebecca would be delighted with the news that the soon-to-be newly weds were having trouble.

"What did you tell her?" I asked.

"Nothing," Fionn replied, a faint blush creeping up her cheeks. "I just told her to ask her daddy."

"You see," I laughed, "you are halfway there to being a proper mammy! That was my mother's stock reply to almost anything."

She raised a half-smile, before it quickly faded. "And Alex told her sometimes grown-ups have little arguments – like she does with her friends at school – and that they need some time on the Naughty Step to cool down."

I asked the obvious question, not sure I really wanted to hear the answer: "So, is it your bed or the spare room that is the metaphorical Naughty Step?"

"He didn't say, but I can guess. And I tell you it did nothing at all for my sense of worth to have him going all *Supernanny* on me. If our bedroom is going to be a Naughty Step, I'd at least like to have a say in what kind of Naughty Step that is. I certainly wouldn't be opting for the punishing, stern, reprimanding kind of definition."

"Some people would pay for that," I said. "But seriously though, Alex has now sent Emma back to Mummy Dearest with the notion in her head that you've been naughty and need 'time out'?"

Fionn nodded slowly and sadly. "And the thing is, I don't know what to do about it. If I do nothing, I have a notion that Rebecca will worm her way back into Alex's affections, but if I make a song and dance about it, I'm not sure Alex won't jump to her defence. After all, she is the mother of his child."

"But that's all she is," I replied.

"It's a pretty big deal."

"You're the woman he wants to marry. He never asked her, did he? In fact, they were never really, truly together – not properly.

And, yes, they have a daughter together and fair play to him for being in her life so much but he does not love Rebecca."

"I'm starting to think that doesn't matter. Emma is his priority. He has made that perfectly clear and I'm hardly in a position to tell him I'm more important than his own flesh and blood."

I could see where Fionn was coming from. And I didn't have the answers. If I did, I would have willingly handed over my sage advice – but who was I to advise anyone on anything? I hadn't exactly made a roaring success of my own personal affairs. I had a Life Plan in tatters, a wasted relationship with an egotistical chef and, it would seem, a new staring role as a fuck-buddy in a virtual stranger's life.

"I don't know the answers," I told Fionn, "But you will get through this. You and Alex were meant to be together. I don't think I've ever seen such a sickeningly perfect couple as the pair of you. Have faith, okay? We'll work it out. I promise."

11

There was no booty call that night. In fact, there wasn't so much as a flirty text or a poke on Facebook. There was no word at all from Ant. I felt smug about that for all of about five minutes until I realised that I couldn't really boast to Fionn about it. Sure there had been no booty call – initially, in my mind, blowing the theory out of the water that he was simply using for me for sex. But then, it dawned on me, there had been no call at all. Nothing. No lazy Sunday-evening blether on the phone.

I wanted to send him a text but didn't want to appear desperate. My phone remained silent apart from one message from Pearse saying he had a box of my things he wanted to drop round at my earliest convenience, or if I wished I could collect them from Manna.

I thought about the latter suggestion for all of about three seconds before I dismissed it as a very bad idea indeed. I could deal with splitting with Pearse. I could deal with our life together being over. But I simply could not be coping with the notion of making the Walk of Shame across the floor of the restaurant with my toothbrush, an Abba CD and a selection of clean underwear in a cardboard box for anyone to see. Especially not after our last encounter. God knows what other humiliations he would have in store for me. People were always looking to see what Pearse was up to and that would be scandal in the extreme for the local gossip-mongers. It would look like he was packing me off, rather than the other way around, and I would have to fight the urge to tell everyone – in a loud voice – that it was *me* who broke up with *him* and that I had been having it away with an exceptionally virile Donegal man. On reflection, I realised that particular plan of attack might not paint me in the best light so I decided against the whole idea and sent a quick text message back saying I would check my diary and suggest a suitable evening for him to call over to my place. I had nothing more exciting planned than washing my hair but I couldn't have him knowing that.

So I washed my hair, and had a soak in the bath, with the phone in easy reach, and then I took to my bed like a lovelorn lady on the brink of death from self-pity and ate my Maltesers in record time.

I should have put that in the Life Plan, I thought wryly: Breaking the World Record for the Fastest Consumption of a Family Bag of Maltesers. I would have achieved that for sure. I could see the entry now. Me, bloated, chocolate-stained, looking as if I might actually explode but with a smug smile on my face.

Lifting my Life Plan out from its sad little resting place under my chest of drawers, I decided to read through it once more. It was a bit pointless really. I knew every page in great detail. I could recite the longer passages by heart if necessary.

I remembered when I had made each entry – how during one particularly anally retentive phase I would get ridiculously excited if I saw something which would look good in the book, and rush home to get my glue-gun out.

I remembered sitting and writing down my hopes and dreams – as if writing it all out would make it real. I was making my very own catalogue for life. My personal Argos book. Now, if only achieving what I wanted was as simple as writing a few digits down on a slip of paper with an eeny-teeny pen and handing it to a cashier . . .

"White wedding, house in the country and three children?" the cashier would ask.

"Yes, yes," I would nod, adding a pack of batteries to my order at the last moment.

"Will that be all?" she would enquire.

"That's all for now," I'd smile, handing over my credit card, and then I'd wait for my order to arrive at my collection point.

I didn't know where Ant was going to slot into my perfectly planned life. I didn't even know if he would. Surely it wasn't a good sign that he hadn't phoned that evening? We had spent the last two nights lost in each other – you'd have at least thought he would have phoned to see how I was.

Does that make me sound stalkerish? Because I did start to think that I was perhaps obsessing about it a little too much. I had spent fifteen minutes earlier that evening Googling his name – but all I could find was a picture of him at some corporate do, which ironically enough had been held at Manna.

I would have phoned Fionn just to discuss in intimate detail if I was indeed obsessing about it a little too much but I was aware she was dealing with Rebecca-gate at present and with bedtime approaching she would be busy enough discovering whether or not she was still on the proverbial Naughty Step. The last thing she really needed was me bending her ear once again.

The only other option was that I phone my sister, Darcy (also named after a John Denver song) – but as I had yet to tell her about the big split with Pearse I didn't think she would be particularly in the mood for listening to me wax lyrical about the new man in my life (who might, or might not, simply be using me for sex).

Sighing, I slipped between the sheets, imagining my dream wedding dress, and went to sleep.

Of course I didn't sleep particularly well. I blame the sugar rush from the Maltesers. At 4 a.m. I was sitting at my dining table Googling self-help books for hopeless cases like me. After spending £40 at Amazon and a further £150 on the Monsoon website ordering an amazingly beautiful dress which I planned to use as motivation to help me avoid any future Malteser binges, I crept back into bed and stared at the ceiling till six thirty.

I got up and battered off a quick email to Darcy. Just a short one, pretending nothing at all was wrong and attaching a J-peg of the dress. She would tell me whether it was a fashion pass or fail.

I got back into bed and then I fell asleep. And woke, with a start and a sense of impending doom, at 9.10 a.m.

It was then I achieved my second Guinness World Record by managing to get dressed, get in the car and get to work by nine thirty.

I may have looked rough and I may have had to bring my entire hoard of make-up with me for emergency repair work as soon as Bob stopped firing me dirty looks, but I had made it all the same. Just thirty minutes late. Which, in fairness, wasn't at all bad for me on a Monday morning.

"Traffic was a nightmare," I declared loudly, walking into the office. "I think there was an accident on the bridge or something. I've been in my car since eight thirty!"

Someone snorted but I ignored that as I took my seat and switched on my computer. I may well have been running late but I had a busy day ahead of me – phone-calls to be made, client meetings to hold, Bob to avoid at all costs etc. I was just internally telling myself what a brilliant PR guru I was when my email pinged to life with a message from Fionn. Glancing across the office at her before clicking open, I saw that she looked even more tired and worn out than she had the previous day. It didn't take a genius to work out that perhaps Rebecca-gate was still very much ongoing.

"He slept in the spare room last night and left me a message saying we have to talk. I have a very bad feeling about this," her email read and if I'm honest I had a very bad feeling about it too. "We need to talk," four weeks before a wedding, was never a good thing. Especially when there was a cow-bag of an ex waiting in the wings and the normally very nice fiancé seemed to have morphed into a complete tit who was putting the supposed love of his life on the Naughty Step.

Fionn looked pathetic. Her eyes were red-rimmed – which I could spot even from my vantage point across the office. There was a kingsize bar of chocolate on her desk which meant this was a major emergency. Fionn didn't do chocolate. Not much anyway.

She really was of the belief that, apart from the odd glass of wine and our sausage baps on a Sunday morning, her body was a temple. She was disgustingly disciplined with food so the kingsize chocolate sounded real warning bells with me.

I was starting to realise that I needed to take action – and soon.

"It will be okay," I fibbed in my response. Truth was, I didn't know what else to say apart from offering to accompany her on an FSB at ten thirty, by which stage I hoped to have formulated some sort of plan to help my friend out of her truly horrible situation.

My options were, however, a little limited. I could hunt Rebecca down in the hospital and dangle her by her ankles from the top of the multi-story car park until she agreed to back off. I could take Emma hostage until both Rebecca and Alex realised they were acting like children and sorted it out. Or I could do the unthinkable (not that enacting an act of violence or kidnapping a child was exactly thinkable) and go behind my friend's back and have a word with Alex myself.

Such actions were surely against the Friendship Code? I was sure if there had been an eleventh commandment it would have been "*Thou shalt not meddle in thy friend's relationship*". But surely God would have realised my motives were pure and with the best interest of said friend at heart?

Alex and I got along quite well. We had shared many a foursome night out together with Pearse and they were always quite jovial affairs. I had only once made a complete eejit of myself in front of him and that was when they got engaged and I drank just a little bit too much champagne and decided to tell the entire room of well-wishers just how much I loved them.

Pearse had gone rather puce as I babbled on and he had stepped up, taken the glass off me and finished the speech on my behalf while I cried with emotion in a corner. To give him his due, Pearse was the consummate performer and of course the assembled masses were only too delighted to have a local celeb do the talking and not a drunken advertising sales rep. Pearse had said all the right things – even down to offering to bake the wedding cake – which reminded me that I really should check whether or not he was still going to do that. I could imagine his generosity of spirit might have waned as soon as we split and his invitation to said big do became null and void. He would probably tell me to stick my cup-cake tower where the sun doesn't shine, but nonetheless I would have to bite the bullet and ask him anyway.

So that left me three things to be getting on with that day – speaking with Alex, speaking with Pearse and convincing Fionn during our FSB to share some of that chocolate with me.

The whole thing was, at least, distracting me from worrying about Ant. I mean I had barely thought about him at all – well, at least not in the last ten minutes.

Work, it would seem, would have to sit on the back burner for that day. Sure I'd make a few calls, and I should still be able to make my four thirty appointment but the rest could wait. I was pretty sure Bob wouldn't really mind . . .

The ten thirty FSB went okay. Fionn seemed relatively calm. She said she had resigned herself to a life without Alex and was planning on selling her wedding dress on eBay. She would be keeping the pink shoes.

I told her, as kindly and subtly as I could, that she would do no such thing – apart from keeping the pink shoes which she absolutely had to do because she would be marrying Alex. And I would be wearing the most gorgeous dress in the world ever when I was their bridesmaid.

"I don't want to take away from what you are going through," I said as I took a Marlborough Light from my prop packet and pretended to light up, "but you are meant to be together and as God is my witness you will be."

I thought that sounded suitably reassuring and Fionn didn't laugh, or cry, at my comforting words as we headed back to the office.

12

Alex worked as the manager of a local sofa workshop – you know the kind, permanent sale, half-price sofas, three years interest-free credit. He was very good at his job and knew absolutely everything there was to know about Italian leather which was, sadly for Fionn, not half as kinky as it sounded.

Like Pearse, he and his company were represented by NorthStar. In fact, that was how he and Fionn had met. She had been out cold-calling round local businesses for new projects and their eyes had met over a three-piece recliner. She said he dazzled her straight away with his confident sales-patter, nicely fitted suit and sparkly blue eyes. He could have sold her anything, she said, and he must have felt the same because that month Fionn added his business to her ever-growing portfolio.

They had their first date at Manna, but of course, and I managed to swing it so that they got the best table in the place and an upgrade on a bottle of wine to a bottle of the restaurant's finest fizz. I had never seen Fionn so alive. She had been, she said, a month away from buying a couple of cats and officially resigning herself to being on the shelf forever. I told her she was ridiculous. Thirty-five wasn't a bit old but a horrible part of me was already thinking of names for said cats.

Fionn just never seemed like the settling-down type – not until she met Alex anyway and then it felt as if she was always meant to settle down and be a step-mammy. She even started talking about when they would have kids of their own. They wouldn't be wasting any time, she said, not with her being on the cusp of thirty-eight when they married. She was, it had to be said, ridiculously happy.

There was no way I was going to allow this to go wrong and that is how I found myself outside Sofas To Go at eleven thirty on a Monday morning. I had my clipboard and briefcase with me. I looked every ounce the professional PR rep. I had even managed to make a half-decent attempt at my make-up before leaving the office.

Fionn, of course, had no idea that I was where I was. She would have forbidden me from getting involved, but she needed help and I was just the person to offer that help.

Alex, his curly dark hair flopping seductively over his eyes in a Colin Farrell style, was flicking through a sample book of leather and fabrics when I arrived. He smiled when he saw me but that look was quickly replaced by a look of confusion. It was unheard of that I would visit him. Understandably Fionn usually took care of all his needs – professional and personal.

"Is everything okay?" he asked. "Fionn, is she all right? Is something wrong, Annie?"

Bless him. He looked deeply concerned. He looked very much like a man in love and certainly not like a man planning to feck off with his ex. Then again he didn't look like a man who had sent his thirty-seven-year-old fiancée to the metaphorical Naughty Step for the last three nights.

I had to take a deep breath and remind myself that, floppy Colin Farrell hair and concern for Fionn aside, he had been acting like a feckwit the last few days and I was here on a mission.

"Fionn's okay. Well, when I say 'okay' I mean she is stressed to the eyeballs and wondering if her wedding is going ahead, but physically, yes, she is okay."

He looked mildly stunned. A cross between a guilty man and a rabbit (an admittedly very handsome rabbit) stuck in the headlights.

The showroom was relatively quiet and one of Alex's sales assistants looked at us with a look of vague amusement on her face.

"Maybe we should talk about this in my office," he said.

I nodded. "Yes, maybe we should." I followed him to the cosy back office, where I knew for a fact he had bonked my best friend on at least three occasions.

I tried not to think about it as I sat down opposite him at his desk. I tried not to imagine him taking her over the photocopier/fax machine but you know it was a little like when someone tells you not to think about pink elephants and then all you can think about are pink flipping elephants – and in this case the elephants were bonking.

"Annie, I don't know really why you're here, apart from the fact you seem like you're pissed off about something . . ."

"I'm not pissed off as much as worried," I replied haughtily. "Fionn is going through the wringer and I know that this is probably not any of my business but she is my best friend and I'm worried about her. She's convincing herself that you are putting Emma and Rebecca above her and while she knows that Emma will always be your number-one priority she is feeling pushed out by Emma's mammy. She thinks Rebecca is pulling your strings, if truth be told, and I happen to agree with her. You need to put Fionn first, or at least second, just now and believe her when she tells you that she loves Emma and she loves you and she wants this to work."

I felt quite proud of my speech, even if I was turning a slight shade of blue by the time I'd finished it. I felt I had made my point, clearly, concisely, breathlessly and without making too much of a tit of myself.

It was a bit of shock then when Alex just shook his head and started to look for all intents and purposes as if steam was about to start pouring out of his ears.

I might, I realised with a sinking heart, have just made the whole situation worse.

"You are absolutely right, Annie," he said in a voice that shook with anger and resentment. "It *is* none of your business. None of your business at all. This is just beyond ridiculous. I can't believe Fionn has sent you here to tell me off like some naughty schoolboy!"

Of course my appropriate response would have been to tell him that of course Fionn hadn't sent me there and had indeed no knowledge whatsoever that I was there but, and here is where I fecked up yet again, I saw red with the naughty-schoolboy comment and let him have it.

"You're a fine one to talk about naughty," I snarled, "with all your talk of Naughty Steps like *she* has done something wrong! All she wanted was a honeymoon with you and you may well not remember this but I'm pretty sure you wanted that too. But now, somehow, it has turned into a battle of wills with bloody Rebecca!"

There was a pause during which I glared at Alex who was making visible efforts to control himself.

"Please don't ever refer to her as 'Bloody Rebecca' again," he said in an icy fury. "You don't even know her. Now, you had really better go because I have work to do." And with that he got up and stalked out.

I was so shocked, and so embarrassed, that I left straight away and it was only when I was in the car that I remembered, with a nasty sinking feeling, the "Fionn has sent you" bit and realised that, no, I hadn't corrected him. I had left him, steaming angry, thinking Fionn had sent me over there to give him a verbal dressing-down.

This was bad. This was very, very bad. This was about as bad as it got – especially at the start of a week.

I should have gone back in and corrected him. I should have at least phoned if I was too chicken to face him again, but I didn't. I decided to give him a chance to calm down.

I drove on to Manna with a heavy heart and, as I parked up close by, I realised that me arriving there to ask Pearse if he was still going to make the wedding cake might just be a bit premature, given that we no longer knew if there was going to be a wedding.

"It will be fine. It *will* be fine," I told myself loudly, as I got out of the car. I would make this better. I wasn't sure how in the hell I would, but I would. I straightened my skirt, checked my tights for ladders, glanced in the wing-mirror to make sure my lip-gloss was on straight and then I walked into Manna where it was clear all eyes were very much on me.

Toni, Pearse's maître d', was at her usual position by the cash register. She glanced at me – a look on her face akin to that you would give to a child with a stream of green snot sliding down towards their lips.

"Toni," I started.

"Annie," she started back – and believe me that woman could make you think she was picking on you just by the very way she said your name.

"Is Pearse in?"

"Hmmmm, I'll see if he is available for you," she said snootily, turned on her perfectly polished court-shoe heel and walked towards the kitchen.

I looked around and saw a few of the younger waiting staff nudge each other and whisper. One young girl replicated the river-of-snot look perfectly before she too turned on her heel and walked away from me.

It was as if me, and my fecklessness, were contagious.

I should have known this was not the best place to have this discussion. I should have remembered that Pearse had been planning to visit me later that week anyway – but since when did good sense have anything to do with my decision-making?

If I thought the night I shacked up with Ant was perhaps the most ill-thought-out experience of my life, I might just have been wrong. It was clear that that particular Monday morning was going to eclipse that lapse in judgement entirely.

Everyone loved Pearse. Especially his staff. They thought he was God – even when he was doing his best Gordon Ramsey grumpy-hole impression. I should have known that meeting him here was never going to be a good idea. To be honest, I was lucky not to have been beaten to a pulp by his legion of minions and put through the mincer or something equally macabre.

Pearse walked out of the kitchen, a look on his face as if I had just kicked his favourite puppy to death, and headed towards me.

"Annie," he sighed and I could see the same young waiting staff almost swoon at his vulnerability. It was easily seen that they'd never had to deal with his garlicky advances or obsession with Yankee Candles. There had been times when all I wanted was a moment of raw passion without a lingering stench of cooking by-products or natural-scented candles.

"Pearse," I replied. "We need to talk. Can we talk?"

"Of course, Annie," he said, that wounded look stepping up a gear. "Let's go to my office."

So we went to his office, where *we'd* had sex at least three times and all of a sudden those damn pink humping elephants were slap-bang back in my thoughts again.

"Is everything okay?" he asked. He looked genuinely concerned – so genuinely concerned that I felt a real pang of guilt that I had hurt him. He might have been perhaps the most boring, and possibly the most self-obsessed man on the planet, but he wasn't a bad person and he didn't deserve to be hurt.

It struck me that I was hurting a lot of people at the moment, intentionally or otherwise, and I suddenly just felt unbelievably sad and unbelievably disappointed in myself. And I'm ashamed to say that I cried huge, fat tears all over Pearse and his office.

13

Pearse paid for an extra big slice of PR that month. That kept me off the hook with Bob at least. Because I never did make it back to the office.

The furthest I made it was back to Pearse's house where, somehow, we managed to end up back in the sack.

It had started when I broke down. He put his arms around me and I breathed him in. In that moment – in the horrible feeling that I was not, and never would be, good enough for anyone or anything – I let him hold me tight. It felt nice. I knew just exactly where on his chest I could lay my head comfortably. I knew the contours of his strong arms and let them envelop me and when he kissed the top of my head I let him. And it felt nice.

This wasn't a booty call. This wasn't any sort of a game. This was a man who loved me once, letting me know he still cared. And in my loneliness – in my longing to feel as if I could do just one thing right in my life, I lifted my face toward him and brushed my lips against his.

His intake of breath let me know he was surprised by my gesture but amazingly, given what I had put him through, not horrified. He kissed me back His lips were as soft as they always had been. Soft and full – and his kiss was deliciously tender.

I should have stopped it. I knew that. But it felt nice to be wanted and to know it was for more than just a quick shag.

When the kiss grew deeper, I let it. In fact, I kissed him back. Quite hard, if the truth be told. And when he pushed me back onto the desk and pushed my skirt up so that my legs wrapped around him, I didn't resist. I didn't resist one little bit. I pulled him closer to me, allowing me to feel the warmth of his body ripple through my own.

"We can't do this here . . ." he said breathlessly as his hand crept up inside my blouse, making my skin tingle and my body ache for him.

My mind was buzzing. I wasn't in control. I didn't really know what I was doing any more and all I knew was that even if we could not do it there – in his office with Toni no doubt stood at the door with a glass held against the wood – we had to do it somewhere.

"Take me home," I muttered and he groaned in a remarkably sexy way. I hadn't heard him groan like that in months – perhaps even in years – and it made me feel quite dizzy.

He stood back, picked up his car keys, took me by the hand and led me to his car. Toni gaped open-mouthed as we passed and even though I was in some sort of a daze I had to physically restrain myself from saying "Ha!" in a very childish sort of a way.

We didn't talk the whole way home. I'm not sure if it was because we both knew that we could break the spell if we actually spoke to each other or if we were both just so damn horny that we wouldn't have been able to say anything remotely sensible. Sexy talk was not a strong point for either of us – no matter how in the mood we were. We had tried it a couple of times and it had always been disastrously tragic.

But what I do know is that we did it in the hallway, against the wall, and that for the first time in a long time, with Pearse, the earth moved. Boy, did it move.

And twenty minutes later, in his kingsize bed, it moved again. A couple of times. In a row. Not that I'm boasting, or anything.

We fell asleep then, spooned together, his hand cupping my breast which was, I have to say, a little odd. My boobs should not be used as comfort blankets. And yet it was nice to be there and to feel as if I belonged. It allowed me to forget that I had made a mess of huge, giant proportions and that my life was spiralling so far out of control I couldn't see it ever getting back on track again.

I could pretend, in his arms, that I wasn't just being used for sex (as in, by a hairy Donegal man). I could pretend that I was both good at my job and valued for it. I could pretend that I wasn't one step away from being marched out of Bob's office with my P45 and a one-way ticket to the dole queue. I could pretend the last few weeks had all been a bad dream à la Bobby Ewing in the shower, and that my life plan was still intact. I could pretend that I hadn't neglected to get back to Alex to clear up the little "Fionn has sent you" misunderstanding. I could pretend that Fionn wasn't going to kill me and that I hadn't just messed up her life even more spectacularly than I had messed up my own.

I could pretend a lot of things – not least that it was a good thing I had ended up back in bed with Pearse – a man I had been so utterly sure I had fallen out of love with entirely.

I woke to Pearse kissing my stomach, moving his tongue in small and delicious circular motions across my abdomen, making every part of my body tingle with anticipation.

If only he had done this a few weeks ago, I thought wryly, maybe things would be different. As much as my body screamed for me to let him continue on his glorious journey around my lower body, my head had somehow managed to alert me to the fact that it could be a very big mistake. *A. Very. Big. Mistake. Indeed.*

This hadn't sorted anything out. This, while it had been really quite impressive, had probably just made things a lot worse.

I glanced at the clock beside the bed. It read 4.34 p.m. Knowing that Pearse always set his clock thirty minutes ahead of the actual time, I was able to ascertain it was just gone four and we had been in bed for almost the entire afternoon.

There was little point in me heading back to work now. I felt vaguely nervous about that but not half as nervous as I felt when I thought of how Fionn would now be absolutely raging with me or how I felt when I thought about what I had just done, four times, with a possibly fifth time on the near horizon.

As Pearse's fingers – long and lean – followed the path of his tongue and I felt my body win the battle, I resolved to put all my doubts to one side and think about it again later. One more time wouldn't hurt. Not at this stage.

At five thirty Pearse got up and walked to the shower, leaving me to get dressed and check my phone for messages. There were five missed calls from work – which could have been Fionn or Bob or a combination of both. None of them were likely to bear good news. There were two voicemail messages but I didn't have the guts to listen to them. Needless to say, there was still no word from Ant. Ironic really that just a few weeks ago I had cheated on Pearse with him and now it seemed I had cheated on him with Pearse. That is, if you could cheat on someone who was possibly just using you for sex.

"Do you need to get back to the restaurant?" I called to Pearse as he walked out of the shower, towelling off his body and then reaching for some facial moisturiser.

He glanced at the clock, and shrugged his shoulders. "I don't have to. I'm the boss. I can take the night off if you want."

My jaw hit the floor. Pearse? Take the night off? It didn't happen. It never happened. Once again I found myself thinking that if this had happened a few weeks ago, perhaps things would have been different. But it hadn't happened, and things were how they were.

Pearse must have noticed the look of shock on my face because he sat beside me, towel dropping to the floor and his wanger hanging limply – as if it were pleading with me.

He took my hand and looked into my eyes. "I know what you're thinking, Annie. I've missed you. And I know what you did was horrendous and hateful, but it has been so nice to be with you today and I could try – if you wanted me to – I could try and find it in my heart to forgive you."

He chatted on for a while but my brain was stuck on "horrendous and hateful". What I did was wrong, yes, but horrendous? Hateful? No – I was lonely. Things hadn't been right for a very long time. I had felt as if I was worthless, if the truth be told. He had loved his restaurant more than me. And Ant – for all his equal feckwittedness – had made me feel worth something. No, I hadn't acted hatefully or horrendously. I had made a mistake – something which I had a real habit of doing these days.

"Well?"

I tuned in to Pearse. I could have agreed to what he had said, but I had no idea what it was. I just wanted to go home – and soon.

"No, Pearse," I muttered. "There's no need to take the night off. Manna needs you. My car is parked outside the restaurant and I better pick it up and get home. Thanks anyway."

He looked wounded. But hey, what else could he have expected from a "horrendous and hateful" person such as me?

"Are you sure?" he asked.

"Yes," I nodded, standing up and walking out of the bedroom, leaving him and his wanger to get dressed.

I felt a headache coming on, so I went to the alphabetised bathroom cabinet and got some paracetamol. The bad ("hateful and horrendous") part of me then moved the Ibuprofen to where the Zantac should live and the Lynx to the Calvin Klein shelf and smiled to myself that he would be really pissed off when he found out what I'd done.

I don't know why I did it. I didn't know anything any more and when he walked into the room, in fresh chef whites, and kissed me on the cheek, I felt as if I was in some alternative reality.

I leaned my head back and closed my eyes as we drove to Manna, so he would think I was in post-coital slumber, and when we got there I made a convincing show of groggily waking up.

"I'll be in touch soon," he said. "Don't worry about having the afternoon off work. I'll sort it with Bob – throw some extra money his way . . ."

I walked back to my car, feeling very much as if I had just prostituted myself.

I climbed the stairs to the flat, my body aching from the excesses of the afternoon, and was shocked to find a huge bouquet of Cala Lilies waiting on my doorstep. It was perhaps the biggest bouquet of flowers I had ever seen. It was certainly the biggest bouquet of flowers I had ever received. Pearse had been really damn quick off the mark, I thought, as I struggled to haul it through the door and onto my dining table.

Flopping down on the sofa I opened the card. But it wasn't from Pearse. Of course it wasn't from him. It was from Ant.

"Thanks for a couple of great nights. Can't wait to see you again!"

It was then, and exactly then, that I picked up the phone and called Darcy. Desperate times called for desperate measures.

I had always thought of Darcy as a fixer – but not in an illegal *Pulp Fiction* kind of a way, you understand. She was just the sensible one. The one who could solve any and all problems with what often appeared to be a cool wink and shake of her magic Filofax. She was a Mary Poppins for the noughties – able to make all of life's problems seem infinitely more palatable.

She wasn't a walkover, however. No way. She wouldn't be too happy with the mess I had made of things. She would give me that very-disappointed-in-you look that was usually reserved for our parents and she would in all probability give me a lecture also. But then, when her temper had cooled a little, she would set about helping me put it to rights.

So, as much as I was dreading the lecture and the disapproving look, I needed her as my go-to person.

She would, she said, be with me the following day after work. She lived and worked in Dublin – doing something utterly fabulous in the fashion industry which I had never quite understood as I was too jealous of her success to listen properly. She said she had some time off coming up so she would pull a few strings and make it north of the border for teatime. She hadn't listened to all the details. In fairness she could have listened all she wanted but she was unlikely to be able to decipher much amid the flurry of tears and snotters which shot forth from me down the crackling phone line.

"You can tell me about it tomorrow," she said. "But don't worry. Everything will be fine. Life has a way of working out."

While her words should have comforted me, I couldn't help but feel she was talking the biggest load of bollocks known to man.

I put the flowers in water and sat down on the edge of my bed. The voicemails on my mobile were still unanswered so I guessed now was as good a time as any to listen to them.

The first was from Fionn. At 2.30 p.m. She sounded surprisingly chipper.

"Hey, chicken! Wondered when you might make it back to base. I'm dying for a fake fag. Let me know the score."

I breathed a sigh of relief.

The second message was from Fionn. At 3.18 p.m. She sounded less chipper.

"Annie, what have you done?" she breathed – and that was that.

I crawled into bed – my usual hiding-spot – pulled the duvet up tight over my ears and ignored my phone when it rang. I can't say I slept – not when there was so much to think about. Tomorrow, I sensed, was going to be a long and interesting day. And, by interesting, I meant utterly terrifying.

14

Four missed calls. One from Fionn. One from Ant (mini-yay!) and two from Pearse.

No messages.

I should have tackled it all head on, of course, but hey – that's what Darcy was for. I just had to get through the day without doing any more damage to my life than I had already done. It should be relatively easy, I thought, as long as I just kept my head down, talked to no one and got my work done.

Adopting a distinct must-fly-under-the-radar approach, I dressed conservatively in plain black trousers, a white pussy-bow blouse and some low slingbacks. I tied my hair back from my face in a loose chignon and slipped a black jacket on. Make-up was minimal – some Clarins foundation and loose powder and a slick of lip-gloss. I even left for work early – in time to beat the school-run traffic and avoid attracting Bob's attention by arriving my usual ten minutes late.

I stopped at Starbucks on the way and picked up a grande latte, then stopped in and bought a newspaper to adopt that educated-and-interested-in-the-world-around-me appearance.

By eight fifty, I was at my desk and my computer was on. And no, I wasn't on Facebook or Twitter or Bebo or any social-networking site. I was working.

I checked Bob's end-of-day report from the previous afternoon and saw one of his patented smiley faces beside my name. Once again I felt like a complete whore. The dull ache in my thighs reminded me of my misdemeanour as I realised I had slept with two different men in the space of forty-eight hours. This was an unprecedented level of hoor-dom for me. And it didn't feel good. I didn't feel racy. I didn't feel like an empowered woman. I probably should have. I mean I was a feminist – surely I was setting the agenda for my life but the truth was that I had slept with one man who might, or might not, have been using me for sex (flowers confused that particular issue) and another man who, despite having rediscovered his mojo in the bedroom, left me cold everywhere else. Neither were particular good choices.

On any ordinary day this would have resulted in a specially extended double FSB with Fionn but this was no ordinary day. This was no ordinary day at all.

Fionn arrived just after nine and she took to her desk without so much as glancing in my direction. Whether that was because she was in a big giant huff or whether she knew there was generally no point in looking in the direction of my desk before 9.10 a.m. was anyone's guess at that moment. I just put my head down and kept on working, following up leads and making a list of must-calls for the day.

There were two more missed calls from Pearse. None from Ant (not yay).

By nine thirty Bob had arrived and had smiled beamingly at me as he walked into the office. In a slightly creepy voice (the same one he used when he was thinking about me and the red lingerie) he said: "I don't know what you did yesterday, but well done. Feel free to do it again any time soon."

For a minute or two I imagined the call he must have taken from Pearse. "Hey, Bob, I'm just calling in to double our PR this month for Annie. Ads everywhere, please. Yes, double page, colour, centre-spread. Yes, repeat ad next month. Budget? Feck the budget! You set the price, Bob. She has just fecked me sideways – no, really! Seriously it was out – of – this world!"

I cringed.

I was sure (almost) that conversation hadn't happened but it felt as if "dirty hoor" was written all over my face.

At nine thirty-five the silence from Fionn was deafening. So I took the coward's way out and sent an email.

"I was only trying to help," I typed.

"I know," *s*he typed back and yet when I sent my usual half-ten FSB email she replied that she was too busy. And she had something to do at lunch-time. And then she was too busy again in the afternoon.

I was in the shit. I might have made a lot of mistakes in my life recently but it was clear that I was right when I thought that our relationship was perhaps fatally wounded.

Balls.

At three, Bob called me into his office. He had a sly grin on his face. He knew – damn it – he knew exactly what had happened the day before.

"So I hear the big romance is on again?" he said with a wink.

"I don't think that is any of your business," I replied with fake confidence. I knew exactly that his "business" was exactly what it was all about for him. He didn't care about the wellbeing of his staff as long as the figures were right.

"Well, if you are off conducting *business* on my time, then it is," he said.

And he had a point. And God knows he had given me enough chances.

"So while I'm delighted with the sales figures from yesterday, Annie, I have to let you know you are on your final, final warning. There are people out there who would kill for your job – if you don't want it, someone else will."

"I'm sorry," was all I could muster, and I left his office, tail between my legs, in a vague state of desperation.

When I got home (two more missed calls from Pearse, one from Ant), I poured a glass of wine and drank it in approximately 3.5 seconds. I needed it. I didn't care much if I would be three sheets to the wind by the time Darcy arrived. My plans to cook her dinner and prove to her I wasn't a complete waste of effort had gone out the window. I would order Chinese, or pizza. Or make toast.

Fionn hadn't said goodbye when I left the office. I'd felt wretched. I had almost cried. But I didn't. I kept my head held high and managed to stave it off till I got home and then I snottered into my glass of wine (not literally) and curled up on the sofa and waited for Darcy's arrival.

There was one more missed call from Pearse. And a message on my voice mail.

"Annie, it's me. Just wondered if I could call round later, after the restaurant closes? I miss you already."

I looked at the flowers from Ant and my heart lurched just that little bit. There were no more missed calls from him. Nothing at all. And nothing from Fionn. I didn't know whether she was still on the proverbial Naughty Step, whether her wedding was still on or completely off and whether or not I was permanently banned from Sofas To Go (that thought crossed my mind as rather selfishly it dawned on me how shabby my current sofa was).

Two glasses of wine in, I was text-happy. Pearse got a text saying I would call him the following day (yes, I chickened out like the dirty big fecking chicken that I was). Ant got a text thanking him for the flowers. And Fionn got three texts.

"I'm sorry," read the first.

"I'm really sorry," read the second.

"I'm so sorry I can't even begin to say how sorry I am," read the third.

I was typing out a message about how I was so sorry I couldn't even look at myself in the mirror when my doorbell buzzed and heralded Darcy's arrival.

It would all be okay. My big sister was here. The Fixer had arrived.

Darcy was three years older than me. But it might as well have been thirty. She was so together – ridiculously, perfectly together. She wasn't married but she had a lover. She never referred to Gerry as her partner, or boyfriend – always just as her lover.

They had no children. She didn't want any. Never had, she said. I couldn't imagine her with any either. She wasn't at all maternal – which was strange because she was perhaps the most caring person I knew. She was my go-to person. If anything was going horribly, drastically wrong (which it did, a lot) she was the person on the end of the phone shushing me and assuring me it would all be okay. Luckily she had a very understanding employer (in the fancy fashion thingummy) and a very understanding lover who knew that on occasion she would have to hightail it over the border to sort out yet another mess for me. She was the Hardy to my Laurel.

It had been a brave while since she'd been called up North on a mercy dash. A month or two before, she had commended me on being so in control of my life at the moment.

She knew about the Life Plan. She didn't know I still had it, of course. But she knew about it in our teenage years and ribbed me mercilessly about it. When she made her grand speech about how I seemed to be in control of my life, she had quipped: "Hey, you might even make it down the aisle in line with your big grand plans after all!"

We had laughed (well, I had blazed with embarrassment and then laughed) but we had felt she might just be right. I could have been heading for my happy ending – random acts of feckwittedness aside.

Darcy could get away with wearing the sorts of clothes that would make mere mortals like myself look as if we were on day release from the local mental institution. When she arrived that night she was wearing a multicoloured pair of leggings, an oversized jacket and some very colourful plastic beads. If I had tried the same ensemble I would have looked like a mad Irish Floella Benjamin – but Darcy looked cool. She had "fashionista" written all over her and I was a little jealous. I just about managed to wear the Next workwear range with a certain degree of style – anything out of the ordinary just didn't work.

"Hey, baby sister," she said, enveloping me in a huge bear-hug.

I breathed in her perfume – Chanel No. 5, perhaps not the coolest perfume on the planet but one which Darcy could of course carry off.

I felt myself breathe out. It would be okay. I knew then it would be okay.

"Hey," I replied. She handed me a plastic bag – complete with a bottle of Jack Daniels, two litres of Coke and a bag of crushed ice from the local off-licence. She headed straight to the kitchen, took out two tumblers and set about mixing us some drinks.

"I have to say, Annie, you get yourself into some messes, but this sounds particularly impressive, even for you."

I shrugged, glancing momentarily at the display of flowers from Ant on the sideboard. Someone still liked me – even if I was dropping friends like a hoor drops her knickers.

Darcy walked in and sat on the floor, crossing her legs in front of her and sipping from her glass, before exhaling slowly and leaning back against the sofa.

"Okay, babes, you might as well start talking now and let's see what we can do."

So I told her. I told her about Pearse, and Ant. I told her how things had been far from perfect with Pearse for a long time. She nodded, as if she knew all along. And when I thought about it, it was unlikely that Darcy – even with 200 miles of distance between us on a day-to-day basis – wouldn't have known things hadn't been perfect. Darcy knew everything. I would almost swear she had my house bugged. And then again she had an inbuilt radar for feckwits and Pearse was indeed a feckwit.

"I thought you liked him," I said with a sigh and she smiled.

"I did, in a way. You have to admit he has a certain charisma, but there was something . . . I dunno . . . just something about him which kind of creeped me out."

"Like what?"

"Like the fact he is full of himself. And he talked down to you. And he thought he was only person in the whole of Ireland who ever cooked a fecking spud before."

"And you kept these feelings to yourself? Your only sister in a relationship with someone who creeped you out and you didn't share your concerns?"

Darcy shrugged. "Why would I? He didn't appear to creep you out at all. In fact, you seemed quite besotted. And would you have listened to me anyway? You always were your own person, Annie."

Darcy was right – of course she was. I wouldn't have listened to her. I probably would have had a huge screaming row and Mum would have phoned me in a state that the pair of us had fallen out and would have insisted on some big family get-together to sort it all out. Pearse would have been invited, as would Gerry and it would have been very, very awkward.

No, Darcy had done exactly the right thing by letting me figure it out for myself. I just wished I had figured it out earlier. And even if I hadn't realised it earlier I wished I hadn't allowed myself the moment of weakness which led me back into his arms and into his bed.

And I told her about Fionn and Alex. I told her how my intentions had been good – how I wanted to make it all better and how I had in fact made it worse.

She resisted telling me I was a complete disaster and made lots of "poor Fionn" noises, which was fair enough as Fionn was indeed the biggest victim in all this even if I was the one selfishly feeling very, very sorry for myself.

I told her that it was particularly crappy because friends at work were few and far between – in fact, friends everywhere were few and far between. And then I told her how Bob had warned me not to mess up again and how – knowing me – it was unlikely that I could manage not to mess up again.

She nodded again – which did not fill me with confidence. Surely she should have reassured me that I was being overly dramatic and that of course I could manage to stay out of trouble if I just focused. She was supposed to give me a plan – a new Life Plan (not necessarily laminated), with ideas of how to get out of this sorry mess.

Instead she finished off her JD and Coke, then got up and went back to the kitchen where she rummaged through my cupboards until she found two of perhaps the largest tumblers in the world and poured two very large drinks.

Walking back in and handing one to me, she said matter of factly, "Annie, my dear, we're gonna need these."

I nodded. I didn't question Darcy. No one ever questioned Darcy. "I'm sorry," I muttered. "Dragging you all the way up here, away from Gerry and work."

She shook her head. "Sure isn't Gerry glad to see the back of me for a while? He gets to lie in his scratcher all day now, and drink all night if he wants. He'll be glad of the break – and, besides, don't they say absence makes the heart grow fonder?"

"And work?"

"Never mind, petal. They owe me big time. I've been working my arse off lately so don't worry about that."

It must be nice, I thought to myself, to have your work value you so much they agreed to your every request for time off because they could rely on you the rest of the time.

Of course I always promised myself – every Monday – that this week would be the week when I gave work My All. But there were always too many distractions.

I gave a weak smile.

"Annie. Don't worry. We'll sort it all out. I promise. There is nothing here which can't be fixed. You just have to figure out what you want and we'll work out how to get it. But, first of all, you need to start sorting out some of the mess you've made with Fionn, and work, and yes, even Pearse."

I nodded. I had hoped in my heart she wouldn't say that. I had hoped she would have some magic formula which would sort it all out without the need for me to go grovelling to anyone – but I suppose I had always known in my heart that was never going to happen. I took a long swig of my JD and Coke and lay back. This was going to be interesting.

15

By morning I had managed about four hours of sleep. Darcy and I had sat up chatting. It was going to be simple. I was going to apologise to Fionn and I was going to do it like a proper grown-up in a face-to-face capacity and not via email or text, like the big fat chicken I was. I would grovel. I would tell her it was all stupid and that I had been a tit of the highest order and then I would visit Alex (in my lunch break so as not to annoy Bob any further) and explain that it wasn't Fionn who had sent me and that I was sorry for sticking my nose in their business in the first place. I would grovel. I would tell him it was all stupid and that I was a tit of a highest order.

As for Pearse – you can probably see where this is going. There was no point in stringing it out, Darcy said. If I didn't love him (and I didn't) then I should be straight with him. I would invite him round though – I didn't want to act the cow in Manna in front of Toni and nor did I want to give him the chance to humiliate me in whatever way he saw fit. I didn't want him to act the big man and make a scene – as he was likely to – and for us to be subject of gossip-mongers the city over.

"I don't understand why you ended up back with him," Darcy had said.

"Don't you?" I'd asked forlornly. "I was lonely and he was there and he knows me and I know him and yes, he might be a complete eejit, but he was a big part of my life for a long time and he wanted me."

I cringed slightly at telling my sister – regardless of how cool she was – that a man wanted me. It felt all a little bit "too much information" but the JD and Coke had loosened my tongue and I was letting as much of these feelings out as possible.

"And the new man? Doesn't he want you?"

"Fionn thinks he's using me for sex."

"With those flowers? I don't think so."

"But I've not spoken to him in a couple of days."

"But he has sent flowers. And texts. In this day and age that's a full-on courtship. What some of my single friends in Dublin wouldn't give for that sort of attention!"

I smiled in spite of myself and bit back the feeling of something just not being right about the whole situation.

Darcy had a way of making things seem simple – almost too simple. I went to bed believing that things were not half as bad as they really were and that it would all be okay.

Despite the lack of sleep I even managed to make myself look respectable for work the following morning. Although, of course, Darcy laughed at my "terribly pedestrian" dress sense as I slipped into my Next trousers.

"Not everyone can get away with your look," I said as she mocked my tailored black trousers, cerise pink T-shirt and satin neckscarf.

She sat there, eating toast in my living room, her hair a mess of frizzy curls, but still looking fabulous and her long skinny legs creeping out of some vintage cropped denim leggings while an off-the-shoulder tunic completed a look which screamed: "I used to be in Bananarama!"

I hated – but loved – that she looked amazing in her outfit and, yes, I did feel a little boring in mine, even though I had tied the scarf in a very "in season" bow and teased my hair into a funky beehive.

"You should try my look some time. It could work on you, petal," she said.

"Maybe," I said with no intention of ever following through on her suggestion. "But for now I must go and throw myself on my proverbial sword and hope that Fionn forgives me."

I lifted my non-designer bag and left with my spirits high.

In fact, as I drove to work, all set for telling Fionn what an utter eejit I was etc, I even had a smile on my face. I listened in to the radio, laughing along with Chris Moyles and his morning crew and arrived at the office early (seven and a half minutes) once again.

I was the first person there, which made me feel nicely smug and superior. I switched on the lights and the coffee machine and even went so far as to sort out the post and put it on Bob's desk which would earn me brownie points without a doubt.

I then sat down, switched on my computer and tapped out an email to Fionn.

"Fionn

Please can we meet for a FSB at 10.30?

I know you have cause to be annoyed with me but please let me explain properly, and I promise you I will do my very best to sort it out and not make it any worse.

Axx"

She replied, shortly after she arrived, with a simple okay and the scene was set. I texted Darcy to tell her that I had sent the initial email of apology and she replied with a "Good luck!", which buoyed me up. Good old Darcy – with her ability to make things seem infinitely surmountable.

I just had to kill the time before the FSB and I was determined that whatever it was I would do, I would impress Bob. So I set about looking up the latest campaign for my cosmetics client, Haven. We had become so used to plugging their products that we rarely did anything above and beyond the usual mail-out of freebies to greedy journalists with nicely designed press releases – so I set about brainstorming (with my brain competing against itself) for something which would launch their latest twelve-hour-lasting lip gloss into the stratosphere of the public consciousness.

I was kissing my thirty-sixth piece of card – for the press releases – when Bob walked in and looked at me strangely. Whether it was because I was snogging paper with a shade of bright pink lippy slapped across my mouth, or whether it was because it was before nine twenty-five, I'll never know, but I think he looked impressed. It was either impressed or amused.

Fionn and I took our usual place in the corner of the smoker's hut. She looked at me expectantly and I tried to remember just exactly what it was I had planned to say to her.

"Fionn, look, I'm sorry."

"You said," she replied, without so much as a glance towards her prop pack of cigs.

"I thought I was helping," I ploughed on. "I thought if Alex knew how much you were upset and how much you thought of him and Emma, he might reassess how he has been behaving and things might get better for you. I know I do things in a slapdash way sometimes but I was doing it with the very best of intentions."

"Well, he reassessed his behaviour all right." Fionn took a cigarette from her prop packet and lit it for real. She inhaled slowly, the warm curl of smoke catching in her throat and making her cough. "He's talking of postponing the wedding. Not calling it off mind, just 'postponing' it until we can get ourselves sorted. He said it is clear there are major issues in our relationship and that he will not subject Emma to a wobbly relationship. She needs security in her life, apparently, and at the moment he is not sure if I can offer her that."

I felt my heart sink to my boots. Actually, it sank below my boots – right down through the ground. I knew I hadn't helped and I knew Alex had been pissed off but I didn't realise it was this bad.

"Is there anything I can do? Should I talk to him again? I could explain that you hadn't sent me? That I had gone and then just not even realised I had given him that impression? I could even buy a sofa – a really expensive one?"

I hoped injecting a little humour – however badly timed – could help the situation but I was wrong.

"You've done enough, Annie."

"I really am sorry," I replied.

"You said," she repeated as she stubbed her unsmoked cigarette out in the overflowing ashtray. Then she walked off, not looking back.

I knew Fionn was too kind-hearted to stay cross at me forever. I wasn't devastated that our friendship was over. I knew it wasn't. But I did know that it was badly damaged and I needed to do something – feck knows what – to make it better.

It was with slightly less enthusiasm that I went back to my desk and resumed the task of snogging press releases. Somehow my fervour for high-gloss lipsticks had waned and, I'll admit, a few smudged.

I sent Fionn an email just before lunch.

"Things will get better. I know they will. And we'll all laugh about this in times to come. Well, you probably won't laugh about it. And I certainly won't. I'll be too busy trying to make it up to you forever. But, you and Alex, you will get through this."

She replied shortly after.

"I hope so, Annie. And I know you were trying to be a good friend, but sometimes, just sometimes, I wish you would engage your brain before you speak. It's all well and good to be Quirky Annie who messes things up from time to time, but you can't meddle in other people's lives. Imagine if I decided to take a visit to Manna and tell Pearse your innermost thoughts and fears?

It's not my place, and I wouldn't do it.

I love you. You are my best friend. But there are times when it is very, very hard to be around you. I need a little time – I have to concentrate on what really matters to me. I have to make it work with Alex because, even though he is being a dick of the highest order just now, I love him and can't imagine not having him in the rest of my life.

So give me some space and understand that I'm angry with you – and rightly so."

I couldn't argue with her email, no matter how badly it stung.

I took myself out for a solitary FSB and when I returned I clicked on the reply button.

I tried to think of what else to say but all I could think of, once again, was that I was sorry and that just seemed trite.

"I'm here when you are ready to talk again," I typed hesitantly and clicked *Send* and looked up. She gave me a half-smile. It wasn't the progress either I or Darcy had hoped for, but it was a start. My plans, however, to visit Alex in my lunch break were well and truly scuppered. That would break things entirely and, while I wanted to let him know that Fionn had nothing to do with my impromptu visit, I would have to find another way to do it.

Next on my list was to arrange my liaison with Pearse. I called the restaurant and Toni answered, her snooty tones clearly indicating that Manna was a very posh place to eat indeed and that she was a very important person in the workings of the place. I kicked myself for not just calling his mobile.

"Hi, may I speak with Pearse, please?"

"Who may I say is calling?" she asked and I mentally slapped her square across the back of the head. She knew it was me. She had spoken to me a lot over the phone in the last two years. She was just being a smart-arse and I was in no mood for smart-arses.

"It's Annie, Toni. Is he about?" I asked, biting my tongue.

"I'll just check," she muttered and I heard her put the phone down and click-clack off across the marble floor in her fancy shoes.

I knew she didn't actually *have* to check. The same woman would have known, at any hour of the working day or night, exactly where Pearse was. Be it the kitchen, the dining room or in the loo having a quick dump, you could bet your Crème Brûlée Toni would know about it.

A minute passed before I heard her click-clacking back.

"I'll just put you through," she muttered and I wondered why she hadn't just patched me through to the kitchen in the first place. Surely one of the other chefs could have told me if he wasn't there.

I guessed she was just looking for an excuse to gaze lovingly at his face.

It crossed my mind that this shouldn't annoy me. After all, even though he had taken me to heaven and back again just a few days before, I had well and truly concluded that Pearse and I were going nowhere as a couple. It shouldn't annoy me one touch, but it did, and mentally she got another slap.

The phone beeped and Pearse answered. He sounded stressed.

"Work or pleasure?" he barked.

I didn't know how to answer. I wasn't calling for work but I certainly wasn't calling for pleasure.

"Erm, Pearse. Can I see you some time?"

"I can call over in half an hour."

"No, not today. This evening? I'm at work just now."

"That's never really been a problem before. Tell Bob you're meeting me, his biggest and best client. I'm sure he won't mind."

"Actually, Pearse, if there is one thing I am sure of, it is that he will. And no, l-look, we n-need to talk properly." I stumbled over the words, my nerves at this whole sorry mess getting the better of me.

"Talk? I thought you might have been looking for something more than just talking."

I could hear the smirk on his face and I could swear I heard one of the other chefs laughing. The fecker probably had me on speakerphone – he often did when he took calls in the kitchen. He didn't like to dirty the phone with flour or oil or blood or whatever.

I had to be careful how I played this. He was under the illusion – and why wouldn't he be? – that we were well and truly back on again, in which case, no, we wouldn't just talk when we met. But I could hardly break it to him, over the speakerphone in his restaurant, that we needed not only to talk but to have *The Talk*.

"Pearse, could you just let me know when you might be free to come over?"

"I'll try and get over tonight – after we close – is that okay?"

"Yes, fine, p-perfect," I stuttered.

He told me he was looking forward to it (to a distinct "Way-hey!" from the chef in the background) and I hung up feeling like a complete and utter bitch.

In fact, I felt so bitch-like I had to immediately text Darcy and ask her what she thought.

She replied that I was not a bitch, but I was an eejit and asked me to bring home two Wispas and some bottles of Pear Cider. The woman had her priorities right.

I climbed the stairs to the flat with a heavy heart and a heavier carrier-bag. I hadn't bothered to get in touch with Ant. I'd had enough of things going wrong and I didn't see the need to make it a hat trick of disasters.

Darcy was lying on the sofa, her funky outfit now accessorized with a pair of fluffy bedsocks. She was watching *Home and Away* and as I walked in she greeted me with a very chipper "G'day."

"Hello," I replied, throwing myself ungraciously into the armchair.

"What's wrong, Sheila?" she asked in a dodgy Australian accent.

"Nothing," I sighed. "It's just been a tough day."

"Well, how about I throw a couple of shrimps on the barbie and open a tinny or two?"

I raised my eyebrow.

She dropped the accent. "Okay, then how about I whip us up a quick spag bol and we crack open a bottle of this cider?"

"I have to keep my faculties about me. Pearse is coming over later to have *The Talk*."

She responded with an ominous sounding "*Duhn duhn duuuuuhn!*" and I had to smile.

"A wee drop won't hurt you," she said, her accent now transformed into a Mrs Doyle from *Father Ted* impression. "Ah, go on – go on, go on, go on, go on, go on, go on!"

Of course, being Darcy, she was right. A wee drop wouldn't hurt me – but a couple of bottles would. And we skipped the spag bol, choosing to sustain ourselves entirely on Wispas and alcohol for the evening.

At eleven twenty-one we were just reminiscing about our childhood, and how our father had actually made us believe John Denver was our uncle, when the intercom buzzer bleeped and I nearly had a small coronary.

"Oh shite – Pearse," I muttered, stumbling to my feet.

"Oh yes. Pearse. Pee-Arse," Darcy said, before falling into hysterical laughter.

"Darcy, behave!" I chided before the giggles got the better of me too.

We were struggling to keep straight faces when he arrived at the front door – a look of wanton expectation etched across his face and his crotch.

"Annie," he began, reaching his arms towards me and enveloping me in an embrace, "I've been thinking about you and about us all day."

I struggled to focus, feeling giddy from both the pear cider and the effort of trying to stifle my giggles.

I pulled back from him and stuttered, "I-I don't know about 'us', Pearse –"

"Ah, Annie, you *know* we make a good team," he cut in. "And yes, I know we've both made mistakes but I wouldn't change you – faults and all – for anything. And I believe we can get through this and I can forgive you."

He reached a hand to my stunned face and I heard a snort from behind me.

"Pee-Arse, how lovely to see you again," Darcy said, walking towards us, and it was Pearse's turn to look a little stunned.

"Darcy," he said, stretching his hand out to shake my sister's.

He didn't say it was lovely to see her and I wasn't surprised. He had clearly been expecting something a little more sexually gratifying than a chat with my sister.

"Here, come and sit down," she said, gesturing towards the living room and the sofa.

"Can I get you a drink? A pear cider? Although on second thoughts I think we might have finished the cider. There might be some Jack Daniels, or beer or –"

"Malibu?" I offered – knowing there was a dusty bottle of the coconut-flavoured liquid festering in the back of my cupboard.

"No, thank you," Pearse replied, tersely, taking a seat. "Actually, Darcy, lovely and all as it is to see you, I'm really here to talk to Annie, as I'm sure you'll understand."

"But of course," she said with a strange drunken bow before turning to leave the room. "You know where I am if you need me," she mock-whispered to me over her shoulder, and walked into my bedroom, closing the door behind her.

I'm sure I heard Pearse let out a small whimper. The bedroom door was closed: there would be no hanky panky.

I took a deep breath, steadied myself as best I could, and sat down beside him.

"As I was saying," he said, "we can get over this. Haven't we already made a good start? I can't remember the last time sex was so good."

Whatever wild hopes I'd had that he knew what I was going to say, and would let me off the hook, evaporated as he went on telling me just how lucky I was to have such a wonderful, talented, forgiving man on my arm and that he was horny as hell.

"We have let things slide," he continued. "You know, got stuck in a rut. You've let your appearance go a little – but that's okay. That often happens a few years into a relationship, I suppose. And I know, well, your lifestyle isn't quite the same as mine, but don't they say that opposites always attract and . . ."

He wittered on. To be honest I had to stop myself from listening. As he chatted, I didn't see us moving closer together, I saw us drifting further apart. I didn't want this – no matter how good the sex, or how comfortable I felt with him, or how well he was doing. There was a reason I had slept with Ant and one bonk on a lonely afternoon was not going to fix it. Nor was the experience of Pearse pointing out my faults under the pretence of doing me a favour.

And it dawned on me that when I created my Life Plan, the man I imagined standing beside me as I reached that altar wearing that very frou-frou dress was not one who could only point out that he loved me in spite of my faults. The man I imagined marrying was one who would shout all my positive attributes from the rooftops.

I never wanted to be any man's second best – the one he settled with because it was the easier option. I wanted to be his be-all and end-all and it was clear that I wasn't for Pearse. Regardless of how I felt or didn't feel for him, *he* didn't love *me*. He probably never really had. He may well have been fond of me in his own way, but love – no. It dawned on me that the only person Pearse was in love with was himself.

He wittered on as my eyes filled with tears.

"Don't cry," he said. "It's okay. I'm okay with what's happened. It will be okay now."

I shook my head, struggling to find the words I needed.

He reached his hand out to me but I couldn't bear to let him touch me. It didn't matter that his hands were familiar to me. It didn't matter that not so long ago I had let him caress every inch of my body. I didn't want him near me now.

"Pearse," I said. "It's over. I need you to go."

He didn't look shocked. In fact, a smile was dancing across his face. "Here we go again! Annie, don't be so dramatic!" he said, as if he were merely humouring me. "You *need* me."

"No," I said firmly. "I don't. I don't need you, and I don't want you. I never meant to hurt you and I'm sorry things got so confused. I never should have come to Manna. I never should have gone home with you. It can't be right between us again."

"Yes, it *can*," he said firmly. "All it will take is some effort."

"I'm sorry. Genuinely. But I can't do any more. I've done enough, Pearse."

He still didn't look shocked. He didn't look hurt. He didn't really look anything. He sat, expressionless, his eyes moving slowly around the room until they arrived at the bouquet of flowers on the sideboard.

"It's him, isn't it?" he muttered.

"No," I said, with as much strength as I could. "It's not him, Pearse. It's you. It's us."

I could have sworn I heard Darcy cheer from the bedroom. Pearse just stood up and fixed me with his gaze.

"You'll regret this, Annie. You'll never get better than me. You were punching above your weight as it was – and that's saying something, considering . . ." And he looked me up and down, taking in every inch of my less than svelte body.

Finally I was able to put a word to all those looks he had given me over the last year: contempt.

If I needed any confirmation that I was doing the right thing, I'd just had it. There wasn't even a trace of love. There wasn't a trace of the man who had once spent an hour just lying beside me in bed stroking my hair and telling me he loved my smile.

The man who had promised one day that between us we would take on the world was long gone.

And yet, when he left, slamming the door behind him, I felt myself crumple.

Darcy opened the bedroom door and came out to me, taking me in her arms as I all but fell to the floor.

"It's okay," she soothed simply, kissing the top of my head just like our mother used to. "It's going to be okay."

16

I was only five minutes early for work the following day but it gave me the chance to compose myself suitably before my colleagues arrived.

I had plastered on my very best make-up and had Darcy help me pile my hair up in a semi-complicated up-do. I had consumed a litre and a half of water on the drive in and had eaten three apples and two bananas for breakfast – all mushed together in some kind of slimy slushy type of concoction.

I still felt wretched however. And I'm sure I looked it too. And you have to believe me when I say arriving into the heady world of PR, where a smile and jaunty attitude counts for everything, feeling deflated (I wouldn't want to say heartbroken) was not good.

Darcy had held me the night before until I stopped crying. She'd told me that Pearse was an awful bastard and I was to take no notice of him but I wasn't convinced. His nasty remark about me punching above my weight had stung, every way you took it. In my heart I feared it was true.

But now I had to plaster on a smile. I had to be chipper. I had to pretend it was all okay because I could not have yet another crap day at work.

Bob arrived and smiled in my direction. "Well done, Annie. This is what I like to see. The old you back and giving it your all. Great stuff altogether. Come and see me in an hour. I have a topnotch new project which has your name written all over it."

He walked on, whistling as he went, and I at least congratulated myself on being in his good books for a change.

When Fionn arrived she gave me a half-smile before sitting down at her desk. This could mean things were resolving themselves between her and Alex and our friendship would be back on track soon. It could also mean that she had hired the assassin/made the voodoo doll/let the air out of my tyres or worked out some other devious form of revenge for my misdemeanour.

I half-smiled back, my cover-up foundation at risk of cracking. A minute or so later an email pinged onto my screen.

"Are you okay?" Fionn asked.

"Yes," I typed back. "Well, sort of. Pearse and I are over, completely."

Then, of course, it dawned on me that she didn't know Pearse and I had been "not over" for a while and that there had been a need for me to break up with him all over again.

"I'll explain it later, if you'll let me," I added.

"FSB?" she replied.

"It will take a bit longer than that. Maybe a drive at lunchtime? I'll buy you a sandwich."

Of course there was a very real possibility she would just tell me to go scratch but I thought it was worth a chance anyway. I hoped, if she was willing to go on an FSB with me, there was a chance she would join me for a lunchtime drive down towards the coast complete with wilted salad sandwich from the local garage.

I took a deep breath and pressed *Send* and I swear I almost cried in relief when she said yes. I didn't deserve her. I really, really didn't.

Ten minutes had passed and I found myself knocking on Bob's door, wondering what on earth he could have in store for me. Ah, the thrills of life in PR! One week dealing with a local wannabe shooting for the stars, the next standing in your smalls outside a sex shop. I always felt a flush of excitement when a new project landed on my desk – sometimes it exceeded expectations, sometimes it made my heart sink and I had to take a deep breath, fake-smoke three cigarettes and promise myself a stiff drink just to get on with it.

Today was one of those days.

"Annie, sit down. You'll love this. It's so much fun." He was almost glowing with excitement.

I believed he might have overdone it on the moisturiser that morning. He perched on the side of his desk in what was a definite invasion of my personal space and started.

"We're bringing the NorthStar smack bang up to date with funky café culture and relationship co-ordination."

Relationship co-ordination? I wracked my brains to try and figure out what the feck he was talking about. This was clearly one of those cases where he was thinking outside the box again and I would have to try and decipher his gobbledegook.

"What we want is to bring a new concept in finding love and passion to the people of this city."

"I thought we did that with 'Love, Sex and Magic'?" I countered and he gave a weak laugh – as if the sex shop was so, like, fifteen minutes ago.

"No, Annie, this is about more, much more than making sure people have fun in the sack. This is about getting them into the sack in the first place."

Prostitution? It would certainly be a good PR challenge to try and make that palatable to the masses. I could imagine that wee doll in her twin-set and pearls choking on her false teeth at the very thought.

"Let me explain more," he continued. "A singles' night."

"That sounds a bit cheesy," I answered and it did.

We had tried it once before – created a great campaign for one of the local supermarkets to have a night where they openly encouraged single people to come along and have a sneaky peak at a stranger's basket. It hadn't really taken off – turns out there is only so much conversation half a pound of Doherty's mince and a bottle of fine wine can generate. Not enough women showed up and the women who did couldn't be described as very alluring – so we were utterly fecked. Not to mention the fact that the singletons who did turn up were all annoyed that they had to make two trips to the supermarket a week – one to buy their fancy goods which would attract a partner and another to buy their essentials like loo roll, Preparation H and tampons.

"Well, it's not," Bob said defensively in response to my "cheesy" accusation.

I sat back, determined to keep my mouth shut, at least until he had finished talking.

"Speed dating!" he shouted and I tried not to swear in fright. "Our client has a very clear idea what they want and we are going to help them make it happen. Picture it: Manna – a week night. Mood lighting – some classy music. Hordes of young, eligible, well-off young people all looking for love. Clear dress code – no trainers. Market it as *the* place to meet someone who is not a total loser – as somewhere that will take the pain out of dating. Champagne – strawberries – maybe even oysters. Designer beer and designer clothes. Designer relationships."

Bob had a habit of doing that – brainstorming out loud and coming out with a series of increasingly random short sentences. I nodded attentively throughout as he waffled on but my brain had gone into a complete meltdown at the third word of his vision.

Manna. He wanted me to arrange a night in Manna. Which would mean working with Pearse, and Toni, and trying to be professional when I had clearly pissed Pearse off and he clearly found me lacking in so many ways.

But there was no way I could tell Bob I wouldn't or couldn't do it. Not without landing myself a P45 for my trouble anyway. As I sat and listened, taking notes and smiling when he looked particularly excited, all I could think, over and over again on a loop, was that I was well and truly fucked.

Fionn clearly saw my pallor as I walked out of the office just before lunch. She lifted her coat and bag and sauntered over to my desk.

"C'mon then, Annie. You can tell me all about it when we get to the car."

It took ten minutes of me shaking my head and muttering inaudibly before I was able to talk properly to her – and I did feel horrible that I was off-loading on her. She would be perfectly within her rights to tell me it served me right and I should suck it up and enjoy what the Karma Fairy was throwing at me.

But Fionn isn't like that. She is much too nice for her own good and even though she was still clearly annoyed with me (she told me as soon as we got in the car that she did not wish to talk about Alex and that, yes, she was still annoyed with me), she said I could offload to my heart's content.

So I started, where all good stories do, at the beginning. I told her how, after the disastrous meeting with Alex, I had ended up getting it on in the back office of Manna before being whisked back to the big house on the hill for some rather lovely sex. And how that had distracted me from the need to repair the damage done with Alex asap. I told her how, almost immediately, I had realised that sex with Pearse was a huge mistake and how Darcy had arrived to sort it all out.

And of course I told her about the previous night's meeting with Pearse at the flat (and how Darcy was now calling him Pee-Arse) and how Bob now was wetting himself with excitement at the thought of using Manna for his latest PR coup.

"Oh Annie," Fionn said as I finally stopped to draw breath, "this is really quite a spectacular mess, even for you."

I nodded, as we stared out across Lough Swilly eating our salad sandwiches. "I'm trying to make it better but it seems no matter what I do, it just seems to get worse."

"And Ant? What about him?"

"I haven't done him since the weekend. In fact I've not even spoken with him."

"Has he been ignoring you?"

"Quite the opposite. He's texted a few times, but I can't bring myself to reply to him. Everything I touch turns to crap at the moment and I'm not sure he isn't just using me so I'm giving him a wide berth."

"Probably for the best," Fionn said, nodding as she sipped from a can of Diet Coke. There was a short pause. "I think you need to get yourself sorted first before you concentrate on other people. What are you going to do about work?"

"What can I do? I have to do the godawful speed dating thing," I sighed.

"Even though it is at Manna? But that will be dreadful."

"Well, it will be but if I say no I might as well just hand in my notice now. Bob won't tolerate any more feck-ups from me and I can't say that I blame him. I've not exactly been on my game lately and this has to be perfect – even if it means me prostrating myself on the floor of Manna and letting Pearse humiliate me in whatever way he sees fit."

Fionn sat her Diet Coke down on the dashboard and opened the car window to draw in a deep breath.

"Maybe it won't be so bad?" she offered.

Now the Fionn of old would have told me to pull myself together and not to put up with any shit from Pearse. She would have offered to stand (or sit) by my side at the speed dating and she would have made it all fun and a great laugh but it was clear – perfectly clear – from how she was reacting that our friendship was far from repaired.

When I went home that evening I felt even more wretched than I had the night before. In fact I would have thought it impossible that I could have felt more wretched but I surprised myself by feeling utterly pathetic to the point that, when Darcy asked how my day was, I swore, lifted a bottle of wine from the fridge and locked myself in the bathroom for a long soak.

I lay there in the bath, submerging my head under the suds time and time again for as long as I could before gasping for breath. It dawned on me that this was how I always felt: in and out of the water – as if I was on the brink of drowning. My life was one long intake of breath – holding on as long as I could and seeing what happened, pushing myself further and further and achieving nothing from the whole process apart from a sore chest and a growing sense of panic.

I sat up, breathing in as deep as I could, then put my wineglass to my lips, sinking as much of it as I could without choking.

I pulled the plug out with my toes, lying there as the water seeped out and the cold washed over me and then, when I found the energy, I climbed out, roughly dried myself off, slipped on my dressing gown and topped up my wineglass.

There was one thing I had to do before I went to sleep, or tried to go to sleep. I walked into the bedroom. Darcy was lying on the bed with her back to me, reading a glossy magazine. I reached under my chest of drawers and surreptitiously pulled out my Life Plan – my ridiculously stupid and childish Life Plan – and hid it under my dressing gown. Then I left the room and quietly exited the flat.

Just outside there was a fire escape which crawled up to a small roof "garden". It wasn't anything to write home about – no nice planters or fancy wicker chairs. It was basically a bit of concrete on a roof with a couple of plastic chairs and a discarded barbecue in the corner. I sat down, swilling the wine in my glass and looking through the pages of my Life Plan, mocking myself for my foolish optimism.

Happy endings didn't really happen. This was not a fairy tale and I sure as feck wasn't Cinderella. There was no such man as Price Charming. There were no happy ever afters – the best any of us could ever hope for was just to get through life relatively unscathed.

But at the moment it was looking as if even that wasn't a remote possibility for me.

I needed to get real and give up on my foolish dreams of a big dress and a big wedding, followed by a big house in the country and a big family of gorgeous children to look after me in my dotage.

I flicked on my lighter and held it to the corner of my Life Plan.

It took a while to catch – laminate can be a bugger to burn – but it did catch and I lifted the lid of the rusty barbecue, sat the book down and watched the flames start to lick each page, curling each tacky picture of ivory duchesse satin gowns and designer interiors.

I raised my glass to it, and breathed out for the first time in weeks.

I had just put the glass to my lips when I became aware of Darcy standing behind me, a look of bewilderment on her face.

"Do you want to tell me what the fuck that is all about?" she asked, taking the glass out of my hand and putting it to her own lips, downing the contents in one.

I didn't answer.

"I can't believe you still have that tatty old scrapbook." Darcy was staring at the growing inferno in front of her. "And I can't believe you are on the roof half-naked drinking wine. Are you having some sort of breakdown?"

"A midlife crisis," I answered, wrapping my dressing gown tighter around me before warming my hands on the fire.

"You're only thirty-two."

"I feel older."

Darcy sniffed. Or snorted. It was hard to tell which. Either way I could tell she was just a little bit amused.

"Annie, why do you have to be so dramatic? Why does everything have to be a big deal? I mean, for the love of God, everyone goes through shitty times and this is just a shitty time. It's a very shitty time admittedly, honey, but no shittier than what any of the rest of us go through."

I turned on my slippered heel and pushed my way past her and back down the fire escape to my flat.

I heard her footsteps follow me and I knew she had more to say but, feeling very childish and very much reprimanded for my supposed overreaction to having a whole heap of crap poured right on my head, I walked into the bathroom and locked the door behind me.

I heard her rap on the door but I didn't answer. And I heard her sit down by the door and take a deep breath.

"Annie, I didn't mean to be dismissive . . ."

Well, feck me, she was doing a good job of it.

"And I'm sorry if I hurt your feelings . . ."

Not so sorry that I couldn't detect, I thought, a slight sense of humour in her voice.

I wanted to answer – I really wanted to shout (perhaps overdramatically) that she didn't care one jot about hurting my feelings and that no one ever did. But I sat there, in silence, listening.

"But you need to get yourself out of this slump and out of this mess. I can only help so much. You are thirty-two. You are a grown-up. You can't keep running to people for help . . ."

She said it softly – all hint of humour gone – but she might as well have been shouting and my desire to keep quiet in the bathroom left me.

"Running to people for help?" I threw open the door. "I don't run to people for help!"

"No," she said. "You have them run to you instead."

"That's not fair, Darcy! You offered to come up – and it's not like you're here every week, or every month or even once a season. You left Derry as soon as you could and even Mum and Dad didn't stick around. I rarely see any of you. Mum and Dad haven't been home in three years. This is the first time I've seen you this year. For all intents and purposes I'm alone up here and have been for years."

"You're a grown-up," she reiterated. "You shouldn't mind being on your own. You have a good life, Annie. You just don't see it."

"So sue me for feeling lonely!"

"Annie, I can't talk to you when you're being like this. I never could. It's like your teenage years again – all self-pity and mooning about like the world has done you some great wrong. Any second now you'll be sticking on a Morrissey album and donning some black eyeliner. You need to realise that this – this whole sorry situation – is only as bad as you let it become."

"God, Darce, are you ever downhearted? Do you ever just think 'fuck it' and have a bad day? Christ almighty, woman, just because you can cope with everything life throws at you, doesn't mean we all can. Fair bloody play to you for being perfect. But I'm not and I make mistakes, and I regret things and have a stupid Life Plan which, yes, might be exceptionally childish and immature of me but it's just all gone to shit and I feel down. And I'm *allowed* to feel fecking down!"

I sat down on the sofa, rearranging my dressing gown to curtail an unfortunate flashing incident.

"I never said I was perfect," Darcy said. "For fuck's sake, Annie, you know I'm far from perfect, but what is different about me is that I just get on with it. You don't know the half of it because you never ask."

"I ask!" I protested. "I send emails every day asking how you are."

"No," Darcy said, sitting down across the room from me, and to my amazement I suddenly saw tears glistening in her eyes. "You send emails every day telling me how *you* are and what is going on in *your* life. If I'm lucky you might, somewhere, have stuck in a 'What about ye?' or a 'Hope you are well' –" A tear rolled down her cheek and she brushed it away. "But it's all about you, Annie. And I love you, with all my heart. You are my baby sister and you mean the world to me, and I would never see you hurt, but sometimes you need to get the hell over yourself and get on with things."

I got up, walked into my room, slammed the door and climbed into bed. I was just drifting off when my phone peeped to life with a text from Ant.

"Hey Sexy. How r u?"

"Fuck the feckity fuck off," I shouted at the phone, throwing it across the room before I pulled my pillow over my head, wondering if it would be at all possible to suffocate myself with a memory-foam pillow and sheer brute force.

Darcy came in two hours later and climbed silently into the bed beside me. I wanted to say sorry but something in me just couldn't bring myself to do it.

I couldn't find the words. I couldn't trust myself to know what to say – because, no matter how hard I tried these days, I always seemed to get it wrong. And that wasn't me being over-dramatic and nutso – that was me being a complete and utter realist.

I listened to Darcy breathing softly beside me and I wondered what she had meant by "you don't know the half of it" and what had made her cry and my heart started to ache for everyone who wanted a happy ending and didn't seem to be able to find it.

17

She was still sleeping when I woke up. She didn't stir, not even when my alarm burst into life. I figured she was ignoring me and I couldn't blame her.

I got up, dressed quietly and put my make-up on in the bathroom. Before I left the flat I took one of the flowers out of the arrangement Ant had sent me and put in a glass on the worktop. I scrawled a quick note: *"I'm sorry and I'll make it up to you. We'll talk later. Love you, sis."* and left them both there together and then I set off for work where my first day without my Life Plan would start and where, I realised, I would have to start piecing together a whole new plan for my immediate and not-so-immediate future.

Gone were my dreams of fancy wedding gowns, chair covers and pink champagne. Now I had to sort things out, once and for all.

~ First I had to make this Speed Dating Night the best darn success NorthStar had ever seen – even if it meant humiliating myself entirely in front of Pearse.

~ I had to stop feeling guilty about what had happened with Pearse. He was indeed, as Darcy said, a Pee-Arse.

~ I had to make it okay with Darcy. She was clearly upset about something – and I had a feeling it wasn't just that I was an immature fecker.

~ I had to make it okay with Fionn – which I realised might have to mean I just bided my time and crept around her where possible. I was to absolutely keep my nose out of her business and I wasn't to either talk to Alex or make a voodoo doll of Rebecca – even if I thought Fionn would be secretly happy about the voodoo doll.

~ I had to either tell Ant to feck off completely or spend more time with him. It was time, as my dear daddy would say, to shit or get off the pot. Not that I was comparing the time I spent with Ant to either voiding my bowels or sitting on the loo for any other reason.

~ I had to prove to everyone – myself included – that I could do this. I could be a successful, happy, confident grown-up who didn't need anyone else other than herself to be happy.

The last of those, I guessed, would probably be the hardest but I was determined that I would make it happen. Perhaps Darcy was right – it wouldn't be the first time – and I needed to just get the hell over myself.

I arrived at work feeling a mixture of excitement and fear at the very thought of what could, or wouldn't happen. I was very good at making lists. I just wasn't very good at following through.

I sat down, switched on my computer, opened my contacts book and set about making the Speed Dating Night at Manna the biggest success story NorthStar had ever seen.

I arranged an appointment with the clients – one of those exclusive dating agencies who charged a fortune for the privilege – and I called a few event planners we had on our books. I discussed themes, and chair covers, and pink champagne. I called some of the local press – the same greedy journalists who this morning or the next would be swooning over their free samples of lipstick – and promised them press releases and invites if desired. I tasked a photographer with getting us a great image to use for the releases and spoke to the printers about a leaflet drop in the city's fanciest bars.

By lunchtime the only thing I hadn't done was actually book Manna but I had decided to take my life in my hands and do that in person that afternoon.

Fionn invited me for an FSB and I nipped out feeling strangely enthused and it obviously showed.

"You look happier?" she offered.

"I am and I'm not," I replied. "But I'll get there. I just have to take it one day at a time."

"Good way of thinking. I'm trying to adopt that approach myself. I'm trying to just keep going and hope that things right themselves."

I felt myself cringe. I knew that while I wasn't entirely to blame for the problems in the Fionn/Alex relationship, I couldn't escape the fact that I was partially to blame.

I didn't know what to say to her to make it better so I just nodded. At least that way I couldn't make it worse. I figured she would talk to me, and tell me more, when she was ready to and until then I would keep my head down and do the best I could. I vowed to myself that when I nipped out for lunch I would pick up a packet of Maltesers and drop them on her desk when I returned.

And I vowed that on my way back from Manna, I would stop off and pick up something really yummy for Darcy and me for dinner and then maybe we would chat. She hadn't called or texted that morning and I hoped she wasn't still mad at me. I hadn't called or texted her either but I had at least updated my Facebook status to say that I loved my sister very much, in the hope she would check in and see it. If I was lucky she might even click the wee button which would indicate she liked my update and that things weren't terminal between us.

But it seemed I just wasn't that lucky.

I sat outside Manna trying to slow my breathing. I had to remind myself I was a professional woman. I was more than able to deal with a business transaction. Pearse was not stubborn enough to turn down money being poured in his direction and, for the moment at least, Manna was still a client of NorthStar and had recently promised a wodge of cash to us in return for us upping its profile.

And it was still on my books. I was still the account manager and I could do this. I could show myself – and Pearse – that I could make a success of this night and that I wasn't the useless lump of nothing he thought I was.

I fixed my make-up in the rear-view mirror – reapplying my lip gloss and dusting my face with some pressed powder. I lifted my bottle of perfume from my bag and sprayed it liberally on my pulse points. I ran my hairbrush through my hair, before twisting it and clipping it up high on top of my head. As I did a final check in the mirror, I noticed the pearl studs I was wearing were ones given to me by Pearse and for a second I contemplated taking them off – but even though he had been a complete prick to me, and I wasn't exactly his favourite person in the world, I thought some memory of our time together might be a nice touch.

Stepping out of the car I straightened down my skirt and jacket and slipped my feet out of my flat driving shoes into impossibly high heels. Then I tottered – briefcase in hand – into the lion's den.

Toni was in her usual place – propping up the reception desk, a pencil pushed through the loose bun on her head. I could see she had just had her hair highlighted and, if I wasn't mistaken, her upper lip waxed. Her pristine white uniform blouse was also opened one button lower than normal with just a glimpse of black bra showing. She clearly knew Pearse was now absolutely and completely single and yet that did not stop her doing a double take when she saw me walk in.

I was almost tempted to tell her, right then and there, that there was absolutely no chance whatsoever of repeating that dry hump on the office desk and that she was welcome to Pearse and all his garlicky, arrogant, candle-obsessed, wankerish git-dom from here on in.

But that did not scream professionalism at me and I was, I reminded myself, to remain professional at all times.

"Toni, is Pearse around?"

She sniffed and looked at me mutely as if she was desperately trying to find a way to tell me to feck the hell off.

"It's purely business," I offered and she nodded before lifting the small Bakelite phone on her desk and dialling through to the kitchen. She turned away from me when she spoke, however, and placed her hand over the receiver before whispering (not that quietly) that "Annie – yes, Annie – is front of house. She says it's business." I heard a slightly raised voice swear down the line at her before she turned to me, face blazing, to say Pearse would be out shortly and I was to take a seat in the bar.

I smiled at her and picked up my briefcase before taking a seat at the bar and ordering a fizzy water from the friendly barman. I didn't know him – he was new – but he obviously knew who I was and what had happened, as he told me with a wink that the drink was on the house.

I had worked out how to pitch this and I actually felt really empowered, knowing that I had come up with some top-notch ideas. I sipped my wine and waited for Pearse. And waited. And waited. After twenty minutes Toni approached to say he had been held up with a kitchen emergency and would be held up for a while yet, but I could wait if I wanted to.

So I waited, and waited. An hour had passed and my fizzy water had been topped up (still on the house). I had even nipped to the loo, hoping that the old adage that a watched kettle never boils also applied to a narky chef bothering himself to show up for a business meeting.

My lip gloss was once again reapplied and I was just reading through the proposals for the fifteenth time when I heard footsteps approach from behind. I took a deep breath, steadied myself and turned to find myself face to face with a clean-shaven but otherwise very hairy Donegal man.

He smiled, a slow sexy smile which may have started in his lips but twinkled in his deep blue eyes.

"We have to stop meeting like this," he drawled and I felt my legs turn to jelly.

I knew this was bad. Very, very bad. Here I was, with not even the excuse of having drink taken, feeling incredibly turned on by a very virile and hunky man while waiting for my ex to walk out of his kitchen and conduct what was bound to be a very terse business meeting with me.

I once again took a deep breath – realising I was now at risk of hyperventilating – and smiled back at Ant. "I'm here on business actually."

"Hmmm, that's disappointing. There was me hoping you were stalking me."

"But I was here first. Maybe you're stalking me?" I offered with a raised eyebrow.

"Maybe I am. After all, I've tried every other method of getting your attention – phone-calls, texts, flowers . . ."

I blushed (ignoring the fact he might actually really be stalking me). "I'm sorry. I've been very busy."

"But you're here now," he said with a wink, sitting on the bar stool beside me.

"And I'm working," I repeated.

"Anything interesting? Any other sex – sorry, adult entertainment shops to promote or the like?" He looked most amused.

"Actually, I'm planning a Speed Dating Night and we're hoping to use this place as a venue. Manna is one of our biggest clients."

"It's a nice place all right. I've just had lunch here with a few colleagues. But watch out for that Pearse Campbell. I hear he's a complete tosser. All mouth and no trousers."

I laughed – a strange strangulated high-pitched effort – just as the very same all-mouth-and-no-trousers effort came walking out of the kitchen in his chef whites with a face on him like thunder.

"Annie," he said, "what could you possibly be doing here?"

Ant looked at me, and at Pearse, and then blushed every so slightly. "So I take you are acquainted then?"

"I would say that is one way to describe it," Pearse said and a small voice in my head just begged him not to say any more.

"What other kind of way would you describe it?" Ant said with a raised eyebrow.

This was not the professional start to the business meeting I was hoping for.

The wee voice in my head got louder.

Pearse looked at Ant, at me and then back at Ant. "And you are?" he asked.

"Anthony Dunne. A friend of Annie's."

"Well, I'm Pearse Campbell, an ex-friend of Annie's." Disgust was written all over his face.

I knew I had to say something very quickly before he worked out that Ant might well be the new friend who had been the catalyst to our relationship going to the wall.

"Oh but Pearse," I said, plastering a smile on my face, "we don't have to be friends to do business."

"That much is true," he said.

Ant watched, vaguely amused by it all.

I turned to him and excused myself. "I'm sorry, Ant, but I really do need to talk to Pearse about a business matter. We'll catch up later."

"Yes, I hope we do. You have my number, Annie. Use it."

The meaning behind his words was obvious and as he sauntered away I had to forcibly stop myself from staring at him until he was out of the room.

"Is that *him*?" Pearse asked.

"Don't be stupid," I replied quickly. "Look, Pearse, I have a proposal for you."

"Annie, be honest with me. Was that him? The one who sent the flowers?"

"No," I lied, desperate to get this meeting back on track as quickly as possible.

"Well, if it is him," said Pearse, "you really are scraping the bottle of the barrel now, aren't you?"

I bit my tongue. I would not rise to his bait. I would not tell him that actually when I was seeing *him* I was scraping the bottom of the barrel and, in comparison, Ant was floating somewhere near the top of the barrel even though he might, or might not, simply be using me to get his end away.

"Pearse, can we talk please about the real reason I'm here? I'm here on NorthStar business – a proposal which could benefit both Manna and our newest clients . . ."

Pearse listened, his head for business once again becoming more important than anything we had ever shared on a personal level.

I outlined our plans – canapés, wine, chat, candles, press coverage and maybe making it a regular event.

"So what you are proposing is getting all the losers who can't get a date elsewhere lumping into my restaurant and salivating over each other?" he asked.

"No, not at all," I replied. "Our clients are high end. There would be a considerable fee for people looking to take part in the events. We are aiming this at the professional market. And, as I've said, we could go for it on Thursday nights which are traditionally on the quiet side for Manna. Initially we'll market it as a one-off – just to see how it goes – but if it goes well this could be big news. Think of the revenue. Our clients will be paying top dollar for a selection of your finest canapés – maybe you could put on a tapas spread or something, I'll leave that to you. You know what you're doing, Pearse. You could do this in your sleep."

Pearse nodded. I knew I was winning. I knew him well enough to know that appealing to his ego was the absolute best way to achieve anything.

"Right, one time. And tell Bob it better work. And it had better be classy. Manna is not a knocking shop and I won't have my name dragged through the mud. I'll draw up a sample menu – you can return that to your clients – and we'll take it from there."

"Great, Pearse. You won't regret it," I said, standing up and shaking his hand. I wondered why I had never noticed before how limp his handshake was. It made me feel funny and not in a nice way.

I walked away feeling proud of myself – after all, despite the very dodgy scenario of running into Ant, I had managed not to make anything worse in the last couple of hours. Given how things had gone recently I figured that was a major achievement.

I would go so far as to say I was almost on a high as I drove back to the office to move the plans on to the next stage with Bob.

I stopped on the way and picked up some delicious treats from M&S and knew that when I got home I would be able to sort things out with Darcy.

And my heart felt lighter still when I walked back into the office to find a huge giftwrapped box of goodies from Ant. There was wine. There was chocolate. There were edible knickers. The sentiment was unmissable but just in case I needed some clarification the card read: "*Was lovely to see you today. Can't wait to see to you again sometime soon.*"

Yes, it was kind of dirty. And it kind of reinforced the notion that he might just be using me for sex but it felt me feel nice all the same. Fionn smiled at me from across the room and when I checked my email there was a note from her proclaiming that I was a lucky bitch. Smugly, I admitted to myself that I did feel like a bit of a lucky bitch in that moment.

Darcy was sitting on the sofa watching *Home and Away* and painting her nails when I arrived home laden with my M&S bags and my huge box of goodies from Ant.

She looked up as I stumbled in the door. "I'm pretty sure he's interested in you," she said with a wink. "I'll put the kettle on make us a brew." She got up and hobbled, wet toes curled upwards, towards the kitchen.

"Naw, sit down, Darcy. I'll make dinner. I've brought a lovely, gooey, cheesy pasta thing and then for afters a lovely, gooey, chocolatey pudding thing. And if you are really good," I said, delving in the gift box, "I'll share my edible knickers with you."

She let out a roar of laughter, hobbled back to the sofa and sat down. "I'll go for the pasta and the pudding. The sweetie thong you can keep for yourself. Will be nice to have someone cook for me. Gerry isn't up to much in the kitchen."

"Least I could do after being a cow last night," I said with genuine remorse.

"I think I was the cow," she said.

"No . . . well, maybe we were both cows . . . but I'm worried about you, Darce," I said, sitting down beside her and kicking off my shoes.

"Nothing to worry about," she said with a smile. And, while the smile was still Darcy's trademark all-teeth-and-gums grin, her eyes gave away the fact that something *was* amiss.

"Is it Gerry? Is everything okay there?"

"Annie. Honestly. I'm fine. Must be PMT or something. I just had a bad day. I have them sometimes, like we all do. But it's grand. Honest." She turned her head back to the TV. "Not been the same since Pippa left," she said, nodding at the residents of Summer Bay and I knew the discussion was over for the evening.

An hour later we were at the table eating the creamy, cheesy pasta, and making suitable yummy noises while discussing the merits of *Home and Away* versus *Neighbours*, when the intercom buzzed to life.

"Expecting anyone?" Darcy asked.

"Maybe it's Scott Robinson come to take me away from it all? I always fancied changing my name to Charlene," I joked, shovelling one more spoonful of dinner into my mouth before answering the buzzer.

"Annie, it's me. Can I come up?" Fionn asked, a distinct waver in her voice.

"Sure, course you can," I answered, shooting a confused look at Darcy.

"Not Scott then?" she asked as I hung up.

"Nope. It's Fionn and she sounded funny."

"Funny ha ha, or funny peculiar?"

"Definitely peculiar," I said, walking down the hall and opening the front door, just in time to see Fionn lumping what looked like her entire earthly belongings up the stairs.

"It's over," she said dramatically. "Or at least that bastard is going to think it is until he wises the feck up!"

I doubted my gob had ever been so smacked before.

Fionn staggered in as I held the door open. She walked down the hall, dumped her bags on the living-room floor and sat down at the table, spooned some of my lovely pasta in her mouth and took a deep breath.

"Darcy, how the hell are you?" she asked with a grin and I wondered if it was her turn to have some sort of breakdown.

"Fine," Darcy replied, mildly amused.

"Great, great. Annie, is there any more of this? I'm fecking starving! I've hardly eaten a damn thing in the last three weeks because of that wedding dress so, seeing as I might not actually get to wear the damn thing at all, I might as well eat whatever the shag I want and grow to the size of a house. So if you have any garlic bread, or parmesan, or even lard, then bring it on because I don't care any more."

I nodded mutely and walked to the kitchen and dished her up a plate of pasta before grating a small mountain of cheese on the top.

"Will this do?" I asked, presenting it to her.

"Perfect, absolutely perfect," she said and turned her attention back to Darcy. "So what is it you were talking about before I lumped in?"

Darcy looked at me, at Fionn, back at me and then back to Fionn again. "Are you sure you're okay?"

"You know what," Fionn said, "I'm about as okay as I've been in a long time but I really don't want to talk about it just now. I just want to eat this, talk some utter rubbish and then go to sleep. Annie, I take it's okay if I crash here?"

"Of course," I said, thinking of the one bed in the flat which was already populated by me and Darcy. I wondered if could we fit a third person in.

"One of us will have to take the sofa though," I said, "I don't mind if you two want to share . . ."

"I don't mind sharing," Darcy said and Fionn shrugged her shoulders.

So it was sorted.

The rest of the evening was spent in a weird conversational zone – *Home and Away* vs *Neighbours* vs *Coronation Street*. We had just about covered every birth, death and marriage in Summer Bay, Ramsey Street and Weatherfield by eleven when there was a mutual decision to go to bed.

I climbed into my jammies, pulled a blanket over me on the sofa and lay there with thoughts of mixed-up relationships, sisters with secrets and edible underwear running through my mind.

19

It was unusual for me to get up early on a Saturday morning. Usually – unless I had a shopping trip planned with Fionn – I would laze about most of the morning, dozing, reading, watching TV. I'd get up around eleven and maybe go for a run through the park to get some fresh air into my lungs. It was rare for me not to have a little buzz of a hangover so the fresh air helped with that and then I would go home, eat something yummy for lunch and watch a tacky film before getting ready for a visit from Pearse after hours or a trip down to Manna to sit like a spare part at the bar waiting for him to come and talk to me.

But this was no usual Saturday morning. I had spent the night tossing and turning on the sofa – at one stage rolling off and landing with an almighty thump on the floor. I'd been so tired I'd just stayed there for a while, hoping it would be more comfortable than my sofa. I vowed, at 4.36 a.m., that if both Fionn and Darcy were with me that night there would definitely have to be drink involved. A good feed of wine would at least ensure a decent night's sleep.

So I rose at seven thirty and headed for the shower – figuring I might as well take advantage of the calm before the storm. The last time I had shared with two girls had been during my university years where it became a fine art to get up and in the shower first, without waking my housemates who would have used all the hot water had they beaten me to it.

So I crawled off the sofa, stretching so that I could actually hear my bones crack and click back into place, headed for the bathroom and switched the shower on.

It seemed terribly selfish of me and probably a bit bitchy, but knowing that Fionn and Darcy were having their own problems (even if, admittedly, Fionn's was a little of my making) comforted me. For a long time, I thought as I let the water pour over me, I had felt as if I was the only person in my wider circle of family and friends who wasn't dancing her way towards a happy ending. All the books say that your thirties are meant to be the happiest decade in your life so when they rolled around – and I said goodbye to my drunken twenties – I embraced the new beginning. This was where it was all going to happen. *Cosmo* said so, so it must be true. And I had hauled that bloody stupid Life Plan out on my thirtieth birthday and gazed at it again and convinced myself this was when it would all happen and all I had to do was chase after it.

I felt a bit of a failure when it hadn't all come together. Sure I had met Pearse and we had been in love for a while but it had become increasingly clear to me that he was A): An asshole, and B): Never likely to commit anyway.

I rinsed my hair and tried to shake the feelings away as I knew that feeling happy at anyone else's misery was a recipe for disaster. It was bound to anger some giant big karmic being and misery would be heaped upon me by the bucketload.

I stepped out of the shower and lifted my towelling dressing gown from the back of the door. Padding to the kitchen, I flicked on the kettle and rummaged in the fridge to see if there was anything there that I could use to hammer together a decent breakfast for my houseguests. All I found was some cheese, one egg, the chocolates from Ant and a suspect-looking yoghurt. A trip to the shops was going to be necessary but, as I was naked apart from a towelling dressing gown and the only item of clothing outside of my bedroom was a pair of edible knickers, I knew there was no way I could sneak out without waking Darcy and Fionn.

Still I tried my best to be deathly quiet as I crept into the bedroom and rummaged about for a pair of jeans, clean T-shirt, underwear and some flip-flops. I looked at the bed. Darcy was sound out to the world, her blonde curls messy over her face, and only drooling slightly.

She was my rock and my heart ached a little to think that there was some unhappiness there that I didn't know about. I was struck by an awful sense of guilt for my earlier comforted feelings and I gently moved her hair from her face.

She opened her eyes and smiled. "You okay, sis?" she asked.

"Yes, Darce. Love you. Just nipping out to the shop. You sleep on."

She nodded, her eyes drooping again as I closed the door softly behind me. I was so lucky to have her here. To have someone in my life who would drop everything and travel 200 miles to be at my side. It dawned on me that no man had ever done that for me. For the love of God, it had been nigh on impossible to get Pearse to travel four miles to be with me. I remembered one time I had been violently ill – feeling as if I was going to die – and I called him, begging him to come over. "Annie," he said dismissively, "you know I can't come near you when you're sick. What if I bring something into the kitchen? Jesus, do you want to get me shut down?" I knew there was some logic in what he was saying – but that didn't stop me doing a horribly ugly cry when I put the phone down. All I wanted was someone – the man who loved me preferably – to hold me and comfort me, and hold my hair back when necessary and ply me with Lucozade. Instead I sat alone weeping into my pillow, feeling horrendously sorry for myself, and it was Fionn, and not Pearse, who had eventually called round and brought supplies. She had tidied the flat, bleached the loo and opened the windows to dissipate the smell of sick before changing my bed sheets to tuck me back in and then she had promised to tell Bob I would be off for at least twenty-four hours post my last boking fit and he would just have to make do.

I vowed, as I stepped out into the fresh morning, that I would cook them both a breakfast they wouldn't forget in a hurry and that we would have a deliciously girly day.

My culinary skills weren't a patch on Pearse's, but I could fry a mean egg. I had already grilled bacon and sausage and buttered a small mountain of delicious scones and pancakes. I had squeezed some fresh orange juice (okay, I had bought some freshly squeezed orange juice, but the sentiment was there) and I had brewed both tea and coffee. I opened the window in the living room to allow in the fresh morning air and put the radio on softly in the background.

Darcy had been up when I returned from the shops and was now on the phone to Gerry in the bedroom while Fionn was in the shower. I had tidied her cases away to the bedroom and made the bed. I had even made tentative plans, with myself, to load the three of us into my car and go for a long drive once breakfast was out of the way.

I figured we could do with some sort of distraction – not least, for me, from the increasingly insistent texts from Ant.

I set the table before returning to the kitchen and taking out my mobile.

"I have guests, Ant. Sorry. No can do midnight feast," I typed, referring to an earlier message from him referencing the edible knickers and the chocolates.

"Shame. I've quite an appetite," he typed back. And I felt myself shiver – even though it was far from cold in my over-heated kitchen.

Darcy walked in and smiled. "Smells good, Annie. All those years with Pee-Arse must have had some positive influence on you after all."

I smiled back and replied that I hoped she was hungry, trying not to think of just how hungry Ant was and how I had turned him down once again.

Fionn followed and I ordered her to grab a plate of toast and follow me to the living room where the rest of my feast was waiting.

"So, ladies," Fionn asked, biting into a slice of smoked bacon, "what are the plans?"

"Well, I was thinking we could get in the car and go for a drive. Maybe we could grab lunch somewhere and then go for a walk and when we get home I was thinking wine, pizza and a good old gossip."

"Sounds like a plan," Darcy replied with a smile. "But let's not go too hard on the wine. I'll have to get back to Dublin tomorrow. Duty calls."

Of course I knew that Darcy couldn't stay forever and she had already been here for four days but I couldn't help but feel that familiar sadness as she declared she was leaving. It was the same every time we parted, not knowing when we would see each other again. And even though she wasn't my mammy and even though I was big woman now, every time Darcy left a part of me (a big brattish part of me) felt as if I had been orphaned again.

Noticing my crestfallen face, Darcy reached across and rubbed my hand. "You'll be fine, sis. You're on your way now. You've got rid of that eejit. Work is going okay and you have made up with Fionn." She nodded in Fionn's direction and Fionn nodded back. "You don't need me any more but I do promise not to leave it so long till next time. Or, you know, you could always go crazy and get that bus down the road to Dublin. Just a thought."

I blushed – of course she was right. I was more guilty of not visiting her than she was of not visiting me. I should really make the effort too – I mean Dublin could be good. There were great shops, fab bars, lovely restaurants. And I wouldn't even have to endure the latter with Pearse who would no doubt spend the entire time passing comment on everything that was set down in front of him and posing, hoping that someone would recognise him as "that bloke off the telly".

"I will," I said. "I promise."

"I'll make sure she does," Fionn added.

"Great, that's that sorted. Now, where will we go?"

Fionn didn't talk about what had prompted her to walk out on Alex and Darcy didn't talk about whatever it was that had been upsetting her. I even managed to spend the day in their company without talking about Ant and his masculine ways.

Instead we walked along the shore at Portrush and stopped for candyfloss. Then we had a go on the bumper cars where I inflicted minor whiplash on a bolshy teenage girl who was getting on my wick as she flaunted herself in her wee electric car like it was a top-of-the-range sports effort.

We stopped at the Silver Sands for a lunch of egg and chips, complete with a thick slice of buttered bread and a cup of tea, and we sang all the way home along with the *Dirty Dancing* soundtrack. When we reached Derry, I stopped at the off-licence and stocked up, feeling absolutely high on life. My life certainly was a rollercoaster and I was thankful that at least at the moment it was on the up.

I was on my third glass of wine and my tongue was loosened when I decided to ask Fionn outright what had happened. While she had been in good form all day, I hadn't failed to notice her checking her phone every ten minutes and the odd faraway look on her face when it was clear there were no messages to read and no missed calls to return.

Darcy shot me a look, warning me not to go overboard with my questioning.

Fionn sat back, curled her feet up under her and sipped from her glass. "He came home from work – he had himself all in a fluster," she said. "Seems he had lunch with Rebecca. He needed someone to talk to – you know – about me and him. So anyway he chose to speak with *her*, which is laughable really."

Fionn wasn't laughing.

"So apparently, surprise, surprise, she told him that she agreed postponing the wedding was for the best. She said it would be unfair to put Emma in a position where she could be hurt in the future and that if Alex had any doubts whatsoever he should take his time. If I loved him, I would be fine with this."

"So after you killed him, what did you do?" Darcy deadpanned.

"Well, after he dropped that one on me, I once again asked why Rebecca had such a big say in our relationship. I asked why he couldn't have talked to me about it, and that was when he really fecking pushed his luck . . ."

"Oh crap, Fionn, what did he say?" I asked, sitting forward, my radar on full alert.

"He said he couldn't talk to me about it because ever since we got engaged I've become a big fecking Bridezilla obsessed with getting married, getting pregnant and planning the rest of his life . . ."

I didn't know what to say. If there is one thing Fionn wasn't it was a Bridezilla. Sure she did have a certain glazed look on her face when she tried on her dress but the rest of the time she was as laid back as they come. As brides go. She didn't care about huge floral arrangements, favours, buttonholes and chair covers. She just cared about marrying Alex. And as for obsessed with getting pregnant – of course she wanted to have a baby with Alex but she was happy to let that happen in its own good time.

"What the fuck?" I said.

"I know," she replied. "I'm not a Bridezilla, am I?"

I shook my head. "You're not even a Bridezuki," I said solemnly. "You're the most chilled-out bride-to-be I know. He's talking through his rear end."

"And I'm not obsessed about wanting children. In fact, we've hardly mentioned it. Just once, I think, when we agreed it would be cool when we're ready."

"So where is he getting all this nonsense from then?"

"I don't know. I know Emma is desperate for a baby brother or sister and she has been rabbiting on about it a bit lately – but that's her, not me. And suddenly Alex thinks I'm plotting how to poke holes in his condoms and flush my pill down the toilet!"

"And I suppose you told him he was talking bollocks?"

"You know what?" she said. "I'm fed up telling him he's talking bollocks. He should know me well enough by now to know where I'm coming from and what I want. So I told him as much and went and packed up my bags."

"And did he try to stop you?"

"No," she said, sadly. "He went out. Slammed the door behind him. And I've not heard anything since."

"What a fucking asshole!" Darcy said, breaking her silence.

And it was then that Fionn burst into tears.

I looked at Darcy, slightly aghast at her outburst even if it had been what I was thinking. I kind of expected her to do her usual big-sisterly thing of putting her arm around Fionn and comforting her. But no.

She just sat bolt upright in her chair and continued: "I mean, he's supposed to love you. You're supposed to be his everything and yet he'll listen to some ex rather than you. Maybe he should just fecking marry her."

This, of course, prompted yet another bout of weeping from Fionn. "Do you think he will?" she asked, her large eyes pooled with tears. "Do you think that's what he wants and he's just trying to push me away? He hasn't the balls to finish with me so he's pushing me away and then he can set up home with Rebecca and Emma and have the perfect little family?"

Darcy shrugged her shoulders while I reached out and gave Fionn's hand a gentle rub.

"Don't be so silly," I said. "If he didn't want you then he never would have proposed."

"But that's just the thing," Fionn said. "He never did. It was me who did the asking."

Fionn had never told me this before. Fionn had told me almost everything else about her life but she had never mentioned that it was her, and not Alex, who had got down on one knee.

She had just come into work one day and announced she was engaged and that he was taking her ring-shopping. Sure, when I asked her what the big proposal was like she had been hazy on the details. "It was really romantic, but if you don't mind it's kind of personal so I'd rather keep it to myself."

I had assumed that he had asked her during a sexy personal moment or something, not that she had actually been the one to pop the question.

"He seemed happy about it," she said now. "Genuinely happy."

"Yes," I said, remembering how he had grinned his way through the engagement party. "He did seem happy."

"Let's cut to the chase," Darcy interjected. "Tell me, he did at least pay for the ring, did he?"

Fionn blushed. "We went halfers."

"See," Darcy, proclaimed, standing up and raising her wineglass in her own personal toast. "Proof positive that all men are bastards!"

"No!" Fionn proclaimed, taking to her feet. "He's not a bastard. I just wanted a really nice ring and he couldn't afford the one I wanted and so I offered to help pay for it . . . I mean a lot of people buy engagement rings for their menfolk these days – I just did a double whammy on myself."

"Atta girl!" I declared. "Might as well keep the bling to yourself."

"Well, at least the bling won't let you down," Darcy said, sitting back down.

"Are you okay?" Fionn asked my sister.

"Perfectly fine," she muttered. "Now don't be deflecting the attention away from yourself. You can at least tell us the details of how you proposed to him."

Fionn shot me a look and I shrugged my shoulders. It was clear that Darcy wasn't fine and that all was not well. Could it be that there was trouble between her and Gerry? It seemed unlikely – they were the most together couple ever. But I also knew my sister well enough to realise it would do me no good to ask her any more. She would tell me when she was ready to. That was her way and I had to respect that. Or, to be more accurate, I just had to accept that there was no way I could get Darcy to talk about such matters even if I begged and pleaded.

Fionn sat back. "I need a top-up," she said and reached for the bottle on the floor – sloshing cool white wine into her glass, then taking a long drink. "We had talked about it. A few times. Within months of being together he said I was the kind of woman who would make him break his no-marriage rule."

"There was a rule?" I asked.

"Oh yes. He said he couldn't ever bring someone else into a mammy role for Emma so he was going to be a confirmed bachelor forever more. He said that every woman he had dated since Emma was born had either been completely horrified at the thought of taking on another woman's child or had become ridiculously gushy about children without ever even having met the wee pet."

"And you?" Darcy asked.

"I let him introduce me to her when he was ready. And I didn't spoil her – although I did watch those fecking Disney Princess movies two and a half thousand times. But leaving that aside, we fitted, all of us as a family, you know. I knew he loved me. Loves me," she paused. "I know he loves me."

"Of course he does," I soothed.

"Just not enough to make a commitment," Darcy said.

I glared at her. "Jesus, Darcy, you really are in a man-hating mode at the moment, aren't you?"

"Well," she said, adopting her best Lloyd Grossman impression, "let's look at the evidence. We have Alex, who is a commitment-phobe who creates a hundred and one stupid reasons not to go ahead with his marriage to the lovely Fionn here but does it in such a way that we end up blaming Rebecca for it. That's a clever kind of bastard if you ask me. And then, we have Pee-Arse. The most self-centred, up-his-own-hole, sanctimonious excuse for a celebrity wannabe there is, who thinks he can land every woman he wants just because he's been on *Ready Steady fecking Cook*. I tell you what, I could shove his green pepper right up his ass. The alternative though – well, what a catch he is! The kind of man who sends edible knickers to a woman's work place!"

"You said you liked him!" I protested.

"Annie. I've not even met him. How the feck can I like him? All I said was that he might not actually be using you for sex but now, looking at the evidence, ya know what – he *might* just be after your body!" She reached into the box of goodies and extracted the edible knickers, then bit off some of the wee sweetie beads before sitting down and raising her glass once again.

She was, I realised, more than a little pissed.

Fionn, equally tipsy, was more than a little pissed off. "And what about you, Darcy? And the perfect Gerry? Surely you are not including him in this wee tirade? Are *you* immune to feckwit men then?"

"No, not at all," she said. "Not one bit." She threw the knickers to the ground. "I'm going to bed," she said, standing up and walking towards the bedroom.

"You can't leave it like that," I said. "Darcy, talk to us!"

She looked back. "No. Look, I'm sorry. I said too much and I went too far. I'm just going to sleep. Never mind me. Never mind me one bit."

She walked into the bedroom and closed the door behind her.

"You should go after her," Fionn said, lifting the sweetie knickers and biting off some of the g-string.

"No point," I said sadly. "There's no point."

We sat in what could hardly be described as companionable silence for a little while. I tried to process what Fionn had told me. I thought of how she had proposed to Alex. How they had seemed deliriously, stupendously happy but how he might actually be a shitehawk commitment-phobe trying to sabotage his own wedding even though he did love Fionn. And I thought of Pearse and his shitey ways but I quickly pushed them to the back of my mind and thought of Ant. I had a longing to be with him. It wasn't that I (God forbid) loved him or anything ridiculous like that – it was just that I knew that if I was in his arms – or in his bed – I wouldn't be able to think about anything else other than being there in the moment. And my brain could use a break.

"Penny for them?" Fionn asked, breaking the silence.

"You wouldn't really want to know," I said, casually biting a sweet off the knickers. "It involved me, a hairy man and some very dirty things . . ."

"There was me thinking you were going to say something deep and meaningful there, Annie."

"I'm too damn tipsy for deep and meaningful and it hasn't got us very far tonight, now has it?" I stood up and stretched. "In fact, fuck it, Fionn. Balls to meaningful!" I raised my glass and walked to the sideboard where my iPod sat in its dock. "What do you fancy? Something to sing to? Something to dance to? Something to chill us out?"

"Dance," Fionn said, climbing to her feet. "But hang on a minute – we have to get the attire right." She picked up the half-eaten knickers and pulled them on over her jeans. She looked like a weird, sexually depraved Superhero in the making and I couldn't help but howl with laughter as she pointed one arm in the air and sang the *Superman* theme tune.

"Now, music!" she said as she finished her lap of the room and I searched for something suitably upbeat. As the opening strains of "I Will Survive" blasted across the flat I lifted the now-empty wine bottle and adopted my best singing pose while Fionn conducted her very own Elvis style hip-swivel in time to the music – sweetie beads gyrating here and there.

We were just launching into the chorus when the bedroom door opened and Darcy, in her pyjamas and with her make-up scrubbed off her face, stormed across the room.

I braced myself for an outburst. I shielded the iPod from her fury. But she simply lifted her wineglass from where she had left it, took a long drink and shot us a glance which said "Let's not ever talk about my big huff again" before launching into the chorus loudly and tunelessly and dancing with her trademark lack of rhythm. That was one of the things I loved so much about Darcy. She was physical perfection, with her long legs, glossy hair, flat stomach and amazing sense of style. She had boobs that could make grown men weep and grown women want to gouge her eyes out. She had skin that had never seen a spot or blemish – not even when she was fourteen and pumped full of hormones. She was one of those jammy bitches who could get away with not wearing make-up and not only did she not look any the worse for it – her skin was so damn peaches and cream perfect that no one really noticed. I swear she produced her own lip gloss naturally, secreting it from her Angelina-Jolie-like pout effortlessly. Simply put, she was gorgeous. But she couldn't dance. Not even a little bit.

As she flailed and flounced to her own beat while Gloria Gaynor got into full Disco-Queen mood, I smiled to myself. And then, I got funky.

Soon it was the case that our conversation was behind us and we were just having fun – dancing, singing and ignoring any of the big issues which might have been holding us all back.

The same shit would still be there to deal with tomorrow, as my mum would have said.

20

I groaned as I opened my eyes and tried to look at the clock. Light was poking through a gap in the curtains and I realised there was an awful ache in my back. I was on the floor. I had obviously fallen off the sofa again but had been too drunk to notice or care. It was 9.17 a.m. The flat was in silence. There wasn't even so much as a hum from the road below. It was Sunday morning and everyone was sleeping. The room was spinning just that little bit. I looked to the dining table where we had lined up the wine bottles the night before. Six bottles. Two each. That was a lot, even for me, although I did have a hazy memory of pouring at least one full glass into my bamboo plant when I simply didn't feel I could take any more.

The elastic from the sweetie knickers was wrapped around my wrist like a sad little bracelet. I hoped Ant wouldn't still want me to model them for him.

I tried to sit up and groaned – half through the stiffness in my back and half because of the spinning room.

Water. I needed water.

I hauled myself to my feet and walked to the kitchen where the bright daylight hurt my eyes. I lifted my sunglasses from the worktop where I has discarded them on our return from Portrush the day before and put them on. I downed a pint of water, gagging slightly as the cold liquid hit the back of my throat and then I padded back to the living room, opened the curtains and threw myself back onto the sofa where I decided I would spend at least an hour moaning and groaning in front of the *Hollyoaks* omnibus.

It was just getting particularly juicy when Darcy, looking flawless but proclaiming she was murdered with a hangover, came in. I looked at her and let out a particularly dramatic groan while rubbing my stomach and putting my other hand to my forehead.

"At least," she said as she slumped beside me, "you don't have to do four hours on a bus to Dublin. I may die." She put her hands to her face and took a deep breath.

I reached out and rubbed her knee. "I would say soothing things but I'm rather afraid that if I said soothing things I might throw up. Not because they are soothing . . . just because I feel *bleuurrggghh*."

"Morning, lovely ladies," Fionn trilled, walking into the room looking surprisingly wide-eyed and awake. "Are youse ready for a walk in the park and a sausage bap?"

"*Euuurrgh!*" Darcy grimaced.

I just shook my head, trying not to talk, while Darcy outlined the whole soothing-things-throwing-up scenario I had just explained to her.

"You girls are no fun," Fionn said. "No fun at all."

"Is she always like that?" Darcy asked me, eyebrow raised. "Is the woman immune to hangovers?"

"Not usually," I muttered, curling myself up into a ball and cuddling a cushion to my stomach. "She usually looks just like I look now."

"What has you so chipper?" Darcy asked her. "Saucy dream about Colin Farrell?"

"Actually," she replied with a wink, "I got a text from Alex. He wants me to come back to chat. He said he's sorry."

"So are you going?" I asked.

"Like feck I am. He can sweat it out for another while. I told him I needed a little time to think. He's not the only person who can play it cool."

"Good woman, yourself," Darcy said.

"But, are you sure you want to be playing games?" I asked, hoping not to burst her little bubble of happiness.

"I'm not playing games. I do need a little time to think. And I want him to know that I'm not a Bridezilla who comes roaring into view every time he calls. I did tell him I would call over later to see Emma – maybe take her for an ice cream – but I wasn't ready to have any big conversations with him just yet."

"Well, as long as you're careful," I said.

"I'm always careful," she said with a wink before standing up and walking to the kitchen. "Fried egg sandwich anyone?"

And Darcy and I both groaned in unison.

Darcy got on the bus at two clutching a bottle of water, a bottle of Lucozade, a packet of Tayto Cheese and Onion crisps and a couple of spare Tesco bags just in case she was sick. She had her oversized sunglasses on and her iPod loaded with soothing tunes.

"Just in case I don't make it back to Dublin in one piece," she said with fake dramatic emphasis, "you can have my Jimmy Choos. They are the only pair of proper designer shoes I have and I love you so much that I mind not a jot bequeathing them to you."

I smiled and hugged her close. "You'll be fine. I don't envy you, but I know you'll be fine. Your shoes will be safe."

She groaned slightly and hugged me back. "You take care, Annie. And try not to sleep with anyone else unsuitable or break up with any chefs, or get any more work-warnings. You'll get there, my darling. You'll get your happy ending." Her eyes were misty and I hugged her tighter as she let a few tears fall. "Damn DT's," she said. "I always get overly emotional after a few drinks. But anyway, sis, I love you."

"I love you too," I said, my own eyes filling, and she gave me a final squeeze before climbing on the bus and taking her seat.

I stood and watched the bus pull out of the depot. Her iPod

earphones were already in her ears and her eyes were already closed. She didn't wave or look at me and I sighed, turning and wrapping my jacket tightly around myself before walking back to my car.

I sat there for a while just looking out at the river. I should have gone home, of course I should have. But I knew home was empty. Darcy was gone and Fionn was off supposedly eating Knickerbocker Glories with Emma while trying to conceal the fact she had a whopping hangover. I checked my appearance in the mirror and slicked on some lip gloss before lifting my phone and typing a text to Ant.

"What's your address? I need to see you."

He answered – with an address fifteen minutes' drive away just across the border, overlooking the beach at Fahan, and I drove to him, trying not to think about whether or not it was a good or a bad idea.

He answered the door dressed casually in faded jeans and a white V-neck T-shirt. A tuft of hair poked out just below his neck and before even speaking I found myself reaching out to touch it.

He didn't talk either. He just looked at me and I noticed how dark his eyes were and how full his lips were. He took my hand in his and grazed my fingertips along his lips and then I allowed him to kiss me – right there in the doorway in full view of everyone on a Sunday afternoon drive to Buncrana.

"I'm glad you're here," he said as he led me through the wide open-plan hallway to his solid oak staircase. "Really glad."

I didn't speak. I couldn't speak – and it was no longer because the hangover was making me feel queasy. Yes, my stomach was full of butterflies but it was for an entirely different reason.

"It's amazing here," I said, lying in the crook of Ant's arm on his kingsize bed, staring out his dormer window as the waves crashed to the shore.

"Why, thank you," he mocked, "Always nice to be described as amazing."

I laughed and jabbed him gently in the ribs. "Amazing and all as *that* was, I was actually talking about the location. How do you ever leave? I'd spend all my time just here staring out at the waves."

"I can think of better things to do with my time," he said, snuggling close so that I could feel exactly what better things he was talking about. I laughed again. "But yes, it is great here. You should see it on a stormy day. The beach is deserted, apart from a couple of die-hard dog-walkers and the spray batters against the window. Very atmospheric."

"I like that," I said, turning to face him and kissing him.

He pulled me closer again but I knew I had to get up. It had gone five and Fionn would no doubt be full to the gills with ice cream now and would be waiting for me back at the flat. Lord knows how things would have gone with Alex and she might need someone to talk to. I had to be unselfish and leave this terribly sexy man and his very atmospheric bedroom behind.

"I have to go," I said, pulling away from him and scrambling around the floor for my clothes.

"That's a shame," he said, sitting up.

"Yes, it is," I said, slipping my feet into my shoes.

"Can I call you?" he asked. "Or send any other edible goodies?"

"Calling is good," I said, kissing him on the forehead and leaving him there in bed while I headed home into the balmy summer evening.

Fionn was dozing on the sofa when I walked in. She looked at me, half-asleep, and I pulled the throw from the back of the sofa and draped it over her.

"No, s'alright, I'll get up now," she said, struggling to open her eyes.

"You sleep on for a bit," I said. "I'll get dinner organised and we can chat."

"I bought some food. S'in the kitchen," she muttered.

I nodded before going for a good rummage in the fridge. There were all sorts of healthy treats in there so I set about whipping up a nice salad with some garlic bread.

Putting the food on the tray, I called to Fionn to meet me on the roof and I climbed the fire escape to sit by the old rusty barbecue.

"I'm never, ever drinking again," Fionn commented as she sat down.

I laughed. "I've heard that before."

"But I'm serious this time. I wasn't fit to deal with Emma. And I don't know how I managed to get that Knickerbocker Glory down me." She shuddered at the thought and picked up her plate of salad. "This looks good."

"Thought it would be the best option," I said as I munched lettuce. "Get something healthy into us after the excesses of last night."

"And today," she said. "I had to attempt to eat a McDonald's as well as the Knickerbocker Glory. For one so small Emma can fairly pack away the food."

I smiled. "And Alex? Was he there?"

"Yes, he was there. And he didn't even comment on my greenish pallor and intolerance of sunlight. We didn't talk though – we couldn't really with the wee woman there listening to our every word. But he looked, well, fed up and when I left he told me he missed me."

"That's good," I said.

"Yes. Yes, I think it is very good indeed. But what about you, missus? Where were you all afternoon? Darcy's bus left at two."

"I went to the beach," I half-lied. I'm not sure why I didn't tell her the entire truth – it just felt easier not to for some reason.

"Needed to clear your head?"

"Something like that," I said, staring out over the rooftops at the city. I definitely needed to clear my head. I was just not sure my afternoon in Ant's arms had helped me do that at all.

I enjoyed spending the night in my own bed, even if Fionn was beside me. It was nice not to wake up with a crick in my neck and a pain in my back, but I groaned when I realised it was a work morning.

"Rise and shine, Valentine!" I chimed at Fionn.

"Please, Annie," she whispered back at me. "If I mean anything to you at all, please tell me it is not Monday morning and we don't have a full week ahead of glorious promotion of all sorts of weird and wonderful things?"

"I wish I could," I said. "But come on, Fionn. Where's your *va-va-voom*? Let's get up and kick some public-relations arse! I've this mad singles' night to get sorted, a new promotion at Love, Sex and Magic and another presser for Haven Cosmetics to get out in the post. I have fifty-six press packs to put together – including tying little ribbons around mascara wands. What more could a girl want?"

"Oh feck off," Fionn said with a wry smile.

I climbed out bed and dived for the bathroom. I was still determined that, houseguest or no houseguest, I was getting in the shower first.

As the water poured over me, I could swear I smelled a faint hint of Ant and his musky aftershave. I sighed. He had texted me the night before – to thank me for my company and telling me that the beach was gorgeous at sunset. There had been no sexual innuendo at all and I liked that.

"We better take both cars," Fionn said, grinning, after we were dressed. "We don't want rumours starting about us spending the night together."

"Could you imagine the scandal? Bawb would wet his knickers. He'd think we were running off together! It would almost be worth it, you know."

Fionn shuddered. "I don't fancy being a part of Bawb's lesbian fantasy. Jeez, could you imagine it? Him getting himself all hot and bothered . . ."

I burst out laughing. "There are some things I really, really don't ever need to think about!"

"Right, well, separate cars then," she said, lifting her keys from the hall table.

"Deal," I agreed. "I'll pick up some coffee and Danish pastries on the way in."

As I drove to work I mused on how things were always changing, life always turning, and we never really knew from one day to the next what was ahead. Some things would always be the same though – like Monday-morning traffic, the chatter of the DJ on the radio and the smell of coffee in the local Starbucks.

Bob's Monday-morning enthusiasm was also something which would never, ever change. He walked in, head held high and greeted us all as his team.

"Let's make miracles happen!" he chirped before grabbing a latte from my desk and heading into his office. "We'll meet in ten," he called from the door to everyone and there was a small but audible groan from my colleagues.

"Where does he get the energy from?" Fionn asked the room and there was a general shrugging of shoulders and moaning about Monday being the absolute worst day of the week.

But for once I felt quite energised myself. I set about curling ribbon for the Haven Cosmetics press release and was twenty-six ribbons down (curling in record time) when Bob called his meeting.

We met in the boardroom and Bob was in highlighter-pen overdrive, with his flipchart already colour-coded for each employee and their client folders.

"Right, let's make it a good week, people. Our clients are happy at the moment but we want to keep them happy. I've circulated the press cuttings from the relevant magazines and newspapers regarding our clients and a few of you will see there are interview requests. Could you coach your clients? We don't want them blowing all our good work by saying the wrong thing. Fionn and Annie, that in particular refers to the LSM crowd. For the love of God ask them not to use the word 'fucking' live on radio again. Much as it generated a bit of a stir, the local Council were not a bit impressed and were talking of pulling licences etc."

Fionn and I nodded. It wouldn't be easy. Max and Maggie, the couple behind Love, Sex and Magic had to be persuaded to tone everything down. If they had their way they would have had lap-dancers shaking their wares in the shop windows day in and day out. Still, if we had managed to persuade them to stick with the magic theme as opposed to the sex theme for the launch, we could hopefully persuade them to lay off the swear words.

Bob rattled through the other projects and upcoming events before landing on the big Speed Dating Night. "Right, well, our client – Dream Dates – are very happy with how things are going so far. We have a great venue, some brilliant publicity ideas and Annie has had some brilliant ideas to make the night go with a bang." He laughed at that – a little joke all to himself. "We really want this to work. This is our first event for Dream Dates and as they are going for the young professional demographic it is a big coup for us. So I want everyone to be on board here."

Everyone nodded and I beamed. I was in his good books. Even though I thought he was an awful gobshite, it was definitely good to be in his good books for a change.

"Teacher's pet," Fionn mocked during our FSB.

"Don't be so ridiculous," I replied, secretly delighted. "You heard what he said. He wants everyone on board. So we can all be his wee pets. God love us."

Fionn laughed. "Ooh, guess what?"

"What?" I asked.

"I had an email from Alex. He never emails me. He's email-phobic. But he said he misses me. And that he is an eejit. And that Emma misses me too."

"Did he think of that all by himself or did Rebecca tell him to say it?" I asked and immediately regretted it.

Fionn's face darkened at the mention of the Evil Ex.

"Shit, I'm sorry," I offered. "I was trying to be funny but obviously I wasn't one bit. That's lovely, Fionn. Honest. I'm glad he is missing you. He should miss you. You are eminently missable."

"You can stop creeping, Annie," Fionn said with a wry smile. "You're forgiven. It's just a good thing I love you so much, otherwise I might just have murdered you by now."

We walked back into the office and I didn't tell Fionn that Ant had texted me earlier saying that the sunrise too was lovely at the beach.

I couldn't believe it when I answered my phone to find Rebecca on the other end, her voice laden with grief and pity-me vibes.

"Annie, I know you don't really know me," she started, "but I need your help."

I knew her much better than she thought, that was for sure.

"Things are bad between Fionn and Alex now, right?" she went on. "How bad are they? I'm terribly worried – you know, for Emma and all."

Like feck was she worried. She was probably sewing her own wedding dress as we spoke and reapplying her crazy-assed lipstick so she could snog a well-worn photo of Alex in her pyschotic little shrine to him.

"I think they'll be okay," I lied – because the truth was, I didn't know if they would be okay. I hoped that it would all work out but, given that I was proving myself to be a hopelessly rubbish judge of character these days, that didn't count for much.

She sighed – a gutwrenchingly exaggerated sigh – and I actually feared what she might say or do next. "Well, that's good then," she said. "Because you know Emma wants to know and I was really worried about them. Poor Fionn – Alex really has messed up this time, hasn't he?"

Oh, I knew what she was at – for absolute sure and certain – she was waiting for me to confide in her that, yes, Alex had messed up somewhat spectacularly so that she could run back to him with tales that Fionn had been badmouthing him to me. There were just two problems with that, however. The first, of course, was that Fionn had *not* been badmouthing him to me and the second was that it was me who had messed up. Regardless of the cause of their disquiet, I wasn't going to give anything away to Rebecca – not without the aid of a very bright light and some instruments of torture anyway.

"Well," I said, "you know these things just happen sometimes. I'm sure it will be fine."

She sniffed. I could sense her lip curling. "Really? It seems pretty bad."

"Ach, sure the path of true love never runs smoothly," I offered and put the phone down before I had a chance to say the wrong thing.

At a quarter to five I had just packaged up my last mascara wand and set up an interview between a glossy magazine and Max and Maggie when Bob opened his office door and called me in.

He looked rather flushed and his tie was loosened. There was a light film of sweat on his brow as he sipped from a plastic cup of water.

"Sit down," he gestured, his tone solemn.

I began to feel uneasy. The four walls of his small office seemed to close in around me little.

"There is no easy way to tell you this," he began and my head started to swim.

This had to be bad news and by the look of horror on his face it was really bad news. Oh God. Not Darcy. Please let Darcy be okay. And Mum and Dad, of course. My heart started to beat faster and, while I could see his lips moving, I could not quite work out what he was saying. My brain was running ahead of itself. I was thinking back to how, just that morning, I had thought of how life can turn itself around in a heartbeat. How it could all go wrong, or go right or just go.

Bob paused and I focused on him again.

He took a deep breath and said: "It's Manna. And Pearse."

Well, at least it wasn't Mum, or Dad or Darcy . . . but, if he had his most serious face ever on, it still wasn't going to be good.

"Manna?"

"Well, I took a call from Pearse. He said either we take you off the Dream Dates account or we find another restaurant. He said he can't work with you any more."

I felt sick. "But I manage the PR for the restaurant too. He can't want me to walk away from that?"

Bob nodded. "Look, Annie, I'm sorry. I know this is tricky and difficult."

I snorted, and nodded. I was afraid to say anything because I knew that if I did I would cry and I so didn't want to cry, especially not in front of Bob.

"But I have to protect the interests of NorthStar and both these clients put a lot of money our way. I could keep you on, but we would lose business and in the current climate that would be suicidal. There are other clients who are more than happy with your work and they remain yours – but Manna and Dream Dates, I'm sorry. I'm going to have to reassign them."

I thought back to Friday – how Pearse had agreed with me that business was business and that we could work together. Something had obviously happened to make him change his mind – and maybe it had been naïve of me to think that he would be happy for things to continue as they had been.

But this was my job – my career. Manna was the biggest client on our books. There was a certain prestige in managing their PR – in fielding calls from admiring journalists looking for fifteen minutes with Pearse, or a free meal for a review. I had worked my ass off to make sure the restaurant was one of the most high profile, not only in the city but throughout the North. It was for nothing though. It was being taken away from me and I had to suck it up or leave my job. I would have to turn in a few minutes and walk out of Bob's office and look at my colleagues and then they would receive an email telling them that I was leaving the Manna portfolio behind to concentrate on promoting hugely overpriced skin-care products and a shop run by two sex-addicts with a desire to swear at every given opportunity.

I felt the tears well up and, even without the effort of trying to justify myself, or fight for my accounts, I felt them start to fall. At first it was just one slowly sliding down my cheek and I tried to wipe it away quickly while glancing towards the window.

But another followed and another.

"It's okay," Bob said, in an uncharacteristically sympathetic manner. "These things happen, Annie. It is no reflection on your work, but you do understand why I have to do this, don't you?"

I nodded, as a big fat tear plopped right off the end of my nose and landed with a tiny little splash on my trousers.

"And, despite the fact you haven't exactly been on your game lately, you are a valuable member of this team."

I nodded, and the little splash became a puddle.

"Look," he said, moving his chair around so that he was sitting close to me, "I don't know what has happened between you and Pearse. But I do know he is a bit of a knob and, if it weren't for the credit crunch and us all fighting to keeping our head above water, I would tell him to shag off."

I was moved, and if truth be told a little disturbed, by Bob's sudden non-knobbish behaviour. I looked at him, rubbing at my eyes, and he clearly saw the confusion etched all over my face.

"I'm not the arse you think I am, you know," he said with a half-smile. "I am paid to keep you all on your toes and that's what I do. But don't think I don't notice what goes on here, Annie. Don't think I haven't noticed that all isn't well with Fionn or that for the last couple of weeks you've been on another planet. I don't pry into my employees' private lives but I will say this much – he isn't worth it. I've known many men like him in my time – truth be told, I've slept with a fair few of them too – and while they are perfectly useful for a short-term fling they are never going to be The One. Pearse loves himself, Annie. He will never love anyone else. I doubt he even really knows anyone else exists."

To say I was gobsmacked was putting it mildly. I gaped at him, trying to digest all this information. Bob was caring. Bob was gay. Bob slept with men like Pearse (but not actually Pearse, which was at least something) and it looked very much like Bob was actually going to hug me.

And he did.

And I let him, crying watery tears on his designer shirt.

"Why don't you take some time off?" he said. "You have the annual leave – take it."

He didn't need to tell me that there wasn't actually much for me to do in the office at the moment anyway.

"Go away for a few days. Get your head clear and then come back and we'll find you the biggest and best client we can lay hands on."

"I'll think about it," I said. "I'll definitely think about it."

"Do," he said. "And, Annie, don't let the bastards get you down."

I stood up and straightened my hair with my hands. Taking a deep breath, I plastered a smile on my face, nodded in Bob's direction and left his office, picking up my bag without talking to anyone and going straight to my car.

Lifting my phone, I texted Fionn. "Going for a walk on the beach. Am okay. Won't do a Reggie Perrin and throw myself in or anything. Promise. Will see you back at the flat."

He was still wearing his work suit when he opened the door. The faint smell of cigarette smoke hung in the air and he was holding a cold beer in his hand. He looked at me and smiled.

"To what do I owe the pleasure?" he asked.

"I wanted to find out more about those sunsets," I replied, taking his bottle of beer from him and leading him upstairs.

"I should have probably asked this before," Ant said, stroking my arm gently as I lay in his arms looking out again at the waves below. "But are you okay?"

"I'm fine," I said.

"It's just I wasn't expecting to see you. Twice in two days, it's very unlike you. And I didn't even have to send any gifts."

"I just needed to see you. Tough day at work."

"Want to talk about it?"

"No. Not now. I needed to absolutely not talk about it for a while and that's –"

"Why you came here? I'm your distraction, am I? Are you just using me for sex, Annie?" He had a cheeky glint in his eye and I couldn't help but laugh.

"You should be so lucky," I replied.

But as I drove home I wondered what on earth had taken me to his house, and his bed, when a large part of me was screaming that I needed to take it slow or perhaps just not go there at all. Ever.

But I could not deny that I had felt content there. Even, dare I say it, happy, and I could ignore everything that was happening with work entirely. So no, I didn't want to talk to him about it.

"Are you okay?" Fionn asked. "I know you said you weren't going to do a Reggie Perrin but after Bob sent that email round . . . well, fuck me, Annie, I didn't see that coming!"

"Didn't you?" I asked, even though I hadn't seen it coming myself. "In hindsight it was pretty obvious Pearse would pull something like this. It was much too much to think he would let me get away with dumping him. And he knows where to hurt me."

"He's an asshole," Fionn said, pulling me into a hug before offering a choice between wine or tea.

Thinking that if I started drinking just then I might not ever stop, I opted for the tea.

"That must have been some walk," she said, pouring some chocolate biscuits onto a plate. "It's dark out."

"I had to watch the sunset," I offered. "It really was magnificent."

She carried the biscuits to the living room and sat down on the sofa. "Bob called me into his office after you had gone. He wants me to keep an eye on you." There was a look of confusion on her face. "Is he okay?"

"I think the old Bawb may have been abducted by aliens and replaced with an imposter," I answered. "He was actually very, very lovely today."

"Ah, that will be because he wants in your knickers then?" Fionn said, referring to our earlier lesbian-fantasy conversation.

"That actually couldn't be further from the truth," I said and then I let her have it straight. "He's gay."

"He's gay?" she repeated stupidly.

"Yep. Queer as a bottle of chips. Camp as a row of tents. Gay as a . . . very gay thing. He says he's slept with knobs the likes of Pearse and it's never worth it."

"Well, feck me!" Fionn was reeling. "Really? Gay? He told you that? Did he tell you more? Does he have a boyfriend? Even though the thought doesn't sit well with me – and not because he's gay, just because he's Bawb and the thought of him with anyone . . . eek!" She shuddered. "Do we have to stick to the tea? Because I'm thinking wine would be good around now. For the shock, you understand?"

I smiled. "Tea is just fine, Fionn. And no, he didn't mention a partner. He didn't say much more than I told you. I was as shocked as you. He just seemed so utterly asexual that I never imagined him with anyone else."

We sat in stunned silence for a while before Fionn spoke again. "So what now? Bob said you might be taking some time off?"

"He thinks it would be good – just a week or so to get my head together and wait till the rest of the office gossips have moved on to a new topic."

"A week off sounds like bliss!"

A thought struck me.

"Why don't you take it too then? We could go away somewhere? Go on – a girly holiday. One last fling before you settle down to married life with Alex and I settle down to a life of spinsterhood?"

"I could, couldn't I?" Fionn asked. "I could do with a break away."

"Great then," I said, clinking my teacup against hers. "It's a plan!"

Darcy answered the phone with her trademark cheerful "Hellloooo!"

"Hey, sis," I started. "You know when you said I never visited you and that I should at least make some sort of effort to get down to Dublin some time?"

"Yes?"

"How about Wednesday?"

"This Wednesday?" she asked, clearly surprised.

"Yep. Me and Fionn. A girly break. We won't get under your feet, promise. You won't even know we're there. Honest!"

"Is something wrong, Annie?" Darcy asked. She knew me so well.

"Something and nothing," I answered. "I'd rather tell you face to face."

"I'd have to work," she said. "And I need to run it past Gerry – you know, just as a formality – but, darling Annie, of course you are welcome. You are always welcome."

And I wondered if I heard a small sob catch in her throat.

21

Fionn had promised Emma she would bring her back something gorgeous from Dublin. Alex had been surprised at her impromptu break away and had hugged her and told her he would miss her terribly.

"Ha, Rebecca! Stick that in your pipe and smoke it!" Fionn had cheered when she came back from saying goodbye to them.

"Are you sure you want to go?" I asked. The absolute last thing I wanted to do was be responsible for things getting worse between her and Alex. Although from the sounds of it, absence certainly had been making the heart grow fonder.

If Alex had been commitment-phobic before now, his enforced separation from Fionn was changing his mind. Now, as long as Rebecca kept her nose out of it, it was possible they could come back stronger – jaunts to Dublin aside.

"Of course," she said. "I'm really looking forward to it. It's been yonks since I was in the Big Smoke. I can't wait to hit the shops and – result!" She flashed a piece of plastic at me. "Alex pressed this into my hand before I left and said to enjoy myself! *Cha-ching*!"

Oh, how I loved Mastercard!

I grinned and gave her an impromptu hug before zipping up my case.

"I'm looking forward to it as well. Apart from the bus journey."

Fionn grimaced along with me. It wasn't necessarily that the bus was uncomfortable – it was more that the journey was long and arduous and – before you hit the motorways in the south – very, very windy. Even the most settled of stomachs would struggle to stay calm between Omagh and Monaghan. But at least we had the glorious surroundings of the Monaghan bus depot and their ice-cold toilets and impressive sandwiches to look forward to midway through the trip. It took a brave soul to risk the cold seat of their breeze-block toilet-building at any time of year.

We could have driven of course, but I was nowhere near brave enough to face the traffic in Dublin. It certainly required someone made of sterner stuff than me to take on the bus lanes and taxi drivers of the city centre. I even broke out into a cold sweat when approaching the toll-booths – just in case I was all out of euro. Besides, there was limited parking at Darcy's apartment and she and Gerry had already taken up their two designated spots.

It would have to be the bus – there was no choice. We just loaded up with Polo mints, bottled water and magazines which we wouldn't read as they would make us feel even more travel-sick.

By the time we arrived in Bus Áras in Dublin, I was half-demented with exhaustion and bursting for a pee. I would have to face my demons – namely the public loos in the bus centre. With Fionn's support, I did, and emerged in better form to face the city if still a bit anxious.

The thing is, visiting the big city showed me up for the yokel I really was. I liked to think Derry was all very metropolitan and chic but, truth was, in comparison to Dublin it was little more than a village. Whenever I visited the big city I instantly became a gobshite tourist who walked about clutching her bag to her in fear of the pickpockets (I even felt the urge to pick up my trolley-case and hug it to me) and looking on in shock at the beggars on the street and the sheer number of people bustling in and out of every building at any hour of the day and night.

I tried not to make eye contact even though the locals were supposed to be friendly and, if truth be told, I was afraid of my life that everyone would hear my Northern accent and rip me off. And as for euros – it was like Monopoly money and I would find myself standing like an eejit searching out the appropriate coins to pay for a Mars bar while mentally trying to work out how much it would cost in sterling. I was not a good traveller whereas Fionn was in her absolute element with her oversized sunglasses perched on her head and her Orla Kiely trolley-case trailing behind her effortlessly. She wasn't even one bit tempted to lift it up and hug it to her. She knew it would take a brave person to try and mug her.

"Darcy won't be finished work for another two hours," I said as we walked towards O'Connell Street. "So we have some time to kill? Any ideas? Shopping? Something to eat?"

"How about the pub? We are on our holidays after all."

I thought about it for a moment and nodded. "Sure why not? Why not treat ourselves after that journey? I could do with a drink or two." All I had to do was make sure I kept our cases tucked under our table and never let them out of our sight.

We headed to the delightfully named Hairy Lemon where I declined Fionn's offer of a pint of Guinness.

"No," I said, pulling a face. "A bottle of ordinary beer will do me just fine."

"Ah, but you're on your holliers!" Fionn replied in her best faux-Dublin accent.

"Fionn, we are only 200 miles from home – where we can drink Guinness any time we want! Now stop acting the eejit and bring me beer!"

She headed to the bar, not even stopping to dig out the right amount of euro first.

I was glad she had come with me – and not just because it saved me from having to endure the long journey on my own. It had been a long time since I'd been to Dublin and longer still since I'd been away on any kind of a girly holiday. Pearse and I had devoted all our free time to each other over the last two years – with me planning my holidays from work around his schedule. My last break had been a weekender to London where he was filming some Saturday-morning cooking show. I had wandered around the shops on my own, occasionally phoning Darcy to ask which clothes shops were in my league and which I should avoid like the plague, or texting pictures of random touristy things to Fionn.

I had spent the afternoon in the hotel bar, curled up with a good book and a glass of wine, while Pearse met with agents and journalists and then that night we had gone to dinner at another celebrity chef's restaurant so that he could make notes for Manna and how he could promote it. I had enjoyed myself – I couldn't deny that – but it had not been the same as sharing a break with someone and just relaxing and letting go.

Briefly I wondered what kind of place Ant would take me to – or even if he would take me anywhere at all? Perhaps all I was good for was his bedroom in Donegal?

I had texted him to say I was going away for a few days and would be in touch. I had been hoping – after the tenderness of the weekend – he would text me back to tell me he would miss me or maybe even to ask me not to go. (I would have gone anyway, for the record, but it would have been nice to have been asked.) He had texted back a simple "OK".

I didn't know how to take him – and because of that I had managed a full four-hour bus journey to Dublin without talking to Fionn about him at all. He was giving me very mixed signals, running hot and cold, and I didn't know if I needed the hassle of something else to worry about just now. But when I thought of him, and how it felt in his arms, I thought maybe he was worth the risk.

"Beer for the lady, go on – get it into ye!" Fionn said, placing a bottle of cold beer on the table in front of me. Sitting down, she raised her pint of the black stuff and clinked it against mine.

"To us, and freedom, and being better than all the feckwit men on the planet!"

"I'll drink to that!"

"You'd better! Alex is paying for it," she said with a wicked smile.

"Is he one of the aforementioned feckwit men?"

She shrugged her shoulders. "You know, I don't think so. I think he's a fairly decent sort but he has definite feckwit qualities. I just hope that by realising what he might lose he may want to hold onto it tighter. Of course, it could all blow up in my face and I could end up back on the shelf again. And you know what has shocked me most about it all? The thought that Emma could be out of my life. Shocking, isn't it? You'd think I'd be doing cartwheels at the thought of no more Disney nonsense, or *High School Musical* or My fricking Little Ponies but . . ." her eyes filled with tears, "the wee shite has really grown on me."

"Course she has. She's a cute one," I said, reaching out and giving Fionn's hand a reassuring squeeze. "But tell you what, darling, even though my faith in happy endings has been really shaken lately, I just know you and Alex will work it out. He loves you. He's just being a commitment-phobic arse and it doesn't help that Rebecca is getting her nose in wherever she can."

"I can't honestly say that I blame her, though," Fionn said. "I mean, why wouldn't she love him? Feckwittedness aside, he's good man, a great daddy and a great catch."

"But she didn't love him before you came along. From what you've said there was never really any big relationship there?"

"That's the thing. I just presumed she never loved him – he told me they were never meant to be together and it was all pretty casual. But, if Alex was the same commitment-phobe then as he is now, maybe he was the one who made the decisions about whether or not their relationship was serious – baby or no baby."

I sat back and sipped from my beer. "Fionn, have you ever considered the possibility that, even if she did love him, she is not the woman for him anyway? I mean, he may not have done the asking when it came to your proposal but he did say yes. He did agree to marry you and he was – is – happy about it. He was glowing on the night of your engagement party."

"That could have been," she said with a sly grin while wiping her tears away, "because of the damn good seeing to I gave him before we went out."

I laughed. "Sex and love are not the same thing, Fionn," I said, thinking of my time with Ant. "Trust me. I should know."

Darcy joined us shortly after five. Even though she had just completed a long day at work, she looked positively glowing. Her blonde curls were twisted high on her head and she wore a tunic that most of us mere mortals could only get away with wearing teamed with trousers. She, however, teamed it with opaque tights and delightfully clunky shoes. A thick belt accentuated her virtually non-existent waist and a plethora of chunky jewellery last seen in the 1980s completed the look. She made me and Fionn look positively granny-ish in comparison. My low-slung jeans, vest top and bolero cardigan could never compete with her in the fashion stakes. Instinctively I ruffled my hair and repositioned my sunglasses on the top of my head.

"Hey, babes," she said, a broad grin spreading across her face. "I can't believe I've finally got you to come to the Big Smoke. You survived the journey okay then?"

Fionn grimaced. "Just about!" She got to her feet. "I'm going to the bar – what will you have?"

"Pint of Magners on ice," Darcy replied, slipping into the seat beside me and stubbing her toe on my case. "Still hiding your bags in case of wanton thieves and pickpockets?" she said with a wink and I blushed. "You really need to get out of Derry more," she laughed.

"How was work?" I asked.

"Oh, busy – manic really. But great. I was talking to some new buyers today about the Spring collection. It's all very exciting – well, for me anyway. You would be bored shiteless if I told you all the details. And I hate talking shop at the end of a day – let's just enjoy a quick drink and head back to the flat."

I nodded. I was suddenly beyond tired, the combination of the long drive down from Derry and the beer making me feel a little woozy. "Sounds like a good idea. I'm beat."

"Well, I thought we would just order in some Chinese and get a good rest tonight. I figured you might be wrecked. I've booked a half day tomorrow – maybe we could head out somewhere and have a good natter." She smiled warmly at me and I knew she was concerned for whatever it was that had enticed me out of Derry and down the road to Dublin.

"I'd like that," I said as Fionn walked towards us with a tray of drinks and enough packets of Cheese and Onion crisps to sink a small ship.

"They had Tayto. I love Tayto from the South – much nicer than the Northern variety," she said with a grin, opening a packet and cramming a few into her mouth.

Darcy's apartment was, appropriately, like my flat's bigger, more stylish sister. On the top floor of a beautifully huge Georgian house, it had all its original features – but with a fully up-to-date modern kitchen that could fit at least six people in and a bathroom which was not ridiculously over-sized. It had two bedrooms in comparison to my own cavernous room and each was stylishly decorated with sash windows which didn't rattle in the wind.

Even better, it was only a short walk from the city centre and some very trendy pubs. Darcy had an apartment that would make most young professionals in Dublin seethe with jealousy – indeed, it made me a little green around the gills. I vowed, within five minutes of walking onto her polished oak floors that I would absolutely have to clean my own home more. I would also have to buy some proper grown-up furniture and ditch some of the hand-me-down efforts which littered each room.

"Oh Darcy, it's gorgeous here," Fionn said, staring around her wide-eyed. "It's so stylish. You should go into interior design!"

Darcy laughed and thanked her for the compliment before showing us to our bedroom – complete with king-sized wrought-iron bed, Egyptian cotton sheets and a very sparkly light fitting which made me gasp in admiration.

"Seriously, girls," Darcy laughed, pulling the curtains over, "you need to get out of Dodge more. Now, I'll leave you to get freshened up while I dig out the Chinese menus – if you aren't too stuffed on Tayto crisps, that is. Gerry is finishing work soon so I can get him to pick it up on his way back."

"Sounds fab," I said and she left.

Fionn flopped down on the bed. "Forget Alex getting cold feet – I think I want to run away from it all and live here forever. Seriously, Annie, I could die happy in this bed."

"If you could at all help it, then please don't. I really don't fancy waking up beside a corpse."

Fionn pulled a face and sat up, arms outstretched before her, in a pretty pathetic attempt at a zombie impression. "I'll do my very best," she said, "but, if I do cark it, can you do the *Thriller* dance at the funeral? It would be a laugh."

I threw a perfectly fluffed cushion at her face and sat down on the other side of the bed. "I'm worn out," I said. "I'd love to just lie down and have a good sleep."

"I'm sure Darcy wouldn't mind," Fionn offered. "You've had a tough few days, petal. Why don't you just take it easy? I'll help Darcy demolish the Chinese, you have a lie-down."

"I think I will," I said, slipping off my flip-flops and climbing onto the bed. The pillows felt so soft against my cheek and I was pretty sure I was asleep before Fionn even had the chance to walk to the door. It was only when I woke several hours later, needing the loo, that I realised just how completely bone-tired I was.

Fionn was asleep beside me. I hadn't heard her come into the room and it was now dark outside. Lifting my mobile from the side table, I flicked it open to see the time. It had gone twelve.

I stretched before digging in the dark, with the light of my phone to guide me, for my pyjamas and wash-bag and I quickly changed and wiped off my make-up. Picking up my toothbrush, I crept out of the room towards the bathroom, stopping off at the kitchen first for a long, cold glass of water. As I stood there, rubbing my eyes and trying not to fall back asleep standing up, I heard the chatter of voices from the living room. Darcy and Gerry must still be up, I realised, and I made to go and say a quick hello in case Gerry thought I was a complete ignorant gulpen for falling asleep before even showing my face. As I padded quietly towards the door, my brain managed to tune into what they were saying just before I walked in on what was clearly a very personal conversation.

"Darce, can we not have this argument again? Please!" Gerry pleaded in his deep Dublin brogue.

"It doesn't have to be an argument. It's a discussion," Darcy replied, her voice equally pleading.

I know that I should have walked away and minded my own, considerably complex, business but I couldn't. I couldn't just leave and not get to the bottom of what it was that had been upsetting my sister so much lately.

"You know, no matter how it starts, it always ends in an argument," he retorted. "I'd love if we could talk about this calmly but we can't, Darcy. Experience has shown us that."

"But it's not going to go away, Gerry. I'm not going to wake up one morning and think 'Feck me, I've changed my mind. I'm happy as I am after all.' If it were that simple then I'd have done it by now. But it's not."

I heard my sister's voice start to break and I had to fight every urge in my body not to run into the room and comfort her while shooting death-ray stares at Gerry who was obviously being a complete bastard.

"And I'm not sure I'm ever going to wake up and feel differently either, Darcy. You know that. You know we talked about this when we first got together and we were both certain we wanted – or didn't want – the same things. It isn't me who changed."

"I didn't change to hurt you," Darcy said, almost defeated.

"I know, I know. And I'm trying to work round it but I'm tired now. I've had a long day. I'm just not up for going round in the same circles all night – it won't get us anywhere. Don't you understand that?"

There was silence and I felt as if my heart might just pop right out of my chest. I stood there, not wanting to move but really, really not wanting to listen any more. Even my nosiest of instincts was screaming at me just to get to the bathroom as quickly as possible and as far away from scary conversations which sounded terribly grown-up and serious.

Suddenly I was seven years old again and thirsty as hell. I'd climbed out of bed and headed to the top of the stairs to call Mum or Dad to fetch me a glass of water. But as I stood there I heard their raised voices – an argument – and I felt my centre of gravity shift.

"We're not taking the girls anywhere," Daddy had said.

"Why not?" Mum's reply was almost petulant. I imagined her stamping her foot and tugging at her dress in mock rage.

"Because they are settled here and they deserve to feel secure."

"What about me? Don't I deserve to be happy?"

Daddy had sighed. "Of course you deserve to be happy – but we have these girls to think about now as well. No matter how much we want to, we can't be selfish here."

"Couldn't we put them up for adoption or something?" Mum had said and Dad had laughed.

And I cried. And went back to bed thirsty.

As an adult, of course, I realised they were joking – sort of. But I spent the rest of my childhood trying my very best to behave so that they would want to keep me. When, in my twenty-fifth year, they announced their relocation to Spain I felt gutted but, at the same time, relieved. They were finally doing what would make them happy – even if it wasn't what would make me happy. Happy endings didn't necessarily work for everyone – and now standing in Darcy's hall I saw her happy ending slipping away from her too.

Creeping to the bathroom I stood and looked in the mirror, my pale face staring back at me. It might have been a monumental mistake to come to Dublin after all.

As I crept back into bed, Fionn stirred. "Are you okay?" she asked sleepily.

"Fine," I lied. "Just fine."

22

By the time I got up Darcy was dressed – in some ridiculous concoction with shoulder-pads – and Gerry had gone to work. She was smiling and singing to herself as she danced around the kitchen preparing breakfast.

"Morning, sis!" she said cheerily. "Sleep well?"

"Yes, great, thanks," I fibbed, wondering if perhaps I had just imagined the previous night's conversation. "Gerry gone already?"

Her face didn't darken. "Yes, he likes to hit the gym before the office. Has to keep his body in trim to keep me happy," she said with a wink.

I laughed out loud. I was quite happy, if truth be told, to pretend last night had simply been a figment of my imagination.

"Where's Fionn?" she added.

"Shower," I replied, picking up a piece of toast and slathering it in butter.

"So, while we have five minutes to ourselves, do you want to tell me what has prompted this highly delightful trip to see your favourite sister?"

"Trust me. It would take more than five minutes."

Darcy sat down beside me and poured two cups of coffee. "Well, this afternoon then. For definite. But please just tell me it doesn't involve Pee-arse and his ability to get you back in the sack."

"Not directly," I said with a grimace.

"And what about the knicker guy?"

I blushed at the memory of our last meeting, and just as quickly cringed at the memory of his last text. "He's still on the scene."

"In a starring role?" she asked, eyebrow raised.

"I don't know is the easy answer. I don't think I know an awful lot any more." To my absolute disgust I felt tears spring to my eyes. Quickly I took a deep breath, forced myself to get composed. Darcy was due to leave for work any time – and anyway it seemed she had enough of her own worries.

"Oh, petal," Darcy said, "it will be okay, you know. It always is." But she didn't sound wholly convinced.

I wanted then to ask her was *she* okay – maybe even ask if everything was okay with Gerry but, just as my mouth opened, Fionn walked in, broad smile across her face and best faux-Dublin accent on. "Top o' the fecking morning to yese. Let's hit the shops!"

"Oh Jesus, Fionnuala," Darcy said with a grin as she set about pouring a third cup of coffee and sticking two more slices of bread in the toaster. "Whatever you do, do *not* talk like that to anyone who actually comes from round these parts. You might actually get lynched."

"What has you so chipper this morning?" I asked Fionn.

"Oooh, text from Alex. He misses me. He loves me. He loves me a lot," she said with a wave of her left hand and a grin on her face that was positively contagious.

"You see, treat 'em mean, keep 'em keen," Darcy piped up, biting into a piece of toast as she lifted her bag from the worktop and headed towards the door. "I shall see you lovely ladies after lunch. I'm thinking picnic at St Stephen's Green. Bring a good book, some sunscreen and something yummy to eat. It's going to be a hot one out there today so I'm thinking basking in the sun could be just perfect."

Fionn gave the thumbs-up while I promised to include some

lovely chocolate in the picnic and to bring along the nice picnic blanket from the back of the airing cupboard.

I even promised to wash up while Darcy was at work, which was very unlike me, but I figured she deserved a break. Emotional upheaval really does fuck up your desire to keep the house in check.

Darcy left and Fionn and I looked at each – a glorious air of "What do we do now?" in the air.

"Shopping?" she offered.

I shook my head. The heat was oppressive in the city and I didn't fancy traipsing through the crowds in Grafton Street, clutching my bag to me for fear of being robbed by some faceless pickpocket with sneaky fingers and brass neck.

"Sleeping then?" she offered, eyebrow raised, and that sounded good to me. After all, in normal circumstances at this time of a morning we would both have been at our desks under Bob's watchful gaze, listening to his joyful Americanisms and business clichés. At times like that we would have probably killed to be back in our beds – so it seemed lovely and decadent to be able to creep back into bed now.

"Hang on a minute till I text Alex," Fionn said as she climbed under the covers. "I'll tell him I'm off to bed with a hot woman and get him all a-flutter. Absence not only makes the heart grow fonder but the you-know-what grow harder."

I blushed, embarrassed by her honesty, and wondering if Ant was thinking of me at all – and indeed if his you-know-what was getting harder at the thought of our time together. No, I chided myself. I had to put thoughts of him out of my head. This was my new beginning – my new way to a happy ending. This way would include only occasional dalliances with men and would never again mix business with pleasure. I had tied myself in knots since his "OK" text message, wondering how many other ladies had seen the sunset over Donegal from his bedroom.

No, it would do me no good whatsoever to think of him now.

So I laughed – tried to get the image of Alex and his penis out of my head – and stretched out for a snooze.

I dozed on and off for an hour before getting up and padding back to the kitchen where I cleaned up as Fionn slept on. Opening the fridge to get a drink of orange juice, I spotted a postcard on the outside from Spain. I knew it had to be from Mum and Dad – the image on the front was of their nearest beach.

I suddenly had the urge to see my mother's handwriting so I turned it over and saw her familiar scrawl. I didn't need to read the words. I just held it to me, comforted by the thought that she had once held it in her own hands. I also knew that once I read it any sense of comfort would most likely leave me. Mum and Dad – lovely as they were – were not blessed with the usual parental qualities of gushing adoration for their offspring. I looked and found it was covered in simple instructions to Darcy (they wouldn't have trusted me) regarding the rental of the old family home and a quick mention of me with a comment that they hoped I was behaving myself.

If only they knew! Mum would have had a mild coronary at the very notion of me having casual sex with a hairy man from Donegal on a semi-regular basis.

I smiled anyway at the card – and the way my parents dealt with everything practical first of all. Maybe if I was more like them and less inclined to have my head in the clouds, I would live in a lovely practical house with decently proportioned rooms and spend my day working at a sensible job where nipple-tassel-wearing was strictly off limits.

I took some money from my purse, pressing it as deep into my pockets as possible, and nipped out the door towards the local market where I stocked up on all sorts of goodies for our picnic. It really was a glorious day and the city was alive with visitors and locals all making their way around, getting on with their life.

I felt like a very small cog in a very big wheel and for once that feeling was just fine with me. I even stood still, just for a few seconds, outside the market and let the sun beat down on my face.

Whatever had brought me here, whatever I would find out about Darcy and Gerry, whatever would become of Fionn and Alex, I was overcome by the sure and certain feeling that it would all work out just fine.

23

I could feel my skin warm and start to sizzle. I knew I should probably move – cover up a little or add more sun cream but I was too blissed out to do anything. I was lying on the cool grass in St Stephen's Green while Darcy sat, her back rested against a tree, reading. Fionn was lost in some sort of sexy text loop with Alex who was clearly missing his wife-to-be.

"If I had known all it would take would be a midnight flit to Dublin, I'd have done it a week ago," she'd said dreamily as we scoffed some chocolate-covered strawberries and sneaked a wee sip of wine from our Thermos flasks.

Darcy had looked at me and rolled her eyes and I had shrugged my shoulders.

"The problem hasn't gone away though, has it?" Darcy had said and Fionn looked most taken aback.

Of course Darcy was right. The problem – the big Rebecca-shaped problem – was still there. Just because Alex wasn't being held to ransom by her just now didn't mean that she wouldn't rear her head again.

"Oh for goodness sakes," Fionn had said in a more than exasperated tone of voice. "First of all Rebecca is a problem. Then it's Alex that is the problem – him and his commitment phobia. And then it's me because I let him get away with murder. And now it's Rebecca again . . ."

Darcy shrugged her shoulders and Fionn looked to me for back-up.

"Look, darling," I replied as supportively as I possibly could, "I'm delighted Alex seems to have his act together and seems to be getting over his fear of commitment but you have to accept Rebecca is still there – the Woman Scorned and you know what they say about that . . ."

"And," Darcy interjected, "Alex is horny. It doesn't mean he has grown up. It takes a lot for a man to grow up, believe me."

Fionn had raised her middle finger and said she didn't want to talk about it any more and Darcy had gone back to reading her book – or at least doing a very good impression of someone reading a book. I looked at the back of her book (which was obscuring her face) and wondered what on earth was going on with her and Gerry and what I could do to make her tell me. Chances were there was nothing I could do until she was willing to tell me herself, so I lay back and started reading until my eyes grew a little heavy and I fell into a half-doze.

It was only when my skin started to singe that I forced my eyes open and sat up.

"Isn't this lovely?" I asked, stretching my arms to the sky.

"It sure is," Fionn replied. "And it beats working for a living."

"If only it could be like this all the time," Darcy added with a smile, putting her book down and pushing her glasses to the top of her head. Her long legs were already deliciously golden and I felt quite self-conscious of my milk-bottle variety splayed out in front of me.

"Funny that you don't realise how much you need a break till you stop for a while," I added, realising that for the last few weeks I had been like a tightly coiled spring and that it was only here that my body and mind were starting to relax.

"So are you ever going to tell me what finally got you to leave Derry behind and head down the road to see me? Must have been something big," Darcy asked and Fionn sat up, crossed her legs and put her phone down.

I explained how Pearse had messed things up for me at work and how I had lost out on my two biggest clients because of it. I told her I blamed myself in some ways for treating him so poorly. Of course Darcy dismissed this entirely – he was an arse, she reminded me. And if he had been so annoyed with my behaviour he shouldn't have agreed to continue working with me and been so sociable during our meeting at Manna. She said that even though things had ended badly he could have still done me the courtesy of talking to me first rather than talking directly to Bob.

While a part of me agreed with her, I also wondered whether I would have offered him the same courtesy if the roles had been reversed. After all, I had slept with someone else while we were still together – regardless of the state of our relationship, I would have been utterly devastated if he had done that to me.

As I told her this I felt very ashamed of how I had acted and the sheen of the day in the sun started to fade.

"Annie, you have to stop beating yourself up about things. What is done, is done. Pearse knew your relationship was in trouble. He more than likely knew that it was never going to last. He might be hurt but in the long run he will thank you for it. Believe it or not, you will even thank yourself." Then she added with a wink, "You must already feel better knowing that you never have to sleep with him again."

"Is that how you would feel if Gerry dumped you after sleeping with someone else?" Fionn asked and I felt my face redden, aware that Fionn might well be closer to the mark than she realised.

"It's a different situation," Darcy said. "You can't compare the two."

"Why not?" Fionn asked, playing devil's advocate and still clearly irked by Darcy's judgements on her own relationship.

"Because Gerry and I are different. We are different people. We have a different dynamic to Annie and Pearse. He wouldn't do that and neither would I."

"Oh, so you are perfect then?" Fionn asked and I started to feel nervous.

It was entirely possible that my sister and my dearest friend were going to have a full-on bitch-fest in the middle of a public park in Dublin.

"I didn't say that."

"But you implied it. Darcy, you sit in judgement of everyone else. My relationship is a joke, my fiancé a commitment-phobe, me a walkover. Annie here is a tart who had no respect for her partner, who was an arse anyway. But you, you in your fancy apartment and your designer clothes and your lovely boyfriend – well, nothing could ever be wrong in your world, could it?"

My heart started to thump. Surely Fionn had been privy to the same conversations I had. She knew something was wrong with Darcy and yet she was pushing her – and being downright nasty with it.

"I didn't say that," Darcy replied, quieter this time.

"But you didn't need to, Darce. It's there all the time in everything you say. You don't even know Alex and yet you are there judging him like no one's business and judging our relationship. And you didn't know Annie and Pearse together – it was good sometimes, you know. Sure it wasn't going to be forever, but that doesn't make him an arse."

"No," Darcy said coldly. "Him being an actual arse is what makes him an arse. That has nothing to do with how long he dated Annie. And I'm not judgemental – I just don't walk around with my eyes closed all the time."

I didn't know what to say or do. I wanted to challenge her about what was going on with Gerry. I wanted to tell Fionn to stop picking on her. I wanted to get up and walk away from the scene that was unfolding and do something altogether less uncomfortable – like stick those fecking nipple-tassels on again and go five rounds with the old biddy from the protest group.

"My eyes are very much open," Fionn said. "I know Alex isn't perfect but he is perfect for me. And yes, we have our issues but I would really appreciate it if you would stop casting aspersions on what we do have, because he is the man I'm going to marry and spend the rest of my life with. He'll be the father of my children, my best friend, my everything . . ."

Her voice started to falter and I hoped this would be enough to put Darcy off, but no, my sister was about to pull an absolute blinder.

Slowly she started to clap, a fake, insincere but loud clap. "Well, fair fucking play to you, missus, and your happy life and your best friend and your everything and your fucking children!"

"Darcy!" I pleaded as Fionn's face fell.

"What?" said Darcy. "If you can't handle a healthy dose of reality then that really isn't my problem."

"So what is *your* fucking problem then?" Fionn almost roared.

Darcy stood up, dusted herself down and lifted her bag.

"*You*. You two and your self-obsessed little world. That's what my problem is. Get over yourself, ladies."

And she walked off, leaving Fionn and me once again open-mouthed in disbelief.

This time we knew she wouldn't be walking back in ten minutes later to apologise and dance badly to "I Will Survive".

Darcy had always had a temper. We had our fair share of scraps in our childhood and teenage years. I still remembered the time she emptied a waste-bin over my head when I had dared use her make-up during a particularly dodgy experimentation-with-colour stage in my early teenage years. I also had a small scar on my left hand where she had stabbed me with her fork when I tried to swipe a chip from her plate. There were various other mental scars too – she could turn nasty when she wanted – but mostly, since we reached our adult years and stopped sharing the same house, things had been hugely improved between us and I looked on her – perhaps unfairly – as the mother our mother never really was. She was the person I could confide in and who could make things right, except now things were very not right and very, very mixed up.

"Know any good hotels?" Fionn asked and I sat there, rigid with shock, shivering in the heat of St Stephen's Green.

"I know nothing about Dublin. Nothing at all."

"Well, I'm not staying," Fionn said. "I'll go and get my case and find somewhere else to stay. You can come with me if you want to."

I shook my head and dragged my fingers through my hair. "Hang on, Fionn. Darcy was a bitch, I'm not going to say she wasn't, but there is obviously something very wrong in her life."

"Okay then, let her walk all over you just like you let everyone else do," Fionn said, packing her things in her bag and standing up, then storming off in the opposite direction to Darcy while I was left there like a cold snotter (and a cold snotter with a pathological fear of pickpockets and big cities) in the middle of a park, not entirely sure what the hell had just happened.

I couldn't phone Darcy. I couldn't phone Fionn. I couldn't phone Pearse and it would have been laughable to phone Bob even though he was the only person who had shown me even an ounce of warmth and compassion in the last few days and who I was still speaking to. I couldn't – or wouldn't – phone Ant. There was nothing I could say to him anyway and, at that moment, on a bench in the park crying like the fecking loon that I was, I wasn't even sure I would make sense.

Coming to Dublin was supposed to sort everything out. Darcy was supposed to say soothing words. Fionn and I were supposed to be having a great *craic* and being all *Sex and the City* with ourselves. It was not supposed to be crap. I was not supposed to be stranded in the middle of a park unsure of how to get back to Darcy's apartment and unsure of the reception I'd get there even if I found it.

I had tried calling each of them and got no answer – both were obviously in mega-huffs which was fine by me as I felt myself sink into a mega-huff as well. They had abandoned me, right in the middle of a city I barely knew. Could I even remember Darcy's address? Not without my address book and, as my luck would have it, I didn't have it with me. I really didn't know the way back to Darcy's. Should I head in the direction in which Fionn had stormed off?

Part of me wanted simply to feck the lot of them and walk to the nearest bar and get scuttered – but I figured that getting scuttered would not help me find my way to wherever on earth it was I was going to spend the night. I felt tears prick in my eyes as I gathered my belongings and started walking, hoping for a glance of something familiar to lead me to the city centre. Spotting the Shelbourne, I headed towards it only to be confronted by the most manic traffic imaginable. There was Luas, three thousand taxis, people on bikes, people walking, ordinary cars with grumpy drivers all going in a jillion directions and leaving me dizzy with confusion.

Which probably explains why I ended up walking out in front of a Dublin taxi driver driving his very own Dublin taxi which might as well have had "Killing Machine" written all over it.

You know how they say that in those moments your whole life starts to go in slow motion? Well, that's bollocks. It all speeded up – too fast. The car was too fast. My life was going too fast. My breathing was too fast. The person shouting at me to be careful was shouting too fast. The only thing that wasn't going too fast was me. I was in slow-down mode. As I tried to turn, my body seemed to freeze as if my feet were stuck like a wee Lego man on a Lego board to the road. My feet felt as though they weighed six stone each – which I was pretty sure they didn't but they wouldn't move and all I could do was twist a little and gasp a lot and then – in a very fast way – pray that what was about to happen wasn't going to be too godawfully painful. I mean, seriously, my life was pretty shit as it was – did I have to add the trauma of all my bones being smashed to smithereens into the mix?

I closed my eyes, knowing that was the only thing I could do and felt a body-blow against mine – but it wasn't a metal body-blow. More a human-y one. Someone had pushed me out of the way and as I hurtled towards the pavement, twisting my stupid Lego ankles and grazing my knee, I heard him land with a similarly inelegant thud on the pavement beside me.

"Are you okay?" he asked, standing up and brushing himself off. He reached his hand out to mine and, when I glanced up, he was there all floppy-haired and besuited.

"Fine, just fine," I muttered and then burst into snottery tears.

"Are you sure?"

"My ankle hurts," I sniffed. "And I cut my kneeeeeeeeee," I wailed.

He helped me to a chair outside a nearby coffee shop at the top of Dawson Street.

"Have a seat. I'll get you a hot cup of sweet tea," he offered and as I watched him walk to the counter my head started to swim. Whether it was with shock, or stress or the effects of the wine we had sipped out of the flask earlier I didn't know. Whatever it was, however, I wasn't taking any chances. I put my head in my hands and started to breathe slowly and evenly – which actually ended up more like mad hyperventilation.

"Calm down," he soothed me, sitting a tea in front of me.

I looked at him – this stranger. This stranger who had saved my life. This stranger who had bought me a hot sweet tea. This stranger in a big city who I didn't know at all.

"Thank you," I stuttered.

He smiled, his eyes crinkling, and he offered me his hand.

"Owen," he said. "My name is Owen Reilly. And don't worry about thanking me. I'm glad you're okay."

I noticed his hand was grazed and had an urge to touch it – but this was shock. This was definitely shock. I shook my head and shivered, despite the heat.

"Drink your tea," he urged, making to leave.

"Do you have to go?" I asked, rather pathetically, but I figured if I couldn't get away with pathetic, just after I'd almost been run over, then I never would. "I mean, go if you want to. You must have somewhere to be. I'm sorry. I'm not usually a complete psycho. I'm usually quite normal. I'm usually in control." All of which prompted a fresh flurry of tears as my ankle throbbed in time with my hyperventilation.

He didn't look embarrassed, or awkward. He simply sat down and asked me to look in his eyes (in a non-creepy way) until my breathing evened out.

"Now . . ."

"Annie. Annie Delaney," I offered back.

"Well, Annie Delaney, drink your tea and think about your breathing and when you've calmed down we'll have a look at that ankle of yours."

I nodded and did what I was told and my breathing did settle down and my ankle throbbing eased.

I asked him if I could buy him a cup of tea, or maybe a bun.

"A tea would be just fine," he said and smiled.

"And then I'll let you go," I promised. "I'm sorry for taking up your time."

"Stop apologising. You've had a nasty shock." He smiled slowly and I couldn't help but smile back.

"But you must have things to do?"

"To tell you the truth I had a date with a frozen meal and the telly. I probably shouldn't have told you that – it makes me look like a saddo but tonight was going to be all about a beef curry and *Top Gear*."

I laughed, immediately relaxing, and I sipped my tea feeling the colour return to my cheeks. I was just about to ask him who his favourite *Top Gear* presenter was when my phone burst into life with the ringtone I reserved for Fionn.

"Annie," she began, "I'm in the Westbury. Alex's card. Come and join me. I'm getting our cases sent over in a taxi. Darcy wasn't home yet – Gerry sorted it. Come and meet me and we'll figure out just what in the hell we're going to do next. Okay? Room 114? See you there." And she rang off without even giving me the chance to talk.

"The Westbury," I muttered.

"The Westbury?" he repeated.

"Where my friend is. Where I need to go. Do you know the way?" I glanced around me as if I should see a sign right there pointing the way.

"I'll walk you there if you want," he offered. "After all, the beef curry can wait and I wouldn't be comfortable leaving you and your battered ankle to make it there on your own."

"You don't have to," I stuttered.

"I know," he replied and I knew that he was going to walk me back to the hotel.

He lifted my bags and I didn't even for one second worry that he was going to run off with them.

"It's not far," he said. "Is your ankle up to it?"

Tentatively I stood up, grimacing slightly as I put pressure on my foot. Yes, it hurt but I would be able to walk on it – or at least waddle in a very undignified manner on it.

"I'll manage," I said. "Although I might need to grab onto your arm from time to time."

"My arms are very grabbable," he said with a smile as we headed slowly towards Grafton Street. "So, the Westbury? What has you there?"

I shrugged my shoulders. "It's a long story."

"At the speed we're walking, I have the time," he said with a wink.

"Well, to cut the long story short – so that I don't bore you senseless – we were staying with my sister but there was a bit of a falling out and so my friend has decamped to the Westbury instead."

"Very fancy," he said.

"Her fiancé is paying. That's a long story too."

"I'm a good listener."

"I sensed that but seriously you have better things to do than listen to me waffle on."

"Like what? *Top Gear* and the beef curry? Because much as I like Jeremy Clarkson, I like a bit of real-life scandal more."

"Well, if there is one thing I can do, it is scandal. Trust me, falling in front of a speeding car is just one in a long line of disastrous events in my life lately."

"You can talk to me," he said. "I'm a therapist."

I felt my heart sink to my swollen ankle. If there was one thing I hated more than wannabe celebrity chefs, it was therapists. Even if they were dashingly handsome and had just saved my life.

"I don't need to be therapised," I stuttered.

"Is that even a word?" he laughed.

"It is now – and believe me I don't need it."

"It's okay. Your secrets are safe with you. My therapising skills are strictly reserved for wayward teens and, while I realise this may well alienate me from you further, I'm guessing you are not a teen."

I smiled, relieved, and my heart left my ankle. Although it was a bit of bruise to my ego that random strangers on the streets of Dublin very obviously knew that I was well past my teenage years. I'd liked to have thought that in the right light I could have passed for a mature nineteen-year-old.

"You guessed right. And thanks for not pushing. It might traumatise you entirely if you knew the full extent of my disastrous life."

"Okay, we'll save it for another time. And beside, we are almost there – that's the Westbury. You'll like it. It's a great hotel – very swish."

"I don't usually do swish," I said, fearing he might think I was a godawful snobby cow who regularly stayed in plush hotels in the centre of Dublin – especially when I had spent the last half hour telling him what a yokel I was.

"I know the kind of woman you are," he said. "You are effortlessly swish."

I laughed. In truth, I almost choked. Was he actually flirting? Had we moved from life-saving knight-in-shining-armour territory to flirting-at-a-fancy-hotel-ville?

"That proves you really need to brush up on your people skills – because nothing I do – apart from putting weight on and make an eejit of myself – is ever effortless."

"My people skills are spot on," he said, his face serious for a moment, and I felt a little flutter of something somewhere.

I knew I absolutely had to make my move then and there before complicating my life any further.

"So here we are then," I said.

"It would seem so."

"Thank you kindly, Mr Reilly, for your company and for not robbing me or trying to sleep with me."

"Not trying to sleep with you?" he laughed. "Do you always just say the first thing than comes into your head?"

"Mostly. Yes. I did tell you – I am a disaster."

"Well, you are a most welcome disaster, Ms Delaney," he said with a twinkle in his eye.

I almost didn't want to walk through the door. I could have stood there for ages – if only I didn't have an urge to pee and an ankle that had decided that it actually really did hurt after all.

"This might be a little pathetic, but how about I give you my business card?" he said. "You know, in case you ever turn into a fourteen-year-old with an image crisis?"

I smiled and rifled in my bag. "And I'll give you mine in case you ever want to shamelessly promote your therapising skills."

He smiled as he kissed me on the cheek and turned to walk away. It would have been terribly romantic if I wasn't almost sure that I was never going to see him again.

Fionn was lying prone over what was perhaps the biggest bed I had ever seen in my whole entire life. She was wearing the hotel robe and sipping from a glass of champagne.

"Have a bath," she said. "You absolutely should have a bath. That is perhaps the deepest, most scrummiest bath in the whole world. And have some champagne while you are at it. Alex is paying – again."

"Actually I'd just love a glass of water and some Nurofen," I replied, sitting down on the bed and rubbing my ankle. It was only then I noticed the graze on my arm which was really quite bloody nasty-looking and bloody sore to boot.

"What the bejesus happened to you?" Fionn asked, sitting up and grabbing at my arm for a closer look.

"Nothing much," I shrugged. "Just a rampant taxi and a near-death experience."

I gave her a quick rundown on my nearly being run down,

mentioning my rescuer only as a nameless faceless stranger with quick reactions. Nor did I mention he had walked me back to the hotel.

"Jesus, Annie. Are you okay?"

"Fine. Just fine. Worried about Darcy, and you, and a little sore and battered, but fine." There was more than a hint of fecked-offness in my voice and Fionn visibly bristled.

"I'm sorry," she said. "I know she is your sister but she was a right pain in the arse today. In fact, she was a nasty bitch today if the truth be told. And she has been a right pain in the arse quite a lot lately."

"There's more to this than meets the eye, though."

"Like what?" Fionn asked.

"I don't know. But you must realise this is not what she is usually like. You spent time with her and Gerry last night – did it seem strange?"

Fionn shrugged: "Not really, that I can think of. We had something to eat. Gerry was a bit quiet but he said he was tired. Nothing which would justify her biting the fecking head off me over nothing anyway."

I felt torn. I knew that Darcy had been out of line, but I also knew something else was going on and, while I was angry with her, I was also worried stupid about her.

"I overheard something last night," I confided and then told her what I had heard when I got up to use the bathroom.

Fionn was silent when I'd finished.

"I'm not trying to excuse her behaviour," I went on. "I'm not trying to say we should be lovely and nice to her when she is being a cow, but I think something is seriously wrong, Fionn. And I'm worried. Did Gerry say anything at all when you got the bags sent over?"

"He said she had come home in a foul mood and had gone to bed. He'd wondered had there been some falling-out. In fairness to him, he asked me to reconsider, but I was so bloody angry that I said to send the bags over anyway. And I don't regret it for a minute. I couldn't play nice with her after that, Annie, surely you understand?"

I nodded sadly and sighed. "I don't know what to think any more. I'm going to get that bath and that glass of water and a couple of Nurofen and then we can talk about what to do."

"I'll run you the bath," she said. "And I'll order us some room service – although Alex's patience might only run so far – and we'll work it out."

"Okay," I nodded again, starting to resemble one of those stupid dogs people sit on the parcel shelves of their cars.

As she left the room I lifted my phone and tried to call Darcy. There was no answer. Part of me was damned angry that she wouldn't take my call, regardless of whether she was lying like a wounded swan in her pit. I hung up and waited a while before calling again. Still no answer.

This time I left a message. It was a simple "Darce, call me." But when I called back a third time it was more angry: "Darcy, call me now. You're acting like a madwoman. Shouting at my friend, running off on me. What the feck are you at? I nearly died by the way, but I doubt you'd give a damn about that just now."

I was pretty sure if I listened very, very carefully I could hear the sound of my big sister falling square off her pedestal and landing flat on her perfect hole. I hung up just as Fionn walked back in to ask me how much bubble bath I wanted and I sighed.

"Let me just get a shower first. You know how I hate lying in a bath when I actually need to be cleaned."

She smiled and handed me a towelling robe. "Okay, pet. I'll just watch some telly, you take your time."

24

I lay back and allowed the bubbles to soothe my battered ankle. I had my phone beside me but it stayed ominously quiet. No messages from Darcy, no calls from Ant. No nothing. I tried not to get all paranoid but it was a losing battle.

I tried to quell the uneasiness in my head with thoughts of Owen Reilly. I tried to remember him – to lock away that glint in his eyes in my memory, the softness of his hands and the strength of his arms. And then I tried to forget him. He was a nice man. He was a good-looking man. He had saved my life almost definitely but he was a man all the same and I was off men. Even, I thought, Ant who seemed only interested if I could be with him and in his bed right then and there. Sighing, I sank under the bubbles, holding my breath and listening to the rhythmic thumping of my own heartbeat echo in my ears.

Fionn may well have been right – this was perhaps the most glorious bath in the whole entire world. I could die happily right there – which of course I was at risk of doing if I didn't actually sit up and breathe soon. Gasping for air, letting it sink in my lungs as I brushed the bubbles from my face, I decided that I was not going to give any more headspace that evening to Ant – who hadn't called – or Owen – who had saved my life. Instead I was going to be a strong, independent woman in a Beyoncé style and I would set about helping my sister to stop being such a cow to everyone and I would try as much as possible to discourage Fionn from completely bankrupting Alex even though this was perhaps the nicest bathroom I had ever set foot in.

I climbed out of the bath and dried myself off before wrapping up in my robe and padding back into the bedroom where Fionn was now drinking a cup of tea – and where one was waiting for me.

"Have you tried calling her?" she asked.

"Yes. No answer."

"Hmmm," she shrugged.

"I left a message. A pretty nasty one. I might have told her to fuck off or similar."

"Good enough for her," Fionn said.

"I know," I said, but I felt uneasy all the same.

I hated fighting with Darcy. I needed not to be fighting with her, even if she had been a bitch. I knew what she would be up to now, locked in her room, maybe a glass of wine, hopefully feeling sorry about her actions. Memories of our childhood years once again flooded back. After the great bin-upending incident she had locked herself in the bathroom for three full hours. And not even Mum's best efforts at coaxing her out with promises of extra Arctic Roll or a kick up the arse worked.

And we only had one bathroom. And I really needed to pee. I ended up walking the five minutes to our grandparents' where I battered on their door as if someone was dying and didn't even say hello before battering up their staircase to their bathroom and relieving myself.

I stayed in my grandparents' house until I heard that Darcy had come back out of our bathroom but when I went home I wished I had stayed there even longer. She was in a mega-sulk and spoke little more than the occasional one-syllable word for the next three days – but no one gave out to her because we all knew that was just Darcy's way and she would come round eventually and in her own good time. Of course we were also afraid that if we wound her up again she would lock herself in the bathroom for a whole other three hours and then, well, we'd have to run round to granny's to pee or take to using a bucket in the back hall. Neither of which was ideal if the truth be told.

So I told Fionn how I felt, how I knew my sister was acting awfully – how finally I was realising, maybe painfully, that she was far from perfect – but that I was worried about her.

"The problem with you, Annie, is that you are too damn forgiving," said Fionn. "I don't think I could be. But if you want to go round and sort it out, of course I'll support you. I don't have to like it but I'll support you."

I hugged her and cried on her shoulder while babbling incoherently about how she was the best friend ever and how I didn't deserve her and how I absolutely would make Darcy say sorry if it killed me – which it just might.

"Are you feeling very brave then?" I asked.

"Hey, I just put more money than is acceptable on Alex's credit card. Of course I'm feeling brave. Brave is my middle name. I'm the bravest person in the whole entire universe, don'tcha know?"

"Right, well, let me get dressed and we'll head off."

"But we can still come back here? Can't we? I mean, it cost a lot of euros and the beds are ridiculously big and the bath is the very best bath in the whole wide universe. And besides, try as I will to play nice, I don't think I could stay a night in Darcy's, not after all those things she said."

"Yes," I said. "We can come back."

"Thank you," she said.

I wondered what she was thanking me for. It was me who needed to thank her.

I dressed in jeans, a T-shirt and a cardigan – slipping sneakers on my feet to help protect my bruised ankle. Hair still wet, I tied it up in a ponytail and just brushed some loose powder across my face which had a distinctly pink glow from the afternoon in the sun.

"Is your ankle up to the walk?" Fionn asked, slipping a light cardigan over her shoulders.

"Not a fecking chance. But, please, could you deal with the taxi-drivers? You know I have a pathological fear that they're going to take me the long way round just to fleece me."

"Seriously, Annie, how on earth did you ever get a job in PR with such a serious distrust of people?"

"I got my job in PR – and am damn good at it – precisely *because* of my serious distrust in people. Sure isn't our job all about lying in the most impressive way possible?"

"Oooh," she said with a cackle. "Don't let Bawb hear you talking like that. He'll have you excommunicated from the righteous clique of PR gurus. Never a free lip gloss or a meal for two in a fancy restaurant will pass your way again."

"I've had enough of meals for two in fancy restaurants and I've enough lip glosses in my possession to sink a small to medium-sized ship. That's not even to mention the buzzing little freebies I got from Love, Sex and Magic – I will never see a fluffy little rabbit in the same way again." I raised an eyebrow and the smile on my face just about said it all.

Fionn was discussing the merits of the Rampant Rabbit when we arrived at Darcy's. I had been trying to change the subject, aware of the rising colour (and feck knows what else) of our taxi driver – but she was most insistent.

"I don't like the twirly bit," she said. "It's too much. Alex fears the neighbours will complain."

I nodded and smiled, my own colour rising which was making my face a strange shade of red, never mind the pink I had been before. I could see it all in the wing mirror. The glass or two of champagne had clearly lowered Fionn's inhibitions just a tad. It made me wonder just what she would be like when she got in front of a fragile Darcy. Lord only knows what she would say to my sister and how it would be received. I knew I would have to change the subject before we reached the door but everything suddenly seemed laden with innuendo – from pressing the buzzer, to going upstairs, to getting it all out in the open. Fionn was practically purple with the exertion of laughing by the time a serious-faced Gerry let us into the flat. At least, I thought, Fionn was laughing and not spoiling for a fight.

"Ladies," he said, a strange looked on his face as if we had just caught him on the toilet or something worse.

"Gerry," I said, realising this was the first time I had actually seen him since my arrival in the Big Smoke, "how are you?" I moved to air-kiss him and he pulled away. I was startled – after all, I hadn't done anything to him or Darcy – well, except move out of course. His body language was giving me a big old feck-off and he looked fed up – tired and fed up and not at all the ruggedly handsome Dub I had come to know and love.

"Right," was all he said, before looking towards the bedroom and almost whispering, "She's in there."

Fionn had composed herself and the firey look was back on her face. I knew she wouldn't be impressed with me pussy-footing around my sister as if *she* was the wounded one.

"I'll sort this," I said to her and then, to placate her further, added, "I'll get her to say sorry." I gestured towards the living room, thinking it would be safer for her to wait there instead of coming into the lion's den.

She nodded and left me to it.

I felt a shudder as I walked towards the bedroom door. I half-expected it to be locked or barricaded.

I rapped on the door gently, but there was no answer. So I whispered Darcy's name. Then said it. Then almost shouted it. I heard a grunt in return which I took to mean "Oh, hello, lovely sister. Please do come in and talk to me. I feel the need to unburden myself on your wise ears." Or something.

Gingerly I opened the door and saw her lying on the bed watching *Coronation Street*. "Do you think they drink a lot in *Corrie*?" she said. "I mean it feels as if they go to the pub every day – a couple of times a day. I would be pissed as a fart if I drank as much as they seem to do. And did you ever notice how cheap the drink is? You wouldn't get a glass of wine for that price at Searsons.

But then, do you know how fecking lucky you are – up there in the North with your cheap drink and your cheap food and cheap everything?"

"You couldn't wait to leave it," I said gently, sitting down beside her and watching a scene unfold with Rita and Norris in Roy's Rolls.

"Aye, but I miss it sometimes."

"Like a hole in the head."

"Maybe," she said, turning to face me and muting the telly. "Was I a complete bitch today?"

I shrugged my shoulders. "Not a complete bitch. No. Maybe a ninty-nine per cent bitch but certainly not a complete one. You need to say sorry to Fionn. You were out of line."

She cringed visibly, curling her knees up towards her chest. "Oh God. I'm sorry. I'm not usually so godawful. Am I?"

"No. No, you're not," I said, lying back on the bed beside her and brushing her hair from her eyes. "What's wrong, Darcy? And please don't tell me nothing because I know something is up. You've been acting out of sorts for a few weeks now and I heard you and Gerry talking last night. Not all of it, mind. Just some of it. Enough to know that something is really quite wrong."

She half-laughed and half-cried a response. "It's wrong and it's not wrong. Oh but Annie, I envy you and your eye on the prize. I envy how you've always known what you wanted and gone for it and never once shifted the goalposts. Your Life Plan? I need me one of those."

"But you have a great life. Gerry loves you," I said, my eyes pleading with her to tell me that he still did. "You have this amazing flat with its perfectly proportioned rooms and a job that most people would kill for."

She nodded sadly. "But it's not enough, Annie. Don't you realise that? It's just not enough."

Darcy was more maternal than my mother. My mother was lovely – don't get me wrong – but she was one of those women who wanted to be best friends with her daughters rather than mother them. So Darcy mothered me. She made sure I had the right-sized bra, wore clean underwear, had a decent packed lunch and did my homework. She listened when I cried about the fact that Jason Donovan was never, ever going to love me and she encouraged me to go to university when a decent enough proportion of my school friends were getting jobs which paid actual money. She even subbed me when I wanted to go out with them and my grant had been frittered away on luxuries such as rent and food and textbooks.

But even at that, she was never maternal. She never wanted children. That was something she was one hundred per cent certain about.

Until now. Now, everything had changed.

"I know you think I'm an eejit. I know you think I could never do it anyway. I know that I probably would crack under the pressure but I can't help it. I want a baby. My baby. Our baby. And I've been trying to ignore it because it was never in the plan – not for either of us. I mean, one of things which drew me to Gerry in the first place was that he didn't want kids. He never treated me like a freak for not having the desire to procreate. He was too busy feeling relieved. But then, you know, as time went on it started to creep in. I'd see a pram and think 'I want one' and at first I thought it was just because the pram was particularly stylish but then I started to see the babies in the prams and think 'I want one'. Something. A child of ours. Part of me. Part of him. And I realised that when I said I didn't want children, the truth was I hadn't wanted children. I could never see myself as a mother. Not until I met Gerry and I realised I didn't want just any child. I wanted *his* child. But he doesn't, you see. He's happy with things the way they are and, Annie, I don't think I'm going to be able to talk him round and that terrifies me. Because I can't imagine life without him or without our baby."

Of course I should have immediately been able to say something witty and reassuring and supportive and all those other things which sisters are supposed to do. But truth was, I didn't have a baldy notion what to say. The thought that my sister – my Darcy – could ever want to have kids was alien to me. She spent so much time mocking my Life Plan and my ideal of one of each sex that I just assumed she would always be the auntie and never the moaning mammy. Seeing her face, crumpled and filled with misery, everything made sense. What she was facing was just simply unthinkable. Whatever way she played it, she wasn't going to get what she wanted. My heart sank and at the same time broke just a little which left me feeling really quite sick to the stomach.

"Oh Darcy, why didn't you say? Why didn't you talk to me about this before?"

She shrugged her shoulders. "It only got bad recently. Until then I wrote it off as me being peri-menopausal or something – ya know, my biological clock having one last laugh before it stopped ticking. I thought it would go away and Gerry and I would be happy carrying on just as we were – but it didn't go away. It just got stronger till I was contemplating poking holes in condoms with a pin or flushing my pill down the toilet, like Fionn said. But I couldn't do it. I wouldn't do it. I didn't do it. I was just contemplating doing it. Gerry would have had a blue fit."

"And he's not for changing his mind?"

"The boy is not for turning," she said sadly. "I just can't believe that I may have to walk away from him. That we may have to split up because we can't work through this."

"Darcy, you're thirty-six. You have years left in you."

"It really doesn't feel like it. There is a part of me screaming out that I need to do this and I need to do it now. I know," she said with a wry smile, "you'd never have thought it of me, would you? Me that was always so bloody against breeding and was always happy with my life. God, I was such a smug cow when I met Gerry and realised he felt the same and I wouldn't have to explain to him that I was going against nature and had no desire to procreate."

"If you can change your mind, he can change his," I offered – not sure if I was saying the right thing and helping or saying exactly the wrong thing and making things worse.

"I wish I could believe that, but I know. In my heart, I know." She lay down again and sobbed and all I could do – bar saying the wrong thing again – was to lie down beside her and hug her while she sobbed. My heart hurt perhaps more than it had ever hurt before. I could deal with my own feck-ups, but to know that my sister was hurting and that there was nothing I could do – that killed.

"Have you spoken to Mum?" I asked eventually and Darcy spluttered loudly – a mixture of a big dirty cry and a raucous laugh.

"Now what exactly would that achieve? You know Mum – she'd have a blue fit if I so much as told her I was *considering* making her a granny – never mind if I told her I was thinking about leaving Gerry to do it."

I knew she was right of course. Mammy was not the person you turned to in a crisis. She generally *was* the crisis. I imagined that was where I got my own penchant for creating a crisis or two from – which made me think. If Mum was off bounds in a crisis and I was just as likely to be causing one myself, then who did Darcy turn to when she was feeling like the world was falling in on top of her? I guess I'd always assumed it was Gerry – but he was clearly not available for support on this issue. She must have felt so utterly alone.

"He doesn't want to lose me," she said eventually. "He said he loves me like he has never loved anyone else in his entire life but a deal is a deal and no matter how much he wants to, he can't change his mind. It's complicated."

"I wish there was something I could say," I offered.

"Don't worry. I know there is nothing."

I lay there with Darcy for another fifteen minutes or so and then she did a typical Darcy thing and stood up, straightening herself out and heading to the bathroom to freshen up her face.

"You go on through," she said. "I'll follow you when I've thought just how on earth I can apologise to Fionn for being such a godawful fucker."

I wondered how I would walk back into that room, back into

Gerry's company, and not immediately get an urge to knee him straight in the knackers. Or, alternatively, not drop to my knees and beg him to reconsider and impregnate my sister and make her happy again.

But I did it. I walked in and smiled and told him Darcy would be out in a minute. But he looked at me and he knew. He knew that I knew and he blushed a little while Fionn chatted on about the Westbury and how absolutely fabulous it was.

"Tell him, Annie. Tell him about the baths. Tell him how deep they are. And tell him about the beds and how big they are and the champagne and how –"

"Nice it is?" I finished and she nodded.

"I'm waffling, aren't I?" she said.

"Just a bit."

Gerry smiled. "It's okay. I know how you yokels like to be all impressed by the big city."

And I wanted to slap him – even though I was a self-confessed yokel – and tell him to stop being smug and laughing and having a bit of *craic* with me and my friend when he was being so utterly, utterly selfish with his sperm. Fecker.

And I hated that I was cross with him. Up until now I had really, really liked him. I mean, if I had to choose a brother-in-law (in a non-married way) out of a big catalogue I would have picked Gerry. Tall, but not too tall, with the kind of rugged good looks owned only by trendy Philosophy lecturers. Drunkenly I had once told Darcy that I thought Gerry had a very nice arse, which she had delighted in telling him and we couldn't look at each other straight in the face for several months after.

He was smart, funny, and, up till now, caring, and he had sparkly green eyes. I could understand why the majority of his undergrads had a crush on him and why Darcy loved him so much. But I couldn't really understand how, if he loved her as much as he said he did, he couldn't just give her the one thing that would make her happy. The fact that they had initially both agreed they didn't want it was neither here nor there.

I did a half-grin, half-grimace thing which I imagine was not at all attractive and I think he read the signs.

"I think I'll go out for a pint in Searsons," he said. "Sure you girls can join me in a while if you feel up to it."

"Sure thing," Fionn said with considerable enthusiasm.

But he looked at me – his eyes kind of pleading – and all I said was "We'll see" as if he were an errant child being promised a possible treat if he behaved. Which was ironic, really, given the circumstances.

He picked up his jacket and keys and said his goodbyes, while Fionn turned her gaze to the floor, increasingly aware something very, very bad was happening. When the door slammed she turned and asked me just what exactly was going on, and I was just about to launch into it when Darcy walked into the room, looking suitably abashed.

"Fionn," she said, "I'm not going to try and justify what happened. I'm sorry. I'm really sorry. I was a bitch from hell. I can't say more than that," and she burst into tears.

Fionn looked at me, more than a little alarmed. First she had seen Darcy shouting like a madwoman and now she was crying, equally like a madwoman.

"You can tell her," sobbed Darcy to me. "Sure you can tell everyone. It's no big deal. I'll be okay." But the look on her face said she was definitely not going to be okay.

25

Back at the Westbury I buried myself under the duvet of the gigantic bed and listened to Fionn gently snoring. I couldn't sleep – my head was buzzing. It certainly wasn't because the bed was uncomfortable or the room wasn't dark enough or all those usual distractions which would normally keep me awake. It was because I couldn't stop thinking of Darcy and trying to find a solution in my head.

We had stayed with her for two hours after Gerry had gone out and I had told Fionn exactly what had been going on.

"Annie knew there was a reason you were acting like such a godawful bitch," she said to Darcy and I felt myself tense. But my sister just nodded and gave a half-smile.

"If the shoe fits," she said. "I'm sorry. There isn't really an excuse but if you really want to know, Fionn, then, yes, I'm jealous of you and Alex and Emma and your readymade happy ending."

"Ah, but I'm the Wicked Stepmother and the Fairy Queen is waiting the wings. There is no guarantee at all that I'll have my happy ending."

"But you already have it," Darcy said, sitting down opposite us. "You and Alex. You want the same things."

Fionn sat there, silent for a moment. "You're right, and you're not right at the same time. It's more complicated than that."

"Isn't it always?" I sighed.

"Hey, don't you be getting all bitter on me, Mrs Happy Ending," Darcy said to me. "You *have* your Life Plan. You *know* what you want."

"Correction, I *had* a Life Plan and I *knew* what I wanted, Now, I haven't a clue."

"Oooh," Fionn said, sensing possible juicy gossip. "Tell me about the Life Plan? Did it involve celebrity chefs or hairy men or anything else intriguing?"

"It was laminated and everything," Darcy said, stifling a giggle while my face blazed.

Fionn looked incredulous. "Laminated?"

I nodded slowly. "I wanted to keep it good," and at that moment it sounded ridiculous to me too. I mean I was grown woman – in her thirties with a mortgage and a job (albeit one that was going to absolute hell at the moment) and all sorts of adult responsibilities like too much credit-card debt, a car with a slightly dodgy habit of breaking down when I absolutely needed it not to and perhaps too much of a fondness for white wine.

"Tell me about it? Do you still have it? Can I see it?" Fionn pleaded and I blushed harder as I explained how I had burned it in a fit of pique over my relationship breakdown with Pearse and my growing belief that I would end up on the shelf.

"And don't tell me that ending up on the shelf is okay and that I'm a modern woman who shouldn't worry about such things. Don't tell me that as a feminist I'm a damned disgrace to crave my day in a white frock and my big romance, because I don't actually care if that makes me weak or pathetic or just a sad oul' boot – I want it. I've always wanted it."

"Ending up on the shelf is okay," Fionn said while Darcy snorted, "but getting the big white dress is nice too. It's okay to want those things, you know. But," she added with a wicked grin, "I'm not so sure it is okay to make a book about it and laminate it."

"Oh feck off," I grimaced, but then I couldn't help but smile.

"I'd love to get married," Darcy said, glancing at me, no doubt checking my jaw for its inevitable dropping action.

Darcy had never wanted to get married. She took immense joy out of teasing our mother that she would always live in sin – even when she was eighty-seven. At the age of sixteen she had insisted that every single piece of mail which ever arrived at our house for her was addressed to Ms Darcy Delaney – none of your "Miss" nonsense for her. Mum just couldn't understand it, but Darcy would go into one about the repression of women and a bit of paper not being worth anything and how a wedding ring was as oppressive as if you had been branded with a red-hot poker.

So here she was, talking about getting married so I should have been shocked. But then, she had not that long ago told me how she also wanted to have children so I was, by this stage, far beyond shockable and I recovered quickly from her announcement.

"Would I be bridesmaid? If so, then I'm not wearing pink. Or peach. Just so as you know."

"I don't think there is much chance that you will get to be bridesmaid, because there is feck all chance I'll actually get to be a bride. But all I'm saying is that I would like it. I can see the appeal now. And it's not just about the big dress and the party – I like the idea of being someone's wife. Does that make me sound very 1950s?"

"Well, if you are then so am I," I said.

"And me too," Fionn added.

We sat in silence for a moment or two before Fionn looked at me again. "So the laminated Life Plan? Did it have pictures and everything?"

"Many many *Modern Bride* magazines died to make that Life Plan," Darcy replied with a snigger.

"Mock all you want," I said, "but both of you would kill to have a pictorial collection of the finest in bridal couture and don't you forget it."

It had been hard to leave. Part of me just wanted to creep back into her gorgeous spare room and sleep but she said she was going to try and talk to Gerry again when he came home and I figured it was best we stayed out of the way. Besides, I think Fionn would have actually cried real tears if she hadn't got to spend the night in the Westbury after spending a decent whack of Alex's money on the room.

I had hugged Darcy as we left, climbing into a taxi with Fionn assuring me she had enough euro to pay the fare and that she knew enough of Dublin to know if the driver went the long way round to try and rip us off. I probably hugged Darcy a little too tightly, but in the absence of having anything remotely useful to say I thought a hug was good as anything.

When we reached the hotel, Fionn coerced me into stopping in The Marble Bar for a cocktail before retiring to our room. I was pretty sure that my attire of jeans, flip-flops and swollen ankle was not typical of the clientele of the bar but Fionn told me we had to. We were on our holliers, after all, she said, and the cocktails were said to be fab. The bar, she said, was the thing of dreams and it was indeed exceptionally pretty. It was the kind of place Manna aspired to – classy art-deco-influenced interior and beautiful leather chairs which begged you to lounge across them while you sipped your cocktail and waggled your Manolo Blahniks on the end of your toes. Me? I crouched into a chair, trying to hide my fat ankles in my very non-designer flip-flops under me. The cocktail, did however, take the sting off the embarrassment and as I sat back, I tried to relax – but my mind was back with Darcy and Gerry and whatever was happening there.

At least, I thought, it took my mind off the fact that I still hadn't heard so much as a peep from Ant and that Pearse was sabotaging my career and that my ankle hurt like the bejaysus.

"Should we go shopping tomorrow?" Fionn asked and I shrugged. The thought of the fine boutiques and designer stores of the capital did give me a frisson of excitement – but the thought of hobbling around same with my sore ankle left me a little cold. Not to mention I just wanted to be with Darcy even though she was going to be at work and it would look very strange if I lumped along with her. I don't think – even though in my head I liked to think I looked seventeen – that I could pass for a work-experience intern. Besides, I knew feck all about fashion. I was a Primarni girl through and through, and while the thought of the boutiques excited me, I doubted I would spend much money. After all, I didn't have Alex's credit card to use and for some reason Pearse no longer let me use his.

"We'll see," I said, sipping my Cosmopolitan.

"Humph! That's what I say to Emma when she asks to do something I have absolutely no intention of letting her do."

"Yes, Best Mammy in the World."

Fionn's eyes misted over momentarily. "Do you think so? I mean really? God, just talking to Darcy tonight made me realise how lucky I am. Do you think, Annie, that Alex and I will be okay?"

"Apart from the credit-card bill? I'm pretty sure of it. We just have to find a way to deal with Rebecca."

"All I can do is be myself," she said determinedly. "Would it be bad if I phoned her now?"

"Rebecca?"

"No – Emma! I miss her. Although I would probably have to phone Rebecca to get through to her. Would that be bad?"

I looked at my watch. It was almost nine. There was every chance in the world that Emma would already be in bed and given that Fionn was on a rather potent cocktail it might not be the best way to try and win over Rebecca's affections.

"Leave it till tomorrow, darling."

"But I miss her. God, Annie. I love her so much. She's a right wee madam but I miss her all the same. And God, can I admit this, I'm jealous as fuck of Rebecca!"

I'm sure my eyebrow raised itself to a new height. What did Rebecca have that Fionn didn't? Fionn was the one getting ready to walk up the aisle with Alex, and Emma would live with them at least half the time. There was nothing at all to be jealous of, as I saw it.

"But why?"

"Because she gave him something I'll never be able to. His first child. Even if we do have kids, he'll have been there before. He'll have heard another woman tell him she's pregnant. He's already held someone's hair back as they threw up. He's rubbed a pregnant woman's back. He's held a hand as his child – his first child – was born and his life changed in that moment in a way I won't ever be able to change it. We might have children, but he is already a father. It's a bit of a 'been there and done that' situation."

"But he hasn't done it with *you*," I answered. "Surely it would be different."

"Emma is his number one. She always has been and she always will be."

"He'll love your children just as much, I promise."

She shrugged her shoulders before looking around to catch the attention of a handsome barman. "Enough of the doom and gloom," she said to me as he walked over. "More cocktails, please?"

He smiled back, telling us in a cheeky Dublin accent that he would be right with us.

Fionn looked around her. "Right," she said. "Let's see if we can spot any wannabe c'lebs and ask them if they need PR representation? We can go back to Bawb and become the toast of the office and Pearse and his wanky restaurant can go to hell!"

"Sounds like a plan," I said, clinking my glass against hers.

Back in the room, and back under the duvet I tossed and turned a bit more before drifting off into a thankfully dreamless sleep. It had been a strange day indeed. Darcy and Gerry were on the rocks. I was nearly killed. Fionn was jealous of Rebecca the Witch and I learned that two cocktails in a very swish bar could knock me three sheets to the wind.

26

Fionn was not to be appeased. She wanted to go shopping. And she wanted to do lots of shopping. She had already planned a route down Grafton Street and Henry Street and then a trip on the Luas to some of the finer out-of-town centres.

While I tried to squeeze my still swollen foot into a flat sneaker, she slipped her dainty little toes into a pair of impossibly high heels.

"Are you serious? You'll be murdered!"

"Fashion knows no pain," she said stoically. "If I'm going to swan into some posh boutiques I want them to think I mean business – even if I'm only window-shopping. Flat shoes do not say 'serious shopper with bags of money'."

"No, they say 'feck me, it's a long walk down that street and I almost got killed yesterday so I reserve the right to wear flats'!"

"Well, don't be getting all annoyed with me if they do a *Pretty Woman* on you and tell you they've nothing for the likes of you."

"I don't intend to visit anywhere fancier than H&M, so I'm sure me and my inferior trainers will do just fine."

"Even if I promised to treat us to something very fancy for lunch?"

"Sorry, Fionn, but I'm hoping to meet Darcy for lunch," I said, conscious of the fact I hadn't heard how she was doing. "And besides, we need to decide what we're doing, whether we're going back to hers for tonight or staying another night here."

"True. But I don't think my suitcase would go well with the fancy shoes as I traipse around the city. And I don't think we should be annoying Darcy just yet – or at least I shouldn't be annoying her anyway. I'm thinking I'll keep this room for at least tonight – you can stay here, or there, depending on how things are which means you absolutely can go shopping with me this morning *and* meet Darcy for lunch. Everyone's a winner."

I could tell that there was no way she was going to be dissuaded from her shopping plans and I figured it might well distract me from the worry. At that moment my phone beeped into life and my heart soared. It could well be that Darcy was texting to tell me everything was just okay with her and Gerry and things were going to be exactly how they should be.

But no, it was an unfamiliar number – a Southern one – and I wondered had it been sent to me in error.

"How are you today? Recovered from your brush with death?"

I stared at my phone, confused.

"What? What is it?" Fionn asked.

"A text. Not sure who from, but whoever it is knows about my brush with death yesterday."

It wasn't Darcy's number and I wasn't expecting a cheery text from Gerry any time in the next century.

Owen. It had to be Owen Reilly.

"Well, who did you tell about that?" Fionn wanted to know.

I texted the number back with a quick "Who is this?" message. It bleeped back "Owen".

"Owen," I said aloud.

"Owen?" Fionn echoed. "Who is Owen?"

"Erm, Owen . . . Owen Reilly . . . the man who saved me."

"He introduced himself to you?"

"Yes. Didn't I tell you?"

"I think I would remember if you told me about making the acquaintance of a handsome stranger."

"I didn't say he was handsome."

"But he is, isn't he?" she said with a wicked glint in her eyes.

"I suppose," I said, shrugging my shoulders "To be honest, I was too busy trying not to pass out with the pain, and shock, to really notice."

"You always notice," Fionn said. "It's one of the things I admire about you so. The ability to notice who is around and how they rate out of a ten, regardless of whatever else is going."

"Near-death experiences are an exception to that rule."

"Whatever," she said, flicking her hair and turning to face the mirror to touch up her make-up. "But tell me about him anyway. I need whatever details you have and I need them now."

"Well, he's Owen. He's a child psychologist – which means he works with children, not that he is some Dougie Howser type of character. He is quite strong – I mean he was able to knock me out of the way of the taxi and that's no mean feat. And he walked me back to the hotel to make sure I was fine."

"And now he's texting you. It's all so romantic."

I rolled my eyes. "To be honest, Fionn, I've had enough of romance."

"Pish!" she said emphatically. "I know all about you and your plans – your Life Plan, your dreams of a big white wedding. You can't tell me that you, Annie Delaney, are off romance – especially not when it charges into your life in a Superman style and literally sweeps you off your feet."

"There was no sweeping off feet. He actually bashed into me and knocked me down. And no romance. He helped me because he was there and he could. And he walked me back to this hotel because he is a gentleman. And, believe me, after Pearse and Ant, I'm done."

"Ant? I thought he was done a long time ago? Was he not simply a two-night wonder?"

I blushed, remembering how she didn't know about my afternoons in his bed at the beach and how I had kept that from her for some inexplicable reason – how I had kept from her the fact that he hadn't been at all bothered at my clearing off to Dublin and that it seemed, when I wasn't there to service his every whim, he really wasn't interested at all. In fact, of all the things I was sure Ant was interested in, romance was certainly *not* one of them.

And as for Owen – he was nothing. He was a nice man who was kind enough to enquire after me the day after my accident but that was all – a nice man, with a nice smile and nice manners who lived 200 miles away from my home and who I would most likely not see again – never mind run off into the sunset with.

"Ant? No. Well, yes. Well, actually, I don't want to talk about it just now. I thought he was more. But he wasn't."

"You can't just leave it at that."

"Yes, yes, I can."

"No. You want to know all the details of my relationship and Darcy's and you need to tell me about yours."

"It was hardly a relationship."

"But it was more than just two nights and some edible knickers?"

"A little – but not much. Not as much as I thought anyway. Look, Fionn, really. Do I have to go into this? You were right, it seems. He was using me for sex. And while I wanted to think it was something more and I suppose I hoped it would be in a way – even though he has a disgustingly hairy back – it's not. And that's done. Just like Pearse is done and just like Owen is just a nice man who didn't mind risking his life to knock me over. The only aisle I'll be walking up any time soon will be the one you walk up when I'm wearing my gorgeous dress and being the very best bridesmaid in the entire world. I burned the Life Plan for a reason, Fionn. Because it was bollocks. All of it. I was never going to get my perfect ending. Life doesn't work that way – Jesus, look at me now – five minutes from losing my job, relationship-less with a sister and a friend in the shit with their love lives. If you two – sensible heads that you are – can't get it right, then I have feck all chance. So that's that then. Discussion over."

"You should still text him back," she answered with a wink and I threw my phone across the room in a fit of pique before locking myself into the unbelievably gorgeous bathroom and saying more bad words than I had ever said before in my life. And it felt fucking good.

We were walking down Grafton Street when my phone (rescued from under the gorgeous bed in the gorgeous hotel room) beeped to life again.

"Taking the rest of the day off. I need you," Darcy had written and I felt my heart sink again.

I showed it to Fionn.

"Darcy?"

"Yep."

"I need to go, alone," I said and she nodded.

"Okay, I'll shop on and I'll see you whenever. You know where I'll be – spending up a storm. There are a few wedding boutiques I feel the need to visit."

Her words were light but she looked as emotional as I felt. We knew that chances were Darcy and Gerry had not come to some happy conclusion overnight. I hugged her tightly and limped off in the direction of a taxi rank to find a cab to take me to Waterloo Road (I had now memorised the address) and I didn't even care if he took me the long way round or overcharged me. Darcy was worth it. Suddenly I was glad my own life was in the shitter and that I had come to Dublin to get my head sorted. At least, for once, I could be there for Darcy when she needed me although what the feck I was going to say to make her feel better was beyond me.

I felt slightly sick as we wound through the busy Dublin streets, veering in and out of the bus lane and dodging cyclists, while I watched the taxi-meter clock up the fare at a shocking rate.

I was not looking forward to this. Not one bit.

27

"Gerry is moving out," Darcy said in a very matter-of-fact manner as she switched on the kettle and sat two cups on the worktop. "So I'm going to have to get a room-mate. I think one of the younger girls at work might be interested. I mean, it's a great location, isn't it? And our – my – spare room is lovely. Just no way I could pay the rent on my own."

I didn't know what to say, so I said nothing – just stared at the teacups and tried to still the thumping of my heart.

"I'm going to go to work tomorrow, even though it's a Saturday. I'll find something to do. He's picking up his stuff then. Best I'm out of his way. But I'm hiding all my favourite CDs and DVDs tonight – there's no way he's taking those. I might pack up some of his books. Feck knows he has enough of them. Still, I'll be able to fill the bookcases with photos and trinkets like I always wanted. Waste of the good floor-to-ceiling cases, if you ask me, all those books in them. He's staying with his mother tonight. So, you know, you are welcome here."

"I'll be here," I said.

"It's no Westbury," she said with a half-smirk and poured the hot water into the cups before dunking some teabags into them.

"The Westbury can wait," I said.

"Grand job. You can help me pack then. Feck knows I'm useless at it. I'd break something, no doubt. But best I sort through his clothes. I mean, wouldn't want you handling his smalls."

She was being very, very jovial about it all, but she wasn't making eye contact which meant that really she was just about holding it together. It was going to come crashing in around her soon and I knew that I absolutely had to be there when it did, even though the very thought of it scared the absolute shite out of me.

"I've no biscuits," she said, opening one of the shaker-style cupboards and lifting out a packet of Ryvita. "Will this do? Don't suppose it will, really. I mean, who eats Ryvita with their tea? Even if you put something nice on it, it's still not a good dunker, is it? I mean, I should have got some chocolate biscuits in when I knew you were coming. Come to think of it, I asked Gerry to pick some up on his way home from the college on Tuesday night and he didn't bother. He must have forgotten."

"Darcy," I said softly, as she stared into the cupboard and back again at the Ryvita.

"I fucking hate Ryvita," she said.

"Darce . . ."

"Seriously. I always buy it, but I never eat it. Well, I eat one or two pieces and then it sits in the cupboard till it goes soggy and I throw it out and then I buy some more and the cycle repeats itself. You'd have thought I'd have learned by now. You'd have thought I had more sense, wouldn't you?" She was still staring into the cupboard and her voice was starting to break. "I could go to the shop. In fact, I will go to the shop and get some nice biscuits and sure you sit there. It's only down the street."

"Darcy, I'll be fine without biscuits. Honest."

"No," she said, turning to face me, her foundation streaked with her tears. "How can you say you'll be fine without biscuits? You need a biscuit with your tea for the love of God! Everyone needs a biscuit. I need a fecking biscuit!" She was half-shouting by this time and I knew – in a rather proudly perceptive way – that she was not talking about fecking biscuits any more.

I stood up and walked to her and put my arms around her and hugged her as the sobs racked her body.

"I'm sorry," I said.

"It's not you who's run out of biscuits," she answered and all I could do was nod, although in fairness my biscuit barrel (metaphorical or not) was as empty as Darcy's right now.

Darcy had gone to wash her face and I carried our teacups into the living room and sat them on the chunky whitewashed table in the middle of the room, between the two facing chocolate leather sofas. I looked at the majestically gorgeous white marble fireplace and at the picture of Darcy and Gerry at the centre of it. He was standing behind her, his arms wrapped around her while she looked up at him. They were both laughing in the picture – it was gorgeous, like an advertisement for what love should be like. It was then I realised that the old song was right: sometimes love just wasn't enough.

Darcy walked into the room and sat down opposite me, pulling a fluffy cushion onto her knee and taking a deep breath.

"It wasn't horrible. Well, it was horrible. He cried. I cried. But it wasn't angry. I told him how much I loved him but that I didn't want to start hating him and that I was sorry I had changed."

"And what did he say?"

"He said he was sorry I had changed too and sorry that he didn't feel he could. Kids had never, ever been on his radar and he said he loved me too much to end up hating me. It's kind of crappy really – we're splitting up because we love each other too much and we don't want to hurt each other. But it still hurts."

"Of course it does."

She ran her fingers through her hair, twisting it and turning it in the way she always had done when she was nervous and on edge.

"Am I mad, Annie? Should I just have kept going?"

"Would it have been any easier to break up three weeks down the line, or three months, or three years?"

She shook her head. "But it's hardly easy now."

"Is it definitely over? I know that's a shitty question to ask but, you know, is this it?" I suppose part of me just couldn't start to fathom that they were actually done, even though I had seen the hysterical falling-out for myself.

"Yes," she said. "Oh arse. Annie. Can you believe it? What am I going to do without him?"

It was one of those questions that I simply could not answer, even though my usual response would be to try and say something witty to lift the mood. I guessed that would not be appreciated just then.

"And now I have to find a man to have a baby with, when the truth is I'm not even sure I want one any more. I mean, it wasn't just that I wanted a baby – I wanted *his* baby. I wanted us to be a family. I wanted me to be the mammy – and a nice, maternal one – and him to be the daddy. And we would have been great parents."

She sipped from her tea and I could see the confusion etched across her face as if the events of the last twenty-four hours kept repeating on her, hitting her with a new wave of shock every time. Twenty-four hours ago she had been part of a loving, long-term relationship. She had got up in the morning and kissed her partner and cooked his breakfast and then she had dressed for work in their joint bedroom before making the bed and even fluffing his pillow. He had packed her something for her break at work and kissed her on the forehead as he left. She had phoned him, just like she always did, between lectures mid-morning, and they had laughed and planned what they would do that weekend. And they had been together – and even though of course she knew there were underlying problems in their relationship and one big problem had recently reared its head – she had reasonably believed that they would still be together twenty-four hours later.

But something had changed and then everything changed and now Darcy was planning an ad in the paper for a room-mate and thinking about packing up her old life into cardboard boxes.

"Will you stay here?" I asked.

"In this flat? Long-term? Not sure. Depends on whether or not I can get a lodger or cope with sharing with a near stranger."

"No, in Dublin? Will you stay in Dublin? Would you come home?"

Darcy smiled. "Annie, pet, this is home to me. I didn't come here to be with Gerry – and him leaving, us breaking up, won't be the reason I leave. My life is here – my work, my friends, my flat. What would I do back up North? Derry isn't actually famed for leading the way in the fashion industry and I'm experienced in buck-all else. And besides I would go off my head back up there – I'd miss the rush of the city, the noise, the nightlife."

"If you change your mind, you can come and stay with me," I offered and she laughed.

"And risk our mammoth rows again? I don't think so, darling, but thanks anyway for the offer. It's very kind of you, but us Delaney women are made of strong stuff and I'll be fine here, honest."

She sniffed and sat back before declaring she was off for a soak in the bath. That was her stress relief – an hour in the bath, soaking in the bubbles – and I figured that, even while she didn't want to be alone, she needed some time to herself.

"I'll cook some dinner while you soak."

"I'm not hungry," she said.

"You will be, in a while. I'll just make something to tide us over. Anything you need, honey, just shout."

"Thanks," she said and sloped off to run the taps and even though she ran them at full power I could still hear her sobs echo around the gorgeous high ceilings of her flat.

Looking at my watch, I saw it had gone six and realised Fionn would be wondering where I was. Lifting my phone I called her and waited for her answer. As she picked up I could hear the chatter of the Marble Bar in the background. She answered cheerily.

"Hey, doll, how are things?" she asked.

"Not so good," I replied. "I'm going to stay here."

"I thought you might," she said.

"You don't mind?"

"Course not. You need to be there for Darcy and, besides, I have some news of my own."

Although I knew she was concerned for my sister, I also could hear the excitement in her voice.

"What is it? Found something delicious and wedding-y in one of the boutiques? Survived a day on your heels? Won the Lotto? Bumped into Colin Farrell in Stephen's Green?"

She laughed, a deep throaty laugh. "Who needs Colin Farrell when I have my very own hunk driving down the M1 right now to spend a night with me in the Westbury? I hope you don't mind but I just knew you wouldn't be back and, well, he is paying for it. And he said he couldn't wait any longer to see me and I thought that since he *is* paying for the room – and indeed for the disgustingly sexy underwear I bought today – he might as well have the benefit of it. I figured you need time alone with Darcy now without me ploughing in and no doubt saying the wrong thing so Alex is going to drive me back up North tomorrow and we are going to sort this whole situation out once and for all."

She sounded hopeful and happy and filled with excitement and that cheered me up. Lord knows we all needed some cheering-up just now.

"I'll send your bag round in a taxi, and I'll even pay the fare," she went on. "You just take it easy and come back when you can and you know where I am if you need me at all – for anything."

"Except for later tonight when you'll be indulging in all sorts of make-up sex?"

I could practically feel her blush down the phone line.

"Well, maybe. Actually, I really hope so. I've ordered some champagne for our room and I'm determined to make the most of that gorgeous bath."

"Too much information, my sweet," I said before telling her I was delighted for her really.

"And Darcy – is she okay?"

I shrugged. "You know Darcy. She gets her practical head on so she is being very matter of fact but she is hurting. A lot."

"Give her my love," Fionn said and we said our goodbyes.

So here I was, back in the gorgeous flat at Waterloo Road,

feeling about as much use as a chocolate fireguard – although the thought of all that deliciously melty chocolate was actually quite appealing right now. This was a crisis, after all.

So I took my life in my hands – and my purse with my collection of unfamiliar notes and coins – and headed to the shop. This called for emergency supplies – wine, chocolate, carbohydrates galore in whatever form I could find them. There was no way we were going to start sorting through Darcy's love life without these essential supplies – not a fecking chance. Oh and tissues, we would need some tissues even though Darcy was anal about such things and always had a supply. It would have been utterly remiss of me as a sister and friend not to stand in the Eurospar counting out my coins, like a five-year-old learning to count, so that I could buy tissues in a crisis.

As I walked back, laden down with shopping, I felt my ankle ache and I thought of Owen and the text he had sent that morning. I should really reply, I thought. After all, he had saved my life. But not tonight – tonight had to be all about helping Darcy – that and trying not to think about what exactly Fionn would be getting up to in that hotel room.

When I got back to the flat Darcy had dressed in a T-shirt and Capri pants. Her hair was pulled back off her flawless face and I felt a momentary pang of jealousy. She could even do "heartbroken and devastated" with grace.

"We'll just sort through some photos and the like. He can do the rest tomorrow," she said.

I waved the bag of goodies in her face. "I brought supplies," I offered.

"There isn't enough wine or chocolate in the world," she replied, lifting the bottle out and taking it to the kitchen to get two glasses.

"You don't have to do this, you know."

"What, drink? I'm pretty sure that, of all the things I have to do right now, drinking is right up there on the list."

"No, sort things out. There's no rush."

"But it needs doing, and we might as well start. I could put it off but it won't fix things. Me sitting here and moping won't make him decide that he was wrong after all and actually he does really, really want to have children with me."

I shrugged. She was right of course and maybe it was me who was putting it off. Lord knows I didn't do relationship break-up well. I had ended up back in bed with Pearse, with him thinking we were destined for a permanent reconciliation and I kept ending up in bed with Ant even though I doubted his motives were entirely honourable. In fact, I was shite at making a clean break and I didn't really understand how anyone could do it. I was a clinger-on-er. I think I had watched too many romantic comedies in my time. I truly believed that, even when the leading man had exited stage left and the heroine was sobbing in her bed, it could still all turn around and be okay. I had real issues separating that from real life. Maybe I did need therapising after all? Although unless I was able to express those feelings through crayoned drawings and playing with dolls, it was unlikely Owen Reilly was going to be able to help me. And besides, I didn't want him to help me. I wanted to sort this out in my own head for once. I mean, if Darcy could be all grown up and just get on with things, then wasn't it about time that I did the same? I mentally made myself up another, very compact Life Plan: cop myself on and get my life in order.

First, however, I would have to help Darcy.

Gerry was a keen photographer and it seemed that he had snapped almost every moment of their time together. There were shots of him, shots of her, shots of them both. There were shots of the flat – looking more than a little seventies-tastic when they moved in before they had a chance to make it their own. There were pictures of stunning Italian sunsets and African sunrises. There was a picture of a sleeping Darcy, slumbering under a mosquito net, her hair wild on the pillow and her skin dewy as if her skin naturally secreted Clarins Beauty Flash Balm. She was wearing a plain white camisole and the cotton sheets were ruffled around her. That picture

– the moment frozen in time – said everything to me that there was to say about love. And it made me cry. Darcy handed me a tissue, refuelled my wineglass and assured me it would be fine.

My mission to help her was failing miserably.

"Do you remember when we were little and Mammy and Daddy used to dance around the living room?"

"God, yes, I thought they were the best dancers in the world."

"And Mammy was the best singer?"

"Christ, yes. I thought she was better than Madonna. Less slutty of course, but better all the same."

Darcy laughed. "I used to be jealous of them, in a way."

"Don't be getting all Freudian on me," I cringed.

"Not in that way, for God's sake! They just seemed so happy and all they needed was each other. Do you think they ever really needed or wanted us?"

"I'm pretty sure they loved us. They still do. You'll always be Daddy's Girl, Darce. But did they need us? I'm not sure."

"I miss them. Ya know. At times like these. I wish Daddy was here to get all enraged and threaten to knock Gerry's block off. I even miss Mum and her annoying little ways. She would be out researching sperm-banks and buying turkey-basters and telling me it was all for the best."

"Do you think it is? All for the best, I mean? I can go and buy you a turkey-baster if you really feel the need?"

"I don't know, pet, if it's for the best. But it's happened and that is that. All done and dusted."

She looked down at the pile of photographs placed in a file-box and closed the lid – but not before I noticed she had taken the picture of her sleeping in some African boudoir and slipped it into the pocket of her trousers.

I woke in the early hours, as the sun rose over Dublin, and walked into the kitchen. Darcy was still sleeping. She had cried herself to sleep and I had stayed beside her in her bed in case she woke – but now I got up and did what all good Derry ones do in a crisis: tidied. I loaded the dishwasher with the remains of the day before and brushed the floors. I pulled open the large sash windows in the living room to allow the cool morning air in and I made myself a cup of tea.

Sitting on the sofa I lifted my phone and tapped out a message. "My ankle is getting better. Thanks for asking – and thanks for helping" and I pressed *Send*.

Then I picked up my phone – and against all better judgement – typed out another message. "I miss you. Do you miss me?" and also pressed *Send*.

The cavalry arrived shortly after nine. A procession of exceptionally fashionable girls – and a few men who looked like girls – traipsed into the flat on Waterloo Road and hugged Darcy in a very solemn fashion before taking over the kitchen and making some fancy egg dish with Bucks Fizz.

Contrary to her previous belief, Darcy would not be going to work today. Work had come to her and they were going on an emergency team-building trip to the pub – just as soon as it was a respectable hour to swan in and get hammered.

I felt a little like a spare piece – not to mention I felt woefully underdressed. Even though I was in my best River Island skinny jeans with a funky floral top from Monsoon (via eBay), I still looked like I had fallen off the table at a jumble sale in comparison to the assembled fashionistas. It was slightly mortifying – I might as well have had some straw sticking out of pockets and a sunhat with the word "*Doofus*" written across it in big letters.

Darcy introduced me to various people with exotic and interesting names – some of which I was sure were made up and to a man named Dermot (I was pretty sure *he* hadn't made his name up) who was as flamboyant as any of the women in the room.

I smiled back and declared, without invitation, that I worked in

PR – just so that they knew that under my vanilla exterior I did actually have quite a trendy job. I offered to put the kettle on, but they pooh-poohed the very notion.

"We have fizz. That's needed more on occasions such as these," someone called Summer told me.

So I stood back and watched them swarm around my sister, soothing and chatting and hugging and shaking their heads. She didn't tell them, of course, the reason behind the break-up. She just told them there had been irreconcilable differences which she figured they could interpret in whatever way they saw fit. They tried though – Summer and Dermot and some people with names I could barely pronounce, never mind spell. But I knew she would never tell them. All the same she lapped up the sympathy and while to my yokel eyes it at first seemed a bit OTT and insincere, it was clear that Darcy felt at home with these people. And while their dress, their mannerisms and their very names were impressively exuberant, they did at least seem to care about her. No wonder she felt at home here. If you're going to have anyone nurse you through a crisis, it might as well be exceptionally hip and happening young folks.

I walked through the living room and sat on the sofa, my eye glancing at the mantelpiece where the picture of Darcy and Gerry used to stand. Used to. It had been moved. I wondered had Darcy packed it away with the picture of her sleeping in Africa – and a small sob caught in my throat.

"Are you coming? Say you're coming?" Darcy called in to me as I brushed my tears away and painted on a smile.

"Where?"

"To the pub? Come on, it will be fun. Honest."

"I think I would stick out like a sore thumb."

"Don't be ridiculous."

"I'm not. Honest, Darcy, you go with your friends. I'll hang out here for a while and when Gerry arrives I'll go for a walk or something."

She looked at me incredulously. "You? Go for a walk in Dublin? Now that is funny!"

"I can walk," I said defiantly. "Look, Darcy, you go and be with your friends. Maybe I'll join you later?"

She gave me a look which begged me to reassure her I would be okay and I stood up to hug her.

"Sure what do I know about fashion anyway? And no doubt you will talk shop and I'll be there embarrassing you with tales about my bargains from Dunnes Stores and Tesco."

She smiled and kissed me on the cheek. "Be good. And be careful. And don't do anything stupid like knee Gerry in the bollocks or the like."

I nodded, but little did she know that I had already done something stupid. The text messages I had sent earlier remained simply sent – no replies, no phone calls, no reassurances that I was missed.

I didn't mind so much with Owen. He wasn't important to me. But, well, with Ant it was different. Not that he was important to me, but I kind of wanted to believe that he could have been. I had wanted to prove Fionn wrong – that his gift of flowers (ignoring the edible knickers) had been born out of some genuine sense of affection. I had wanted to think that the hours spent in his arms in his house at the beach meant more than just mind-blowing sex. A wee small part of me had wanted it to work more than I had ever wanted anything to work. Because then he wouldn't have been just another mistake and I could have believed that I was worth more than just a fuck buddy.

And I suppose I had wanted something of the last few weeks to have been salvageable although maybe I would have contented myself with the salvageable thing being Fionn and Alex's relationship. I should really text her but there was still an hour to check out and I was pretty sure she would be making use of her time in the hotel fully. The fact that she had not called or texted me in a fluster led me to feel fairly sure things were okay for her. At least that was something.

I slipped on a cardigan and lifted my bag. My ankle felt okay so I figured I could risk a walk. I would have to be brave some time and I really didn't fancy running into Gerry so I set off walking, only stopping once every five minutes to check if I had missed a call or a message on my phone.

I had walked and window-shopped for ninety-three minutes and was rewarding myself with a coffee and a Danish when my phone did actually beep to life. And it was from Ant. He had responded! My heart leapt and I clicked open the message, bracing myself for some flirty or dirty reply about just how much he missed me and what he wanted to do to me when we were reunited.

"Annie, sorry if you thought this was more than it is. I thought we were just having fun. I'm not ready for romance or a commitment but any time you feel those gorgeous urges of yours then please get in touch."

Even though nobody but me could see the text message, even though no one but me could feel the rise of heat and shame on my neck, I felt more exposed than I ever had done. I had played with fire and I had got burned. I should have known Ant wasn't the type – he never pretended to be – so I shouldn't have been surprised or disappointed. But I was – and I was humiliated beyond words and, unlike Darcy with her harem of oddly named friends, I had no one to turn to. Fionn was off with Alex. Mum and Dad where a million miles away (or so it felt) and that was really about it in my list of people I could call on in an emergency.

What would I tell them anyway? That I had fallen into the bed of an exceptionally hairy and well-endowed Donegal man on several occasions and it turns out he was just going along for the ride and nothing more?

I left my Danish untouched and picked up my coffee, then walked towards the park where I vowed to find a big shady tree to sit under and drown my sorrows with a latte, a good book and a sinking sense of failure.

Although in fairness my sense of failure had now sunk so low it was virtually impossible to see how it could sink any further without actually ending up in Australia. In fact, if I was robbed now, or hit by a car or just the victim of some random self-combustion type of event it would probably be the perfect end to a perfectly shitty few weeks.

Of course I was never going to allow myself to have those "urges" Ant spoke of again – not with him anyway. In fact, it crossed my mind to go back to find Darcy and tell her we could both forsake men for life and a buy a baby from the internet and raise it together. We could be Derry's answer to the *Golden Girls* only we were not so much golden as a bit turd-coloured at the moment. Still, it could work. Us and our weird non-lesbian relationship. Just two sisters, with a shared child who could call her "Mum" and me "Mammy" so no one would get confused. And any time anyone with a penis came within five foot of us we could shout – or just show them our T-shirts which would be embossed *I'm single. I'm sad. Get used to it.*

Except we wouldn't be sad because we would have no feckwitted men getting on our wick and Darcy would have her child and I would no longer find myself in this repeatedly humiliating position. And Alex could supply us with new sofas every couple of years so we didn't come across as completely man-hating – although of course we would be – and wouldn't that all be grand?

I was in the middle of contemplating just exactly how much it would cost to buy a brand new baby – as opposed to a toddler or an older child in a Madonna style – when my phone peeped to life again.

"No problem," Owen wrote and it took me a split second to realise he was referring to my earlier text and not to my plan to buy a child. (He was a child psychologist after all. He had to have an excess of children in his presence at any one time.)

No problem. Not a fizz. Easy for him to do. To save people. From death. And walk them to nice hotels. Like he did that every day. Then again, he probably did. Beneath that suit there was probably a Superman-style costume and a secret aversion to Kryptonite. For a split second (there were a lot of split seconds that day) I hated him – just for being lovely and life-saving, because I knew just like every other man I had ever met in my entire life there was no doubt some underlying level of bastarditis I was heretofore unaware of and which would undoubtedly come to the fore just when I least wanted it to.

I muttered "No problem" to myself in a very childish and whiny voice and then laughed at myself before realising my behaviour was most probably making me look like a complete mentalist. Taking a deep breath, then sitting back and drinking my latte, I decided today was the first day of the rest of my life, which of course I realised sounded particularly wanky. But feck it. If I couldn't do wanky when my life was in the toilet, then when could I?

By mid-afternoon I was hungry and tired and wondering if it was safe to go back to Darcy's. I decided to head for the very same coffee shop Owen had taken me to after my near-death experience and grab a sandwich. What I didn't expect, however, was to see Superman himself striding towards the self-same coffee shop in search of a cappuccino.

I hid my head behind my magazine, but I stilled feared my swollen ankle would give me away. Although I would be the first to admit that random strangers in random coffee houses in Dublin generally don't look at people's ankles first of all.

I heard him order. I watched him smile. A little part of me wanted to get up and reach out and stroke his arm, or something equally weird. But I didn't. I just hid behind my magazine until he turned and walked away with his coffee and even though there was a part of me that wondered if I had done the right thing, there was a bigger part of me that was deeply proud of not throwing myself headlong at another stranger.

Yes, Darcy and I would be just fine in our spinsterhood.

I wandered around for another hour before making my way back to Waterloo Road, reasoning that Gerry was most likely to have gone by then. However, my reasoning was once again up the left and when I opened the door he was there, walking towards me carrying what looked like a very heavy box of books.

I should have offered to help. I knew that, but it felt that if I did I would be betraying my sister so I didn't. I just nodded in his direction and he tried to shrug his shoulders, but failed under the weight of the box.

"I'm sorry about this, Annie," he said.

"You don't have to apologise to me," I said coldly and walked past him into the kitchen where I poured myself a long, cool glass of water.

I heard him put the box down and follow me.

"Any chance I could get a drink too?" he asked and it felt very weird that he was asking me if he could have a drink in what was still his own flat and his own kitchen – and out of one of his own glasses.

"Help yourself," I said, stepping out of his way and watching him reach for a glass. I noticed his hand was shaking slightly. He stood back, sipped from the glass and looked at me.

"I never wanted it to end this way, you know. I didn't really want it to end at all."

"I know," I said.

"How's Darcy?" he asked, not looking me in the face.

"Probably as you would expect her to be. Bit of a mess. Trying to keep it together."

He sighed, and rubbed the bridge of his nose. "How did it come to this, Annie?"

But I knew he didn't need or want me to answer. There was no point.

"I love her so much, you do know that?"

I nodded.

"Can I talk to you?"

"Sure isn't that what you're doing?" I said sourly.

Much as I tried to stay neutral, and tried to realise that leaving must be as painful for him as it was for Darcy, I couldn't hide my disdain. He was hurting my sister and, regardless of his reasons, that made me want to hurt him. Sure he had never stood before a church and promised to love and cherish forever, but as far as I had been concerned he was my brother-in-law all the same and I had trusted him not to fuck this up and yet here he was – fucking things up.

"I want you to understand."

I shrugged.

"No," he said, "I need you understand. Otherwise you'll just think I'm some godawful gobshite and, while I will admit to a degree of gobshitedness, you need to know the full facts."

"I know what Darcy has told me – that's enough."

"But it's not," he said, his face etched with pain. "Don't you realise, we – that's both of us – never wanted kids? I never expected Darcy to change her mind. How could I? She changed, not me."

"But people do change. No one is the same person they were five years ago. Can you say you've never changed?"

"Not when it comes to whether or not to be a dad, Annie. I can't do this because I don't want to make the same mistakes my own father did. Not that, to be fair, I know too much about him. But he messed up so badly I never want to risk doing that to any child of mine. I know the damage that causes. I feel it every day."

I stood, open-mouthed, unsure what to say. Here Gerry was, pouring his heart out to me while I stood giving him bad looks in his own living room. Surely this was a situation where he could at least sit down and yet he stood, awkwardly swaying from foot to foot, unable even to look me in the eye.

"I can't take the risk. I can't risk bringing a child into this world and it all going horribly wrong and then my child ending up with no da like me. I've only met him twice since he left, you know. Once when he lumped in drunk after my Confirmation and asked me for a loan of money and once when he sat at the back of one of my lectures and started roaring and shouting about me being an ungrateful bastard halfway through. I'm not sure what I was supposed to be ungrateful for to this day . . . but . . ."

He sighed, looking so broken I felt embarrassed.

"Does Darcy know this?" If she did, she should have told me. Gerry was right: it made a difference to know where he was coming from.

"She does and she says I'm a different man to him, but who knows, Annie? I couldn't make that call. Children change things."

"You *are* a different man," I said softly and he shrugged.

"I can't take the risk," he said sadly. "No matter what, I can't take the risk."

He placed his glass in the sink and gave me a weak smile before going back to lift the impossibly heavy box. But this time I helped him carry it out to his car and I even hugged him when we got there. It didn't feel like a betrayal then and there. Gerry had been a part of my family for a long time and I felt genuinely sad that it hadn't worked out and that I probably would never see him again.

"Take care, Gerry," I said.

"You take care of my girl, okay?" he asked and I nodded.

And then he left and I went back to the flat to wait for Darcy's return which I knew would be deeply horrible indeed.

The phone rang just before six. I stared at it for a bit, wondering if I should answer it. Conceivably it could be someone for Gerry who didn't know that he didn't live there any more and I wouldn't want to have to try and explain what had happened. It could also be someone for Darcy who might be enquiring how she was and the truth was I didn't really know. It made me realise how little I actually knew about my sister's day-to-day life – who she knew, what she confided in them. Did they know she had wanted a baby? Did they know her relationship had been in trouble? I looked at the phone and bit my lip. Whoever it was wasn't giving up easy. Lifting the handset, I offered a fairly weak hello.

"Darcy," Mum's voice started and momentarily I was floored.

My mother's voice. I hadn't heard it in ages.

"Mum." It was hardly deep and meaningful but I was fighting the urge to tell her I really, really needed her.

"Thank God you're in. I tried to get you earlier in the week. Dad and I aren't coming back this year, Darcy. We've decided to go to Mexico for Christmas. I know you were hoping we could come back and meet that man of yours and maybe go up to Derry but we got a great deal. And Dad has always wanted to see Mexico, so I know you won't mind."

I listened to her ramble on. There was a part of me that was gutted that she hadn't instantly recognised my voice when I had called her "Mum". Surely it is a mammy's job to recognise the voice of their child – even if we spoke less frequently than I spoke to my bank manager. I wanted to jump in and tell her it was me but, as I listened to her put her once-in-a-lifetime cheap package holiday to Mexico ahead of Darcy and ahead of me, I just couldn't bring myself to do it.

"You don't mind, do you, Darcy?"

She sounded a bit like a child looking for reassurance and I realised she had been like this for a long time. And Darcy and I – well, Darcy mostly – had been picking up the pieces for a long time.

"No," I said. "Not at all."

Four words. Surely it would have been enough for her to catch on to the fact I wasn't actually Darcy after all. It wasn't. Her voice brightened and she signed off . . . there was a jug of sangria with her name on it or something. And that was it, Mum was gone. Our first conversation in three months had lasted one minute and thirty-four seconds and she had mistaken me for my sister. All in all, as conversations with my mother went, this one had been a success.

Dermot and Summer carried Darcy into the flat at gone seven. She was still conscious and still had some make-up on her face which had not washed down to her knees. However, she crumpled when she saw the slightly emptier flat and I held her while Dermot brewed a pot of coffee.

"Did you see him?" she asked.

"Yes."

"And how was he?" She had the same pathetic look on her face that he'd had on his.

"Okay, considering," I answered, not sure whether it was the right thing to say or not. I could have told her about his shaking hands, but it would have made her feel awful – but somehow I think me telling her he was okay also made her feel awful. Maybe I just had to accept that there was frig all I could say in that moment that would make her feel better.

"Did he mention me?"

"Yes, he did. He said I was to take care of you."

And that prompted a fresh flurry of tears – so full on that I wondered if she would actually become dehydrated.

"She was okay in the bar," Summer offered. "She even wanted to start a sing-song. Life and soul of the party. We thought she was coping remarkably well."

Summer looked a little shocked, and a little scared. She was obviously used to seeing Darcy cool and in control.

"She's just a little tired and emotional," I soothed.

"*Hellooooo!*" Darcy yelled. "I'm in the room. Don't talk about me as if I'm not in the room. I am very much in the blasted room and hearing everything you say. I am not 'tired and emotional', I'm pissed and single and wondering if I have made the biggest mistake of my entire goddamn life!" She waved her hand around for emphasis, narrowly missing knocking a large lamp from her side table.

Summer looked scared – as if Darcy could start waving her hands in her direction soon and narrowly missing her. She looked at Dermot as he carried the coffee cups into the room with a pleading expression on her face which screamed: *"I'm a fashion intern. Get me out of here."*

"Maybe you should go. I'll take over from here," I offered and both Dermot and Summer were out of the door before I could say, "No, honestly. We'll be grand. You go on."

By this stage Darcy was lying across the sofa, a cushion over her face and her legs splayed on the arm of the settee.

"Annie. Tell me I did the right thing. Tell me it won't always hurt. Tell me that I'll get over it and be fine and not turn into a mad bitter oul' doll who shouts at couples snogging in the street and tells them they are dirty wee shites."

"You did the right thing."

"And the rest . . ." she waved her hand. "The not hurting? And the not shouting? And the not being bitter?"

"All that, Darcy. I promise."

"I feel sick," she said. "The room is spinning."

"I'll get some water. You get to bed."

"'Kay", she muttered as I left but when I came back she was already asleep on the sofa and it was the sleep of the deeply drunk. I pulled a blanket from her bed and tucked it around her, leaving a basin beside her and a pint glass of water and then I went into the spare room, opened the windows wide and listened to the sound of Dublin in the evening and the snoring of my very drunken sister.

I curled up, and lifted my book and my phone and pretended to read the first, while wondering who on earth to phone with the second. Scrolling through my address book, I stopped at Fionn's number and hit the call button. It rang three times before she answered, sounding deliriously happy if a little tired – from the journey back to Derry and the bedroom antics before and after.

"Hey, babes," she said cheerily and it was lovely to hear someone sound happy. It felt as if it had been one very long day of depressing news, and overwrought emotional interactions and it was just the loveliest noise in the world to hear my friend say "Hey, babes!" in a cheery tone.

"Hey, yourself. I'm guessing by the obvious joy in your voice that things between you and Alex are on the mend?"

"Well and truly. The wedding is very much back on so you will get to wear that gorgeous dress after all and I'll get to wear the pink shoes."

"Well, that is just about the best thing I've heard all day."

"And you want to know what else?

"What?"

"He doesn't even mind about the credit-card bill. Well, not that much anyway."

"That's great, darling. Honestly. It's brilliant."

"I know! But tell me, how are you? How is Darcy?"

"Me? I'm fine – well, I will be fine. Darcy? She's passed out on the sofa. She'll be fine too though. I know it."

"Give her a hug from me," she said, her voice soft and compassionate.

"I will do. And give Alex a hug from me – and Emma too."

"Oh, I haven't stopped squishing her since we got back."

She told me how Emma had thrown herself into her arms when she and Alex arrived at Rebecca's to pick her up. Rebecca had looked a little put out, which in her good mood Fionn had understood. She actually felt sorry for Rebecca, she said – well, a little bit anyway.

And now she was at home, back off the Naughty Step and she and Alex were working out the seating plan for their big do. All was right with the world.

"I'm so glad to hear it," I said honestly, before saying my goodbyes and hanging up. I lay back on the bed, sighed and realised that I felt utterly alone.

Must. Not. Text. Pearse. Or Ant. Or Owen.

So I closed my eyes and tried my damnedest to drift off to sleep, even though it was stupidly early and I wasn't in the slightest bit tired.

In my dream I was standing in Stephen's Green on a balmy evening. Everything was gorgeously green and silent except for the gentle hush of the wind through the trees. I felt scared – exposed – and alone. And then he was there. And he walked towards me and smiled and I smiled back, even though I wasn't sure what his motives were or what he could want from me. He reached his hand to my face, gently grazing my lips with his thumb before gently pulling me towards him and kissing me softly and gently with more love than I had ever felt in my life. He didn't talk. He just breathed deeply in a way that said he adored me and everything about me. I felt my heart soar as his lips softly moved against my own and I felt content, and safe and sure that it was all going to be okay. Then he walked away and I woke – my heart sore because no one had ever kissed me or loved me like that in real life.

Darcy was green – actually really green – around the face the following morning. I found her, still prone on the sofa, when I got up to get a glass of water shortly before seven.

"Have I been here all night?" she asked. "I don't remember coming home. Shit, did I make an arse of myself?"

"No," I lied. "You were fine."

"I need water."

"There's some on the floor, but I'll get you a fresh glass, and maybe some paracetamol?"

"Yes, please," she moaned, sitting up. "That sofa was clearly not made for sleeping on."

I walked back in and handed her the water and some tablets and told her to go to bed for a proper sleep.

She padded off to the bedroom and I settled on the sofa, ready for another long day trying to amuse myself on the scary big streets of Dublin. Figuring that it was still too early for the majority of pickpockets to be up and about, I decided to go for a run while planning to stop off to pick up some croissants on the way back.

The only way to get out of this crappy mood was to run around until I felt like I might vomit and then gorge on baked goods.

So I set off slowly – forgetting that there had always been a fatal flaw in my plan. My sore ankle didn't want to go for a run. In fact, it protested quite loudly at the very notion of doing anything more strenuous than a gentle stroll. Of course, had this been some Hollywood romantic comedy, this would have been exactly the moment – as I stretched over to rub my swollen ankle – that Owen Reilly would have appeared as if from nowhere and commented on coincidences and fate and other such things.

Part of me wanted to believe in Hollywood happy endings, so I glanced around me hoping for a glimpse of him on his way out to get another fix of coffee. But the streets were quiet, so I limped towards the shop and then back to Darcy's flat, feeling really rather sorry for myself.

Boiling the kettle, I made a cup of tea and buttered a croissant while waiting for Darcy to wake. When she did, she seemed like a new woman.

"Right, moping over. I'm just going to have to get on with it, aren't I?"

"Go easy on yourself, petal, but I'm glad you're feeling better."

"Grand job," she said, pouring herself a glass of orange juice. "So what time do you want me to leave you to the bus station?"

Bus station? There was no way I was going anywhere near any buses any time soon – not when Darcy was so emotionally fragile. Although looking at her shoving half a croissant into her face and declaring it delicious, she looked pretty stable to me.

"I was planning on staying."

"But don't you have to be back at work, Annie? Tomorrow's Monday and I'm pretty sure that boss of yours won't be impressed if you don't show up."

It was then that it hit me. The whole spinster plan didn't need to be set in Derry. I could be just as much of a spinster in the Big Smoke as I could in Derry. And I'm sure I could find a job down here – there had to be more chance of a new job in PR in Dublin than in Derry. There wasn't much for me up in the North anyway – an oddly shaped flat, Fionn of course – but no Pearse, no Ant, no good contracts in work.

"I could stay. Here. I could be your new room-mate. You need someone, don't you?"

"Now, Annie, I love you with all my heart. But no. I'll be fine and you need to go home."

"This could be home."

"No, it couldn't. It's not you – the big city and the way things are. And it never would be you. You are just trying to run away from your problems."

"No," I was adamant. "I want to be here to help you, Darcy. And, yes, well, life isn't perfect up North so a fresh start could do me – could do us – the world of good."

"But it wouldn't be a fresh start. We know we can't live together, Annie. We would fall out in no time. And you know that things are just tough back home for you right now but you have to face it head on because if you don't you will be letting Pee-Arse win."

And I realised I would be letting Ant win too. And Bob. More than that I would be letting myself down. Darcy was right – and not for the first time.

"But I don't want to leave you."

"Jesus, Annie, it's only a few miles up the road. I'll be there if you need me and vice versa and I will be fine. Sure don't I have Summer and Dermot looking out for me down here? And you – my lovely sister – will be fine too. You are going to go back up there and you are going to kick some ass and show the world that you can't keep a Delaney down. Do you hear me?"

I nodded as she clinked her glass against my cup.

"That's the girl!"

I decided then and there I would leave telling her about the plan for us to be spinsters raising our bought baby for another day. For now I had to prepare myself for the trek back to Derry and walking into an office where everyone would know my personal business and I would be left dealing with some utterly shitey account while one of my colleagues gloated about the Manna deal. The most exciting thing on my books was Love, Sex and Magic but there is only so much coverage you get for lubricants and nipple-clamps in the Northern Irish media. Believe me, I'd tried.

The big goodbye at Bus Áras wasn't as absolutely horrendous as it might have been. Darcy had given me a hug and told me that I was not, under any circumstances whatsoever, to cry or she would kill me. So I sniffed a bit and stifled my emotions until the bus was pulling out of the city centre and even then I only let out the eeniest of squeaks in case Darcy and her bat ears could still hear me. I was going to miss her, and I was going to worry about her. There was nothing that was going to change that.

29

There was a strange comfort in walking back into my flat – even though it was a pigsty in comparison to the luxury of Waterloo Road. My things were all where they should be. My fridge was still comfortingly understocked. The windows still rattled just that little bit when the breeze hit them and the toilet was still much too far from the bathroom door. There might not have been a hint of a high ceiling, or a marble fireplace or a gorgeous twisted metal light-fitting but that was okay for now.

I lifted the phone to call Darcy just to let her know I was back safe and sound and then I called Fionn to let her know that I would be at work the next day. Both sounded okay. Both said they would talk to me the next day. So I unpacked, loaded the washing machine, made my umpteenth cup of tea of the day, and climbed into bed for an early night. Glancing at my bedside table, I saw the card which Ant had sent with his saucy gift and I ripped it up into impossibly small pieces before throwing it in the wastepaper basket and laughing – just a little maniacally – to myself.

I made it into work early. I figured if I was already there when people arrived it would give them less time to talk about me. So, as my colleagues arrived, I was at my desk, scanning through my client portfolio and wondering how on earth I was going retain even an ounce of dignity. Aside from the sex shop, there was, of course, Haven Cosmetics, a very self-important photographer, a swish clothing boutique which was overpriced and under-stocked, and a handful of wannabes who rarely contacted us for any PR campaigns because they were completely broke. I would have to pull something else out of the bag – and quickly – if I was to continue to justify my position at NorthStar. Without Manna and the rising star that was Pearse to work with, my portfolio looked distinctly lacklustre.

Fionn arrived on time – smiling broadly. She passed by my desk to check I was okay and said she just couldn't wait for our FSB so she could fill me in on the latest developments.

Bob was next in the door. He smiled – just a little one – in my direction before declaring to the room that we would all touch base at ten for a staff meeting and we would see where we could move on from there to get the Star in NorthStar up and shining again. He finished this with a wink and a weird finger-pointy thing and walked on.

It was comforting at least to know that Bob was still 'Bawb'. Much as I had appreciated his compassion the previous week, it had unnerved me. He might be an eejit but a part of me liked him that way.

I caught up with a few emails, had a quick and cheeky look on Facebook and then lifted my prop lighter and headed outside to meet with Fionn.

"Well?" I said, leaning against the side of the smoking shelter.

"Well, everything is going to be fine. Alex and Rebecca talked. She's keeping Emma the week of our honeymoon. And she didn't even complain. Can you believe it?"

A big part of me couldn't. But I didn't say so because I wasn't in the mood for piddling on her parade. Of all the things I knew about Rebecca, I knew for certain it was highly unlikely that she hadn't complained. I guessed Alex had doctored some of the previous night's events to appease Fionn a little, which was okay, I suppose. I certainly wasn't going to go running after him to check anyway. I had learned my lesson.

I smiled and nodded, despite my doubts.

"Oh, I know it's probably not going to be completely plain sailing from now on, but I think he might be over this commitment-phobia thing. Last night he said he couldn't wait to marry me."

"That's good, darling," I smiled.

"I can't wait to marry him either. We are sending the invites out at the weekend. I know I'm ridiculously late with them but they had to be perfect. Do you think we should still invite Darcy? Would it be shitty and insensitive for her to get a wedding invite when she has just broken up with Gerry?"

"What I think is that it would be shitty and insensitive if you *didn't* invite her. You know what Darcy is like. She's a strong woman – she's hurting but she'll be fine and if we all start trying to wrap her in cotton wool she will turn angry and, believe me, you would not like her when she is angry."

"Oh I know. Don't tell me you've forgotten I locked horns with her recently. But, what about you anyway? You doing okay?"

"I'm crapping myself about Bob's team meeting, and I'm feeling a little ego-bruised but I'm fine."

"Did you text him back?"

"Bob? Pearse?"

"No, yer man. The lifesaver."

"Owen?"

Fionn rolled her eyes. "Well, you know, I've forgotten his name – but, yes, if you say 'Owen' I imagine that's the boy all right unless someone else saved your life recently."

I could see Fionn's matchmaking antennae were twitching like mad twitchy antennae-like things.

"I did. I thanked him. And that's it."

"That's horribly disappointing," she said, pulling a horribly disappointed face, so I decided not to tell her how I had seen him outside a coffee shop and hidden behind a magazine. She would not have been impressed.

We gathered in the boardroom at ten on the dot. Bob would not have accepted a minute before or a minute after. I painted on my best smile (with the aid of some heavy-duty lip gloss) and carried a notebook brimming with ideas (or at least looking as though it were brimming with ideas). I tried not to notice the sympathetic looks from my colleagues who obviously knew I had been shafted royally the week before. Instead I looked straight ahead, chin up and tits out, as Darcy would have told me.

"Hey, everyone. Nice to start another week with you all by my side – and to have you all smiling! Great." The charm offensive began. "We want to keep those smiles up all week – especially when you lot are out and about interfacing with clients or talking to the press. We need whatever coverage, whatever deals and whatever money you can bring our way. We all know times are tough and last week was a scary one for NorthStar. Almost losing two of our biggest clients was a kick in the teeth, but thankfully Elise has pulled us back from the edge."

I felt my face burn. So I had taken NorthStar to the edge, had I? And Elise had pulled it back with *my* clients, had she?

"But this is certainly no time for complacency. We'll put last week behind us and move onwards and upwards. Now, folks, what have we all planned? Annie – how is the Haven Lip Gloss campaign going? Will you call around the media this morning and check that they got their samples and see if they are going to run anything?"

The samples. Shite. The samples. A horrible, horrible sinking feeling crept right up through my body from the very nails on my toes to the split-ends of my hair. I nodded to Bob while trying to crane my neck to see out of the door of his office to the vicinity of my desk where I hoped against hope that the big brown box of perfectly presented samples of lip gloss, complete with press releases and kisses from my very own mouth, was not there. I prayed that I had simply forgotten that I had sent them and that it was not the case that I actually hadn't sent them. Straining my neck until my muscles starting to ache, I spotted a trace of brown cardboard and I felt any and all resolve I had start to crumble.

"Haven are really keen that the coverage is in as soon as possible, so let me know by noon how you are getting on," Bob said and I felt an actual cold sweat break out all over my body. Until that moment I don't think I ever really knew what a cold sweat was – but there it was. All cold and sweaty and I felt as if I might actually throw up right then and there. Fionn glanced at me and instantly recognised the look of horror on my face.

"Are you okay?" she mouthed and I kind of nodded and shook my head at the same time and then gasped about needing air and stumbled out of the office.

Yes, the brown box was at my desk as indeed were the press releases that should have been with the country's media already. And there was no way they were going to get there anytime soon – I could hand-deliver the local ones – but the rest of them? Shit. Unless the Tardis was real and was available for hire, I was buggered. I felt the air leave my lungs. Bob might have been considerate and understanding the previous week but there was no way he was going to understand this. This was not understandable. And it was bad enough I had almost lost two of the company's biggest clients the previous week – now I was on course for a hat trick.

I kicked the box out of sight and lifted the bottle of water from my desk and took a long drink to try and settle myself. When that didn't work, I stepped outside to get a breath of fresh air, only to be confronted on the back steps by a concerned-looking Fionn and even more concerned-looking Bob.

"Is something up?" he asked.

I thought about lying for a split second. It would have been relatively easy to lie but he would find out some time and I figured that honesty was the best policy – or at least in this instance the lesser of two evils. I had a notion that fecking up would be bad enough, never mind fecking up and then lying about it. I was skating on thin ice as it was – not coming clean would have been career suicide. Admitting my mistake was more like a gentle career mercy-killing.

"The samples. I didn't send them. I'm sorry. They are all there, ready to go. I kissed all the press releases. I packed them in envelopes with heart-shaped confetti and tissue paper and everything. They look really good. They just didn't get posted. I'm sorry."

Bob looked at me and looked at Fionn and threw his hands skyward. "Annie, how many chances do you want? Haven are going to go mental when they hear this. The products are launching on Thursday and you are telling me not a single beauty editor or journalist has the press release?"

"I'll sort it," I said weakly.

"How, Annie? How on earth are you going to sort this? This should have been out last week at the very latest. There are only so many times I can cover your back."

"I know, I know," I said as Fionn looked on aghast.

"I'll get a courier – get them out as soon as possible."

"A courier is not in the budget," he said matter of factly.

"I'll take the hit. Take it out of my wages," I offered, mentally working out that if I didn't eat, drive or wear any clean clothes for the next month I could just about cover it.

"That's not the point, Annie. Jane from Haven will be on the phone to me later and what am I supposed to tell her? I know things are tough for you at the moment but they are tough for everyone. But I don't see the rest of my staff come in here and make balls-up after balls-up. I let the Manna thing go, because you know I figured your personal life was your own business and that Pearse was a wanker anyway – but this. Annie. I can't let it go."

"I know," I said even more weakly.

"Bob . . ." Fionn started, but he raised his hand in a very clear sign that she was to say no more.

"Go home. You're suspended until I work this out. And we will be getting a courier and it will be coming out of your pay packet and while you are at it, you can draft a letter of apology to Jane."

"I will," I nodded.

"Don't think this is over, Annie. I'll have to talk this through with HR. For now just go."

"I'll just grab my bag."

"No. Stay out of the office. Fionn will get your bag. Just go, Annie. I'll be in touch." He was somewhere between apoplectic with anger and simply at the end of his tether with me and I couldn't blame him. I would boot me out too. I would do worse than suspend me. I would sack me. And I couldn't quite believe that he hadn't dismissed me then and there, on the spot. My fight, I realised, had well and truly gone. All I needed now was the roof to fall in on my flat, or my car to get stolen and my life would be just fecking perfect.

Was it really only a matter of a few weeks before that my life – while not amazing – had at least been in control? I'd been in a relationship. I'd been good at my job. I had been not at all sullied by a hairy Donegal man. Darcy had been with Gerry and all had been right with the world.

I nodded at Bob because I couldn't speak.

Fionn reached towards my arm, but I shrugged her away. "I'm okay," I lied. "I'm absolutely okay."

I went for a walk along the beach. This was probably – if not definitely – another one of my Very Bad Ideas. It was meant to clear my head and stop me from going home and contemplating jumping out the window – but it didn't. In fact it just made me stand, staring at the familiar window of a familiar house and wondering if the fact that there was a car on the driveway meant that he was inside.

It wasn't that I had any urges – at least not *those* kinds of urges anyway. That said, an hour or two lost in someone else could take away my attention from myself and the mess I was in. Even if Ant did not want to marry me, or even love me, I knew that he wanted me in a very different kind of way and that felt nice. I needed someone to want me even if ultimately that wanting would be exceptionally self-destructive.

I looked up at the window and imagined him there – lying on the bed, all hairy and masculine and powerful. I knew that if I went and knocked on his door he could make me forget all about everything. Damn it, when I was with Ant there were times when I wasn't even able to remember my own name, or what day it was or who was the President of the United States or anything. Those were fine moments.

I stared for a few minutes more and walked on, faster and faster along the beach and out of sight of his house, telling myself that if I still felt the urge to do something reckless by the time I had walked the length of the beach and back I would march up to his front door and let him do whatever the hell he wanted with me. And I wouldn't care. Not one bit.

I strode on, the warm sun beating down on my neck. Around me families, with kids on school holidays and cool-boxes filled with egg-and-onion sandwiches, laughed and joked. It struck me that children don't give a damn about the freezing cold water off Inishowen beaches. It also struck me that those parents – those ones shouting like mad people at their children to calm down and not throw jellyfish at each other – had exactly what I wanted. They had what I wanted and Fionn wanted and Darcy wanted. But none of us had it and I wondered if we were bad people in some way. Having that – a family, a car to take you to the beach and a cool-box with egg-and-onion sandwiches – was all we wanted and yet we didn't have it. None of us. What a fecking big lie we had been told when we were promised it all and told those fairy tales over and over again, as if it was our destiny as women to meet our perfect men and run off into the sunset. I'm willing to bet Cinderella never found herself suspended from her job and marching up and down a beach to stop herself sleeping with the wrong man just to take her mind off her cesspit of a life.

I slumped to the sand, kicked off my shoes and let the warm grains envelop my toes. I glanced up and could see those families having their fun day out and I wanted *my* fun day out.

But at least I knew then that I would never find it with Ant. The answer to what was wrong in my life did not lie in his arms, and certainly not in his bed. And no matter how appealing the view from that room over the coast was, it would absolutely, no doubt about it, be the very worst thing I could do at that time. So I ignored the car on the driveway, and the open windows and the general gorgeousness of it all and got back into my car and drove as far from that beach as I could. Which was in fact back to my own house as I had to conserve all my money and energy, being that there was a very high possibility that I would be jobless and perhaps even homeless soon enough.

As I wandered around the flat, I was struck with a whole new love for it. Yes, of course I was being overly dramatic and definitely over-emotional but now, thinking that if Bob decided my job really was a thing of the past I could lose it altogether, I suddenly didn't mind all the quirks. In fact, I loved them. I no longer coveted Darcy's apartment (well, not that much, anyway). I just wanted my own. And my job. And my car. And my life – back the way it was. Except, of course, not really the way it was because I hadn't been happy with Pearse. I reminded myself of that as I poured an emergency glass of wine and climbed to the roof terrace to look out over the city.

It was still work time for the vast majority of gainfully employed – not suspended – people and I looked out at the roofs of their offices and homes and thought about how everyone else in the world was just getting on with things while I seemed to be stumbling from one disaster to another.

I texted Fionn just to ask if Bob had indeed organised a courier and I asked her to email the press list and vowed that I would personally call them all and let them know something special was on the way. I would also send Bob a very grovelling email to apologise profusely and without reservation for my mistake. After that I would probably drink myself into oblivion – but not before deleting Ant's details from my phone in case of drunken moments of weakness.

Climbing back down to the living room I fired up the laptop, lifted my phone and set to work. I might not be able to save this situation entirely but I would go down trying.

By five thirty I had phoned every journalist in my PR list and smarmed them with my best PR smarmy voice. I had talked up the new Haven Lip Gloss to make it sound as impressive as the cure for cancer, an infallible way to predict the lotto numbers and a magic weight-loss tool all at once. All that and it came in a range of colours and trends to suit every mood, every outfit and every woman. I didn't stop until the Haven lip glosses were the most highly anticipated cosmetic product of the year and I had been promised extensive coverage in beauty pages the length and the breadth of the country. I had even managed to persuade one very minor celeb to be seen slapping it on outside a nightclub that week when the paparazzi were sure to be about. She had promised to pout like a good 'un and I had promised to send her enough lip gloss to keep her gob shining for the next three years.

The email to Bob had been more difficult to write. I wanted to get across just how very sorry I was, without selling my soul into the bargain. I wanted it to get to the point without crossing over into the style Bob himself liked to use. I could do creeping to make up for my misdemeanours but what I could not, and would not, do was sink to using clichés and metaphors and other such waffle. I told him I had messed up. I apologised. I explained just how much of a mess my head had been in lately and why – leaving out the details of my interlude with Ant. I stressed to him that I loved my job. I was good at my job and I would be even better at it if he could just overlook this one last transgression. I hoped that was good enough, because if it wasn't I didn't quite know what the hell I was going to do with my life.

I sat back and topped up my glass, looking out the window and letting the gentle breeze wash over me. My head hurt. A tight band of pressure wrapped around my temples, making me feel as if my eyes were just about ready to pop out of their sockets.

I didn't want to think, even for one second, that things could only get better from here on in because that was a sure-fire way of ensuring that they would only get worse. Sod's Law seemed to see me as a walking, breathing example of itself at the moment.

Nonetheless the mad and foolish notion took me to phone my mother. I wasn't going to tell her just how shit things were – it would only confirm her worst suspicions about me – but I wanted to hear her voice and I wanted her to actually know she was talking to me this time.

I listened to the ringing tone of the phone – the one long beep which indicated I was calling overseas. I could imagine her now – laid out like Lady Muck on her sun lounger slathered in Factor Four, her cursory nod to sun safety. She'd be wearing a bikini more suited to a nineteen-year-old and a colourful scarf woven into a turban on her head. She would lift the phone from where it rested always within hand's grasp and answer as she always did.

"*Hola!*"

"Mum," I said. "How are you?"

"Darcy, is that you?"

"No, Mum, it's Annie."

"Oh Annie, darling. How are you? Is anything wrong? Sorry to ask but it tends to be the case that when you call something is wrong."

"No," I lied, "I just wanted to say hello."

"Well, hello, darling. Tell me, have you thought about getting rid of that wee flat of yours yet? Only Dad and I are talking about selling the house and wondered if you would want to buy it? I mean, if you had the deposit and all."

"No, Mum. I'm still here."

"Suit yourself," she sniffed and I wanted to sniff back that my flat was actually lovely but that would start an argument and I was all done with arguing for today.

"Oh, Mum, I love you," I said, and I meant it.

"And I love you too, darling," she said and my heart felt as if it had broken in even smaller pieces than before.

When I put the phone down, leaving the email to Bob unsent for now, I walked to the sofa where I lay down, adopting my very best woe-is-me pose – but not before unplugging the phone and switching off my mobile. If I was going to wallow in self-pity then I sure as hell was going to wallow in style. If I'd had the energy I would have got up and pulled the curtains closed so that I could wallow in darkness. I might even have been tempted to go and put my pyjamas on and maybe my old, fluffy, worn-out dressing gown and go into proper wallow mode. There might even have been a Radiohead CD lurking somewhere I could have listened to. If I had the energy. But I didn't. I didn't have the energy for anything other than low-level wallowing. In fact, by the way I was feeling just then and there, I didn't think I would ever have the energy to lift my head off the sofa cushions again. I could quite happily have just stayed there, forever, until I died and the stench of my rotting body crept downstairs to my neighbours. It would be an awful tragedy and Bob would be sorry – especially when they found the unsent email to him on my laptop. In fairness, with the copious amounts of apologies and details of just how shite my life had been of late it read a little like a suicide note. Could you actually manage to die through apathy and nothing else? Although if I never got off this sofa again it would probably be the starvation and dehydration which would do it. I would make a lovely skeleton.

Swigging the last of my wine, I stared at the ceiling and listened to the traffic on the streets below before pulling the throw from the back of the sofa and pulling it up over my face to block out the light. I was asleep in seconds.

30

It took a while for me to register just what exactly was going on. I startled, somewhere between being awake and sound asleep, as the buzzing noise grew louder. It was dark. I was disorientated. There was a greatly unattractive puddle of drool on the cushion where I had been lying. Sitting up, I knocked the empty wine bottle over and struggled to find the light-switch for my table-lamp.

The buzzing just grew worse and more insistent and I put my hands over my ears. My head, I realised, was thumping and my mouth was like a furry boot. I couldn't figure out what was happening or where the noise was coming from and I just wanted it to stop. Rubbing my eyes and focusing on the room around me, it dawned on me that the buzzer was my doorbell and whoever it was buzzing like a mad person was certainly not intending to go away anytime soon.

I got up and lifted the handset. I muttered a muffled hello and was greeted with a semi-hysterical Fionn on the other end.

"Jesus, Annie. Are you okay? Let me in!"

I didn't answer – my brain still not engaged enough to say anything remotely intelligible – but I pressed the door-release button before stumbling to my impossibly large bathroom and splashing water on my face. Looking up into the mirror I saw a trainwreck of smeared mascara and bed-head staring back at me. My face looked just about as crash-hot as my life felt.

I was just towelling myself off when Fionn burst through the bathroom door, a look of abject panic on her face. Behind traipsed a somewhat worried-looking Alex.

"I couldn't get a hold of you," she said breathlessly. "We couldn't get you. I've been trying your phone all afternoon. And your mobile all evening. And I sent emails and I even phoned Darcy but no one knew where you were and you were strangely calm when you left work and believe me, Annie, I know when it comes to you, strangely calm is never good. Are you okay?"

I must have looked a little puzzled. Fionn looked as if she might throw up. Alex looked more than a little embarrassed by the whole female, over-the-top hysteria unfolding before his eyes.

"I'm fine," I said, even though my make-up streaked face and bird's-nest hair said different. "I'm a little hungover, perhaps, but it's nothing I can't handle."

"But where have you been?" Her voice was several octaves above its normal level. In fact it was so high that "been" came out as a mere squeak.

"Here," I said, matter of factly. "And the beach. I went for a walk. And then I came here and worked. Called all the media contacts. Sorted things out. Didn't you get my text about the courier?"

She shook her head. "Do you think I would have been running around the country like a fecking eejit if I had a text from you?"

"But I sent it. I sent it early afternoon. Or at least I'm sure I did." I lifted my phone to check the message wasn't still stuck in my outbox, but of course it was switched off.

"Well, I didn't bloody get it. And you didn't answer your phone. And your mobile went straight to your voicemail."

"I had a sleep. And a wee drink," I said, nodding towards the living-room floor where my wine bottle was upended. "I needed to drown my sorrows. It's not every day that you finally cross that line between life being just a wee bit shit to life being a complete and utter balls-up."

I heard a mild snort from Alex and Fionn turned and gave him perhaps the filthiest look I had ever had the misfortune to see.

"What?" he protested. "It's not like it's something new for Annie to mess up. It's one of the things we like so much about her."

"Don't you bloody start," I started, feeling my hackles rise. "We can't all be bloody perfect, you know."

"No one in this room is saying they are perfect, Annie," he said, "but trouble does seem to follow you around."

I wanted to be angry. I wanted to maybe slap him across the face or tell him to get out of my flat or just stick my tongue out at him or something equally childish – but the man had a point. It was as if someone somewhere was selling maps to a little town called Trouble and those maps pointed directly at my big fat face.

I looked at him. He looked more than a little scared of what Fionn and I might do next. Then I looked at Fionn, her face taut and pale with worry, before glancing back in the mirror and seeing my own – exceptionally dishevelled – face stare back at me. I tried not to. I really did. But it was either that or cry and I figured a big laugh was better than a big cry any day of the week. So I laughed like a crazy, crazy lady until Alex looked absolutely terrified and Fionn looked exceptionally confused.

"You're right," I managed. "You are right. My life is a disaster and it's all of my own making. I seem to have a self-destruct button that apparently I'm not one bit afraid to use. Oh God, I'm a bloody disaster, aren't I?" I held my ribs as the pain of laughing so hard I thought my lungs were about to come out through my nose took over. Sliding to the bathroom floor, my body shuddered first with laughter and then – perhaps inevitably – with tears. If I had thought Alex looked scared at the hysterical laughing, it was nothing compared to the look of abject horror on his face when I started sobbing.

"I think I'll wait in the other room," he said. "Or maybe in the car. Actually, I'll just go home and, Fionn, call me when you want picking up. I'll come get you."

Fionn looked at him, stricken, but nodded while I watched it all unfold as if it were happening to someone else rather than me.

When he had left, she sat down on the floor beside me and pulled me into a hug.

"You do know it's going to be okay, don't you?" she said.

I shrugged then shook my head, then nodded just to complete the triple whammy. Sniffing very loudly, I told her I didn't know if I knew anything any more. Except that my life was in the toilet – both literally and metaphorically. That one thought made me laugh again, then cry and then declare to Fionn that I truly believed I was having some sort of a breakdown.

"I'm making a pot of tea. You have a shower and then we'll talk."

I nodded, and did exactly what I was told to, because I didn't have the strength to do anything else. That and I needed a shower.

When I was clean and my hair was brushed, Fionn placed a cup of tea in my hands and sat down beside me.

"Right, lady. We do not leave this room until you are sorted out. We do not leave until we know what we are going to do to make it all better and we do not leave this room until you have a whole new, non-laminated Life Plan."

"What if I need to pee?" I said churlishly.

She rolled her eyes. "Then you go pee, but don't think I won't follow you. That's not meant to sound creepy in any way but you aren't going to disappear into that lovely bathroom of yours for ages on end just to escape."

"I'll pee in record time," I promised.

"Good woman yourself! Now – tell me about it."

"Well, I suppose when you think about it, it all comes down to egg-and-onion sandwiches . . ."

It wasn't as hard as I thought it was going to be to tell her about Ant – and the extent of what we had got up to. Sure I left out some of the more salacious details but she got the gist. I had slept with him. Several times. I had even allowed myself to believe it was something more than that – which of course it wasn't. I had allowed him and other things to distract me from actually getting on with my life – from moving on from Pearse, from resurrecting my career. In some ways I had even let him distract me from helping Fionn and being there for Darcy. Even when they were going through the worst of times, my ear was always straining to hear if my phone was beeping to life or wondering just what present might arrive next. I had been, as a woman and a feminist, officially horrified at the present of the edible undies – but as a woman and a hot-blooded creature I had also been turned on by it. I had felt desired. I had felt alive and it had been a long time since I had felt that way. I certainly hadn't felt alive in the last few months of my relationship with Pearse and I had got into such a rut with work that I had stumbled from day to day, not really giving My All to either. But I had given My All – physically at least – to Ant. He had made me feel as if I was perhaps able to do anything and I had invested so much in him without even realising.

Him dumping me – even though technically I didn't think we were ever in a position to be dumped as such – had shocked me more than I cared to let on.

I had tried to hold it together but my core was shaken. Sobbing, I told Fionn how everything that had happened in the last few weeks had shaken me. From her falling out with Alex, to Darcy and Gerry breaking up, to me losing the contracts at work.

"Oh Annie," she said, pulling me in to her for a hug, "it's not as bad as you think it is, you know. It's all fixable. Look at Alex and me – we're back together. We're getting there. Darcy, she'll be fine. And work – it will be fine too. You said yourself Bob is a soft touch at heart."

"But I really messed up, Fionn. Like, big time. I don't think I could have messed up more if I tried."

"Oh, I don't know," Fionn said with a half-smile and I managed to smile weakly in return.

"Oh, I know. I could. At the moment anything is possible. I'm sure someone is listening somewhere and testing me on all this. Just when I think I'm okay to do anything – just when I think I'm getting things back on track – something else goes spectacularly wrong."

"But you said yourself you are working to sort it all. You said yourself you worked all afternoon. Try and focus on that, not on anything negative. I'm all for positive thinking."

I sniffed. "I suppose you're right."

"Of course I'm right. We've been in worse pickles than this in the past."

"Does anyone actually use the phrase 'worse pickles than this' any more?" I said with a smile.

"Yes. I do. And I'm not afraid to either," she said.

"Well, regardless, I'm not sure if we have been in worse pickles than this."

"What about the time we went to check the air in your tyre?" she asked, eyebrow raised, and I snorted at the memory.

If there had ever been an incident which proved the supposedly outdated theory that women and cars did not mix, then that was it. We had gone, feeling very empowered and in control, to check the air of my tyres – except somehow I had managed to deflate the tyre entirely and we had stood looking at each other with a creeping sense of horror as we couldn't get the darned thing to reinflate. In the end we had to beg a favour from the (admittedly hunky) garage assistant who had looked at us as though we were completely cracked. Which of course we were. We were suitably embarrassed and stood – only the heat from our faces keeping us warm – for the fifteen minutes it took him to change the tyre because, of course, we didn't have blasted notion how to do it ourselves. And we had to go back to work but there was no way we could do that with oil all over our nicely cut suit trousers.

When it came to pickles that had been a big one.

Admittedly nothing about it would have resulted in the loss of my job, or my apartment or my ability to find a happy ending with the perfect man. But it was a pickle all the same.

"It will be okay, won't it?" I asked pleadingly.

"Of course it will, darling. Of course it will."

Fionn went home later, after she had encouraged me to press *Send* on the email to Bob and had tucked me into bed. I was, and always would be, eternally grateful that she had sat with me until I actually physically could not cry any more. She had even managed to make me laugh several times. To top it all off, she had made me a cup of hot chocolate and agreed that when I was feeling up to it she would help me make a very hairy voodoo doll of Ant and do weird and wonderful things to it. Of course we probably never would – because my anger at him wasn't actually all that strong – but it felt all girlpower-y and pro-active to be thinking of actually doing something again.

I wasn't sure that I would sleep, given that I had spent a great portion of the afternoon and early evening drooling on the sofa but I needn't have worried. I was out like a light and woke only when the first rays of the new sun started to stream through the bedroom window, gently warming the side of my bed where one day – I had to believe – my special someone would lie.

A watched inbox never pings. That much was true. I knew that Bob would have read my email first thing. He always checked his mail as soon as he walked into the office. You could set your watch by him. So I had switched my laptop on just after nine and opened my email and sat there and waited, my eyes almost crossing over with the strain of staring so hard at the screen. So I waited. And waited. And the waited some more. Then I got up and went to the loo to see if stepping away from the screen would will a reply into my box. It didn't. So I tried something a little longer – like walking to the corner shop for a packet of Hobnobs. I almost bounded up the stairs on my return, sure that by now (10.45 a.m.) Bob would have certainly replied. But he hadn't. Nor had he left any messages on my voice mail. Believe me, I checked. Several times. I even phoned my landline from my mobile to check it was working. Then phoned my mobile from the landline . . . you get the picture.

So I decided to take a bath – well, a shower first, of course, and then a bath. I decided to be exceptionally brave and leave the phone out of my reach and the laptop on the table. I had actually contemplated bringing the laptop into the bathroom with me and sitting it on a stool close to the bath, but knowing how life had been behaving towards me lately I wasn't convinced I wouldn't knock the darn thing over and topple it on top of myself. It wasn't so much the thought of being electrocuted that freaked me out as much as the thought of someone finding me dead – and naked, with frizzy hair and a bikini line in need of a wax.

As I lay in the water I tried not to think about what might or might not be happening to my inbox. I tried not to visualise what thought processes might have been going through Bob's head. I tried not to panic about the possibility that this time had perhaps been the one time too far and that I would have to sell my flat and move to Spain to live on my parents' couch while I tried to scrape together some semblance of a life for myself. On most of those counts I failed miserably, but I refused all the same to get out of the bath until my skin had gone wrinkly and the water had turned cold.

Climbing out and drying myself off, I steadfastly ignored the living room and instead spent a good ten minutes slathering moisturiser on every available bodily surface. Surely by the time that was done he was bound to have replied?

Nada.

Things were getting desperate.

So I tidied my kitchen cupboards, organising my array of seldom-used pots and pans into a neat order after bleaching them to within an inch of their lives. I even put the radio on to try and drown out the repetitive train of thoughts currently rattling through my head.

And still *nada*.

By that stage I was starving with hunger but loath to mess up my sparkling kitchen so I decided to nip out for a sandwich. Texting Fionn, she agreed to meet me to hold my hand. She hadn't spoken to Bob, she said, and he had been enshrined in his office all morning.

I wondered was she lying to me. I wondered had she spoken to him and had he laughed my email right out of his inbox. But, when I saw her, I knew she was telling the truth. The thing with Fionn was that she actually could not lie without giving herself away. There was always a short pause, one or two seconds at most, before she started to talk if she was fibbing.

"Seriously, Annie, I saw him go in there this morning but he hasn't come back out yet. I'm giving him until three o'clock and then I'm sending in a search party. Jeez, can you imagine it? Me sitting here joking about him and maybe he has had a massive coronary or the like and is lying dead over his desk?" She gave a half-smile.

I suppose she thought I would have been comforted by her words, but I was far from it. So, yes, obviously Bob had been very busy all morning and not up to his usual management levels. But, he had also not left his office – which meant he had definitely, absolutely and without doubt read my grovelling letter and chosen not to reply. All of which pointed to the fact that this was going to end in a Very Bad Way. Crap.

I pushed my ham and cheese Panini around my plate a little, suddenly not hungry any more while Fionn chattered on about work and the wedding and the fact that Rebecca suddenly seemed to be the most accommodating ex-girlfriend in the world ever. I was, of course, happy that Rebecca seemed to be changing but I was still suspicious of her motives. However, I knew that if I spoke up now I might just start a whole new row and I figured I had more than fulfilled my quota of annoying the bejaysus out of people for now. I sipped my Diet Coke and listened intently. It was a welcome distraction but no matter how hard I listened, or how much I tried to listen, there was this repetitive drowning feeling which came in waves – pulling me under. It was as if everything in my life revolved around whether or not I would keep my job – whether or not Bob would let me make up for my mistakes – whether or not I could prove myself to be good at something. It shocked me how much I wanted that something to be work It was like a moment of clarity then and there – that the rest of it could all go to hell as long as I could stand on my own two feet. My work was what defined me. When I wasn't making stupid mistakes, I was damned good at it. It had never let me down.

I felt stupidly emotional, right there in the coffee shop, but I was determined that I would not cry. I just sat there, willing lunch hour to be over, so that I could get back home to my computer and to my email and to waiting for a response from Bob.

When lunch was eaten and my Panini had been pushed around sufficiently, I hugged Fionn and she whispered in my ear that it would be fine. I nodded and walked her back to her car before rushing back home and feeling my heart sink with disappointment to find there had been no response.

So I tried, and failed, to sleep. Then I got up and followed up on the emails I had sent out to the journalists the day before – snaring some great coverage in the Sunday supplements and discussing a promo with one of the glossies. Haven would be beyond happy and I hoped it would be enough to save my job – so I jumped on my email once again to send yet another message to Bob – hoping that it might just spur him into putting me out of my misery.

You can imagine how my heart leapt when I saw the little icon on the left-hand side of my screen registering that a new email had arrived. I dared to hope. I actually closed my eyes as I clicked the inbox button and waited to see what was waiting for me. I prayed it wasn't some eejit trying to sell me Viagra, or an email from my credit-card company saying my payment was overdue. I just wanted to see one name flash up on the screen.

I was disappointed.

There was indeed a name – a non-Viagra-selling name – and a non-'We need your money' name. But it wasn't Bob. I sighed as I clicked open an email from Owen Reilly. Yes, that's right. I sighed. And it wasn't a dreamy sigh, or a lustful sigh, or anything remotely of that nature. It was simply a feck-it-you're-not-Bob sigh.

It seemed he was enquiring after my ankle – which was really very thoughtful of him but it wasn't going to help me pay my mortgage. I tutted at the screen and got up to refresh my teacup before sitting back down – checking that there were no new emails – and reading the rest of his message.

"Hi Annie,

I hope you don't find this email too weird, or too stalkerish. I can assure you I'm not a weird ankle fetishist – although the fact that I have told you that I am not an ankle festishist will probably convince you that I am a bit unhinged.

But I'm not. I just wanted to check how you were and since I had your business card with your email on it, I thought it would be slightly less freaky to email you rather than phone you.

Which brings me to my next point. I figure emails are quite easily ignored and I thought I would give you the opportunity to ignore this if you felt you had to or wanted to. I promise that if I don't get a response from this I will take the hint, destroy all contact details and never annoy your head again, but I figured if I did not at least send this I could be doing both me and you a great disservice.

Anyway, I'm rambling and not getting to the point. I'm well aware of the fact I'm most likely making an unholy eejit of myself, but here is the deal.

I'm in your neck of the woods next week for a conference. You can check the details if you like. I've attached a very fancy flier. And I wondered if I could take you out for dinner?

Now, I fully appreciate that what I am going to say next may indeed make me look as if I was lying to you when I mentioned the not-being-a-mad-stalker thing. But I saw you in Dublin, at the coffee shop, two days after we met. You were hiding behind a magazine and I guess you didn't see me (or maybe you were ignoring me?).

I wanted to come over and say hello, but something stopped me. Maybe I just got the impression from talking to you that the absolute last thing you needed in your life was some weird Dublin gobshite coming over and chatting you up while you were trying to read your novel.

Not that I would have been chatting you up. Well, not exactly.

I'm a believer in fate. I know that sounds more than a little wanky but I believe there was a reason you gave me your business card when we met that day.

I kicked myself for not talking to you the second day because I really did enjoy talking with you when we met. I figure if I can get that level of conversation out of you when you are in pain with a busted ankle, we could really have some craic when you aren't in pain.

So if you want to, then please let me know, and if you don't, well, I won't take it personally. Well, not that personally anyway.

Hoping I haven't freaked you out entirely,

Owen"

Okay, so it wasn't going to pay my mortgage. But he liked me. That was perhaps a very smug way to think – but it was nice to have someone like me. It was especially nice to have someone who had never slept with me, nor thought I could further their career, like me. I liked that he believed in fate even though I had seen him at the coffee shop that day and I had hid from him. I liked that he had sent me an email – and not bombarded me with phone calls or sent me edible knickers. I liked his sense of humour. I liked that he made me smile. I liked that there was no pressure to reply – that it was all in my hands. I liked that he liked me and that he had taken the time to actually think out a message, write it and send it. It was very romantic. I imagined, if we had lived in times gone by, he would have sat at a bureau and penned me a letter with pen and ink and posted it off, waited days for my response in a very Mr Darcy kind of a way. I liked that and the way it made me feel. I liked him. And I thought it was entirely possible that I would indeed allow him to take me out for dinner when he visited Derry. What I liked most of all though was that for ten minutes he distracted me from worrying about work, and the email from Bob which had yet to materialise in my inbox.

I lifted the phone to call Fionn – and not just to ask if Bob had come out of his office yet or given her any indication to my fate.

"He emailed," I breathed excitedly into the phone.

"Bob?" she asked, tension in her voice.

"No. Owen."

"Who the fuck is Owen?"

"The ankle guy!"

"The ankle guy?"

"The guy who saved me when I was almost run down by a Dublin taxi for the love of God!"

I could almost hear the penny drop.

"*Oooooh*," she said, a note of delight in her voice, "He emailed?"

"He very much did!"

"And?"

"He's coming to Derry next week. He wants to take me to dinner."

"Whatever you do," Fionn said, "please do not take him to Manna. That would just be tempting fate."

31

Bob didn't email or call. Five o'clock came and went and my phone remained silent. Fionn was able to tell me he hadn't left his office at all. He hadn't so much as uttered a business cliché all day. He didn't even make a weird fingers-as-guns gesture as he left. If Fionn didn't know any better she would have sworn something was wrong.

I joked that he was probably pining after me and she had given a half-hearted laugh in reply and had then turned the conversation back to Owen and his email.

"Have you replied?"

"Not yet. I'm not sure."

"Not sure about what exactly?" she said incredulously. "He seems lovely."

"How can you say that? You know nothing about him!"

"I know he saved your life! The days of knights in shining armour are kind of gone, you know. Most men would have let that damn taxi hit you and then taken a picture on their phone to sell it to the papers."

"Oh, my Fionn, when did you become so cynical? I thought you were well-loved-up at the moment?"

"Well, I am, but I'm willing to accept Alex is one of the last good ones. I wouldn't want to be out there now . . ." She paused briefly, realising what she had said and then apologised. "I didn't mean that, not the way it sounded anyway."

"It's okay, Bridezilla," I soothed. "You're allowed to be smug. Speaking of which – how are things with the Wicked Witch?"

"Rebecca? Fine actually. No major tantrums. I've actually told Alex he can invite her to the wedding if he wants."

I gasped – the vision of Rebecca screaming "It Shoulda Been Me" at the top of her lungs in the church jumping into my head.

"Do you think that is wise?" I said.

"I not only think it is wise, I think it is exceptionally magnanimous of me. It has earned me major brownie points. And just think how excited Emma will be to have her mammy there."

"But what if she makes a scene?" I couldn't help but think this had disaster-in-waiting written all over it.

"I told you, she's a changed woman. She even recommended a hairdresser to me the other day and I checked her out and she's not a madwoman who would dye my hair purple and make me look like I had a bird's nest growing out of my head."

"Just be careful," I warned. "Leopards don't change their spots. Not that easily anyway."

"And I thought I was supposed to be the cynical one?" she said, a smile in her voice, before hanging up.

I looked at my watch and realised that Darcy would be home by now so I decided to call her – just to check she was doing okay and not lying in a lovelorn slump on the sofa sobbing into a hankie.

The phone rang a couple of times and Darcy answered, her voice barely above a whisper.

"Are you okay, sis?" I asked.

She sighed. A deep sigh. The kind of sigh that made me want to get into my battered car and forget my absolute terror at the very thought of driving on the M50 and go and see her right there and right then. Let's face it, I didn't have much else to be getting on with.

"Grand," she said. No more, no less.

"Really?"

"Yes," she said, no more, no less.

"You don't sound okay?"

"Well, I am. Well, I'm as okay as can be. No, no. I'm fine. Honest. A bit tired. A bit emotional. A bit left on the shelf, but we shall overcome. You don't come from Derry without having a bit of fighting spirit about you."

"Good woman," I said, my heart not really believing she was in fighting mood.

"And you?" she asked. "Any goss?"

It was then I had to tell her I was suspended, and waiting for an email, and recovering from receiving another email from Owen.

"Well, cling on to the good," she said. "Agree to meet Owen. He sounds nice. And the rest of the shite – worry about it another day."

"You're probably right."

"I'm always right. Don't walk away from chances like this, Annie. I know you've had a tough time with men lately and maybe you aren't in the right headspace for it, but chances like these don't come along often. Owen sounds like a gentleman. Let him prove to you that he is – and if he can't do that and turns out to be a twat, then at least you will know and you won't have to spend the rest of your life wondering if he was the one who got away."

"Fair play to you, still believing in romance."

"What else have I to believe in?" she asked, and I thought I heard her voice break a little.

"It will get easier," I offered.

"I hope so," She replied. "I just miss him, Annie. I miss the silly things – like how he would have a cup of tea waiting for me when I got up in the morning, or how he would run me a bath if he was in from work before me. I miss how he kissed my forehead. I miss his Dublin accent – which I know is weird because there are Dublin accents all around me. I miss us. I miss being a part of us – a couple. Darcy and Gerry. Gerry and Darcy. I just miss it."

"I know," I said. It was all I could offer and it seemed hopelessly inadequate. "I can come down again? I've nothing else on."

"No," she said firmly. "We've been through this already. I have to get on with my life and you have to get on with yours. Lovely and all as it would be, I need to learn to be okay with missing him."

"Okay, honey, if you're sure."

"I'm not sure at all, but I'm trying to be."

"Darcy?"

"Yes?"

"I love you."

"I love you too."

We said our goodbyes, then I switched on my laptop and opened my email folder. Clicking the reply button, I typed a message out to Owen saying that I would take up his offer of dinner and that I was looking forward to it. I did, however, as recommended, tell him I would book the restaurant. I would opt for somewhere as far away from Manna as possible.

Bob emailed the next day. He thanked me for my work on Haven. He said he would take into consideration my remarks and that he would be back to me as soon as he could. There was no indication whatsoever as to how long "as soon as he could" would actually be.

Owen replied the following day. I liked that he hadn't jumped to reply to my email – even if it had made me like a cat on a hot tin roof the entire day. My flat had never been so clean. I had never walked so far. I had become the queen of distraction therapy – spending time on the phone to Fionn debating whether or not he would reply at all, and time on the phone to Darcy just to make sure she was still coping, which she was. Just.

Part of me, especially now that I knew Bob wouldn't be emailing any time soon, still wanted to trek down there to be with her. But I knew she would kill me if I did and, no matter how bad life seemed right then and there at that moment, I didn't want to die. Not with the prospect of a nice date with a nice man who liked me in the offing.

When Owen replied he said he was delighted to hear from me. He said his schedule was pretty packed but if I wanted to choose a restaurant I could, because he knew feck all about Derry. He did say he would have asked me to eat with him in his hotel but he didn't want to come across as a mad stalker. He knew he was skating on thin ice as far as that was concerned anyway, he said.

I replied back (after an hour) to say I would book somewhere and I looked forward to it. It felt decadently romantic to be conducting our wooing over email. Regardless of what Fionn had to say on the matter, I knew I was not being a "big fat coward" by not just picking up the phone and calling him. I was thinking of self-preservation and nothing else. If I could type my replies into an email there was less chance of me saying the wrong thing – and Lord knows I had said a lot of the wrong thing lately.

Cabin fever set in on Thursday evening – despite my long walks to distract myself from the endless waiting for email inboxes to kick in. So Fionn invited me over to her house where I would help her stick stamps onto the wedding invites and plan her hen night in greater detail.

She wanted to ask Rebecca along which, as you can imagine, I didn't think was a good idea. But as the days passed my darling friend seemed to be morphing into more of a Bridezilla than I'd thought possible. She was even rethinking the pink shoes – worried they weren't wedding-y or designer-y enough. I told her to quit her paranoia and to admire them for the work of art they were. She gave me a death stare that prompted me to spend an hour and a half online scouting the finest of wedding foot-apparel before meeting her that night. (I had the time, and it was a good distraction technique – plus it was one which allowed me to be on the computer at the same time, so therefore in close proximity to my email. Result.)

I arrived at her house with a print-out of ten different shoes – all of various levels of pain-inducing prettiness. I also came armed with a list of the best restaurants in town which weren't Manna and a list of limos for hire for her big night on the tiles.

I also brought two tubes of Pringles which she turned her nose up at because the wedding-dress diet was on in earnest and there was, in her own words, no effing way she was going to waddle down the aisle. I wanted to take her and make her look in a mirror and realise that even if she put on three stone between now and the Big Day there would still not be a hope in hell of her ever waddling anyway. How I longed for her little waist and slim thighs – the ability to wear a short skirt bare-legged without the risk of chafing. I don't think Fionn had ever chafed in her life. The cow.

As we sat down at the kitchen table, Emma came dancing in – her perfect pink tutu bouncing up and down as she pranced towards us.

"Hi, Auntie Annie," she smiled her gorgeous gap-tooth smile.

"Hey, Ems."

"Are you planning Fionn's big party? She said she is going to have a party just for me and her but I can't go to the big night out because there'll be wine and I'm not allowed wine. Fionn says it's cos only big girls are allowed wine, but I'm a big girl, am'nt I?"

"Course you are, princess," I said, just momentarily wondering what it would be like to see Emma just a wee bit drunk on wine. There was a reason no one let me loose on their children. Not that I would actually get her drunk, mind. I wasn't that bad. I would just be tempted. For the *craic*. And, yes, I knew that made me a bad person and that I was probably going to hell for it.

"I'm gonna be a flowergirl," Emma declared proudly. "I have a beautiful dress. It's the prettiest dress in the whole world."

It would have been churlish for me to tell her that in fact, no, it was not the prettiest dress in the whole world and that mine was. It might have made her cry and it started to dawn on me that I was perhaps the most horrible person in the entire world. Not only had I already plotted to get a five-year-old drunk, I was now thinking of making her cry. I bit my tongue. Maybe my spinster-of-the-parish fate was a good thing. I wouldn't make a good mother. I would probably emotionally or physically scar them and that would be a Very Bad Thing.

"I'm sure you'll be gorgeous," I said with a smile.

"My mammy says I will even be more gorgeous than Fionn," she whispered at me, with a wicked grin that made her look *just* like her mammy.

"I'm sure you will both be just as gorgeous as each other," I said, deciding to keep that nugget of information from Fionn.

Emma was clearly not amused. She huffed, blowing the soft curls off her forehead, and went over to her dolls across the room.

It was just as well. I might have had to pull a scary face at her or tell her that not only would she not be as nice as Fionn, she wouldn't even hold a candle to me. Once again I sensed this would be a Very Bad Thing and another step on my road to hell. No, it was very wise indeed that no man in this world felt the need to marry me, let alone impregnate me.

Fionn walked over carrying a couple of mugs of tea. "Sorry I've nothing stronger, it's a work night."

I grimaced.

Fionn bit her lip. "Sorry. Was that disgustingly insensitive?"

"Not disgustingly insensitive, but verging on it," I said with a wry smile. "Well, I have lots to do tomorrow as well. I've to phone more people about Haven – even though I might not have a job any more – and then I have to watch *Loose Women* and clean the grouting in my bathroom. After that I have to shave my legs."

"And email Mr Lover Man Owen," she said with a wink.

"Who's Mr Lovermanowen?" the bat-eared child in the corner piped up. "What's a loverman?"

"It's a grown-up thing, pet," Fionn said.

"Ah, like 'afternoon nookie'," Emma chimed, replaying the conversation from several weeks ago.

"Does that child never forget?" I choked.

"Memory like an elephant. Ears like a bat. A fatal combination in this house, I can tell you," Fionn said, but she had a faint smile on her lips. It was clear she was amused by Emma's turn of phrase. "She certainly keeps us on our toes."

"I bet she does," I answered, deciding that now was obviously not the time to discuss in any great detail whatsoever any ongoing difficulties, perceived or otherwise, with Rebecca.

"Right," Fionn said. "Are you going to help me stick stamps on these damn invitations or not? It's bad enough we're only getting them out now."

"Damn's a bad word," Emma chirped from the corner, and Fionn apologised.

I could see that Rebecca was not going to be the only tricky character in this marriage.

I lifted the invites – exceptionally stylish white card efforts with a single calla lily imprinted on the front. As with everything else about this wedding, these invites had style and elegance written all over them. As I read the wording, the kind words from Fionnuala and Alex to invite their nearest and dearest to their most special of days, I felt a little bubble of emotion rise up. For perhaps the first time it really, really dawned on me that this was not just about nice dresses and pink shoes. Nor was it really about calla lilies, or cute flower girls or even my most beautiful ever dress. It was about Fionn and Alex and them being in love, and even though there were some difficulties there – even though it wasn't perfect – it was enough.

I stamped those damn (sorry, Emma) envelopes and sipped my tea, all the while fighting the urge to cry. I wasn't sure to be honest if my tears were of happiness, or sadness, or desperation, but I wanted so much just to go home and cuddle someone – not just anyone though. For once my brain was working enough to know that standing outside Manna calling for Pearse or driving down to the beach to throw pebbles at Ant's window would be pointless and humiliating. I wanted someone who loved me. Someone who respected me. I wanted someone who listened when I talked, soothed me when I cried. I wanted someone who laughed at the same jokes I did and didn't mind that I sang out of tune or had a weird obsession with bathrooms and the distance between the toilet and the door. I wanted someone who could sympathise with me about how crappy work was and who would wait in the chapel while I performed my bridesmaidly duties on Fionn's Big Day but who would rejoice in scooping me into his arms on the dancefloor and wouldn't mind smooching me during the slow set. I wanted someone who would get up on the cold mornings and defrost my car before defrosting his own. I realised I didn't mind if he snored, or didn't always shave. I didn't mind if he wasn't well off or didn't have a house on the hill, or overlooking a beach. I didn't care if he sang off key as well. I didn't care if he wore boxers and not jersey shorts. I didn't care – as long as he loved me, and I loved him.

When the invites were done, I kissed Fionn goodbye and took them with me to post on my way home. A wee part of me (the same part which wanted to get Emma drunk or tell her I would be way prettier on the day) thought about not posting them at all and maybe just locking them away in my tiny storage cupboard in a half-baked Miss Havisham impersonation type of effort. I would wear my bridesmaid dress every day – especially when I was signing on the dole, or shopping in Lidl or avoiding Fionn who would no doubt hate me for ruining her Big Day.

But no, I was sensible. Jealous, but sensible all the same, and I went straight to the sorting office and dropped the crisp white envelopes in the postbox.

Then I went home, switched on my laptop and emailed Mr Lover Man Owen – sorry, just Owen.

"I saw you too," I typed. "In the coffee shop. In Dublin. I did hide. I'm sorry. I won't hide in Derry."

I pressed *Send* and off it went. I sat back, staring at the screen, wondering but not really knowing what to expect. Did I want him to respond? And if so, what did I want him to say?

Part of me (that wee bastard part again) wanted to email him again and tell him all about my bad decisions lately – about Pearse, or more precisely sleeping with Pearse after we had broken up or indeed to tell him about Ant and his virility and how his pleasuring skills made me lose the run of myself entirely and do stupid things – like him – repeatedly.

Thankfully my Very Bad Thing radar kicked in again though

and I didn't send that second email. Instead I went to the toilet and contemplated if it would be possible to protect my modesty if someone did indeed burst through the door at a crucial moment. My answer was no. There would no doubt be some bum-showing, knickers-round-my-ankles fiasco in the making. I promised myself I would buy an extra lock. To add to the two I already had.

32

When I woke up the following morning I checked my email. There was a message from Owen.

"I'm glad you won't hide. I hate eating on my own."

I typed back. "I hope there will be wine too? Even just one glass?"

"Oh yes. I hate drinking on my own too," he replied and I smiled.

Then I phoned Darcy at work. She sounded chipper when she answered which did my heart good. But then again, what other way would she sound when answering the phone at work? It was her job to be personable.

"Hey, Darcy," I said.

Her personableness continued. "Annie, sweetie, how are you?"

"I have a date. With the Dub. How are you?"

"Still on the shelf, since you asked." At least she didn't sound suicidal at the thought.

"Have you heard from him at all?" I asked, not at all sure if that was the kind of thing I should have asked.

"I'm meeting him tomorrow. To discuss things."

"Things?"

"Yes, things." Her voice was bright and breezy and ever so professional and I knew there was no way she was going to explain further. This was going to be one of the occasions when I would have to ask the right questions to get the right answers.

"You and him things or boring things like electricity bills and phone bills and the like?"

"A bit of both."

My heart did a little flip-flop. Was it possible this was salvageable? I wanted to say that to Darcy – to assure her that maybe he had changed his mind and all would be fabulous – but I didn't want to get her hopes up. Nor did I want to get my own hopes up. Gerry had been pretty determined that children were never in the game plan. Was a week away from Darcy likely to have changed his mind? My heart stopped flip-flopping and started diving again.

"Will you call me after work and talk to me about it?"

"I will," she replied before hanging up.

I sat back, contemplating cleaning the grout on my tiles, and then noted the sun streaming in the window. No, I wouldn't clean this morning. I might still shave my legs, but later. For now I was going to take a book up to the roof terrace where I would lie in the sun and maybe get a little burned while losing myself in other people's dramas. Although in fairness there was enough actual drama around me to keep me going.

At lunchtime I crept back downstairs to a message on my answerphone from Fionn saying she had decided she was definitely going to go with the pink shoes. Then a second asking if I thought that was a good idea? Then there was a third saying to ignore the second message.

Following that was an email from the managers of Love, Sex and Magic to say their end-of-month sales figures were in and all was super. They wanted to thank me for my help. There was a second email from Haven saying they were delighted to have seen their lip gloss papped on said Z-lister's face in the newspaper that morning and there was an erroneous email from the Speed Dating Night organisers asking Elise for an urgent update as they had heard nothing in several days. A further email apologised that I had been sent the first email in error and asked me to disregard it. As if. A fifth email was from the Features Ed of a well-known tabloid looking for an in-depth interview with Pearse. I toyed with the idea of keeping that one to myself but I knew instinctively that would have been the final nail in my coffin at NorthStar. However, there was no way I was brave enough to talk to him, or meet him face to face. So I simply forwarded it on to his address, typing "Hope you are well" at the top.

I figured, all in all, as I gave in and started scrubbing my bathroom tiles with Pearse's old toothbrush, that was as good a day's work as any.

"Don't be getting any romantic notions," Darcy said as I picked up the phone. "I think he probably just wants to evict me from the flat or fight with me over some old CD or some other such nonsense."

"What makes you think that?" I asked, staring at my hands which were red raw from some serious over-application of bleach in the bathroom.

"Because what else would he want to talk to me about? He's hardly going to have changed his mind and be there on bended knee begging me to come back. This is not Hollywood, Annie, it's Dublin and this is not a city renowned for great romantic endings. Now, if we lived in New York, I could imagine him making a grand gesture at the Empire State, or if we lived in Paris maybe he would sweep me off my feet at the Eiffel Tower, but no. We are meeting in the Hairy Lemon. I doubt anything more than an exchange of CDs will come of it."

I sighed, wanting to hope she was wrong but knowing she was probably right.

"Well, you know where I am if you need me," I offered.

"I know, babes. But I'm a big girl. I'll be fine. Which reminds me, I finally broke the news to Mum and Dad."

"And?" I knew, whatever their response had been, it was unlikely to have been as supportive as Darcy needed.

"Mum said I was probably better off without."

Of course Mum and Dad had never met Gerry. They hadn't been home in several years and Darcy knew better than to risk taking him to Spain to spend any kind of extended period of time with our darling parents. Our parents were fine, but even finer in small doses – especially for those not necessarily used to their ways.

"What did you say to that?"

"What could I say? I told her she was probably right and then finished the conversation as quickly as I could. Oh, she said to tell you she was letting the house out to new tenants and to ask you again if you wanted to give up the flat to live somewhere proper?"

We finished our conversation and I looked around me. This was proper. This was home. This was more home than anywhere else I had ever lived – stupidly big bathroom and stupidly small kitchen and all. I felt like phoning my mum and telling her as much but I knew she meant well. She wanted all for me that I wanted for myself – except it was starting to dawn on me that what I wanted had changed entirely. Now I just wanted to be happy. I wondered why it had never dawned on me before that it was as easy as that – to just want to be happy, content, at ease. I don't know why I had always thought to be happy I had to have ticked all the boxes that I'd dreamt up when I was thirteen or fourteen and still living in a fantasy world where Barbie loved Ken and Harry loved Sally and Leia and Han were heading for their happy ending. I'd wanted nothing short of a Hollywood ending – that dance at the end of *Dirty Dancing* where my very own Johnny Castle would lift me above his head and the whole room would cheer and then dance with us. I'd wanted it to be perfect and nothing short of perfect. But, now, I realised I hadn't really known what perfect was all along.

33

I was watching TV the following morning when the buzzer to my flat went into meltdown. I almost choked on the cherry scone I had been eating for breakfast, not to mention that I almost did myself a serious injury as I hobbled – my toenails wet with nail varnish – to the door. Lifting the receiver, I said my hellos.

"The bitch!" Fionn's voice came hurtling up the line. "The fucking bitch! You are never going to believe what she has gone and done! No, actually you will believe it because you warned me. You bloody warned me!"

"You'd better come up," I said, pushing the release button and steeling myself for whatever storm was about to visit itself on my flat.

Opening the door I could hear her stomp her way up the steps, each new tread heavier than the last and a strange groaning and moaning sound going on.

"What is it?" I asked and Fionn just shook her head.

"What have you in to drink?" she asked.

"It's just gone eleven in the morning!" I exclaimed as she tramped past me to the kitchen and opened the fridge.

"Well, the doodah is over the yardarm then, isn't it?" she said, pulling out a bottle of Sauvignon Blanc and fishing in my top drawer for a corkscrew.

"But don't you have to go back to work?"

"It's Friday and the office is quiet – the only thing doing is that damn Speed Dating Night which, for the record, I might go to." She opened the bottle, practically hurling the cork and the corkscrew across the room and filled her glass to the very brim. "Except that would mean she would win and she is *not* going to win. I hope you know that?"

"I know that," I said as she thrust a second glass in my direction and gave me a look which had me under no illusion whatsoever that I had better drink it – otherwise I might find myself hurled across the room like the cork.

I sipped gingerly – no matter how much I loved a drink or two, I was not usually one for drinking before midday. The wine tasted bitter on my tongue but I swallowed anyway, following Fionn as she marched into the living room, cast open the window and took a few deep breaths followed by a few deep sips from her glass.

"She went to the shop. She actually went to his fecking work. She waved the invitation in his face and asked to speak to him *privately*."

By the way the word "privately" dripped from her lips, I became aware it was most definitely not a good thing.

"Did he tell her to feck off?"

"Ha!" Fionn said, and not in a funny "Ha" way. "No. No he did not. He talked to her – *privately*."

"But he has obviously told you all about this – either that or you actually went ahead with hiring a private detective to track his ass."

"He told me," Fionn said, moving from the window to the sofa, where she downed half a glass of wine in one go before topping it up with the bottle she was swinging around like a very heavy, potentially lethal-weapon-like handbag. "But that is not the point. The point is that she went there. And she told him she loved him. And she asked him not to go ahead with the wedding."

I opened my mouth to respond but Fionn raised her finger to silence me.

"Oh, that is not all. That is *so* not all," she said. "She told him that she never believed we would actually go through with it but, now that she has the invitation, she couldn't deny her feelings any longer. She has denied them – albeit not really very well – for five years but now, now when she gets her fecking invitation, she decides this would be the best moment?" Her voice was rising higher by the second.

"Could be worse," I offered. "She could have done it in the church. But, tell me, since Alex told you, I'm assuming he told her to take a long run and jump because, while you are upset, you aren't 'it's all over' upset. Am I right?"

She sighed, running her fingers through her hair. "He wants to let her down gently. Officially he is horrified, but unofficially I think he might just love that he has two women fighting over him."

"But what did he tell her then?"

"He said he told her that he was sorry but he loved me and the wedding was going ahead. But he said he couldn't really talk about it in work. He said he would call over later and then . . ." she was getting animated again, the wine in increasing danger of spilling out of the glass, "then he asked me if I would look after Emma so he could go and talk to her."

"Fuck that!" I exclaimed.

"Persactly my point of view. Believe me, I trust him."

I raised an eyebrow.

"I do! But I don't trust her and with good reason, it seems. I'm supposed to watch Emma while her mammy does her very best to get her claws into him again. You've seen *Misery*, haven't you? A dime to a dozen by 8 p.m. she'll have him trussed to a bed and will be going at his ankles with a hammer. His only escape will be to dump me and be with her. I think the time has come for you, or for us, to go and talk to her."

"Are you fully aware that my history of going and talking to people has been chequered to say the least?"

She nodded, maybe just a little unsure. "Nonetheless, I think needs must."

I sat back. "But what could we say? You know, apart from the obvious 'back off, bitch' thing."

She shook her head. "I don't know, but I think I owe it to myself to be proactive on this one. I'm three weeks away from the biggest day of my life so far – do I really want to leave it to fate?"

I shrugged my shoulders.

"No," she said, determinedly. "No. I don't want to leave anything to fate at all. I've the florist's head done in listening to me rant on about lilies and foliage. I've had four hair trials. I auditioned seven wedding bands. I ordered sixteen stationary samples before I decided on which one to go with. I have the Child of Prague in the garden already for fine weather. I'm leaving nothing to chance, least of all the possibility of a psycho ex-girlfriend fucking things up. I love him, Annie. I know you don't always get that. I know he isn't perfect, but neither am I. I can't think of anything I want to do more than marry him." A single tear slid down her cheek and she wiped away as if it burned her skin. "It shouldn't be this hard."

I sat down beside her and took her hand in mine. "It doesn't have to be. We'll talk to her."

Fionn stared into the bottom of her now-empty glass. "I feel a little bit sick. My head hurts. Who would have thought getting married would be this stressful? I swear I have a migraine coming on. I should have had some breakfast."

"Go for a lie down. Have a wee sleep. We'll talk to her when you wake."

She looked up at me, tears pooling in her eyes. "I *do* love him, Annie."

"And he loves you." I took the glass from her hands and steered her into the bedroom where I pulled back the duvet to let her climb in. Pulling it up over her, I stepped away and closed the curtains. As I left she was snivelling quietly, her anger spent and the two glasses of wine having their effect.

Fionn emerged just after one and just as the discussion was getting increasingly raucous on *Loose Women*. She sat down and stared at the TV, then looked at me and then back to the TV. Colleen Nolan was saying something really interesting.

"So," I said, reaching for the control and turning down the volume.

"I was watching that!" she protested.

"It's not that good, trust me."

"Ah, you're only saying that because you've been off work all week and been able to watch it at your leisure. You've had your fill of it now, but me, I never get to see it." She took the control from my hand and raised the volume again.

"I'll make some tea."

"And some toast!" she shouted after me.

Four buttered slices later she was calmer – and her interest in Colleen Nolan's pearls of wisdom had been satisfied.

"Right," she said. "I'm chilled now. I've had my meltdown. I've had my sleep. I've had toast with real butter. I'm ready to form a plan of action."

"Good woman yourself!"

"Do you think I could get away with hiring a hitman?"

I wasn't entirely sure she was joking. "You know, I wouldn't take the chance. Why don't you talk to Alex?"

She shook her head, and brushed the toast crumbs off her sleek grey tweed trousers and onto my floor. "He would only tell me to leave well enough alone and that he would sort it. And for reasons pertaining to the safety of his ankles as previously discussed I don't want to do that."

"So we need to go and talk to her then?"

"In the absence of the hitman option, I think so."

We planned it as best we could. We wanted to make sure Emma wouldn't be there so there was no time to waste. School ended at two thirty and Rebecca's house was a fifteen-minute drive away. I ordered a taxi just in case the half glass of wine I'd had earlier was still swirling around in my system. The last thing I needed was a drink-driving rap on top of everything else I was dealing with.

"I'll do the talking. You can just be my heavy," Fionn said, slipping her designer sunglasses on and slicking some gloss over her lips. She meant business. Fionn only ever wore lip gloss when she was going in for the kill.

I nodded, secretly a little concerned that she called me her heavy. I looked down at my thighs in my jeggings and was glad I had worn a loose tunic top to hide any little lumps and bumps.

When the taxi beeped to herald its arrival, I followed Fionn downstairs, half-expecting the theme from *Starsky and Hutch* to start playing in the background. It didn't, of course. The taxi driver was listening to the altogether more sedate sounds of Radio Foyle where some businessman was lamenting something or other in a very agitated and exceptionally strong Derry accent.

"Are you sure you want to do this? Are you sure Alex won't go off his rocker?"

"Oh, I told him when he phoned me. I told him that he could talk to her all he wanted but that I was going to as well. He wasn't happy but you know there comes a time when I have to get this straight in my own head and that time is now."

The taxi driver turned down the radio to listen in to our conversation. Evidently we were more exciting than Radio Foyle, which was fine by me.

Pulling up outside Rebecca's house I'm sure I felt my heart-beat kick up a notch. This felt like a covert super-cool operation, albeit one which Alex knew about.

As Fionn stepped out of the taxi, Rebecca stepped out of her front door, her face ashen. I actually felt sorry for her, for just a split second. Her face was pale and her eyes were just a little bit red-rimmed. Most people wouldn't have noticed it, but I was all too familiar with red-rimmed eyes these days. Her dark hair was scraped back off her face and she was still in her nurse's uniform. She shook her head as Fionn walked towards her.

"Alex told me you were coming. I don't want to talk to you. This is between me and Alex – no one else."

"Rebecca," Fionn said, her voice steady, "Alex and I are getting married in three weeks. Whatever – and I mean *whatever* – relates to Alex at this precise moment in time also relates to me. Don't think it doesn't."

Rebecca paled further, and stepped back towards her door.

"You'd better come in. I don't think either of us wants to have this discussion in the front garden." She looked over Fionn's shoulder and spotted me. I nodded at her, somewhat pathetically. It was somewhere between a "How are you?" nod and a "Don't even think about messing with my friend" nod. I'm pretty sure I looked like I had some kind of facial tick.

"You'd better come in then too," Rebecca said to me and I followed silently.

Her house was similar in some ways to Alex and Fionn's. The walls were adorned with pictures lovingly painted by Emma and every chair had a Barbie or other pokey-footed doll waiting to act as a tool of torture – impaling the most unsuspecting of bums when they sat down. Rebecca did a quick sweep of the room, collecting them and throwing them into a wicker toy basket by the radiator. "I was on night shift. I've not had time to tidy up."

"Well, maybe if you hadn't spent your morning with Alex . . ." Fionn said and I swear Rebecca actually flinched at the mention of his name.

"I'm sorry," she said, gesturing to us to sit down. "What can I say?"

"Well, that you'll never do it again would be good start. That you'll stop trying to make trouble between us and start to accept that what we have is real and it's not going to go away. I'm sorry if that hurts you, but I love Alex and he loves me and we *are* getting married."

"I know," she said, eyes downcast.

"But do you? Do you really know? Or is this just going to be another lull in the storm before you turn up and go all crazy-arsed on our wedding day like the big mad psycho you are?"

Whether or not I thought Rebecca was indeed a big mad psycho, I didn't really think that Fionn saying it to her was a wise move. I was right. Rebecca visibly bristled, her back straightening and her entire demeanour changing in a split second.

"Wait a minute. He loved me first," she said. "And I loved him."

Fionn snorted: "You might have loved him. But he never loved you."

"He told you that, did he? And you believed him?" Rebecca snorted back.

There was a lot of snorting going on. I just sat – a little bit terrified – planning my escape route for when it got nasty, which it inevitably would. It would get nasty and possibly bloody and there might be hair and blood flying everywhere and I liked my hair just the way it was, thank you very much.

"I believe him, present tense," Fionn said.

"Ha!" Rebecca sorted. "I'm not the kind of girl who falls into bed with anyone. I thought I meant something to him. I thought he loved me. He told me he did."

"Bollocks!" Fionn's voice was just a shade – a very eeny-teeny shade – below a roar.

"Were you there?" Rebecca barked back. "No! No, you were not. You think you know it all and you are so damn smug. Don't you realise that I am you? I was once right where you are now. Okay, not however-many weeks away from a wedding, but pregnant with his child, with him whispering every promise I could have wished for in my ear. You're not special. Don't think you are."

I had never actually seen a human being dripping venom before but this was exactly what I was witnessing right now in front of me. Rebecca, human and hurt and feeling very vulnerable, spitting venom at Fionn, equally human and hurt and feeling very vulnerable. I felt uncomfortable. Nosy as feck and part of me enjoying the scandal of it, but uncomfortable as if I was intruding on something I had absolutely no right to be a part of.

"He's marrying *me*," Fionn said, her voice less sure this time.

"And I'm the mother of his child," Rebecca retorted, her gaze turning to a picture of Emma, complete with the cutest pigtails in the world ever, on the fireplace.

"And don't I fecking know it?" Fionn shouted, her voice wavering. "Aren't I reminded of it every time she visits?"

"So you don't like my child then? Ha! I wonder what Alex would say about that?"

"I never said that," Fionn protested, her voice breaking.

I could see where this was going and I wanted to step in, honestly I did. But it wasn't my place. I was just an observer. Not a heavy as Fionn had asked me to be. They needed to sort this out between themselves, once and for all.

"I love her," Fionn said simply, her voice at a very reasonable and not at all hysterical level. "What I meant was, don't I always know you are the mother of his child? You've given him the most important thing in his life, Rebecca. Isn't that enough? You have the one thing I never will – his first child. Why isn't that enough for you?" Her voice broke, just that little bit.

"Would it be enough for you? Would you be okay with it? And what about when you have your own children? Will you even want to have Emma near you then? I doubt it."

"That's a stupid question because you beat me to that one and he loves her more than anything else in the world – more than he loves me and certainly more than he loves you. And that is how it should be and it's something I've had to make my peace with. He'll love our children but no more or no less than Emma. You know that. I'm sorry things didn't work out for you and Alex – no, correction, I'm not sorry. I'm sorry you are hurting. I know you might find that hard to believe, but you have to let him live his life and you have to let him be happy with me. We all – the three of us – need to work together whether we like it or not, because the important person in all of this isn't Alex, it isn't me and it sure as feck isn't you."

Rebecca stood up, walked to the window and stared out.

I wanted to say something but what the hell could I say? Was there anything at all I could say that would be a valuable contribution to this conversation? I sighed and sat back, casting a cursory glance at Fionn who just shrugged her shoulders and raised her eyebrows. We both knew this could go either way. Rebecca could accept what Fionn had said and they could work through their issues, or she could go completely mental and start throwing things at us or start boiling bunnies and the like.

The silence was deafening and unnerving and I shifted uneasily in my seat. Rebecca turned from the window and looked at us. It was impossible to read her face. There was no way to judge how this was going to go.

"You're right," she said. "And I mean properly right. Emma is the most important thing in all this. All I wanted was for her to have her two parents together." She sniffed the last sentence, as if it were meant to make Fionn finally give up.

"I'm not trying to take Alex away from her," said Fionn. "I never would. And I'm not trying to be her mother either. I know you do a good job. I know she loves you. To be honest, I'm just grateful she doesn't hate me."

Rebecca sagged.

"You must know that," Fionn said. "And you must know he loves me."

"I do," Rebecca answered.

"Then please just let us be together. Let us just get on with things. I'm not asking you to be happy for us – but just let us be. We didn't fall in love to hurt you. We aren't getting married to spite you. We just want to get married and we would love it if you were there and, while we don't expect you to lead the speeches or start the dancing, if you could just see that we are in this for the long haul and what we have is not going away, that will be enough."

Rebecca nodded and Fionn stood up, walking towards her and giving her a gentle hug. "I'm not trying to patronise you. I know this must be hard for you, but we don't have to be sworn enemies."

Rebecca nodded again and hugged Fionn back, gently also, and I stood and went outside. I figured they deserved a little space.

34

We walked away from Rebecca's with our dignity just about intact.

"Do you think that's an end to it?" I asked.

"Probably not. But hopefully it's enough to get us through the wedding. I feel sorry for her. Honestly I do, but I'm putting me first here."

"As you should."

"I just hope Alex sees it that way," she said, her face a little darker. "He's finishing work at four. We'll talk then. Let's just hope he doesn't put me on the Naughty Step again."

"You shouldn't worry about such things. Not this close to your wedding."

Fionn shook her head. "Look, I know he is a huffy git at times and patronising at other times but I suppose that's where the 'for better, for worse' thing comes into it. You take the good with the not-so-good and hope for the best."

"You paint such a romantic image of marriage, my friend."

"Romance won't change your incontinence pad when you're seventy-nine," Fionn said wryly. "I'm in this for the long haul – and I'm more into realism than idiotic notions of what love should be like. He makes me happy more times that he makes me sad. He rubs my back when I have my period and buys Tampax without blushing. He makes the best scrambled eggs in the world and he pays my credit-card bill for when I'm brassic without ever questioning why my balance never seems to go down. That counts too, Annie, as well as the hot body and the dinners out and all that other stuff. That counts more in a lot of ways."

She was right, of course.

We walked to a nearby taxi rank where Fionn made off to see Alex and I jumped into a second car asking that the driver drop me into the city centre for some retail therapy. I couldn't stand the thought of going home to my flat and I felt like spending some money while I at least still had an income. The sensible side of me knew I should probably hang on to my money – you know, just in case – but I didn't feel particularly sensible. I felt like buying something new and lovely and maybe something I could wear on my big date with Owen. Not that I was trying to think of it as a big date. I was trying to think of it as dinner with a nice man – with strong arms and a nice accent. I wasn't trying to set myself any expectations whatsoever of what could or would happen. The best I was hoping for was a nice dinner and maybe a glass of wine and some pleasant conversation. I wasn't looking for was romance, or sex, or romantic sex. At least, that was what I was trying to tell myself.

Dinner. Chat. Wine.

So when I started traipsing around Foyleside, I told myself there was absolutely no way I was going within a country mile of La Senza to buy any saucy undies. I wouldn't even allow myself near the undie section of Marks and Spencer. In fact, I had already promised myself that I wouldn't even shave my legs on the big night so that there would be no temptation there at all. This was a new leaf in the life of me – not that my slutty leaf had lasted very long. In fact, it had been a bit of a one-hit wonder, but I was more than happy enough for it to remain that way. I had learned my lesson good and proper. No good can come from passionate clinchers with hairy strangers in posh pubs. Well, if truth be told, a little good can come from it. It was a pleasurable, if slightly sordid, experience but one I had no plans on repeating.

As I ran my eye over the rails and rails of high-fashion clothes in the shops, I wondered how to play it. I could go for demure, but I didn't want him to think I was a total no-go area. Sure I was no-go on that night but who knew what could happen later? I was also acutely aware it was August and unnaturally warm – and yet I was still keen to hide my stubbly legs. I chose a pair of wide-leg linen trousers, with a delicate strappy top and some ankle-defying wedges. I planned to scoop my hair up in a high ponytail and accessorize with some oversized sunglasses. I would phone Darcy when I got home to check I wasn't making some godawful fashion faux pas but first I decided to call into Starbucks and grab a quick cappuccino and maybe read the paper or something equally decadent. Smiling to myself, I decided I would also buy myself the biggest, stickiest cupcake I could find and indulge myself entirely.

I was halfway through my cupcake when I looked up and saw Pearse, hand in hand with Toni. They may have been holding hands but it didn't look as if it were in an affectionate way. In fact, it looked more like they were clinging on to each other for dear life. Neither looked happy. Toni looked kind of scared. Pearse looked angry – and he didn't often do angry. Arrogant? Yes. Smarmy? Definitely. But proper angry? Not so much. I so wanted to walk over and ask what was going on but it was a fair bet that whatever I would say it would not take away from Pearse's anger or indeed Toni's misery.

I sat back, lifting the newspaper to hide behind and tried not to strain my ears trying to listen in. The combination of the hum of the cappuccino machine and the rustle of the newspaper – not to mention the twenty or so other customers in the shop all having the audacity to talk loudly to each other – made it difficult. But I did pick up the words "fecked" "arse" "disaster" and "latte" – although I imagine "latte" related to their order and not whatever scandal was visiting itself upon Manna.

I watched as they huddled over a low table, their shoulders around their ears with stress and Pearse being very unlike Pearse and avoiding any eye contact whatsoever with anyone just in case they might recognise them. I recognised this situation as something Very, Very Bad but I knew I couldn't approach them and it almost killed me. In fact, I had to ram several large chunks of cupcake into my mouth to stifle my urge to say something I might have regretted.

I sat there for ten minutes while they supped their coffee and spoke in hushed but urgent tones. There was a lot of headshaking (both Pearse and Toni) and, I'm not entirely sure, but I think there might have been some crying (Toni). There was definitely some overly dramatic hand-gesturing (Pearse) and I'm sure I heard the word "ruined" mentioned.

They left and I waited a suitable amount of time before leaving myself. Damn Fionn for having the day off. I couldn't phone to see what the gossip was and there was no chance I was phoning Elise to see if she knew anything. It would be a cold day in hell before I went to her begging for some gossip, not when I had been so used to being the purveyor of fine gossip myself.

I went home, dumped my bags in the hall and immersed myself in a big dose of *Home and Away* – which reminded that I really, really should phone Darcy. Then again, as she was having her meeting with Gerry, I wasn't sure that me calling her would be a good idea. No, I would wait (perhaps impatiently) for her to call me. And while I was waiting I would seize the day and book the restaurant for my dinner (not date) with Owen.

Emailing Owen was fast becoming one of my most favourite pastimes. It felt a bit like writing in a diary, only this diary would write back and tell me I was witty, or that I'd made it laugh and that it was looking forward to seeing me.

There was something about Owen – and it might just have been the relative anonymity of the fledgling friendship – that allowed me to open up in a way I hadn't done in a while. I wasn't all psychotic about it. I didn't pour out my innermost fears and hopes. But I was honest. There was no bullshit involved. In fact, as I typed him a message telling him exactly how I would not be shaving my legs in advance of our dinner date and to warn him off any form of footsie,

I smiled to myself. I knew he wouldn't recoil in horror. I knew he wouldn't think of me as a tease, or a reformed tart. I knew he would just find it funny.

When he emailed back to tell me he would support me by not cutting his toenails so he wouldn't be tempted to even think of rubbing his razor-sharp claws along my hairy legs, I laughed out loud. Yes, like a loon, in my flat, laughing at a computer. It was wonderfully freeing.

"I will be washing my hair though. And putting on some make-up and trying not to throw myself in front of any taxis," I typed.

"Grand job," he typed back. "Because my back's been giving me gyp this week and I'm not sure I could save you if I tried."

A very, very cheesy voice in my head (which I battered down with a glass of wine) had the urge to reply and tell him he already had saved me. Instead I recommended he try some Radox in the bath but warned him to shower first to avoid the skin-soup scenario, explaining my aversion to same.

When he replied that he always showered before a bath my heart did that flip-floppy thing and I went and had a shower/bath combo myself as a sign of some kind of serendipitous unity.

Fionn sent a text message just after eight. "Wedding still on. Bridesmaid dress fitting tomorrow at 11. Make-up trial at 12. Meeting the choir at 2. Will chat 2morro!"

There was no text from Darcy. When I tried to call her there was no answer. And I tried a few times. I tried at eight, and again at eight thirty. Then I tried at eight forty-five and nine fifteen and then in a fit of worry I tried at nine thirty-two, nine thirty-four, nine thirty-five and nine thirty-seven. I calmed down momentarily before trying again at ten fifteen and texting her to ask her to call me as soon as she possibly could. I went to sleep with my landline and my mobile phone resting on the pillow beside me and jumped at every small noise in the hope it would be Darcy telling me she was absolutely fine and had not thrown herself into the Liffey in a fit of desperation. As the night progressed I found myself in a quite disturbing mind-loop, wondering if it would be the PSNI or the Guards who would turn up at my door to tell me she was a goner. I would then have to phone my parents who would probably be really put out at having to come home for a funeral, asking me if I could bring her over there instead as mourning was so much easier in the sunshine.

As dawn broke, somewhere around four thirty, I promised myself that I didn't care about my job or Owen or my flat or anything as long as Darcy was okay.

I phoned again, imagining the shrill call of the phoning ringing out in her dark and empty flat, and almost died of shock when she answered, her voice heavy with sleep.

"Darcy, darling, are you okay?" I asked, my voice catching in my throat.

"I'm fine," she whispered. "I'm just fine. I can't talk just now. I'll call you in the morning."

"It *is* morning," I said, almost defiantly, like a parent whose initial relief at finding a lost child is suddenly replaced by anger that they had the cheek to get themselves lost in the first instance.

"Proper morning," she whispered. "Not stupidly-early-in-the-morning morning."

"I was worried!" I stammered.

"There's no need," she said, "none at all."

35

I had tried and failed to get back to sleep so when Fionn arrived at just gone ten with a couple of bottles of water and some fruit I was not a pretty sight to behold. My hair had morphed into some kind of kinky afro from all the tossing and turning during the night and the bags under my eyes were of such a size and shape that they easily could have accommodated all of Fionn's honeymoon luggage.

Fionn, on the other hand, looked fresh as a daisy. Clearly whatever storm she was expecting to have brewed with Alex had failed to materialise.

"You look like shit," she said, her voice reaching a new pitch of Bridezilla-ness.

"Thanks," I muttered as she handed me a bottle of water and ordered that I drink. "It's all part of the plan," I lied. "The worse I look today, the better I will look when I escort you down the aisle."

She raised her perfectly shaped eyebrow at me. She didn't look convinced.

"Trust me," I said.

"If I must," she huffed, sitting down at my dining table.

"Speaking of trust," I said as I lifted a hairbrush and tried to tame my hair. "Alex? Rebecca? Tears and snotters? Fisticuffs? Naughty Steps?"

She shook her head. "It was a bit rough but we worked through it."

"I asked about your big talk, not your sex life," I said with a wink.

She snorted. "Just so you know, we are not having sex at the moment. I have him on a ban so that by our wedding night he is gagging for it."

"You do know you'll probably be too tired on the night?"

"No way. No such thing. I'll be consummating our marriage on the day itself if it kills me. Even if I have to whisk him away mid-reception for quickie."

"In that dress, there will be no such thing as a quickie. I'm already mentally preparing myself for having to help you get to the toilet all day, and I'm a girl. I'm used to buttons and zips and corsetty doodahs. Alex will be stumped."

"Where there's a will there's a way," Fionn said with a wink and I realised she was very successfully moving this topic of conversation away from where it needed to be – which was the ramifications of her meeting with Rebecca.

I steered the conversation back, unsubtly and in a cut-the-crap kind of way: "Rebecca? Alex? What happened?"

"I think he was relieved that I took matters into my own hands," she said.

I went to speak, opening my mouth just before she jumped in.

"And no, I don't think that means he's a cowardly fecker. He didn't want to hurt her. He said he tried, and tried, to let her down gently but that he didn't want to do anything that would jeopardise his relationship with his daughter."

"And what did he say about her saying he had made her all the same promises?" I knew this was potentially a very dodgy line of questioning but it was one I couldn't ignore.

She stiffened a little. "I know you might think I'm off my head but I believe him when he says this. He never made her the same promises. He tried. When he found out she was pregnant with Emma, he wanted to step up and be the man. He wanted to be a good daddy to his wee girl and in those early days he thought the only way to do that was to be together with her mammy. So he tried and he wanted it to work, but, you know, it just didn't."

I felt something in me rise up. Sure wasn't that just what had happened with me and Pearse? Okay, so no, it wasn't just what had happened between us. I hadn't got pregnant and he hadn't tried to make it work but nonetheless we had both found ourselves in a pretty unsatisfactory place trying to make something work which deep down we both knew never would. I felt myself choke up a little.

"He said he wanted to love her. He wanted them to be together. But he couldn't lie and in the end it wasn't fair to him, or Rebecca, or Emma. Most of all, probably, Emma. So when Rebecca said he made her all those promises, she wasn't wrong, but he was trying to make it work. He's not trying to make it work with me – it *is* working. Does that sound smug? I don't mean it to sound smug."

I shook my head, wiping a sneaky wee tear from my face. "You don't sound smug at all."

It was I who felt smug an hour later, wearing the most gorgeous dress in the world ever, as the very lovely shop assistant twirled me around checking for the fit.

The dress was as beautiful as I had remembered it. In fact, it may just have been that little bit more beautiful. It was, perhaps, the most beautiful thing I had ever set my eyes on and I had set my eyes on plenty of beautiful things in my time. I'd once even seen Colin Firth in the very real flesh and he was about as beautiful as they came.

"Ooooh," I breathed as I did a twirl, narrowly avoiding a stab in the leg with a funky little pin with a coloured top. The shop assistant looked at me, her mouth full of other delightful little pins with coloured tops and made a noise which I interpreted as "Stand the feck still, woman!"

"It is lovely," Fionn said, standing back and admiring me in my sleep-deprived beauty.

"It is more than lovely. It's gorgeous. Like properly gorgeous. Gorge-malorge, in fact."

"Okay, it's gorge-malorge. Does that make you happy?"

"Indeed it does," I said, stopping myself just before I did another twirl and knocked the poor assistants to the ground.

I'm not one for wearing a lot of make-up. A slick of Clarins foundation, a brush of loose powder, some blusher and a sweep of mascara if I was feeling adventurous and wanting to adopt a slightly wide-eyed and alert look. Normally the entire process takes all of two minutes (with an extra ten seconds if it is a mascara day). I was not used to spending half an hour in a chair having make-up layered onto my face, bit by bit, colour by colour, fake eyelash by fake eyelash. I had to fight the urge to laugh as my lips were glossed, and the urge to sneeze while my nose was powdered. I passed the occasional glance in Fionn's direction and she was serenely sipping from champagne and chattering to the petite perfectly coiffed girl layering the make-up on her face.

"So, are you excited?" The equally petite and equally perfectly coiffed girl layering make-up on my face asked.

"I can't wait. It's going to be brilliant."

"I love doing weddings," she said dreamily. "It's so romantic. Are they madly in love then?"

I paused for a second. Where they madly in love? They were certainly in love. And they were both a little on the insane side. But was it mad and passionate and everything I had always thought I wanted? Well, it was and it wasn't. They were clearly a good pair and if Rebecca was true to her word I was sure they would be very, very happy together. In fact, even if Rebecca wasn't true to her word I was pretty sure they would be happy together. They were made of strong stuff. I felt yet another bubble of emotion rise up inside me and I bit it back.

"They are great together," I answered, glancing over at how bright Fionn's eyes looked and how she flashed her left hand as she spoke with a palpable pride. "It's going to be wonderful."

I got a bit of a shock when I saw myself in the mirror when Miss Petite had finished with her brushes and sponges and (it felt like) trowels. I looked like I had always wanted to look. Blemish-free. Defined. Sculpted. Highlighted. Beautiful. I'm sure I gasped, as in properly gasped. Part of me was waiting for Gok Wan to walk in with his TV crew to tell me I looked fabulous, darling. I wouldn't cry – not even when I looked across at Fionn who looked perhaps the most beautiful I had ever seen her look – but what I did do was book the very same make-up artist to touch me up before my dinner (not date) with Owen.

By mid-afternoon I was sitting in the third row of St Eugene's Cathedral marvelling at the impressive stained-glass window before me. A choir in perfect pitch was singing a hairs-on-the-back-of-your-neck-standing-up rendition of "Ave Maria".

Alex sat beside Fionn, holding her hand. Every now and again he glanced in her direction and a small smile crept across his face. She was entranced by the music of the choir and he was entranced by her. Not for the first time I felt myself well up. I really was getting daft in my old age.

It was only when I got home, made myself a cup of tea and sat down in front of the TV that I realised that not once during my time in the church had I wished it was me.

That's not to say I didn't wish it was me, but I seemed to be evolving into some sort of better human being. My only thoughts in the church that afternoon were that it was going to be a lovely ceremony. It was going to be a great day and yes, even with whatever difficulties they faced, they were going to be happy. I congratulated myself with a chocolate biscuit and a quick email to Owen.

"Restaurant booked. I'm even going to wash my face and get my make-up done."

An hour later I had a response:

"Does that mean I have to shave then? God – you women are so high maintenance. You'll never know the hardships us men go through."

I typed in a hasty response:

"Yes, please shave. For reasons I will go into at a later date I have an aversion to overly hairy men. It's okay – I understand that you men have it tougher than us, the stronger sex."

He replied: "Want to test that theory with some arm-wrestling?"

Now, either this was flirting – like proper sexy flirting and not just harmless flirting – although in fairness I could think of better things to wrestle with. That is, if I was planning on wrestling anything, which I absolutely was not. Therefore I decided I would not reply with "Come and have a go if you think you're hard enough". That would, I guessed, have given entirely the wrong impression.

"Nah," I typed instead. "I might break a nail and you know what we ladies are like. We can cope with childbirth but we pale at the very thought of a shattered nail."

His response was almost instant. "I'm exactly the same. A martyr to me cuticles."

I snorted so loud that a spray of tea shot through my nose and threatened to short-circuit my laptop. And when I stopped laughing I looked at his words again and thought about his hands and felt all funny – in a nice way.

I was thinking about just how exactly funny he made me feel when my phone rang. Absentmindedly I lifted it and muttered a hello.

"And you," Darcy's voice raged, "have the cheek to be annoyed at me for not answering my phone to you. I've been ringing this shagging number all day with not one word of a response! And do you ever actually switch your shagging mobile on?"

Darcy was in a bad mood. A scary bad mood.

"Sorry, I was out. Wedding stuff."

"Don't talk to me about wedding stuff! Sure I got my invitation today to 'Darcy and Guest'. Guest? Do you know anyone called Guest? Cos I sure as feck don't. Apart from the David Gest guy off the telly. You know, the funny-looking one and I don't want to bring him to the wedding!"

I wasn't sure if she was joking, or just actually flipping her lid.

"Well, Fionn wasn't sure . . ."

"Am I an embarrassment without a man on my arm?"

"I've no man on my arm either, don't forget!"

"Ah," she said, her voice filled with a certain amount of glee, "but you have a date with your knight in shining armour!"

"It's not a date," I protested, but I don't think I was even fooling myself.

"Whatever," Darcy puffed. "Anyway, how did the wedding things go?"

"It went well. My dress is gorgeous. The make-up was gorgeous. The music was –"

"Gorgeous?"

"How did you guess?" I said wryly.

"Call it sister's intuition."

"Well, my sister's intuition had me worried sick about you yesterday! You should have called! How did things go with Gerry?"

I heard small cough and a bit of a sniff, as if she was hiding something. I interpreted this in one of two ways. Either she had killed Gerry and disposed of his body in the Liffey or she had slept with him. For a moment I thought she sounded too bitter about the whole "guest invitation" thing to have slept with him and I contemplated life visiting my jailbird sister in some maximum-security jail somewhere. Fecking Darcy would probably still look amazing in a prison-issue orange jumpsuit.

But then I thought of how she had told me I had nothing at all to worry about when I spoke to her in the wee small hours.

"Oh. My. God!" I almost squealed. "You fecking slept with him!"

She coughed again. "It's not what you think!"

"Well, what I think is that you met for lunch and you were both nervous, so you had a drink, and then maybe another drink and then another and eventually you ended up back at the flat shagging the arses off each other and the last week of heartache is for nothing because now you've just gone back to your starting point again."

"You are *so* wrong," Darcy said.

"Oh, right, well, why don't you tell me how it is?"

"I will then," she said petulantly but I was sure I sensed a hint of a smile.

"Oh Darcy," I couldn't help but say, "I hope you've not done anything silly."

"I promise," she said.

And then she told me how they had met. She had been beyond nervous and not at all sure how to play things. It had taken her two whole hours to choose what to wear and whether or not to wear any make-up at all. She had settled for skinny jeans, a loose tunic belted at the waist and some gladiator sandals. And she had tied her hair into a loose ponytail. She was going for casual chic, it seemed. She had been tempted to have a glass of wine before she left but she wanted her wits about her. She knew it would be tough. Gerry always had a strange effect on her. She just had to see him to want to be with him, in his arms, as close as she could be. It had been like that since they had first met and to be honest it used to get quite embarrassing when we got together. There would be Pearse and I, sitting like a pair of dead fish while Darcy and Gerry – both respectable grown-ups in their mid-thirties – would be snogging the faces off each other, with tongues and everything.

So they had met and he had looked wretched, and she had felt wretched. She wanted to reach across the table and soothe him. Every part of her ached. He was her other half, she said.

They had tried to talk about everyday things but small talk just wasn't cutting it – not when there was so much said and indeed so much unsaid between them.

"I miss you," he said, after they finished their first glass of wine. "I promised myself I wouldn't say that to you. I promised myself we would just talk about the practicalities of splitting up but there is nothing in my head now – nothing but the fact that I miss you."

Darcy had sat back, every fibre of her body telling her that she missed him too – as much and as fiercely as he missed her.

"I'm broken without you," he said. "Nothing is right."

Darcy didn't think anyone actually talked like that outside of movies and cheesy American sitcoms, but it seemed even Dublin on a rainy summer's day could offer a hint of a happy ending.

"I couldn't think of what to say to him," Darcy told me. "All my brain could think was that I felt exactly the same. But where would that have left us? We would still have the same problems we always had."

"So what did you say?" I asked, gripped by this unfolding drama.

It seems that even though she didn't know what to say, she said what was in her heart. That she missed him too. They had looked at each other, pain etched across their faces and he had reached across the table and taken her hand.

"Whatever it is," he said, "whatever it takes, I can do it."

She felt the same.

36

"So they did it?" Fionn asked, sipping from her bottle of water (the third of the day) as we had our usual Sunday morning stroll around St Columb's Park.

I nodded.

"So is he coming to the wedding then?"

"She didn't say, but I'd say it's a fair bet it's either him or David Gest from what I could tell."

Fionn looked a little confused but walked on. I have to admit I hadn't been expecting this turn of affairs at all. In some ways I was happy that Darcy and Gerry had decided to see each other again on a strictly "Let's see how it goes" basis. On another level I was absolutely terrified that three weeks, or three months or three years down the line nothing would have changed and the pair of them would have to go through an even more painful splitting-up-for-the-second-time process.

They weren't absolutely and completely back together. He wasn't moving back in. He was, however, going to contribute towards the rental costs for the foreseeable future just until they had an idea where things were going. They were going to go for couple's counselling – Gerry had already made an appointment. Yes, they had ended up in bed and had done the dirty – three times

– but Gerry had left mid-morning and for now they were simply dating again. It was romantic. And Darcy was shit-scared – perhaps the most scared she had ever been in her life – except, that is, for the week he wasn't in her life when, she told me, every day had left her paralysed with fear.

But he had agreed to talk about the baby issue. He had agreed to talk about his relationship with his father and, while he couldn't make any promises, he would try and she would try and hopefully they would make it work.

"You don't think any the less of me because I fell to pieces without him?" she had asked me at the end of our phone call.

Thinking of how my life had fallen to pieces itself over the last few weeks, I'd shook my head before saying, resolutely, "No, darling. I don't."

"I hope they make it," Fionn said, with a smile. "I'm sure they will. They deserve to." I nodded, because they did deserve it.

Fionn walked on, a little too fast for my liking, but when I begged her to slow down she waggled her rear in my direction.

"Do you see this? Do you see my ass?"

"It's a perfectly acceptable ass," I said, confused – and more than a little disturbed.

"Perfectly acceptable is not good enough," she said. "Not when I'm walking down the aisle in three weeks. I want to have the best ass of all the asses in the church and nothing less will do."

She looked as if she might cry as she grabbed her relatively bony rear end and endeavoured to pinch more than inch.

"Fionn," I said, walking up to her and linking my arm in hers, "remember when I told you you weren't even a Bridezuki?"

She nodded, a little tearfully.

"Well, things change. I fear you have gone to the Dark Side, my friend. You are in the full throes of Bridezilladom."

She gasped, as if my words had caused her actual physical pain. "I'm not that bad!" she protested.

"No, darling, you are worse. Your ass is fine. I would kill to have an ass like that. If Argos made a catalogue solely of asses, yours would be the one I would choose. J-Lo wants your ass, it's so gorgeous. There are knickers in this world whose sole ambition in life is to be on your ass. I don't get how you can't see that!"

"But –"

"Funny you should say that," I said with a wink. "Seriously, darling, you are obsessing. I know you want it all to be perfect but you are going to make yourself sick with all this running about. Promise me you will take it easier?"

She nodded, but I wasn't convinced. I was sure that if I turned my back for all of three seconds she would be off and running like a rabbit out of a trap – gathering pace until there wasn't an ounce of fat left anywhere on her body. And where would that leave us? Apart from the obvious fact that I would look like Pat Butcher as I walked up the aisle behind her waif-like figure, it would make her sick. Then the day she had worked so hard for – and fought so damn hard for – would be for nothing. She'd be too weak to join in the Hokey Cokey or raise her arms aloft for an over-enthusiastic singalong to "Sweet Caroline".

"Tea and scones, now," I ordered.

"But –" she started again.

"Have you eaten today?"

"Not yet."

"Well, then, a scone won't hurt. Go on, have a wee fruit one. It's healthy."

"I *am* fecking starving," she conceded. "And if I drink any more water there is a very real chance me and my kidneys will float off down the Foyle."

"Good woman yourself," I said, leading her from the park to my car where we drove off in search of a homely cafe with scones the size of human hands, real butter, and tea served in mugs with full-fat milk.

We took a seat in the corner and sat in companionable silence as we lifted the Sunday papers and started a deliciously wicked bitchfest about who was wearing what and who was going where. I was delighted to see Zara Dunne – "*an up-and-coming name in the acting world"* – papped applying her lip gloss (Haven) while stopped at traffic lights. Hurrah!

I was just buttering the second half of my fruit scone when Fionn made a rather disturbing choking sound. I looked up, alarmed, thoughts racing through my head of the possible tragedy unfolding before my eyes. We would bury her in her wedding dress.

But she seemed to have composed herself just as quickly as she had started choking and she was hastily and rather unsuccessfully trying to hide a newspaper in her handbag.

"What is it?" I asked.

"Nothing," she said, her face colouring.

"Come on, it must be pretty damn juicy gossip for you to want to keep it all to yourself? Is it a three-in-a-bed sex romp? Is it a gay love triangle with some bestiality thrown in for good measure? Is it someone wearing really, really unflattering clothes which make them look like a big eejit?" I had a smile on my face and I honestly, truly expected Fionn to show me some big scandalous tabloid scoop or indeed a picture of Zara Dunne with anaphylactic shock from over-application of a certain lip gloss.

What I hadn't expected at all was for her to adopt a very stony face and tell me that it really was nothing, in a way which let me know without doubt that she was lying through her teeth.

"Fionn. Don't make me hate you. Give me the paper."

She shook her head.

"Fionn, give me the paper, please."

"Annie, it's nothing."

"Clearly it *is* something so please pass me the paper before I do something we both regret."

She looked scared. Proper scared, not just obstinate for the sake of it and I realised that, whatever she was hiding from me, it was something pretty damned serious. And by pretty damned serious I meant even more serious than the possibility of Zara Dunne's throat constricting while her lips ballooned to such a size that she would never even need to consider any kind of lip-filling treatment ever, ever again.

Fionn shook her head but I simply thrust my hand in her direction. I meant business and she knew it.

Gingerly she reached into her bag and pulled out the paper, opening it to the appropriate page and glancing at it, before glancing at me and then back to the paper.

"Are you sure?" she asked and my sense of impending doom threatened to reach fever pitch.

"Well, to be honest, I'm not sure but what I am pretty sure of is that whatever you are going to show me now is going to get to me at some stage and I'd rather be forewarned." A slick, cool sweat broke over my body. What on earth else could go wrong? I dreaded to think.

Fionn passed the paper to me and my jaw dropped when I saw the headline and the accompanying picture splash.

Oh Manna! – Celeb Chef in Kitchen Bonkfest

Oh shit. Oh shit, shit and triple shit. Thoughts of my on-the-desk bonk flooded my brain. Had we been caught? I could barely focus as the newsprint swirled before my eyes. This was it. Done. My career over. There was no way Bob would take me back on after this. And what if Owen saw it? Or Ant? Ant would enjoy this – and he would think I was a dirty slut who bonked rings around me.

Then, looking at it again, I felt air rush into my lungs as I realised the picture wasn't of me. Grainy and all as it was – the CCTV footage of Pearse mid-hump beside the spuds – was obviously not me. Not least because I at least had certain standards and bonking with the backdrop of a catering-sized sack of Maris Pipers was beyond my comfort zone.

Looking closely – and suddenly replaying in my head the scene acted out between Pearse and Toni on Friday in Starbucks – it all clicked into place. Pearse was shagging Toni. And he was doing it in the kitchen at Manna. And restaurant kitchens were generally places which were hygienic. And sex, no matter how safe, was generally not an activity to be carried out in an environment which by necessity needed to be hygienic. All this was ignoring the fact that aside from the unhygienicness of humping over the spuds, Toni was very much married – to a rather prominent businessman with rather suspect connections.

I could see now why Pearse had muttered that he was ruined and I now suddenly knew why that reporter had been so keen to get his number.

Oh dear, this was really a rather huge mess. Once I had breathed my sigh of relief that it was not me pictured with my knickers round my ankles, I actually felt sorry for Pearse and for Toni, even though I had never really liked her.

No one deserved to be humiliated in such a way – not even Pearse who had been mean to me on more than one occasion – or Toni who always looked at me with a disapproving expression.

"The poor bastards," Fionn said.

I nodded. Even though we both worked in PR, and even though we were both used to dealing with sticky situations with our clients, we knew this would be a tough one to get out of. This needed more than NorthStar.

"Her husband won't be happy," Fionn said, shaking her head.

"No. I imagine he won't."

"Christ, the shit is really going to hit the fan tomorrow."

"But that's Elise's problem. Not mine. She is the Manna woman now. I'm just the poor fecker suspended on full pay who gets to read about her ex-boyfriend's antics in a café on a Sunday morning!" My voice was just half a level below hysterical.

Fionn looked scared. "Ex-boyfriend," she said meekly. "This shouldn't annoy you."

I shook my head. "It doesn't. Well, it does but not in that way. It's just a shock. I wasn't expecting to see Pearse's bare arse this morning."

"They've censored the pic," Fionn said, pointing to the page. "You can't actually see his bum crack or anything."

"But I know," I said. "I know it is there."

Fionn nodded.

The whole episode left me feeling very unsettled. Was I jealous that Pearse and Toni were now at it? Well, yes and no. I was a little well, meh, that he had moved on even though I had clearly moved on. I suppose there was a part of me that, even though we were no longer together and I was perfectly okay with that, sort of felt as if his penis kind of belonged to me and really it shouldn't ever bob in and out of anyone else ever again. I pushed that thought right out of my head though. I never wanted to think about his penis ever again and Lord knows if I ever would have if I hadn't just seen that grainy image of him mid-hump in the newspaper.

Another part of me – the part of me that was no doubt destined for hell – felt jealous. Not jealous of Toni – not jealous of the in-flagrante humiliation. I was jealous of Elise and the fact that come tomorrow morning her phone would be ringing red hot off the hook and everyone would want a chat with Pearse. It would be a tough day at work, but one of those days when you buzzed from start to finish, feeling as if you were actually a part of something huge and important. (Well, huge and important in the salacious-celebrity-gossip stakes, but admittedly not really important at all in the grand scheme of things.)

Another part of me just felt heart-sorry for him. He wasn't a bad person deep down. He would be crushed by this. He would probably be sitting in his house on the hill, burning every Yankee candle he could find, getting off his little head on pretentious wine and wondering what on earth he was going to do next.

Trudging back to my flat, my head filled with a hundred and one conflicting thoughts, I stomped up the stairs and then slammed the door behind me before throwing myself onto the sofa very ungraciously. In fact, I landed with such a thump that I knew I would have a phone-shaped bruise on my rear end for the next week. Reaching in beneath me, I pulled out the phone to see the light flashing to indicate there were three new messages. It was a fair bet they were all from Darcy who would no doubt have seen Pearse's pee-arse in the paper and would be dying to chat to me about it and have a giggle at his (and my) expense.

Dialling through to voicemail I was shocked – properly, totally and utterly shocked – to hear Bob's voice on the line.

"*We've gone to Defcon 1. We need you. The past is the past.*

Pearse is in meltdown. His phone is ringing off the hook. Manna is surrounded by paparazzi. We can't lose this contract, Annie. And by us, I mean us. You have your job back. Welcome to the team. Oh and Elise? Seems she has disappeared. Seems she might have got her hands on some contraband CCTV footage. I know you owe us nothing, and you owe Pearse even less – but he needs you. We need you. Call me. Text me. Poke me on Facebook. Just get in touch."

If the hysterical tone in my voice earlier in the café had been high-pitched, Bob's was almost supersonic.

The other two messages? Yes, they were from Darcy. The first was simply *"Did you see the state of that?"* and the second was a request that I call her immediately.

I would have called her – honest, I would – except that my mind was racing. Bob wanted me. Well, actually I think his exact words were that he *needed* me. I was quite happy to be needed, especially in a professional capacity. I steadied myself and I picked up the phone to call him. This was it – my moment.

37

The offices of NorthStar PR are a strange place to be on a Sunday afternoon. The carpark looked almost bereft with only three cars in it – mine, Bob's and Pearse's. We all parked beside each other which was completely unnecessary but strangely comforting.

I had changed from my tracksuit bottoms and T-shirt into something a little more official-looking. I had combed my hair into a high ponytail and slicked on some make-up. I was even wearing heels – which I rarely did on a Sunday. Sunday was a day for flat shoes for sure. I had sprayed on my favourite perfume and had done everything I could think of to make myself look confident. I certainly didn't feel it. I felt like a nervous wreck. The last time I had seen both Bob and Pearse had not been happy times and, even though it was them who wanted to see me on this occasion, I didn't feel in any way as if I had the upper hand.

I took a few deep breaths and steadied myself. I had to prove myself here and now and I had to put all my feelings about Pearse and his penis and the ownership of same aside. I had to try and be the professional PR Guru Bob believed I could be. I had to get this right.

Walking in the door and through to the inner sanctum of Bob's office, I saw Pearse sitting there with his head in his hands. Bob was pouring, coughing and offering soothing words and the phone was off the hook. Sitting beside Pearse was Toni who looked devastated.

I swallowed hard and said my hellos.

Pearse looked at me, his face blazing, and then he took Toni's hand.

"It's not as bad as it looks," Pearse said with a bravado I was pretty sure he wasn't feeling.

"I'm sure it will be fine," I said. "People have survived worse. A good sex scandal here and there has actually worked in some people's favours. We just have to spin this the right way."

"It's not just a sex scandal," Toni piped up, her eyes firey. "We're in love."

Momentarily I was floored. Just a few weeks ago Pearse had allegedly been in love with me. It was a cruel blow to my ego to know that he had moved on so quickly – even though I had moved on myself while we were still together.

He nodded, blushing slightly, and Bob shrugged his shoulders before handing them cups of coffee and sitting down behind his desk.

Ignoring the whole "in love" declaration, he tapped his fingers together.

"Annie is right. We have to spin this. We can make this work to your advantage. But you will be hounded by every tabloid hack in the country. We have to work this so that whoever you talk to, whoever you let take your picture, it has to be someone you trust entirely."

"And the restaurant?" Toni asked

"You open as usual. But you stay away. At least for tonight," Bob said.

"Actually, I think they should go in," I said.

Three sets of eyes, all round and wide, looked at me as if I were mad.

"If you are in love, as you claim to be, then you brazen it out. You go to work. You have nothing to be ashamed of."

"Not even shagging over the spuds?" Bob asked incredulously, losing his cool for perhaps the first time ever.

Toni spluttered in a most unattractive fashion.

"Right, we get on to the suppliers and we arrange a whole new delivery of potatoes through the front door – where all the paps are waiting – mid-afternoon. Then, Pearse and Toni, you two arrive together. I'm assuming you are actually together now?"

Toni nodded. I looked at Pearse and he nodded too.

"We didn't expect it," he started. "It just –"

"Happened," Toni interjected, giving me a look which let me know she had always, *always* intended for it to happen anyway.

"And your husband?" I asked.

"Well, here's the thing. He's not a bit happy. He's spitting venom if the truth be told."

I shook my head. "Harsh as it might sound, we don't worry about him. Not today anyway. Today we get you two back out there. Tomorrow I'll scout around my contacts and see who we can get to do this story properly. And we have to find a focus – something positive at the restaurant so we can shift attention that way."

"There's the Speed Dating Night?" Bob offered hopefully. "Assuming they don't want to pull out now, we could make it unforgettable."

My brain started to whirr with ideas. "You leave them to me. I'll talk them round and we'll make it work. I'll get Zara Dunne and a few of her cohorts to come along and offer their speed-dating services. We'll go all out to make it a sparkling event. You two – are you up for staging a speed date for the press? Could make a quirky piece. We have to make them think this hasn't phased you at all. So what if you got randy in the kitchen? You were just following your instincts. The worst thing you could do is act like you regret it."

"She's right," Bob said. "Absolutely one hundred per cent right. Genius. Let's make the Speed Dating Night the most memorable night Manna has ever had. I'll get the whole team on it tomorrow. We'll get everyone we can to go. It will be brilliant. Roll on Thursday!"

As I drove home there was a small nagging feeling which refused to go away. I knew I could do this – that didn't worry me. I would call in every favour I could and, that aside, I knew there would be no problem whatsoever in getting a journalist to follow up their story. In fact, I already had one in mind – and as for the speed-dating crowd – we could spin this beautifully. Skirting around the whole shagging-in-the-kitchen fiasco we would spin Manna as the place to fall in love. With a few minor celebs on board – and maybe even a sponsorship from Haven (for Super Kissable Lips . . .) it would be the biggest night out the town had seen. It was going to be okay. And yet the nagging feeling wouldn't leave.

Clambering up the stairs once again and into my flat, I sat down and set to work, planning our strategy, emailing a select few reporters and lifting my phone to make a few very important phonecalls.

"Hello?" Darcy answered.

"Hey, babes!" I said cheerfully.

"About fecking time!" she roared. "It's Scandal Central up there and you leave me hanging. And don't tell me you don't know what I'm talking about because I know of your sordid addiction to the celebrity-gossip columns in the *Daily Mail* online. Would you have thought he'd have it in him? The randy fecker!"

"Actually, he could be quite the Mr Lover Man when he got going," I teased.

"Tell me," she said, her voice laden with curiosity, "did youse ever do it in the kitchen? You know, a bit of a *Nine and a Half Weeks* scenario? Some whipped cream, strawberries and a ripe banana or two?"

"We bloody well did not!" I protested. "Now, his office, that was another matter . . . but, anyway, yes, I knew about it. In fact, I have spent the last two hours in his company. And Toni's too for the record. They are in love."

"Shit," Darcy said. "Are you okay? I mean, I know you and him are no more and all – but in love, already? Shit. That's harsh."

"I'm fine," I said, and I was. "And it has actually been a blessing in disguise."

I explained to her how Bob had called and how NorthStar

needed me and how this was going to be the coup of my career and that, perhaps more importantly, it meant I actually did still have a career. Hurrah! I would not have to trade in my lovely flat for a cardboard box or go begging to our parents for a crisis loan. That certainly cushioned the blow of knowing Pearse had moved on.

Sated in her desire for salacious gossip, Darcy rang off and I set about working again. I grinned when an email from Owen popped into my inbox.

"So," he wrote, "tell me you've not booked that Manna place for our dinner? I'd hate to be put off my spuds!"

I grinned and hit the reply button to assure him, without going into details, that Manna was mostly definitely not on the cards.

It was then I realised just what had been giving me that sinking feeling all afternoon. Thursday. The big night at Manna. Thursday. The big non-date with Owen. I couldn't not go to Manna. I had to be there. Absolutely and entirely. If I wanted to keep my job there was simply no choice in the matter.

But it wasn't like I could just reschedule for another night with Owen. It wasn't as if he lived just over town or was always up and around these parts. He lived 200 miles away – which was not exactly an acceptable driving distance for a non-date dinner. Perhaps serendipity was just messing with our heads.

I didn't type a response, because I wasn't sure what to say. It surprised me, more than I cared to let on, that I was annoyed about it. Perhaps annoyed was too strong a word. Disappointed for sure. I knew he would be disappointed too – just knew it. With a sinking feeling I made myself a cup of tea and climbed to the roof terrace where I stared out into the cool evening air and sighed. There was nothing for it. I would have to work my arse off to save Pearse and my job and hope that, if fate was as good at bringing Owen and me together as we had originally thought, it would find a way to make things happen.

38

It had gone swimmingly well. The press had lapped up my calls. Pearse and Toni had done a *Hello*-style photo shoot in the much more desirable location of Pearse's house on the hill. Toni's husband had gone incognito as his own torrid affairs started to jump out of the closet. Zara and her cohorts were lined up for the big night and the speed dating crowd had been easily won over – especially when they knew Elise was off the case. "We never really liked her much anyway."

The team at NorthStar had all pulled together brilliantly, even Fionn who was hurtling towards her hen night and wedding with an increasing hysteria.

If it hadn't been for the fact I'd had to bail on Owen for our non-date I would have been on Cloud Nine. Not only was the night at Manna going to be a success, it was going to be a huge success. I was back, well and truly, in Bob's good books. He'd even promised me a gold star and an Employee of the Month award.

All we had to do was to get through tonight – but I was confident about that. Bob had, as expected, insisted that I be there. I had set aside my proposed Thursday night outfit of linen trousers and a casual top in favour of a glittery tunic dress, footless tights and killer heels. One of the beauty consultants from Haven had given me a make-over – a really fancy one with false eyelashes and everything. It was a joy to have these applied by a professional – my own efforts generally ended up with me spending all night running to the ladies' to make sure they hadn't run off across my face somewhere. I wore my hair in a subtle beehive – very smooth and glam and not at all frizzy. I looked like I knew what I was doing – like I had been born to run around with a clipboard and earpiece at a big celebrity function. The assembled press even wanted to take my picture along with the other organisers which, believe me, was a coup. At a previous similar event I had been asked to step out of the frame of the photo because "I didn't quite fit in".

Fionn was there – equally and effortlessly glam – but nervous. She was finding any time away from the intricacies of wedding-planning hard going.

"Would you take a deep breath and calm down?"

"Table plans," she muttered. "I've been working on it all evening. I was almost there – almost passed the stage of causing an international incident by sitting my Auntie Jean and his Uncle Seán together. Almost. It was all in my head, but it had to come out. Do you think . . ." she mused, her brow crinkling, "that anyone would notice if I just nipped off to the office for a bit and did a bit of work on it? I mean, you have this covered, don't you?"

I gave her arm a gentle rub while simultaneously giving her a look which signalled that I would kill her – with my clipboard – if she so much as nodded in the direction of the office.

"Stay focused, Fionnuala, my dear. Stay focused. I'll help you with the table plan tomorrow – promise – or even after this. But I need you here. You are my wing-man, or wing-woman. Whatever you are, you need to be here. You know what my recent track record is like. Things could still go spectacularly wrong."

And, besides, if I had to give up the chance of a non-date with Owen, then she sure as hell could put her table plan to one side for one night. I loved her deeply, and with all my heart, but I was starting to look forward to getting her whole Big Day over and done with so that, perhaps, her sanity levels would return to normal.

"I'm sorry," she said, blushing. "You're right. But nothing will go wrong. Look at the queue outside – this place is the place to be. And Zara Dunne is sober. That's always a good start."

I looked over to where the beauty queen was pouting for the camera, her long legs making me feel like Stumpy McStumperson. She had three friends with her, all equally glam and gorgeous. They looked like they had walked right off the catwalk. The high-class bachelors of Derry would be swooning after them.

Pearse was looking really quite handsome and definitely back to his usual over-confident self. There was no trace at all of the nervous wreck who had sat in front of me just a few days before in NorthStar's offices. He was walking around, designer suit, open shirt, big smile, with tiny Toni hanging off him like a limpet. They looked happy. He definitely looked like the cat who had got the cream. As they staged their photo – leaning over the table towards each other in deep conversation, hands touching in a wonderfully romantic way, he grinned, and I saw a trace of something I hadn't seen in a long time. It was there and it brought a lump to my throat. This was the old Pearse. The Pearse who I had fallen for – who had been happy – before we had drifted apart from each other. While I was happy to see him smile in that way, I felt a tinge of regret for the couple we had been.

There was no time for regret, however. I had things to do. It was kick-off time – time to swan about making sure the right people spoke to the right people, that the right people had their picture taken and that Manna, Haven and the speed dating crowd were kept happy. I signalled to the burly doormen to open the door – and to be ruthless about who they let in and who they kept out – and I grabbed one of the complementary glasses of sparkling wine and allowed myself a sneaky sip. No more, mind. This was not going to be an Annie disaster.

The place was certainly buzzing and the atmosphere was all we could have hoped it would be and more. Bob was standing on the sidelines, his arms crossed, his pelvis thrust forward in a proprietary manner. The smile on his face had never been wider.

"You okay, boss?" I asked, blatantly fishing for one of his clichéd compliments.

He nodded. "I couldn't be happier even if Colin Farrell walked right in right now, declared his love for all things gay and offered to take me back to his hotel room for some rampant sex."

Not exactly clichéd – but I took it as a compliment anyway.

The pictures were taken, the dates were well underway and my feet were killing me. I knew I should have worn my ballet pumps, but no – I had wanted to go for all-out glam. Well, now I was suffering for it. I had an almost uncontrollable urge to make my way behind the bar, lift the ice bucket and plunge my feet as deeply into it as possible.

Instead I opted for finding a quiet corner, removing my shoes and giving my feet a quick rub while making rather suspect "oooh!" and "aaah!" noises.

"Annie?" I heard Pearse call and I looked up.

"I thought it was you. I recognised the groans," he said with a wink. But it wasn't a flirtatious wink. It was a definite water-under-the-bridge wink.

"Well, sit down and get rubbing," I said, proffering him my foot. It was the very least he could do. Pearse always did give a decent footrub. He sat down, lifted my foot and starting kneading. I sat back and groaned again. But it wasn't a flirtatious groan. It was a definite water-under-the-bridge groan.

"I never said thank you," he said. "For how you dealt with this. You saved our skin."

"That's my job," I said with a salute.

"I think you went above and beyond. After everything. After how I treated you."

"I did a fair share of the mistreating myself," I said with a blush.

"Okay, so we both fucked up," he said. "Not the most dignified end to a relationship I've ever gone through."

"Hey," I said with a smile, "I take it as a compliment that you were so annoyed at the split that you actually tried to ruin my life."

He paled for a second – even in the dark room I could see the colour drain from his face. Perhaps I had gone too far. Perhaps it was too soon for jokes.

"I'm kidding," I offered. "I'm sorry. I've not handled this well at all."

"Neither of us has," he said.

We sat in companionable silence for a moment or two.

"Are you happy?" I asked. It was suddenly important to me beyond everything that he was happy. Everything would be okay if he was happy – there would be hope for us all.

"Honestly?" he said with a hint of modesty most unlike him. "I'm the happiest I've ever been."

The wine was in full flow. The dates had been completed and now the eager datees where waiting to see who wanted to take things further with whom. Pearse had pulled a blinder by offering a free glass of champagne for everyone – and by champagne I mean actual champagne, not some cheap fizzy plonk masquerading as champagne. And it was delicious. I allowed myself one tall, chilled glass and as I sipped I beckoned Fionn over.

"The next time we'll drink champers will be at your wedding! Oh, won't it be lovely!"

Her eyes misted over. "Yes. Yes, it will. I can't wait, Annie. I just can't wait."

We clinked our glasses together.

"To happy endings!" I cheered.

She smiled, leaning in towards me for a hug. "I hope you get yours too, darling. I really do."

I nodded, unable to speak, and was grateful when the compère announced that the final date swaps were ready.

One by one he called each eager participant to the front and handed them a silver envelope with their matches inside. There were squeals of approval and squeals of disappointment and lots and lots of laughter. Bob gave me the thumbs-up and I raised my thumbs back at him.

"*Annie Delaney!*" a voice called, and I looked around trying to locate it.

"*Annie Delaney!*" it repeated as I tried to find my focus point.

"It's your man," Fionn said pointing to the compère. "He wants you on stage. Go on, girl!"

I didn't really want to. I didn't do standing on a stage in front of a crowd very well. And I certainly hadn't speed-dated anyone. This did not feel right. Not one bit.

I walked up, expecting something Very, Very Bad to happen. But it didn't. He just handed me an envelope. I expected some big announcement – some flash of lights or a thunderbolt or something. It was, however, just an envelope and I walked down again, feeling very confused and more than a little subdued.

"Open it," Fionn urged as everyone around me resumed their hijinks.

So I did. I read the words before me, trying to make sense of them.

Owen Reilly would like to date Annie Delaney.

I looked around and I knew he was there. I just wanted to see him. I needed to see him. I looked around, blinking under the bright lights and the camera flashes, until I saw his smile. I looked straight at him and everything else didn't matter. I smiled back – and crossed the room to where he pulled me into a hug.

"How about we get out of here?" he said and I nodded.

I woke as the sun streamed through my bedroom window. I sighed, breathing in the fresh morning air and staring at the clock. It was time to get up for work. Bob was taking me out for coffee and a debriefing session and we were going to plan how to take things further for NorthStar.

First, though, I just had to double-check. I reached across the bed, feeling around and finding the empty space beside me.

I smiled – relieved. I hadn't slept with Owen!

I had remained rational and in control. We had shared a rather amazing toe-tingling snog and he had even agreed to attend Fionn's wedding as my plus one but I hadn't made a mistake. I had taken it slow, and it had been lovely.

When we left Manna, he had taken me back to his hotel – and

we sat in the lobby sharing a bottle of wine and laughing as if we had known each other all our lives.

"Why did you come to Manna?" I asked as I sipped the last of my wine and got ready to leave for my taxi.

"Some things I just didn't want to leave to fate," he said.

And that's when I kissed him.

39

I slipped into the most gorgeous dress in the world ever and stopped to look in the mirror. Hair perfect – a glittering rose clasp glinting amidst a sea of curls. Make-up perfect – complete with false lashes. Fake tan – done to perfection. Nails – manicured to within an inch of their lives.

If this was how amazing I felt, I could barely imagine how amazing Fionn must feel. I looked at her – glowing in her dressing gown. She could walk down the aisle wearing that robe and those slippers and she would be simply breathtaking. Her beauty ran so much deeper than the dress she was about to wear. She glowed from the inside out and my heart swelled with love and pride for her.

Her flowergirls, Emma and her friends Camille and Lucia, danced around at her feet – their chiffon skirts bouncing up and down as they twirled.

"Oh Fionn! You look just like a princess. You look just like Cinderella. Daddy is going to love you so much," Emma trilled while her friends squealed with delight.

For a five-year-old precocious madam she sometimes got things absolutely spot on.

"Oh, and he is going to think you girls are the most beautiful on the planet," Fionn beamed, reaching down to kiss each of the girls on the top of their heads.

Camille giggled, her bright blue eyes flashing with sheer joy, while Lucia grabbed Emma's hand and the pair danced, their curled hair bouncing up and down, as they jumped around in a circle singing a dazzling rendition of "Ring O' Roses".

Lucia and Camille's mother, Hayley, walked into the room, her own eyes misty with emotion at the sight of her girls, entranced on their magical day.

"Come on, Camille, come on, Lulu, and you too, Emma! Let's leave Auntie Fionn alone to get her head together!"

The girls left in a mass of chiffon and glitter, their laughter echoing around the house.

"It's happening, isn't it?" Fionn asked in my direction as her mother fussed around, smoothing down the sparkling gown and preparing it for the big moment when Fionn would transform into the world's most beautiful bride.

"Yes," I nodded, my voice choked with emotion. "It most certainly is."

We stood at the back of the church – Emma, Camille and Lucia solemnly holding their baskets of rose petals as if they were the most precious cargo in the world.

I straightened the back of Fionn's gown, smoothed down her veil and then stood back as I watched her daddy squeeze her arm and mutter, "Okay, sweetheart. Let's go."

The music started up – "Canon in D" played by a string quartet – and I had to bite back a swell of emotion. They started walking – slowly – step, pause, step, pause. After a suitable time I started to follow. Step, pause, step, pause. I smiled as I walked, aware of Alex standing at the top of the aisle, his face beaming with love, but more conscious of those who stood either side of me in the pews, smiling as I walked by.

Darcy stood, her arm looped in Gerry's. His head rested gently on hers and it was such an intimate pose that I believed it would be okay for them too.

And then I saw Owen, grinning at me, winking slowly. He gestured to his head – and I laughed. Just the night before he had told me how this wedding invite had forced him to reconsider his entire male-grooming routine. Not only had he suffered the indignity of shaving, he had also had his hair cut. I should remember that, he said, if ever I felt like we women had a tougher life than men.

Before I knew it, we were there at the altar. Fionn was crying happy tears. Alex was overcome with emotion. Emma was smiling, sitting on her mammy's knee (and her mammy didn't look suicidal).

They made their promises in unfaltering voices and they smiled before they shared their first man and wife kiss.

They were married. She'd done it. They'd done it.

The room was dark – lit by the softest of lights and the gentle glow of a hundred tea-lights, set on mirrors dusted with crystals. The crisp white linen on the tables matched the crisp white linen on the chair covers while just across from where we sat an iron arbour bedecked with fairy lights showed off the most magnificent chocolate cake I had ever seen.

"If I was a cheesy fecker and I could sing, I'd start singing that Eric Clapton song now," Owen said as he handed me a glass of sparkling wine and sat beside me.

I was taking a breather (after a particularly energetic dance to "Tragedy") while Fionn and Alex, and every couple in the place – including Darcy and Gerry – were wrapped around each other doing a slow and steady shuffle to "Angels" by Robbie Williams.

"'I Shot the Sheriff?'" I responded with a grin.

"No," he said, smiling, but almost embarrassed with it. "'Wonderful Tonight'."

I blushed. "Gosh, Mr Reilly, you say the nicest things."

"But I don't lie. You look wonderful – amazing."

"Great what a bit of slap and some false nails can do," I said, wagging my talons in his direction.

"Annie, one of these days you will realise that even dishevelled and lying in a heap in Dublin, with a bruised ankle and your hair all out of place, you still looked wonderful."

I stared at him, waiting for the punchline, but there wasn't one. He meant it. I knew he meant it.

"Fancy a dance?" he asked and I nodded, letting him lead me to the dance floor.

It felt delicious in his arms. I felt as if we fitted, as if our bodies were moulded to be together. I rested my head on his shoulder and I didn't feel the need to speak. I just felt the need to be with him.

"Perfect," he said and I looked up to meet his eyes. "Everything about today. Everything about you. It's just perfect."

THE END

If you enjoyed *It's got to be Perfect*
by Claire Allan why not try
Jumping in Puddles also published by Poolbeg?
Here's a sneak preview of Chapter One.

Jumping in Puddles

Claire Allan

1

Niamh

THINGS I HATE ABOUT MY HUSBAND:

* He likes pea and ham soup – I mean, who in their right mind eats something which looks like snot?
* He waits until he gets to work to shave, so that when he kisses me goodbye in the morning I get stubble rash.
* He drives too fast.
* He died because he drove too fast. Stupid bastard.
* No one else has bought pea and ham soup from our local shop since he died. And I've no way of telling him I was right that he was the only person in Donegal who ate the blasted stuff.
* He never said goodbye. And the last kiss we had was a stubbly one . . . and I had morning breath.
* He makes me cry.

* * *

THINGS I HATE ABOUT MY EX-BEST FRIEND:

* Caitlin hasn't spoken to me since Seán died.

* She doesn't answer the phone when I call.

* She is a bitch.

* She won't tell me why she has become a bitch.

* * *

Niamh had doodled on the top corner of her page. It was a strange picture – her artist's impression of a tin of pea and ham soup. She knew she was obsessed but if she stopped thinking about tins of soup she might just have to think about everything that was so terribly wrong in her life.

Like the fact her husband was dead – and she was now a widow with three-year-old twins. And that her best friend in the whole world had turned into a psycho-bitch from hell precisely half an hour after her husband was buried in a graveyard in the arse-end of nowhere.

And, of course, she now lived in the aforementioned arse-end of nowhere – their dream home, where it was all to begin and become fabulous. Except it hadn't begun at all, it had ended.

This was to be her Wisteria Lane. She was happy to leave the rat race of Derry behind and become a kept woman in their perfect home, with the porch swing and the designer kitchen island. But this wasn't so much Wisteria Lane as Elm Street and her life was the nightmare. The fact that there wasn't actually some psycho with knives for fingers ready to claw her to pieces in the middle of the night was no comfort. She would have quite liked that – at the moment.

Niamh scored through the picture, looked up at three heads bowed over their own notebooks, writing furiously, and she fought the urge to push her pen through her nose till it hit her brain. She didn't even know if it was a painless way to commit suicide, but looking around at her options she thought it might be worth a try.

"Niamh, are you okay?" a ridiculously smiley woman in a long flowing skirt with, Niamh imagined, long flowing underarm hair, asked.

Rolling her eyes like someone half her age in a teenage strop, Niamh nodded. She didn't have the energy to answer that question any more and anyway she had very quickly learned that people didn't really want to know the answer. They expected her to say she was fine. She could occasionally get away with "fine, all things considered" or "fine, given the circumstances" but no one wanted to know that at this stage, three months after her life had changed irrevocably and not in a good way, she woke up every morning seething with rage and confusion wanting to scream at the world and everyone in it.

Nor were they particularly interested in her obsession with pea and ham soup. Even Robyn, the new best friend who had stepped into the shoes of the psycho ex-best friend, had started to openly avoid all discussions on any kind of soup, never mind Seán's favourite flavour.

"I'm grand," Niamh said, and went back to doodling, hoping that Detta O'Neill, the group facilitator, would leave her alone if she looked busy enough.

She hadn't wanted to come here. She'd done it to keep Robyn, her mother and her GP happy. All had been understandably concerned that Niamh had seemed to give up the day Seán died – putting her life on hold in a haze of grief and anger.

"Don't take this the wrong way," Robyn had said, almost afraid to meet Niamh's eye, "but you should think about some form of counselling, or support."

"I thought that is what I had you two for," Niamh said, looking at her friend and her mother as if they had betrayed her. Had they become tired of her grief? Should she have moved on by now? Surely three months was wee buns when it came to loss and longing?

"Of course you have us," her mother had soothed, "but, darling, we feel we can't reach you sometimes. And it doesn't help that we're up in Derry and you are all the way down here."

"It's only an hour away," Niamh pouted.

"That's a long way when you are worried about someone," Robyn said, "and you seem to have become a hermit since – you know – since. And you never get out and talk to anyone."

"These two keep me busy," Niamh said, gesturing to the corner of the room where Connor and Rachel were playing contentedly with their Bob the Builder toys. "I don't need anyone else."

"Of course you do," her mother said. "You must be lonely."

It would, Niamh realised, have been churlish to reply "No shit, Sherlock" to her mother's concern, but counselling wasn't going to ease her loneliness – not unless the counsellor was planning on coming home and stroking her back gently each night in bed just as Seán had done. That kind of loneliness wasn't going to go away.

"Look," her mum said, standing up and moving to switch on the kettle, "I've been talking to Dr Donnelly and she has given me the name of a woman here in Rathinch who is starting a support group for lone parents."

"But I'm not a lone parent!" Niamh shouted. How she hated that title. She was a married woman, who along with her husband had planned her family with scary precision. The twins were conceived in May, born in February, raised in Derry until they were two and then the family moved to their dream home on the Donegal coastline. It was a home she and Seán had designed together, built together and were ridiculously proud of. They had pored over interior-design magazines, taped every episode of *Grand Designs* and made their house the envy of the village. They had done it all together.

Niamh hadn't made any decisions as a "lone" anything and she shrugged off the title now. It was right up there with "widow" in her most hated terms in the world ever.

"Look, we'll leave you her number. She's Detta and Dr Donnelly said she's a dote. Think about it, pet. What harm can it do?"

Niamh shrugged, walking out into the perfectly manicured garden and staring out at the grey sea at the bottom of the path. As the wind whistled around her, she hugged her cardigan and her grief around her.

Talking to Detta couldn't do any harm. After what she had been through lately, nothing could ever harm her again.

And of course her options were limited. She knew her mother was like a dog with a bone and wouldn't leave her alone until she was joining in nicely with village life and at least putting forward an impression of calm and happiness to her new neighbours. It was either the Lone Parents Support Group, Niamh had realised with a sinking feeling, or the knitting club. And Niamh didn't do knitting.

AVAILABLE FROM POOLBEG

Feels Like Maybe

Claire Allan

Aoife is 32 and in an on/off relationship with sexy singer Jake. When she finds out she is pregnant, he decides the relationship is most definitely off and leaves before she has the time to say 'Mothercare'.

Meanwhile her best friend has been keeping a secret of her own. Beth and her husband Dan have been trying to get pregnant for the past two years. According to the doctors there is no medical reason for their failure to conceive. And if there is no reason, there can't be a problem, can there?

Add a gorgeous gardener, an overbearing mother, an annoyingly perfect sister-in-law and a well-meaning aunt – all with secrets of their own – into the mix and you have 'Feels Like Maybe'.

ISBN 978-1-84223-345-0

AVAILABLE FROM POOLBEG

Rainy Days & Tuesdays

Clare Allen

Grace, Parenting Editor of a monthly glossy, was once the glamorous Health and Beauty Editor.
Now she still looks like she's nine months pregnant two years after childbirth and is devastated when the office bimbo, stick-insect Louise, announces:
"I need you to lose weight."
"Grace has been chosen by the magazine to undergo the ultimate make-over for a feature.
Overcoming her first reaction (which is to murder Louise), Grace decides to go for it – not realizing it will involve taking happy pills, crying torrents in front of her hard-nosed editor Sinéad, being weighed in public, and wondering whether or not she wants to stay married . . .
Will it all be worth it?

Can Grace become a Yummy Mummy
and get her life back together again?

ISBN 978-1-84223-311-5